SAMARITANS

SAMARITANS

BOOK I: The Sound of Silence

C. John Carter

Copyright © 2023 C. John Carter Publishing.
All rights reserved.
ISBN: 979-8-9897611-1-1

For everyone who believed I could do it.

TABLE OF CONTENTS

Prologue 1
Chapter I 5
Chapter II 14
Chapter III 31
Chapter IV 40
Chapter V 58
Chapter VI 69
Chapter VII 83
Chapter VIII 102
Chapter IX 109
Chapter X 117
Chapter XI 136
Chapter XII 161
Chapter XIII 183
Chapter XIV 211
Chapter XV 226
Chapter XVI 241
Chapter XVII 252
Chapter XVIII 271
Chapter XIX 285
Chapter XX 296
Chapter XXI 312
Chapter XXII 329
Chapter XXIII 339
Chapter XXIV 358
A Dream of Things to Come 369

Prologue
"Drink the Water"

    Somewhere beneath the black sun, a Girl sleeps curled among flowers.

    In her dream, she floats alone within a vast ocean. She can't see it, can't hear it, but she can feel it: a cold and fathomless blanket of waves, as comforting as it is terrifying.

    Before long, an unseen force starts to pull her upwards, slowly at first, but then with increasing speed. As her body rises, the darkness fades, oppressive blackness turning to the crisp blue of the sea.

    Up and up she is pulled towards the surface, and soon she can see the sky above, grey and overcast and completely clear save for seven distant figures suspended in a ring high above the waves.

    The Girl draws ever nearer, filled with equal parts anticipation and dread. Though she doesn't know why, she *must* reach those figures, even as every fiber of her being screams at her to stay away. Whether she wishes to go or not, the force dragging her along has already made the choice.

    Excitement and panic reach a crescendo in her heart just as she breaches the rolling waves. Above the tide, she sees only the dreams of others.

The Preceptor dreams of marching across a field of ash, Its black hooves leaving dusty imprints along its path. Three headless horses tread wearily along at Its heels. Behind each horse, bound by unbreakable chains, an army of withered husks shamble in silent lines.

The Preceptor does not know where It leads this army of damned souls, but nonetheless drags its captives along on their futile exodus, even as the ash at their feet seems to pile higher and higher.

The Crucifer dreams of kneeling before a mound of dirt. His eyes are covered by a blindfold, but tears of blood still spill down his cheeks. He looks up to the sky, but the blood spills down his cheeks onto the soil below. He prays it will water the seed sleeping beneath.

Nothing stirs.

The Apostate dreams of crawling across the muddy earth. A horde of worms, tiny and weak, scatter before him. He plods along on hands and knees, reaching out every so often to smash one beneath his palm.

The corners of his mouth split open from ear to ear, and his long tongue lashes out to lick the viscera from his hands. Each taste leaves a new stain inside him, mingling with his own filth until all the smut of the world is his to bear.

The Prodigal dreams of laughing as he swings his sword of bone and carves through the enemies around him. They fall upon him from all angles, their bodies embroidered with ivory and gold. They come in many forms, ranging from small and humanoid to colossal and eldritch.

Regardless of their shape, the Prodigal's skeletal blade shreds them mercilessly. Their golden blood splatters his skin, bursting into sacred flames that consume his form. His flesh blackens and cooks, but the swinging of his sword continues unabated. His charred visage never stops laughing.

The Anchoress dreams of lying suspended atop a dead tree that reaches into the starless sky, body impaled on its black branches. Above her, six Beasts rip and tear at her body, greedily devouring all that she has to offer.

Beneath her, the tree's roots carry their poison upwards into her body, replacing what flesh the beasts consume. The Anchoress screams in agony and joy, crying even as she begs her pets to eat until they are sated.

The Sacristan dreams of stumbling down a dirt road with no end. They come across a child in tattered robes huddled on the side of the road, knees drawn and head bowed as if to hide from the world.

The Sacristan approaches and asks the child to raise their head. It complies, and the Sacristan sees that it has no face. The air around its form seems to bend and warp outward, as if existence itself is struggling to pull away.

The faceless child reaches a thin hand towards the Sacristan, asking if they too will reject it.

The Crusader dreams of standing alone amidst an endless field of emerald hills. His long, pearl-white hair flutters in a pleasant breeze that carries the scent of healthy grass across the land. The sun shines overhead against a vibrant blue sky, bathing everything in gentle warmth.

Despite the comfort of his surroundings, the Crusader's expression is cold and emotionless. He has seen this dream before; its beauty will not last.

No sooner does this thought cross his mind than his surroundings begin to shift. He does not look away as the light above begins to magnify in its intensity. He does not flinch as soothing warmth turns to biting heat. He does not glance down as the grass begins to blacken and burn, as sadist flames rise to lick his flesh.

He does not avert his gaze as the blue sky turns to a sea of sheer, blinding white. He does not react to the sound of sickening *cracks* as the heavens can no longer bear the coming weight.

As the flames engulf his body and burn away all remaining senses, the Crusader beholds the white sky webbed with cracks, a single push from giving way. From within the white void comes a dark shape, sharpening into focus as it draws near.

The shadow reaches the fragile wall, opening itself into the form of a vast hand. Fingers splayed, it crashes into the wall and, with one final burst of deliverance, brings all dreams to an end.

All but one.

The Girl in the flowerbed sheds tears even as she sleeps. From nowhere, a white dove flutters down and rests upon her trembling shoulder, gently brushing her closed eyes with its wing.

Her shaking slows, her breathing steadies, and the terrible dreams fade to silence. She will wake soon, and when she does, something may begin to move for the first time in an eternity.

But for now, the dove on her shoulder flies away, leaving The Girl to deep and dreamless rest.

Chapter I
"Black Hole Sun"

As the last phantom sensations of fire and pain dissipated, Creed opened his eyes to the dead waking world. All he could see were vague black shapes, but as his vision slowly adjusted to what little light there was, his surroundings came into clearer—if still dim—focus.

He sat cross-legged in the middle of a crater stretching out nearly a mile in every direction. At that point, the crater gave way to sheer rocky ridges that rose about fifty feet upwards to meet actual ground-level. From where Creed sat, only the tallest of the ruined city's buildings could be seen beyond the crater's ring.

As always, there was no wind. No smell. No sound. Creed glanced up at the sky where the black hole that was once the sun hung motionless as ever, its circular shadow ringed with a pale silvery glow that gave off just enough light to cast the world in perpetual grey.

Unable to even muster a sigh at the depressing view, Creed turned his gaze back to the crater floor before him. The ground had been crushed flat to the point of resembling grey, well-paved concrete, save for several large swathes of space that were burnt a harsh, ashen black.

Creed sat in the largest of these black patches, leather-gloved hands laid flat upon the ground. At the moment, his body was filled with the dull, ice-cold sensation of his life draining away into the dirt. He could feel his power and energy seep from his palms into the ground upon which he sat, as if the roots of some plant drank from the waters of his life.

That's all you get this time.

With that one groggy thought, Creed rose, his heavy leather coat rustling as he did so. His hands met slight resistance as he pulled them from the dirt, like the force trapped beneath was trying to hold him in place. But in the end, it was still just dirt.

Every muscle and bone in his body groaned as he stood, rendered stiff from how long he had been sitting motionless. Despite the pain, he did not flinch or wince at the discomfort. Rather, he savored every ache. Each was proof of how weak he had grown.

Except for where the dirt was blackened, the floor of the crater was littered by an innumerable number of stakes pierced into the ground. They had been set expertly, each standing perfectly straight and arranged equidistant from one another. Separated by less than a foot, they made the most of the available space.

With a quiet sigh, Creed ran a gloved hand across his head. A small part of him expected to feel long, flowing locks between his fingers, but of course that was just a leftover sensation from his vision. Now he felt only the short, cropped style he had worn for ages now.

Pulling his hand away, Creed glanced down to see several small strands of his hair had come away in his hand. They were white, as they'd always been, but unlike the bright luster they'd held in his stronger days, these were dull and sickly-looking.

Rather than feel distressed, Creed again took a grim satisfaction at the sight.

Can't be long now.

Putting those thoughts aside, Creed began to walk towards the closest grouping of stakes he could see. It was more of a slow limp due to how stiff he felt, but it wasn't as if he was in a hurry. In time, he reached a point where one section of ash-black earth ended and the field of markers began.

Reaching down, he placed a hand upon one of the stakes. It was solid and smooth, formed from a clay that had dried to stone.

Elizabeth.

There was no lettering or branding to indicate who the small gravestone was attributed to, but Creed had no need for one. He'd placed each of these stakes himself. Assigned a name to each one. He wouldn't forget whose was whose. Couldn't if he tried.

After a moment, Creed took his hand from the clay marker and placed it upon the identical one next to it.

Adrian.

Thus did Creed begin his ritual: moving from marker to marker, placing his hand atop each one and reciting the name he'd arbitrarily associated with it.

Rain.
Khan.
Faline.

He weaved his way between the rows with practiced precision. All was silent save for the occasional crunching of his boots when he stepped onto the burnt patches. He had taken great care not to place a single stake into the ash; they didn't deserve to be touched by the stains of the creature that had left them.

Yrsa.
Lydia.
Obi.

His path was methodical, an ever-expanding circle starting from the center of the crater and gradually spiraling outward. Focused mainly near the epicenter, the blackened spots eventually dissipated as he wound his way further outward. More unblemished ground meant room for more markers. More names for Creed to recall.

Esther.
Riley.
Héctor.
Zidane.
Judah.

Creed couldn't begin to make an estimate as to how many there were in total. He'd made a point never to count. It wasn't the number that mattered. Only the names.

Lysander.
Howl.

Jesse.
Ramses.
Yomi.

If the concept of time had still held any meaning, Creed might have measured the ritual in things like hours and minutes. But there was no longer a point to such things, and so he merely went about his work without paying heed to how long it might have taken.

Sharru.
Faye.
Ramses.
Duke.
Ladybird.

There was change in his surroundings to indicate the passage of events. The Black Sun above was unmoving and unchanging; if one flew to the other side of the world in an instant, it would still be hanging in the sky, as if they had gone nowhere. Even the movement of stars could no longer be used to measure progression. Wherever it was they had gone, they hadn't been visible since the day time ended.

Sheba.
Delilah.
Blair.
Jack.
Emilia.

Regardless of how long it did or didn't take, Creed found himself coming to the end of his ritual. When he reached the most recent marker he had placed, there were only a few dozen feet left until he reached the walls of the crater. Not much room left, but that was fine. After so many trips, there weren't many more names left for him to add.

But for now, he could still add another. Stepping a few feet beside the last marker, he raised a hand and called upon what scant power he had left. Once, it would have taken less than the span of a thought for it to materialize, but as he was now, Creed had to strain his will to the limit until the clay finally manifested.

It appeared from thin air, summoned from nowhere; a mass of shapeless, formless earth that warped and spasmed as it floated in place. Creed called the desired shape to his mind, and the mass reacted to his will, shaping and solidifying itself until it was identical to the myriad markers scattered throughout the crater.

Taking the miraculous stake into his grasp, Creed leaned over and pierced it into the ground. Another link added to the chain of graves.

Once it was secure in the ground, Creed allowed his hand to rest atop it as he had the others. Reaching into his mind, he saw the ever-dwindling list of names he was incapable of forgetting and grabbed one at random.

Gideon.

And that was all. For no reason at all, this fresh piece of featureless stone was now Gideon's. The last and only bit of evidence in the entire world that someone with that name had once lived.

Despite the contemplation such a thought might have entailed, Creed did not linger. After only a moment—no more than he'd given any of the others—he removed his hand from the new marker and limped away. The high wall of the crater's edge loomed before him.

As he prepared for the stiff and unpleasant climb that awaited him, Creed wondered which he would exhaust first: the list of names, or his strength?

He would prefer each name receive its own marker before he wasted away entirely, but supposed that it ultimately didn't matter. No one but Creed would ever know which of these graves was Gideon's and which was Elizabeth's. Even if he had marked them, no one but he would understand the significance of their presence. And once he was gone, there would be no one at all to remember.

Until then, he would continue as he had. One more visit. One more grave. One more name.

One more failure.

With a small groan of exertion, Creed finally pulled himself up and over the edge of the crater. Falling to his hands and knees, he took a moment to catch his breath before rising again.

His whole body still ached, but not near so much as when he'd first awakened. The further Creed got from the crater's center—and what it held within—the less his body was weakened, though he always recovered a bit less with each visit.

For now, though, he still had life left in him yet. He stood and stretched out the remaining tension in his muscles. There were only two real aches that remained by now: the gash that carved its way down the left side of his face, and the mark branded between his shoulder blades. These were familiar pains, ones that had nothing to do with the void in the crater. Just two old scars that would never be permitted to heal.

Turning, Creed cast one last look over his shoulder at the crater. At this height, he was able to properly see the pattern formed by the burnt portions of dirt below. Rather than random patches, it was the ashen outline of a titanic, inhuman figure.

Spiraling out from the main body at the center were the unmistakable silhouette of six enormous wings. It coated the ground like a stain, a grotesque shadow that remained completely unchanged from when it had been seared into the earth so very long ago.

Facing forward again, Creed briefly regarded the desolate cityscape before him—or at least, those parts which hadn't been flattened by an angel dying at its center.

Reaching to the inside pocket of his coat, Creed pulled out one of the tiny paper sticks he kept on his person. Holding it between his fingers, he focused his thoughts on the tip.

Seconds later, a small, solid sphere of clay swirled itself into existence, fixing itself to the stick as if it had always been there. It now resembled a sort of lollipop, albeit a rather unappetizing grey one.

With a sigh, Creed popped the miraculous sucker into his mouth; as one might expect from candy made of clay, it was utterly devoid of flavor, but would serve as a suitable distraction for the long walk back. Pulling his coat more tightly about himself to block out the perpetual chill,Creed began his march.

He did his best to ignore the desolate surroundings: hollow buildings that had once been homes, businesses, and all other manner of shelter; streets painted in layers of ash so uniform that they almost obscured the cracks and fissures carving through them; charred husks of burnt metal that had once served as means of transport; and of course, the innumerable black shadows of flailing bodies, scorched into the ground and upon the walls in the same manner as the angel in the crater.

Leaving the confines of the city took time, but Creed's well-worn path eventually carried him out into the equally desolate countryside beyond. Ruined buildings gave way to open, stagnant air, and streets to faded dirt roads.

Past the city limits, the terrain became nothing but barren grey hill-country in all directions, with only the vaguest hints of other locales visible on the horizon. It would have been easy to get lost in the boundless plains, but having made the journey so many times, Creed knew which direction he was headed on instinct.

Like with his ritual in the crater, he paid no attention to how long his walk took him, nor how far. There was no schedule to follow, no appointments to keep. He was only returning from the city out of obligation, and would soon be headed back the way he'd come.

Regardless, after going through at least ten of his artificial lollipops and crossing a seemingly endless number of hills, Creed reached the top of a particularly steep incline, at the bottom of which sat his destination.

Had the passage of time still had an effect, the wooden church would have rotted to dust ages ago, but as things were, it was no worse off than it had been left at the end of the world.

Aside from the rather large hole in its roof, it was remarkably untouched compared to most other structures one came across these days. Whatever color it had been painted was difficult to tell in the weak glow of the dark sun, and its steeple knifed into the sky like a beacon calling him inside.

Before continuing his way down the dusty path, Creed turned to glance over his shoulder one last time—he always seemed to find himself doing that. Beyond the miles of hill country, he could still make out the tallest buildings that defined what was left of the city's skyline.

Biting through the rest of his flavorless sucker, Creed tossed the worn paper stick to the ground, turned back, and began to meander down the hill. He came to the church entrance, climbed the rickety wooden steps, and slowly pushed his way inside the large wooden doors.

The spacious main hall looked the same as ever, high-ceilinged and lined with rows of empty, decrepit pews that could have once seated a hundred or so congregants. The hall was dim and dusty, and the only source of light was the faint silver glow of the dark sun glinting through the hole in the roof.

Directly underneath said hole, a flower bed sat atop the elevated rear section of the hall, just before where the pulpit had once been. The grey light washed some of the color from their petals, but not enough to keep them from standing out.

Unable to grow or die—and by some miracle having never been dug up or trampled—someone had planted a mishmash of breeds with no regard to color theory or aesthetics, resulting in an utterly random assortment of yellows and blues and reds and purples. Garish and tacky by the old world's standards, they might very well have been the last beautiful things left in the world.

Creed may not have felt much at all anymore, but even he could not deny a sad sense of comfort when he gazed upon the blooms.

Within the ring of flowers was a flat mound of dirt. A large wooden cross had once been staked in the soil, but Creed had long since disposed of it. The space had been empty ever since, and should have been so now, but Creed was startled to see that, somehow, this was not the case.

Lying in the dirt, curled up into a ball, a girl was sleeping.

She was a small, pale thing, thin and weak even by the standards of humans these days. Creed would have placed her physical body at around fifteen years of age, which was unfortunate for her. To be a young woman, just on the cusp of adulthood, only to find herself trapped in a half-grown body for the rest of eternity—in Creed's experience, only the elderly struggled more in this world of frozen time.

She was clothed in little more than a short, worn-out dress that may once have been white but was now too dirty and stained to qualify. Her feet were bare, filthy with grime and calloused from what must have been infinite miles spent wandering the wilderness.

There appeared to be something tied around her waist, but he couldn't make out what. Her long hair, pale blonde and stringy, fell across her upper body like a blanket. She lay so peacefully in the soil that Creed might have thought her dead if not for the subtle motions of her breathing.

Creed believed he could have adequately reacted to most any other scenario, but in this case, all he could do was stare as he approached, passing by empty pews without thought. By the time he reached the edge of the ring of flowers, he had yet to recall what most people did when they found girls sleeping in flowerbeds.

He wasn't shaken from his stupor until the girl began to stir, perhaps having felt him looming over her. He stiffened as she slowly came to life before him, pushing up onto her hands as if waking from a perfectly normal nap.

Ignoring the bits of soil that clung to her hair, she glanced around the room with bleary, half-lidded eyes until her gaze found Creed.

She gave a few slow blinks, then finally seemed to process what was happening. Her eyes, too large for such a small face, went wider. Even in the dimness, they were somehow brilliant, like twin green lakes reflecting the light blue of a sky that was no longer there. Her unguarded stare gave him the unmistakable view of confusion, fear, and perhaps a little embarrassment.

Against the weak light of the dark sun, those eyes seemed bright enough to burn him.

Chapter II
"Where Did You Sleep Last Night?"

Neveah wondered if this was where she died.

She had been waiting for the day when her luck ran out, of course. The way she lived, it was something beyond a miracle that she'd even made it this far. Now, having nicely presented herself on a platter of dirt for anyone to find, she had no one but herself to blame if this was where it all ended.

The man certainly looked like he could kill. Even from the ground, she could see he was at least two heads taller than her. He was clad in a heavy leather coat such a dark shade of navy blue that it looked nearly black. A pair of thick leather gloves hid his hands, and a pair of leather combat boots encased his feet. Neveah found herself off-handedly wondering if that was the only form of clothing he had, or if he thought all the leather looked cool.

The coat was zipped up to its collar, which was high enough around that it obscured the lower half of his face. He'd clearly been in a hell of a fight once, as a long, jagged scar carved its way from his forehead down the left side of his face before disappearing beneath the collar.

It certainly made him look intense and dangerous, but also drew more attention to his eyes (the left one had somehow survived whatever wound had left the scar). They were shockingly blue, vibrant and sharp like bolts of lightning.

Curiously, his pupils seemed to have a sort of white glint about them, though Neveah wondered if that wasn't just the soft light from above catching them in the right way. Together with his short, chalk-white hair, they contrasted nicely with his skin.

His physical age was impossible to place, having that perfect combination of ruggedness and firmness that made him seem neither too old nor too young. His skin was a flawless mocha shade, ambiguous enough to make his origins equally indeterminable.

All in all, he would have been incredibly handsome had it not been for the slouch in his posture and the dead expression on his face.

Despite the harshness in his bearing, Neveah began to realize as the silence continued that the man was *not* going to kill her outright. In fact, he stood so still that she began to wonder if he was just as lost as she was.

Realizing the silence was shifting from dramatic to awkward, Neveah decided she needed to say something, *anything*, to get things moving. Tilting her head to the side and mustering a weak half-smile, she let her brain pull the first thing it could from her lips.

"Howdy..."

Holy shit, she thought.

Neveah hardly remembered where she came from, but she knew it wasn't any place where they said "howdy." This was probably the first time she'd spoken to someone in a lifetime, and she'd begun with a word she'd never uttered before.

Luckily, her statement seemed to have been absurd enough to startle the blue-eyed man out of his stupor. He blinked once, and his white eyebrows furrowed slightly. When he spoke, his voice was deep but hoarse, as if it had been a very long time since he'd said anything at all.

"What are you doing?"

The obvious question. Deciding any form of obfuscation would be pointless, Neveah replied, "Napping."

"...Napping."

"Yes."

"On a pile of dirt?"

"I didn't want to mess up the flowers." She almost let out a chuckle, but stopped herself. That didn't qualify as a joke. "Are they... your flowers?"

A pointless question. Nobody *owned* anything anymore; if these flowers were here, they'd been here since the end of time.

"I'm sorry if they are. I promise I didn't step on them or anything. I was worn out from walking so long, and when I wandered inside here, I couldn't believe that there were *actual* flowers. I never thought I'd see anything like it again, so I thought I'd sit down between them and... well like I said I was exhausted and it just—"

The man held up a leather-gloved hand to stop her rambling, for which she was grateful. "It... it's fine."

He didn't really sound sure if he thought it was fine or not. His gaze left her for the first time, glancing around as if he was expecting something. "Just, uh... just go."

"'Go?'" Neveah parroted. Had that really been the fourth or fifth thing he'd said to her in a situation like this?

"Yes." The word came slowly, as though even he realized how rude it sounded. After a moment, he hardened his gaze, which made his scar look more intimidating. "You had your nap. Hope it was nice. Time to move on."

Neveah wondered if the shock showed on her face. The first other person she'd met in recent memory, and he was telling her to shove off after a minute of awkward conversation? "You don't have any other questions?"

"Not really."

"*No* other questions for a mysterious girl you found lying in a flowerbed?"

"I asked you about that. You explained."

"Well, I suppose, but—"

Neveah realized she was still kneeling at the man's feet. Pushing herself up, she brushed the clinging soil from her hands and knees before continuing, "It's pretty unusual to find *anyone* these days, especially like... that. Don't you want talk before shooing me out the door?"

"'Talk?'" The poor guy sounded like it was a foreign word to him.

"Yes? You know, have a conversation? I say something. You say something. We ask questions that require answers. Information gets exchanged?"

"I know what—" he snapped before catching himself and continuing in the same dead tone. "Nothing to talk about. You're a wanderer, you wandered into my home, and now you're going to wander back out."

His eyes once again flicked behind her for a brief second, and Neveah could have sworn he seemed anxious. Maybe he had something valuable in a back room he thought she might steal? It wasn't likely, seeing as how "valuables" weren't a concept anymore.

Regardless, it was clear that whoever this strange man was, he did not want her here, and one of the few lessons Neveah had learned in the past eternity was how to take a hint.

She was moments away from giving one last apology and leaving the man to his flowers when the stupid Dove ruined things.

It fluttered down from nowhere, as always, landing atop the man's shoulder and cocking its dumb bird head from side to side. It resembled an ordinary dove in all respects, save for the fact that its feathers were such a clean, pure white that it almost seemed to glow in the dimness of the world.

The man didn't remotely react to its presence, not that Neveah expected him to; she was, after all, the only one who could see it.

It wasn't anything mystical or unique; Neveah just happened to be crazy, is all. That wasn't such a big deal. Everyone was crazy now. They had to be.

Her personal brand of insanity just so happened to manifest as an irritating bird that came and went as it pleased. It seemed to appear whenever she was contemplating where to go next, catching her attention before flying off in some arbitrary direction for her to follow.

Seeing as Neveah had never once had a set destination since she'd begun her travels—and seeing as it was just her broken mind randomly selecting path to walk anyways—she had always followed the dove without much thought, even if it led her right back the way she'd been going. If she couldn't trust her own madness, what *could* she trust?

Naturally, it had been the Dove which led her to the church. It had fluttered into the hole in the roof as soon as she'd crested the hill outside, and when she'd entered, it had been laying right in the middle of the flower ring, as if inviting her to come rest. So, she had.

And now here the irritating thing was again, perched atop this scary man's shoulder as if to say, *This is* right *where you need to be.*

Neveah gave an inward sigh. The Dove was just her own addled mind, and if it was telling her to stay, that meant she was curious. It hadn't happened in quite a while, but she could still remember that "curious" was her absolute *favorite* thing to be.

Resigning herself to her own foolishness, Neveah decided that she would *not* "wander back out," as Blue Eyes had put it. Not until she got enough social interaction to carry her through the next eternity, at least.

"You live here?" she asked, grasping at anything to keep words moving between them. "There's a whole city not too far off, isn't there?"

Blue Eyes' gaze grew distant at that. "Not a *whole* city."

She wasn't sure what he meant by that. "Still, there has to be more there than here, right? Supplies? Maybe even a person or two?"

"No. No people. Not for a long time. There's nothing."

"What happened? Besides the obvious."

At that, the man seemed to realize that he had, in fact, been roped into talking. His gaze hardened again, and he took a step closer to the ring of flowers, heavy boots thumping on the ground.

"It's time for you to go." His tone was the harshest it had been thus far. "I don't live out here because I like visitors. There are no supplies here or in the city. This entire region was wiped clean ages ago. I'm sorry, but you need to—"

The rest of the words died on his lips, and this time when his gaze was drawn behind her, it stayed. He went still, and Neveah naturally turned to see what had caught his attention.

She hadn't expected the most beautiful woman she'd ever seen to emerge from a door in the far back corner.

She wore the habit of a nun, though their monastic nature did very little to hide her curves. It didn't help that the sides of the dress bad been cut rather sinfully high up, exposing two long legs up to mid-thigh.

Her face was flawless in the literal sense of the word, features completely symmetrical and skin nigh-unnaturally devoid of imperfection. Her eyes—an unusually bright shade of violet—had locked on Neveah so intently that she thought they might be about to start firing lasers.

After a moment, the nun abruptly left the doorframe and began marching in Neveah's direction, the modest white heels she wore clicking on the wood floor. Neveah heard Blue Eyes sigh behind her but couldn't tear her gaze from the stunning woman.

As she neared, Neveah saw that several strands of hair spilled from the hood of her habit. She was also blonde, but hers was a few shades darker and *much* healthier looking than Neveah's own. Neveah imagined that in actual sunlight, it might resemble gold.

Suddenly very aware of her dirt-stained clothes and tangled hair, Neveah couldn't help but feel self-conscious. How on Earth did someone this beautiful still exist?

Her thoughts were interrupted as the nun stepped over the ring of flowers and placed herself rather uncomfortably far into Neveah's personal space, looking down at her with wide, unblinking eyes and an even more inscrutable expression than Blue Eyes.

Neveah leaned back as several seconds passed, starting to wonder what exactly the people in this church had against initiating conversation.

"Hello," the nun finally spoke. There was little inflection in her tone, save the slightest hint of anticipation.

"Hello..."

The response came less than a half-second later. "It's nice to meet you. Where did you come from? Did you travel far? Are you tired? Do you need to rest? I'm afraid we don't have any food, but you're more than welcome to—"

"Stella," came Blue Eyes' voice from behind. Neveah finally turned back to see that his expression seemed to have softened ever so slightly, though the scar made it hard to tell. He still looked decidedly un-thrilled at the situation. "Personal space."

The nun looked between Neveah and the man for a few more seconds before backing away just outside the ring of flowers. She straightened, clasping both hands in front of her waist.

"I'm sorry. It's been quite a while since we've had a visitor. I was... excited. My name is Stella. What's your name?"

At last, someone who understood how to converse with another human being! Despite the woman's slightly disconcerting behavior, Neveah found herself feeling more at ease.

For the first time since she awoke, she spoke with a genuine smile on her face. "Call me Neveah."

The nun stood a little bit straighter at her words, as though just speaking with someone was giving her a jolt of energy. "It's very nice to meet you, Ms. Neveah. May I ask what it is that brought you here today?"

"She was just leaving, actually," came Blue Eyes' abrupt response.

At his words, Stella's wide-eyed gaze snapped to him like a whip. She began to mechanically march around the ring of the flowers to where he stood. She brought herself just as close as she had to Neveah, and Blue Eyes seemed to shrink slightly under her stare. The Dove on his shoulder fluttered a bit at the movement but did not leave its perch.

"You were trying to send her away before I could see her." It was not a question.

"That's ridiculous," Blue Eyes responded, though his refusal to look the nun in her eyes didn't give much weight to the claim.

"I don't think there's any other conclusion I can draw from this." The barest hint of accusation colored her monotone. "You have a pattern of not liking to deal with unexpected situations, and your response is to always try and make them go away with as little effort as possible."

Blue Eyes didn't say anything, though the brief glance he shot at Neveah made her pretty sure he *did* wish she'd disappear.

"We're very far from any other kind of shelter." Stella pointed in Neveah's direction. "This girl has traveled a very long way and needs rest."

"She already got her rest. I found her napping in the flower bed."

This appeared to give the nun some pause. "I didn't hear her enter."

"Were *you* resting?" Blue Eyes asked.

"Yes, but... she must have been very quiet."

Why would she have heard me? Neveah thought. All she'd done was walk in and lay down on a pile of soil while the nun had apparently been in another room.

"Look," she spoke up, finally stepping out from the ring of flowers and onto the wooden floor. "I really didn't think anyone would be here. I didn't mean to intrude. I can leave if—"

Stella spun on her heel like a soldier. "Please don't feel like you have to do that." She motioned a hand in Blue Eyes' direction. "He's very rude, so you don't have to listen to him when he tells you to do things."

Neveah almost laughed, though Blue Eyes' unamused expression kept her from doing so.

Stella turned back in the man's direction. "Introduce yourself."

"If she says she wants to leave—"

"Introduce yourself."

There was no difference in tone between the two commands, but something about the second seemed far more compelling. With a defeated sigh, Blue Eyes finally looked at Neveah once more.

"Creed." As soon as he spoke, the Dove pushed off its shoulder and flapped off into the air. Neveah didn't bother following its path with her gaze; she knew that it would be gone if she tried to find it.

Creed. Not much of a name, but Neveah supposed it had more dignity than Blue Eyes. Seeing such a harsh-looking man cave to the much-smaller nun did wonders for Neveah's nervousness, and she started to wonder if this wasn't going to be an unpleasant time after all.

"It's nice to meet you, Creed." She nodded to the nun. "Stella."

The other woman motioned to one of the dusty pews several feet away. "Please sit."

Neveah complied, the wood creaking as she plopped down. The pew wasn't exceptionally comfortable, but given that sturdy seating was a rare find anywhere these days, she couldn't complain.

Stella took her own seat on a pew across the aisle from her. She looked expectantly towards Creed, who reluctantly sat down several feet away from either of them. Apparently satisfied, the nun turned to Neveah once again.

"May I ask what brought you here, Ms. Neveah?"

"Just Neveah's fine. I was traveling. I didn't expect to find anything way out here, and it had been a while since my last stop, so I couldn't help myself."

Stella tilted her head slightly. "Are you on some sort of journey?"

"I wouldn't call it anything like that. I just hadn't stopped to plant in a while."

"What does that mean?" Creed asked. Neveah was surprised he'd actually engaged.

"These." She rose from the pew and reached down to the simple rope cinched around her waist. It was looped through three small brown pouches. She angled her hips toward the two others to provide a better look.

Creed's brow furrowed in confusion, and Stella cocked her head further in apparent curiosity.

"What are they?" the nun asked.

"Seeds."

There was a time when Neveah would never have volunteered that information. She would have done everything to keep her pouches out of sight lest some greedy strangers try and take them.

She'd eventually realized that nobody cared. Seeds weren't valuable in a world where they would never grow, and anyone who found out what she was carrying would typically just look at her with a mixture of puzzlement and pity before moving on.

Creed didn't have that look; his was somewhere between shock and outright disbelief. She might as well have said she was carrying bombs with how deeply his gaze bored into her.

"You're... planting seeds." He said it as if the concept was unheard of.

"Yep," Neveah responded, making sure to keep her tone light and casual. She had to act like her actions were a perfectly rational thing for someone to do these days.

Even Stella briefly seemed at a loss for words. "Are... you aware that —?"

"Of course. I know they can't grow. I don't try to water them or anything. I just go around and find nice places to put them in the ground."

"Why?" Creed asked, making it sound like an accusation. Neveah didn't blame him. It *was* a ridiculous notion, but she just kept a light smile on her face and continued.

"Well, time may be frozen now, but that doesn't mean it won't move again someday, right? If that ever *does* happen, it would be helpful if there were some things already planted."

Creed gave a short scoff. "Time isn't frozen, girl. It's gone."

"Well, if it ever comes back someday—"

"It won't."

There was such iron-clad certainty in his words that Neveah immediately knew better than to try and argue. "Then it's just something to do, I guess."

His eyes widened a bit at that. "Something to..." He let out another scoff, louder than the first. He stood from his pew and took several steps away as if trying to keep his wits about him. Neveah wasn't quite sure why the notion seemed to offend him so deeply.

"What kind of seeds are they?" Stella asked, ignoring yet another scoff from Creed at the question.

"Oh, all kinds. Fruits, vegetables, flowers, herbs; anything that grows in the ground. I don't know where he got them all, but—"

"'He' who?" Creed interrupted.

Neveah hadn't meant to mention that part. In her mind, she heard the kind voice from so long ago echo once again:

Why not make a bet? What's left to lose?

Shooing the memory away, Neveah responded, "Someone gave them to me. It was soon after everything ended, I think; I don't remember much from that time anymore. I told him I didn't really know what to do with myself, and he just handed them over. I've been going around planting them ever since. Never saw him again."

Creed didn't bother to mask his disbelief. "You've been doing this since The End?"

"Oh yes. I used to have *way* more. Started out with five big sacks full of the little pouches, but I'm just down to these three now."

Not sure what I do once they're gone, she thought, but kept that bit to herself.

"How are you even still alive?" Creed asked.

"I'm also curious," Stella added. "Someone like you traveling alone for so long... the odds of not being found by scavengers or caught by an angel during all that time are impossibly long."

It had been longer than usual since someone had brought *them* up. Unable to keep a bit of sheepishness from her voice, Neveah admitted, "Well, as a matter of fact, I've... never actually seen one. An angel, I mean."

A ridiculous notion, but it was true. Frankly, she'd never even *glimpsed* one of humanity's destroyers before. She was perfectly aware of how absurd it sounded, and could very much understand the shock she saw on Creed's face. Stella's expression was more inscrutable, but she seemed equally lost as to a response, so Neveah continued.

"I know what they *are*, obviously. And I might have seen them back during The End. I don't really remember those days anymore. But as long as I've been traveling..." she shrugged, "I've just never seen one. There were a few times where I felt the ground shaking, and I remember once there was this bright light coming from the other side of a mountain. I always assumed that meant they were somewhere nearby, and so I went the opposite direction."

The other two continued to stare at her, and Neveah felt herself shrinking beneath the scrutiny. She was struggling to think of anything that could make her story sound less unbelievable when a light bulb went off in her head.

"Oh!" She held up a finger. "I *did* see an Eidolon once, though. At least, I *think* I saw one. Part of one, at least..."

Creed continued to silently analyze her, but Stella cocked her head to the side again. "Is that so?"

Neveah nodded. "I remember I was walking through some woods, and I came to a lake. Right in the middle of it, I could see this *huge* metal arm sticking out towards the sky. All gears and plates and pistons. I never got to see one in action during The End—I'd still remember *that*, at least— but I'd always heard they were hundreds of feet tall." She shrugged again. "Deep lake, I guess."

Stella nodded at her story. "Yes. That was definitely an Eidolon you saw."

Her certainty piqued Neveah's interest. "Did you ever see one? Walking around and fighting?"

Another nod. "Once."

Neveah couldn't resist. "Was... was it cool? I mean, it was a giant robot fighting demons. I imagine it was pretty cool."

"No." Stella's voice seemed even more toneless than it had been thus far. "I don't think that it was." Her gaze left Neveah and focused on something unseen. "The Eidolons were powerful, but I don't believe that anything created by humans was ever going to be capable of fighting in The End. There were thirteen built in total. None of them managed to have any real effect on the war."

"Oh. That's... a bummer."

"I agree."

Her memories were vague, but Neveah could still recall the excited whispers of other refugees during the war as they spoke about the Eidolon Project. The last of humanity's greatest minds and all of its remaining resources, brought together one final time to produce colossal, mechanical titans which could stand up against their enemies.

Up to that point, only the angels—not yet the insane destroyers they were now—had been able to fight the demons. The Eidolons, people claimed, would be the last and greatest weapons of man, finally allowing them to fight the supernatural invaders on their own level. To Neveah, hearing that they had apparently been far less than that was, indeed, a bummer.

It was then that Creed finally decided to chime back in. "So, you're a girl with seeds that will never grow, given to her by a mysterious stranger, who's done nothing but garden since the end of time, and who's never seen anything interesting beyond a metal hand sticking out of a lake. Have I got all that?"

"Creed..." Stella interjected. Her tone was still neutral, but it seemed like an admonishment.

Creed glanced in the nun's direction, but didn't take the hint. He walked several steps towards Neveah, looming over her and looking her up and down like he was seeing her for the first time.

"Who are you? Really?"

"I'm no one." Neveah was almost surprised at how easily she said it. And how honestly she meant it. "Really."

Creed scrutinized her for another few moments, but whatever it was he was searching for, he apparently couldn't find it. With a sigh, he stepped back and returned to his seat. He looked tired.

"I'm sorry," Neveah said. "I really don't know what to tell you. I just plant my seeds."

"You don't need to apologize," Stella responded. She glanced at Creed as if expecting him to say something, and when he didn't, she continued, "It's just that your claim is... very unusual. The idea of someone having never encountered an angel at this point is difficult to accept."

Neveah couldn't disagree. She used to wonder at her apparent luck. It had even caused her a fair amount of guilt; while the whole rest of humanity was systematically being wiped out, she got to wander the world planting seeds and never seeing a moment of it.

At some point, she had learned to turn off such extraneous thoughts. Her world became walking, digging, planting, and repeating. She'd *had* to become like that; it was the only way to bear the solitude.

Don't think about it, she told herself.

Aloud, she said, "Again, I just plant my seeds. Whatever happens, happens."

"You'd be better off giving it up." Creed didn't sound especially vindictive, rather stating it as a matter of fact. "Whoever gave you those seeds clearly didn't understand what had happened yet."

He looked at Neveah with electric-blue eyes, and she realized it hadn't just been a trick of the light before; his pupils really did appear to be white instead of black. It gave his gaze an eerie glow. "Those seeds are never going to grow, any more than your body will. You might as well stop."

"Stop now?" Neveah forced levity into her tone. She didn't know why, but she felt she *had* to stay positive while explaining herself to this man. "When I'm so close to getting through them all?"

"And what happens then?"

"I suppose I'll have to find something else to do." Vague and non-committal, but it was the best she could do while still sounding like she knew what she was talking about.

"There *is* nothing to do. Not anything worth doing, at least."

Neveah found herself wishing he would be angrier or more venomous in his words. She'd even take him laughing in her face. This dead defeated tone was far more difficult to bear.

"Maybe. But doing something useless is still doing something, right? Finding *anything* to do is rare these days, so I figure as long as I still *want* to do something, then I'm still me." She tapped a finger lightly on her forehead. "Means it's not all gone just yet."

The man didn't appear to have a response to that. He just sat there, staring into her. Stella stared as well, and Neveah found it rather disconcerting how impenetrable each of their gazes was. Normal people shouldn't be so good at hiding their thoughts.

Neveah glanced down. "That's just what I think, anyways. And it's not as if I'm the only one, though. The Samaritans are still fighting, aren't they?"

The entire atmosphere shifted at her words. She looked up to see Creed glowering in such a way that made his scar look positively villainous, and even Stella was now looking at the floor. Realizing she had somehow made a mistake, Neveah felt her body tense.

Creed's voice was low and emotionless. "And what exactly do you know about them?"

"Not much. I know they fight angels, but since I've never seen one, I've never met any of *them* either. There's... seven, right?" Neither of the others responded, and Neveah found the tension almost unbearable. "Have... you ever met one?"

"Yes," Creed muttered.

"I... take it you're not a fan?" Neveah had no idea why she would ask such a question when the man was obviously irritated, but she had never been good at controlling her words.

"You could say that."

"Oh. Sorry, then." As she continued to observe the man and nun in their dark silence, an obvious suspicion began to poke in the back of Neveah's head. Given the sheer unease she felt, she didn't dare give voice to it directly.

"It was never worth an angel attack, but I've always wanted to meet one, I suppose." She stared at Creed for a long while, hoping for some kind of reaction.

He didn't meet her stare. "Sorry to disappoint. But you're not missing much."

"Really? I'd think anyone who can fight off an angel must be very impressive."

"Afraid not. And if you haven't noticed, the angels haven't gone anywhere."

Neveah glanced away from the bitterness in his tone. "True. I guess I just thought... well, at least they're trying."

"Yeah. They've been *trying* for a while." His voice went from bitter to venomous. "Don't let any stories you've heard fool you. They're not saviors. Just a bunch of self-righteous fools who think they're saving the world. But the world's still *dead*. The truth is, they're even more useless than those seeds."

"Creed," Stella interjected once more, and this time her voice managed to snap him out of his burgeoning rant. Unclenching his hands, he glanced down at the floor.

Neveah was still looking at the ground. The silence in the large room bounced around with no end in sight, and after a long enough while, Neveah realized that there wasn't going to be anything else to gain from this discussion.

"Well... I'm sorry again for intruding. I should get moving." She stood from the pew and brushed some of the dust from her behind, trying to look as casual as she could.

Stella rose from her pew. "Please. Don't feel like you have to leave right away. I apologize if we've made you feel unwelcome. If you would like to rest here, you can certainly do so."

The words pulled at Neveah in a way the nun probably didn't realize. It had been so long since she'd even *seen* other people, let alone had an actual conversation with them.

But perhaps it had been *too* long. She didn't seem to be any good at it anymore, and she couldn't escape the feeling that there was nowhere good left for this chance meeting to go.

Forcing a calm smile, Neveah fixed the nun with what she hoped was a pleasant expression. "I appreciate that. But I already got a good nap on your dirt over there." She gave a weak chuckle. "Honestly, I've spent so much time outside that I can't even sleep on regular beds and stuff anymore."

She wondered if such lie was even a little convincing.

"Besides, I don't like to waste too much time in any one place. Planting's just about all I do, and seeing as this place already has enough pretty things," she motioned to the garish flowerbed nearby, "I'd be better off finding someplace else. Thank you for the offer, though. I'll get out of your hair now."

With that, she turned and headed towards the wooden doors. She was about three paces away when Creed's voice stopped her from behind. "Wait."

Neveah half-turned over her shoulder, part of her wishing he'd let her leave and another glad he hadn't. He stood from his seat again and seemed to be struggling to say something.

After a moment, he sighed. "You really shouldn't go towards the city. What's left of it is falling apart. It's dangerous."

He pointed to his left, out one of the church's broken windows towards the miles of indistinguishable hills beyond. "If you head West, there's a forest. It's dead now, but there's no trouble anywhere nearby."

He shifted awkwardly in place and didn't look at her when he continued, "Maybe you can find a few good spots there, or... something."

His tone told her he still didn't give a rat's ass about her planting, but Neveah still found herself grinning at the gesture. "Thanks."

She walked the rest of the way to the door. With a push, she opened the way and stared out at the grey, lifeless world before her. She looked at the black sun hanging where it always did and couldn't stop herself from looking back one last time at the splash of colorful flowers behind her.

"Hey... Creed?" she asked. "What's the world look like to you?"

He regarded Neveah in silence for a long moment, briefly looking past her at the landscape beyond the church threshold. Eventually, he fixed Neveah with a look so empty he looked like a walking corpse.

"It's dark."

Neveah just nodded, then turned and began making her way back up the hill, once again feeling the chill of stagnant, unmoving air. Once she reached the top, she began to follow one of the many dirt paths in the direction Creed had indicated.

She focused her thoughts on her task, glancing around as she walked in case any spot looked particularly aesthetic to her. There would be nothing to gain by dwelling on what had just occurred. It had been just another meeting, another set of strangers, another conversation, and another re-affirmation that what she was doing was right, regardless of what anyone thought.

And yet, as she continued her endless wandering, she couldn't push the images from her mind: that beautifully ugly collection of flowers, and those hollow blue eyes.

He looked like... he was hurting.

Chapter III
"God's Gonna Cut You Down"

Somewhere, high in the starless sky, a monster ran for its life. It had enveloped itself in unholy flame, a hideous combination of reds, blacks, and purples. It streaked about like a comet beneath the grey light of the dark sun, moving at a speed no fathomable force should have been able to match.

Unfortunately, that which hunted the creature was anything but fathomable.

The monster could not see its pursuer, but felt Its presence in every direction. No matter how much distance was put between them, the strength of Its aura did not diminish.

Every so often, the monster could feel the foreboding sensation of *something* reaching out to grab it, like a vast hand threatening to snuff out the flames and dash its body against the earth below. The monster had somehow managed to heighten its speed each time, but though it had thus far managed to evade the ghostly grasp, each escape proved narrower than the last.

Just as it was beginning to wonder how much longer it could possibly continue this fruitless game, a presence flashed into the monster's awareness. A single soul, distant and unexpected, but so familiar that it nearly caused the monster to slow in its desperate flight.

Could it be? Here? Now? In *this* circumstance? The monster had long known that things like "fate" and "destiny" no longer held any sway over the world in which it lived. But to stumble across the very thing it had been searching for? Completely by chance as it fled for its unnatural life? Perhaps those concepts were not so preposterous after all.

The monster struggled to keep a sudden thrill in check. It could not simply charge forth towards the soul it had sensed. Not with the shadow of Death still threatening to subsume it. The pursuer was so close now, close enough that the monster would be followed no matter where it fled.

Deep within its breast, the monster could hear its children scream. A cacophony of pitiful wails, just as desperate for survival as it was. They clawed and tore at the inside of its flesh, demanding their father to set them free lest they share his end.

The monster almost laughed. So weak, its children. So pitiful in their fearful fervor. So—

Wait.

Could that be it? A solution? An opportunity? A chance?

No. It wasn't a matter of "could." There was no other avenue which afforded even the slightest chance at a reprieve. It was a reckless strategy even by the monster's own standards, and yet was now the only recourse that remained.

Summoning even greater speed, the monster focused entirely on closing the distance between itself and the soul it had felt. The shadow of the pursuer's hand came upon it once again, closer than ever. There would be no escape this time. All the monster could do now was make one last, foolish wager.

Just as the pursuer's grasp threatened to enclose it completely, the monster steeled itself and reached deep into its very being. The screams of its children reached a new crescendo.

You want free, little ones? Be careful what you wish for.

With a roar of defiance, the monster tore itself to pieces.

If Joshua still had his eyes, they would have snapped open. Without a second's delay, he rose from where he'd been seated atop a nameless hill in some random part of the world.

The last image he'd seen through his mind's eye replayed in his head: the comet of hellfire, inches away from destruction, erupting in a flash of destructive energy before splitting off into smaller shards that rained down to the earth below.

Didn't think he'd actually do it.

Having been forced out of his viewing by the explosion of power, Joshua tried to re-center himself and locate his target once again, but as he'd suspected, the presence had disappeared. Or rather, it had become so weak that he could no longer feel it.

Not that it mattered. Joshua had seen where his brother's path had taken him. Finding it would be simple enough; all he had to do was follow the nearby presence that he *could* feel.

Joshua grimaced as he realized what was coming. Despite his best efforts, they were going to find each other again. It had been bound to happen sooner or later, but he couldn't think of a worse way for things to come to a head after all this time.

Oh well. No use putting it off.

Resigning himself to the reality of the situation, Joshua fixed the remaining presence in his mind. Around him, space began to shift and fold in on itself. In the next instant, he was streaking across space, barely more than a thought on the wind as he barreled towards a long-overdue reunion.

Creed supposed the basement of the church was in marginally better shape than the main building above, if only because it was hidden away from the stagnant, rotting air.

A large, open box of a room, it had been used for storage by its owners long ago. Originally, it had held the everyday tools and items used in the church's daily functions. Shortly before The End, when the world was still burning and demons lashed out across the land, the space had been used to hide once-holy relics now branded as heretic, becoming a reliquary in which the last of a religion would gather dust.

In time, the evil had found the relics, slinking its way below and swallowing them whole. What little significance the church had left was consumed alongside them, reduced to nothing more than a box of wood and stone devoid of sanctity or sanctuary.

At least they'd been nice enough not to step on the flowers.

As he lay looking up at the ceiling, Creed supposed that the basement was once again serving its purpose: a hidden space for useless relics.

The emptiness of the room in which he rested was exacerbated by the long shadows cast by a pair of primitive yellow lights. They were dim enough not to show off the layers of dust which covered the floor and large wooden table in the room's center.

The basement had perhaps once smelled of must and grime and other forms of age, but so many lifetimes of nothing had erased any scent that might have remained.

Creed found himself glancing towards the top of the nearby staircase, and the door which led to the church's ground floor. Rude as it may be, he wished Stella would remove his head from her lap and head upstairs to her own room. Unlike him, who couldn't sleep if he wanted to, she seemed to need more rest than ever these days.

Furthermore, the nun in question didn't seem to be enjoying the situation any more than he was. She sat straighter than usual on the wooden bench they occupied, gazing at nothing as she supported Creed's head on her legs.

She wasn't moving her fingers through Creed's hair as she sometimes liked to do, which was fine with him. The way she forced him to use her lap as a pillow was silly enough; her occasional attempts at affection only made Creed more uncomfortable.

They had been sitting in silence for quite a while when Creed finally decided he might as well try and talk to her about what had happened. "If you're angry, you can say so."

"Why do you think I'm angry?" Stella's voice was as measured as ever, and her eyes remained focused on some random part of the far wall.

"You only make me do this when you want to make things awkward."

"It's my understanding that most people would consider this a form of reward."

"We're not most people. And you know your lap isn't exactly comfortable"

"I'm not angry."

"You never look at me when you are."

There were a few beats of silence. Then she turned her head down to fix her violet-eyed gaze squarely into his own. "You were harsh to that girl."

Creed didn't feel like arguing. "Yeah."

"You didn't need to be."

"Probably not."

"I know you're only telling me what I want to hear."

Seemed he'd be arguing anyway. "What did you want? Did you want her to stay here and live with us forever?"

"Do not marginalize my concern with exaggerated hypotheticals." It never took her more than a second to think of a response.

"It's not like she could have stayed," he continued. "She had an *important* task to return to."

"It is exceedingly rare to find anyone who bothers to perform any sort of task these days."

"She's not special. There were lots of Lambs who tried to keep up appearances after everything ended. If what she said about never meeting an angel was true, that just means she somehow got lucky enough to make it this far without realizing there's no point."

Stella lifted her head and resumed looking at the wall. If she wasn't mad at him before, she was now. "Regardless. You shouldn't mock her for her desire to accomplish something. Even you have a goal."

At that, Creed allowed the conversation to die. He fancied himself the only one who could see through Stella's limited capacity for expression and grasp the ghostly facsimiles of emotion behind them. The one he'd seen after he sent the girl away was one of frustration, and the one he'd heard in her words just now had been one of accusation.

Luckily, she wouldn't directly engage in the subject of his trips to the city if he himself didn't. She knew perfectly well how such a discussion would go, the circles they would spin while never arriving at a resolution.

So here he lay on her shapely legs, letting their usual silence take over. It had been a novel distraction to meet another person after so many ages, but it was time for them to return to their usual repertoire of conversation topics: which was to say, nothing.

Creed couldn't recall precisely when the last real topic of discussion had been exhausted between them. The complete and total cessation of anything new or noteworthy to discuss between two people was something rare—impossible, even—before this world where time was both infinite and void.

Creed personally found the notion comforting in a strange way; there was a sort of solace in truly knowing everything about another, a certainty that there was nothing left to be said.

Thinking in such a way, he could content himself with lying mute upon his companion's uncomfortable lap. He may not have been capable of sleep, but if nothing else, he could allow his mind to drift in the quiet.

Ssaaaa...

The hiss slithered into Creed's mind, and he stiffened. He fought down a chill through his spine as the ghostly sound tried to slink its way further into his being.

Hssssaaaaaaaa...

Again, longer this time. A sickening whisper of ice and honey. Creed would have liked to pretend that he had no idea what it was, that he hadn't immediately recognized it.

Hssashasaaaa...

The sound became more distinct, as if trying to convey a message. Creed resolved not to budge an inch, to let no indication into the world that this sound existed or that it could affect him.

Ssssaaaaaaa... Shaaaaaaaaaaa....!

It wasn't possible. Creed couldn't lie still with such whispers filling his insides. Trying as hard as he could not to jolt, he lifted his head from Stella's lap and sat up. He stood, ignoring her stare and trying not to let anything show in his posture or body language.

"What's wrong?"

Naturally, he couldn't fool her for a second. She saw every flaw in his posture, every abnormal flicker in body language. Creed tried to rack his brain for a lie, some excuse that wouldn't raise her suspicions.

SHAAAAAAAAAAAHHH!!!!!!!!!!!!!!!!

The whisper turned to a shout of agony, the ice to shards that pierced his insides, and the honey a thickness that clogged his thoughts. The pain that shot through Creed's head was too sudden to withstand, and he clutched at his skull, growling as he hunched over like a drunk.

No, he thought through the pain. *Not this. Not him!*
SHAAAAAAAAAAAAAGHGHGHG!!!!!! BROTH—

The scream reached a crescendo before ceasing altogether. The pain vanished, as did the cold. All was silent, as it had been only moments before. But things were no longer the same.

Creed took several deep, shaky breaths before slowly righting himself. Despair in his heart, he turned over his shoulder to look at Stella, who stared back in silence.

He couldn't bring himself to say the words, but as it turned out, he didn't have to. With a jolt, her head snapped abruptly in another direction. Her eyes widened slightly, and she rose from the bench without shifting her gaze an inch.

"What?" Creed asked, though he already knew the answer.

"Movement. To the West. Three sources." Her voice was even more toneless and efficient than usual. "Demons."

If Creed had a heart, it would have sunk. "Three of them?"

"Close together." A brief pause, then, "They're splitting off. They sprang from the same source, but the source has faded now. The other three have scattered. No unity, no pattern. Power is decreasing rapidly: they're suppressing their presences." Her eyes snapped to Creed. "Do we go?"

A terrifying question. It had been so long since their last encounter of this sort that even she seemed unsure of what to do next.

Three demons, Creed thought. *Why?*

One idea stuck particularly in his mind, and he met the nun's gaze again. "How far have they gone?"

Her eyes returned to that far-away place as she observed. "A half-mile already." She paused, her gaze becoming unfocused for a moment. "Their presences have been fully suppressed. I've lost them." She once again looked to Creed, who had begun to pace.

They shouldn't be able to get that far away from him. Did they escape? Not possible. Then how—?

He started as an absurd possibility entered his mind: *He let them go?*

"Creed," Stella called, pulling him out of his thoughts. "Do we go?"

"Not to them. To where they split from."

"There's no presence there."

"That's how I know it's the right place."

"We can't ignore them."

"I won't. But the source is more important. Tell me where."

There was the slightest of pauses. "I can show you."

"Nice try. You're staying here."

"There are three demons whose presences we can't feel. You will need help."

"They're running away. Won't come anywhere near me."

"What about the source?"

"I can handle the source."

"You're not strong enough anymore."

"And you are?"

The words came out more sharply than he'd intended. Stella's eyes flicked to the floor at his words. Creed felt a slight pang of guilt, but not nearly enough for him to reconsider. Discussion on that matter had *long* since been exhausted.

He softened his tone just a hair. "It'll be alright. Just tell me where."

She didn't look up at him. "The forest. I can't be more precise than that. There is no presence."

"It's enough." He turned towards the dusty staircase leading back up.

Her voice stopped him in his tracks. "Can you really fight?"

Of course she wouldn't just let him leave. He turned over his shoulder. "I can."

She just stared back at him.

"I can *fight*," he insisted. "It hasn't taken everything from me yet."

"The forest. We told her to go there."

Creed saw the ghost of guilt behind her eyes and could not face it. Turning away, he forced any emotion out of his response. "I only suggested it. Going would have been her choice."

"You should look for her."

"She isn't important."

"It would be our fault." Creed heard genuine stubbornness in her voice, which was rare. "It's our responsibility. If she's there, you have to help her."

Creed tried not to clench his jaw. He didn't *have* to do anything. He didn't even *have* to go investigate this disturbance, if not for the fact that he knew it would come find him regardless of what he did.

But a flash of pale hair and green eyes ran through his mind, and Creed had to stop himself from clicking his tongue in annoyance.

"I'll find what I find."

With that, he continued up the stairs, through the main hall, and out the doors.

Joshua stood perfectly balanced on the tips of his toes atop the pointed steeple of the church, arms crossed. Though he could not see it, his mind's eye observed the bitter aura of a man marching out into empty wilderness.

He felt a twinge of disappointment that Creed apparently couldn't feel his presence, though that wasn't unexpected. Things were likely just as bad as he'd feared.

His soul still has some *color left. Might still have a chance.*

Joshua briefly turned his mental gaze from the other man's retreating presence to his destination far to the west. The shape of the land echoed in his senses, telling him it was a collection of twisted trees laying past many rolling hills.

He tried not to feel too anxious about what he knew was waiting in those shadows, nor about the fact that Creed was moving ever closer to it.

Joshua told himself that this reunion had been inevitable. Necessary, even. Resigning himself, he chose to accept that he would finally get to play the role of little brother again after so long.

He wished he could have been excited about it.

__Chapter IV__
"O' Death"

Even by Creed's especially meager standards, the area that had once been a forest was a depressing locale.

In every direction, leafless trees twisted their way into the air. Their bodies had been bleached white by some disaster before The End rendered them frozen that way. Now they resembled gnarled, skeletal hands reaching to the sky, begging for rain that would never come.

No one tree looked meaningfully different from the others, and Creed didn't make it far before giving up on keeping his bearings. Accompanied by nothing but the crunch of dirt and twigs beneath his feet, he marched along in whatever direction he felt, knowing that his shit luck would lead him to his quarry before long.

After what could have been hours or minutes, he came upon what had once been a stream, but was now just a dry scar carving its way through the ground. It must have dried up sometime during The End; had the water survived, it would have still been there, dead and motionless and never again able to flow.

With nothing else to go on, Creed flipped a coin in his head and followed the winning direction. The dry river could have been leading him back out of the forest for all he knew, but somehow he doubted he'd get out of this so easily.

Indeed, after following only a short distance, Creed came to a break in the trees and stepped into a clearing. The scar he had been following gradually widened and opened into a sizable pit. A pond once, perhaps. Now just a bowl of dust. Creed brought himself to the lip of the hole and looked down.

From a distance, it looked to be some kind of worm, pale and shivering in the perpetual chill of the air. As Creed climbed down into the pit and began to approach, the worm took on a slightly more humanoid shape, if only barely.

He came within a few feet of the thing before noticing the ground around it was discolored, wet with some sticky substance fanning out a few feet in each direction.

Coming to a stop, Creed regarded the thing in earnest. He was thankful to be incapable of vomiting, because even his lowest expectations hadn't prepared him for a sight so sickening.

What was left resembled a man, albeit one so withered and ancient that it had more in common with the surrounding trees than a living person. And at least the trees had something resembling limbs; the old man's shoulders ended in bloody, shredded stumps, and his lower half appeared to have been torn off just above the groin.

It was from these gaping wounds that most of the blood had spilled. The rest had likely come from the massive gash in the thing's chest, a gruesome hole right where a heart should be. It would have been the perfect image of a freshly-hewn corpse were it not for the weak rising and falling of the thing's skeletal chest.

Creed stood taking in the gruesome sight for a long moment before—as slowly as he dared—extending an arm out to the side and splaying his fingers. But the moment he moved, so too did the breathing corpse.

A bald head slowly swiveled in Creed's direction, and although the creature's eyes were clouded over, Creed knew full well that the corpse could see him, its gaze boring into him as well as any functioning pair of eyes.

Slowly, its wrinkled mouth opened wide to reveal a desiccated, toothless maw from which poured yet another stream of blood; it seemed the wretched thing's tongue had been shorn away as well.

«Found youuu...»

The voice was not physical. It resounded in the air as if coming from all directions, and that was all Creed needed to hear. He took the last few steps toward the corpse, ignoring the squelch of his boots in the blood-soaked dirt. As he did, the power he had been calling in to his hand materialized.

A mass of shapeless, grey-brown clay appeared in his grasp, warping and elongating. Its edges sharpened to unnatural levels, and in moments, it had solidified into the shape of a spear, approximately six feet long and deathly sharp on both ends.

With no hesitation, Creed raised the clay weapon above his head before bringing it down as hard as he could onto the old man's throat. He felt the impact of the spearpoint hitting dirt, but not flesh and bone. The spot where he struck exploded in a burst of white mist that briefly obscured the thing's ruined face.

Angry but unsurprised, Creed pulled his weapon from the dirt and watched as the fog drew in and reformed, leaving the living corpse in the same state it had been in moments before.

The old man let out a short series of bloody hacks that Creed took to be laughter before the awful voice echoed around him again:

«I have missed you too... little brother... I knew... you would come for me...»

Creed forced himself to speak through his disgust. "Why? Why would you come here? Of *all* places!?"

«Coincidence... mixed with desperation.»

Even in the form of projected words, the creature's voice was sickening and raspy, the sound of pestilence itself. *«I was simply... running. But then... I felt you...»*

"Bullshit, Stryfe. An entire world, and you just happen to land in my backyard?"

Stryfe—for it *was* him, in spite of this mangled visage—made a movement as if he was rolling his blind eyes. *«Perhaps... it was fate...»*

A joke so unfunny it almost made Creed laugh. He ran one hand through his hair, spear gripped tightly in the other.

"Who the hell would you run from?"

«Who else... could it be...?»

Creed pondered a moment before realizing that there was, in fact, only one possible answer. The dull ache of the brand on his back seemed to throb in response to the thought, though that may have only been his imagination.

"What did you do?"

Another hideous smile let fall a mouthful of blood.

«*Nothing... but what was asked of me. My role... was fulfilled. And our jailer... saw no more use for me...*»

Creed couldn't hide his surprise. "'Fulfilled?' You actually gathered them?"

«*Every last one.*»

Creed honestly didn't know what to make of that. A Samaritan's role fulfilled? The idea was nearly comical. Then again, if there was any role that *could* be fulfilled, it was Stryfe's. Unlike the others, his targets were finite, and though it had taken him ages, an end to his task was not impossible.

So this is how It rewards success, Creed thought.

That wasn't unexpected. Their "leader" had always made it very clear their lives would be forfeit one day. Creed was mildly surprised at the brutality of the response, but then again, he could never begrudge someone wanting to kill the monster lying at his feet. Which reminded him:

"Three demons ran from here. What happened? I know you didn't lose them."

«*It was... the only way. He could sense me... anywhere I went. He would always find me. I had to diminish myself. I chose... three of my children. I gave them my limbs... my tongue... my heart... and set them free.*»

He motioned with his chin towards his ruined form. «*This... is what was left. Weak... useless... but undetectable. And as you just saw... unable to die....*»

It made an absurd sort of sense. Without its heart, the thing in front of him was just a shade, a substance-less image of what remained in Stryfe's soul. Too weak to even kill. It might have been clever if it wasn't so asinine.

"What is this supposed to have accomplished?" Creed asked.

«*I've bought time... such as it is. All I need now... is to track those naughty children down again.*»

Creed felt the prickle of danger on the back of his neck. "And how do you plan on going about that like this?"

The old man did nothing but give Creed another sickening smile. The implication was immediately apparent, and his temper grew white-hot once more.

"Oh, that's a hilarious joke, Stryfe. But I'm not laughing."

The demon did not seem especially shocked by the response. «*Have you truly come... to hate me so, brother?*»

Creed responded by taking a booted heel and bringing it down on the specter's head. As before, it burst into a cloud of white mist. When it reformed, Stryfe's bloody mouth was set in an irritated-looking line.

«*A simple 'yes'... might have sufficed.*»

Creed dropped to his haunches and looked the shade right in its clouded eyes.

"After everything you've done, the idea that you think *anyone* would ever help you is fucking comical. We are *all* dead already. You. Me. The others. There was never any doubt in that. Not from the day everything ended. We've all got it coming— you more than anyone. I'm going to leave you in this pit, and either Rictus is going to find your strays and finish off what's left of you, or you're just going to writhe here for all eternity."

He leaned in as close as he dared and hissed, "You've been running from your judgment for too long. No more."

Creed rose to his feet. With a thought, he had the clay spear dissipate from his hand. He turned to leave, but the shade's ethereal voice resounded one last time: «*But I'm not... the only one hiding... am I?*»

Creed stiffened at the words, fighting down the pointless urge to immediately summon another weapon.

«*I think you wish to avoid him... as much as I. Perhaps... even more so.*»

Creed refused to let it show on his face how right the demon was. Since it had first been brought up, Creed's mind had been puzzling out how he was going to avoid their "leader" when Its gaze finally passed over this place. He hadn't worked out a solution yet, but he would. He had to. He could *not* be found. Not now.

Even so, Creed refused to give Stryfe any form of satisfaction. With one last spiteful look, he ignored the question and began to walk away from the wretched shade.

He didn't notice that he had turned directly towards the black sun. He did not think about the grey glow that it gave off, or consider the fact that even such a weak light was enough to cast a shadow.

A sound like sudden wind filled Creed's ears from behind, and he whipped his head around just in time to see Stryfe's broken form burst into mist and seep into the ground that his shadow touched.

"NO!!!" he shouted. But it was far too late.

His entire body seized as he was overcome with the pain of another soul forcing its way into his own. The ice and honey filled him as it did before, magnified a thousand-fold and spreading through every atom of his being.

Creed let out a guttural scream, falling to his knees and clutching his head as the feeling of a nail piercing into his brain overcame him.

His thoughts went haywire, and he suddenly had trouble recalling who he was. Was he Creed? What were these feelings that weren't Creed? What were these two voices screaming from his throat? These two pairs of hands grabbing at his skull?

It stopped.

Creed came back to reality on all fours, panting. Like a switch had been flipped, the pain ceased. His vision returned, and the world around him was quiet again.

He could almost swear that nothing had happened were it not for the cold, sickening weight that now sat somewhere deep within him. A pressure that hadn't been there before.

«*Sorry, brother,*» came a whisper directly within his mind. It was the old man's voice, only now it spoke more clearly and with greater strength than it had before. «*I tried to ask nicely...*»

"Get out."

«*It's too late. I've stitched myself to you.*»

"GET OUT!"

«*Our souls are joined now. And it would seem that I am no longer strong enough to undo what's been done.*»

Creed clutched his head again. This couldn't be happening. It had to be a lie, just like everything that spewed from Stryfe's mouth. "I'll fucking kill you."

«*I wouldn't recommend trying in this state. Perhaps things would be different if I had my full power, no?*»

Creed felt like he was going mad. The sensation of this thing crawling on his back was sickening. The world began to spin, and for once, Creed wished he was capable of vomiting, that he could do anything to—

It found him.

Everything, from his body to his soul to the barren trees and each speck of dirt upon the ground, went completely and utterly still beneath a new presence that suddenly washed over the area. All of Creed's anger and pain evaporated, subsumed by a cloud of pure *dread*.

«*No time,*» came Stryfe's voice. It no longer carried even a hint of smugness. «*It felt that. It feels me now. And you. It's coming.*»

Creed closed his eyes, wanting to scream again. Why was this happening? Why now? He had been so close. Just a bit longer and it would have all been over, so why had these bastards chosen *now* to come and drag him back into their world?

«*What will you do, brother? Will you let It come?*»

No. He couldn't be caught. Not like this, not in a way that would unravel everything he had been striving for.

Stryfe seemed to read Creed's feelings without giving word to them. «*Then there's only one option, isn't there?*»

Somehow, Creed forced the feeling back into his nerves. Swallowing his terror, he rose to his feet and clenched his fists. His damnable, cursed brother had forced the puppet's strings into his flesh, and now he had no choice but to smile and play the part.

«*Run*», said the demon. «*RUN!*»

He did. Desperately, pointlessly, utterly uselessly, Creed ran.

He made it ten steps past the tree line.

Endless miles of hills stretched out before Creed in all directions, but any possible escape they may have promised vanished once he felt the brand on his back ignite.

He came to a dead stop as the feeling of molten lead lanced down his spinal cord, heralding the arrival of the figure that appeared in Creed's path mere moments later.

Appeared was perhaps the wrong word, because that would imply the figure had visibly come from somewhere. That was not the case; they had simply not been there, and then they had. Creed could only stare as they materialized a mere ten feet from where he stood. He struggled not to let despair and the burning of his brand overwhelm him.

The figure wore the body of a man, and Creed supposed it *was* one in its current state. He was thin but stood tall and imposing, nearly a full head more than Creed's own considerable height. His clothing was little more than a collection of tattered pale cloth stitched together to form a ragged set of robes that covered the entirety of his form.

Beneath a tightly-wrapped hood, the vague shape of the man's head could be seen, but any definable features were obscured by a grey iron mask in the shape of a grimacing human skull. The only thing visible from behind its sinister visage was the glimmer of two white pupils within the eye sockets. Those eerie glimmers, a defining trait of all Samaritans, bore into Creed without mercy.

After only a short moment, the man spoke in a voice that sounded scratched and muffled, as if it was coming through on an old radio or outdated television:

"I did not expect to find you here, Crusader."

Creed focused the whole of his will on keeping calm. There had to be a way out of this, but panicking would make it impossible. Controlling his breath and standing straighter, Creed looked into the sockets of the dark man's mask.

"Rictus..." He did not use the other Samaritan's title as he had for Creed. "It's been a while."

The man returned no pleasantries and, as always, spoke without even the barest hint of emotion in his disturbing radio voice. "I shall admit to a sense of confusion, Crusader. Do you have an explanation as to why the Apostate is bound to your soul?"

No time wasted. Fine. Creed didn't feel like talking around the situation either. "I assure you it wasn't by choice."

The brand on his back was positively searing now, but he refused to let the pain show. "He was just a shade, and I let my guard down. Guess he had just enough strength left to force his way in."

"I never imagined you so foolish as to think the Apostate ever short on deceits."

Creed couldn't exactly disagree. "Like I said, it's been a while."

Rictus tilted his masked head. "I am surprised at you as well, Apostate. Such desperation is uncharacteristic of you."

«*It's not as if you left me with many options, leader,*» came Stryfe's voice at last. It resounded in Creed's head, but he knew Rictus could hear it as well. «*And when my dear brother refused to extend his hand, I was forced to take it a bit… forcefully.* »

"Do not think that you have bought yourself a reprieve. Your role has ended, and you will not avoid this last fate which lies before you."

"So it's true?" Creed asked.

"Indeed." Rictus' words stuttered with some unnatural static. "The Apostate has gathered his scattered brood. Every fiend left behind in The End now resides within his flesh. The only duty left to him now is to offer their souls to the Preceptor, as well as his own."

«*You're being too hasty, Leader. I haven't become as useless as you—*»

"Be silent." Rictus had not raised his voice an ounce, but there was a force behind the words that instantly quelled the demon's voice. "You may try and bargain, but it is the Preceptor within me that has lain down your fate; a fate which was made evident to every Samaritan on the day the Covenant was forged. All the souls which remain in Creation belong to *It*, and you have kept yours long past what was destined."

There was a kind of shift in the pressure the man was giving off, and Creed felt confident that a move was about to be made. He quickly held up a hand, surprised he was able to keep it from shaking.

"Hold on." He had to keep a foothold in this conversation, no matter what. "You know me, and you know him. I'm not a part of this by choice. If you want to take him, I'm happy to let you do it. I'll kill him myself if you want. But you've got to get him out of me first. You reap him now, it kills us both."

«Do you think he cares?» came the demon's voice. Creed ignored it.

Rictus appeared unmoved. "I cannot do this. Your souls have been fused, and even the Preceptor's power cannot separate them. We will not let him escape again."

"This isn't even all of his soul, Rictus. It's just a shadow. He gave his body and power to those demons."

"I am aware of the strays. They cannot truly escape so long as they carry aspects of the Apostate within them. They will be hunted, and these aspects will be eradicated. But that shade carries his will and mind. These are things I will not allow to remain."

Creed felt himself take one step back against his will. "There has to be a way!" He found it impossible to keep from shouting now. His mind moved wildly, searching for anything to placate the man, even for a moment. "My role isn't finished yet, right? Killing Stryfe now just means you lose another Samaritan!"

At this, Rictus paused and seemed to give his words some consideration. Creed dared to hope the man might see *some* reason.

"*Are* you still a Samaritan, Crusader?"

Oh no.

"What?" Creed asked, trying to sound incredulous but knowing where the conversation was going.

"When last did you slay an Adversary?" Rictus' unmoving gaze bored right into the core of Creed's being. "When last did you fulfill your duty of defending the Lambs?"

"It's... been a while," Creed admitted, knowing he couldn't hide the truth. "But the fact is I can't even remember that last time I've seen a Lamb, let alone an angel. There's been nothing *to* fight!"

The response was immediate. "Do you think me so gullible? There has not been life here since the day of your failure, and no Adversary would ever fall upon a land devoid of Lambs." Somehow, the weight of the man's gaze grew even heavier upon Creed's body.

"The Preceptor's labors have kept us busy, but not so much that we could not observe you. Given what your battle with the Archangel cost, I was willing to support the Crucifer when he came begging for the Preceptor to grant you a reprieve. And yet here you remain in this lifeless region, even after all this time."

A brief image of green eyes flashed through Creed's mind at the mention of no life, but he kept silent. He did not want Rictus to know of the girl, even if he shouldn't have cared. It wasn't as if the presence of one Lamb could have drawn an angel regardless.

Rictus continued. "I contented myself with our work, hoping that in time, you would begin to move again. But I see now that you have taken advantage of our generosity, and that your true intentions lie elsewhere." He tilted his head again.

"Where have your Colors gone, Crusader?"

The question hung in the air like a guillotine, and Creed had no response.

«*Ah*», Stryfe hissed in his mind. «*So that's why. I thought it was strange...*»

Rictus took a single step forward, prompting Creed to take one back. "You have not broken the rules of the Covenant, but you have ignored them. You have abandoned your duties in an attempt to escape them. You claim yourself a Samaritan but reject your duty. As such, how can I be certain that you still *are* one, Crusader?"

Again, Creed had no words with which to respond. He was finished.

"In the Preceptor's eyes, ending you is akin to ending nothing. There will be no loss in our strength, given that you evidently have none left to give. As such, I see no reason not to let It reap your soul along with the Apostate's."

And there it was—end of discussion. Creed felt numb, and could only lament how close he had been.

Stryfe's irritating voice jolted Creed out of his stupor. «*What will you do? Will this be the end?*»

No. No, this couldn't be the end for him. Creed didn't give a damn what happened to the demon, but he could *not* die here. He could *not* let Rictus and the Preceptor be the ones to do it. Death by *Its* hand was not the release he sought. There was only one way out of this meaningless eternity, and Creed would never reach it if he lost here.

Summoning up an ironic will not to die, Creed snapped a hand out and summoned his remaining power once more. Another cloud of malleable clay churned from nowhere, this time shaping itself into a long-bladed gladius with a simple hilt. He held the earthen sword forward, pointing it directly at Rictus in a futile but defiant gesture.

«*Excellent*», said Stryfe. «*Not so ready to die, then?*»

If Rictus reacted in any way, it was obscured by the skull mask. "Is this truly how you wish to fall?"

Creed said nothing. He knew this action was pointless, that no power he still held could even break his opponent's stride. But it was all he had left, and he would be damned if he didn't at least try. If he was fighting to die, he might as well do so on his own terms.

If Rictus possessed the emotions to elicit a sigh, he likely would have, but instead merely declared: "The Preceptor is the only sliver of fate left in this world. If you seek to struggle against It, I shall not dissuade you."

With that, the world around them began to shift. The presence that had first blanketed the forest returned in full force, like a smothering smog. Rictus lifted a hand towards his mask, and Creed felt the burning of his brand more intensely than before as the man began to speak:

I heard a voice amidst the four beasts—

"Whoa-kay! No need for all that!"

Creed whipped around, eyes wide, at the lively voice that came from behind.

A man was emerging from the tree line at a relaxed pace. He wore a simple pair of black shoes and dark grey pants, and his upper body was covered only by a black wool-lined jacket, unzipped to expose his chest.

His face was disheveled, poorly groomed and covered in uneven stubble. His neck-length dark brown hair, loose and uncombed, was just long enough in the front to mostly obscure the black strip of tattered cloth that wrapped around his head and covered his eyes.

The man sauntered toward them as if going for a stroll, effortlessly ambling across the uneven ground despite the blindfold. A single piece of yellow straw hung from his mouth.

His "gaze," such as it was, never left Rictus, though he did point a lazy finger gun at Creed as he passed. Creed followed the man wordlessly, mouth agape, and thought to himself that this couldn't be what it seemed.

Rictus, against all expectation, had been halted by the sudden interruption as well. The shifting of the air had ceased, and he had dropped his hand away from the iron mask. He gave only a cold black stare as the newcomer placed himself directly in his path.

The unkempt vagrant gave a small, lazy wave, and Creed could have sworn he saw a twitch of annoyance in the Rictus' posture.

"Your presence was not requested, Crucifer."

"And yet..." The newcomer spoke through the straw in his teeth, casually raising hands covered by fingerless gloves, "I am present!"

'Crucifer,' Creed thought. *It can't be.*

«*Now this* is *strange,*» Stryfe chimed in.

Rictus was unamused, not that he was capable of being anything but. "You are merely a facilitator. Your role gives you no authority in the punishment of dissenters."

"Actually, Boss Man, it does. Part of my job is mediating between you schmucks, right? Well, I've come to mediate, and to keep you from blowing what little manpower we've got left to Kingdom Come..." He gave a grimace at the poor choice of words. "Not that it exists anymore. Besides, who could possibly pass up a chance to hear that creepy, old-timey voice of yours?"

The last of Creed's skepticism was erased. There was only one person who could speak so casually to Rictus.

"Joshua?" he croaked, not realizing how dry his throat had become.

The man turned over his shoulder and threw a lazy wave over his back. "Hey there, Big Brother." He gave a slight nod to the demon inside Creed's head. "Bigger Brother."

«*He just can't help himself, can he?*» came Stryfe's voice.

Quiet, Creed thought back. Out loud, he said, "What is this? Why are you—"

He was cut off as Joshua held a finger to his lips. If his eyes hadn't been covered, Creed was sure the man would have winked.

"Details later. Let's get you not killed first."

"The Preceptor brooks no discussion on this matter, Crucifer," Rictus intoned.

"I think you're acting a tad hasty here, Boss Man, and there's no point being hasty in a world with no time! Let's at least *talk* about resolving things in a way that doesn't end with lots of us dead, yeah?"

"You will not change the Apostate's fate. He has fulfilled his role."

"Not asking to at the moment. I'm just wondering if maybe we can give Creed a chance to get out of this mess he's found himself in!"

"The Crusader has abandoned his role. He too is deserving of judgment."

Joshua put his hands up in mock surrender. "Can't argue with you there, but let's not ignore the fact that *you* were the one who signed off on giving him a break in the first place. Not his fault that you never bothered to look up from your desk to see if he was milking the vacation!"

When Rictus did not immediately respond, Joshua continued, "I'm just saying, it's easy to lose interest in your work when the boss never checks in, right? But now that you're here, I'm sure Creed has realized his mistake and is *very* sorry." He turned back over his shoulder to shoot Creed another sightless glance. "Isn't he?"

Creed did nothing but glare, and Joshua turned back to Rictus. "Poor guy. Too ashamed to even speak! But I think he at least deserves a chance to make things up to you!"

"What penance do you believe exists to rectify such a mistake, Crucifer?"

Joshua made a big show of appearing to think it over, even removing the straw from his mouth and tapping it against his forehead as if he had to really rack his brain. "You could start by letting him get Stryfe out in the open for you?"

«*Of course,*» Stryfe hissed.

Joshua pointed his straw in Rictus' direction. "You know you can't take him in this state without also taking Creed. And even then, it's not like he'll really be dead until those pieces he gave the demons have been taken care of, right? Instead of running around doing it yourself, why not have Creed do it for you?"

"What!?" Creed spat, but Joshua held up a finger that politely asked him to shut up.

"Once Stryfe has his body back, he won't be able to hide in Creed's soul anymore, yeah? They'll be split, and then it's back to our regularly scheduled reaping."

Rictus seemed unmoved by the proposal. "What is the Crusader performing this task meant to prove?"

"That he's willing to work hard for you again, I'd say! Just give him a chance to remind you why you had him fighting angels in the first place, and when he's finished, I *promise* he'll go back to his duties. For *good*."

Creed had had just about enough of being spoken for and opened his mouth to protest when he was interrupted by Stryfe's chilling hiss addressing everyone present.

«*Just a moment. I don't particularly care for this outcome of being served on a platter.*»

"You do not possess a voice in this discussion, Apostate. As we have said many times, your role has ended."

«*But does that really mean I have nothing left to offer, Leader?*»

Creed felt a slight sense of unease.

«*I would say that I've proven myself nothing if not capable of fulfilling a role, wouldn't you agree? Can the same be said for my brother here?*»

He wouldn't, Creed thought, panic quickly rising to his throat.

«*I'm certainly in favor of retrieving my body, but once Creed and I have separated again, why not give* me *his role?*»

"Bastard," Creed spat, wishing nothing more than that the demon still had a throat for him to crush.

«*I've an army of demons inside me to fight with, Leader. What better use for them than to fight the Adversaries as my brother refuses to do?*»

"Enough!" Creed barked, utterly infuriated that he was now being forced to bargain for his life like a child convincing their parent to give them a toy instead of their sibling. "Get this thing out of me, and I'll *gladly* kill him for you! I'll kill him and however many angels you want!"

«*What reason do we have to believe that? If nothing else, you at least know that* I *can be trusted to do my duty!*»

"You said yourself he's avoided this for too long, Rictus! Don't you dare let him slip away again!"

Joshua let out a small, tired sigh and held up another finger in Creed's direction, "Hey, big brothers, why don't you let me—"

"Quiet!" Creed shouted.

Silence! hissed Stryfe in unison.

"**Enough.**"

The word was punctuated with the pealing sound of speaker feedback and a rush of power that silenced the three of them in an instant. Creed's brand flared once again, and he saw Joshua wince and grab at the right side of his body, where his own mark was clearly seething.

Rictus crossed his arms, a rare human gesture for him. He remained like that for a long while, and Creed assumed he was communicating with the thing that hid within his soul.

After a small eternity, Rictus fixed the pale white lights of his eyes on Creed and Joshua from behind his skull mask. His words came measured and deliberate.

"The Crusader has abandoned his duty. And the Sacristan has vanished. As of now, the Prodigal remains the only one of the three tasked with fighting Adversaries who still fulfills his role."

Creed started at that. What did he mean, 'The Sacristan has vanished?' Testament had disappeared? Something like that shouldn't have been possible.

"The Preceptor demands a soul," Rictus continued. This is not negotiable. But I cannot deny that losing two Samaritans at once would not be in Its best interests."

Joshua raised his eyebrows at the unexpected concession. "Sooo...?"

"As the Crucifer has proposed, the Crusader will hunt down the fiends that were let loose and retrieve the Apostate's shell.

He will do this alone and unaided, and he will have only as long as my patience allows."

Creed felt relief and despair in equal amounts. It seemed he was going to make it out of this conversation alive, but this was *far* from what he wanted.

"When the Apostate has been restored, he and the Crusader will do battle. The strongest between them shall claim victory and assume the role of protecting Lambs from the Adversaries. The weaker shall fall, and the Preceptor shall claim them."

Creed's heart would have fallen into his stomach, if he'd possessed either. So close. He had been *so* close, and now he was to go hunting for monsters? He was to risk his life bringing his bastard brother back, just so they could tear each other apart again? Defeat meant falling into Rictus' clutches for the rest of eternity, while victory meant being forced back into fighting an endless war long since lost.

He didn't know which outcome he hated more.

A long silence passed between everyone present before Joshua's listless voice filled the air once again.

"Well... I suppose that's about as fair a deal as we could expect, given the circumstances."

"It is not a matter of fairness, Crucifer. I simply wish to avoid diminishing our numbers more than is necessary, and to punish those who do not deserve the destiny offered by the Preceptor."

Creed clenched his sword tightly at the arrogance. If there was any Samaritan he disliked most after the demon currently stitched to his soul, it was their "leader."

He kept his temper under control as Joshua turned and regarded him with a rather blatant look of pleading on his features.

"Well? We in agreement?"

«I have no issues.»

Creed could not tell from Stryfe's tone if the demon was actually satisfied with the arrangement. He looked once more to the sword in his hands, pathetic and dull in the black sun's weak light, and recalled Rictus' words:

Where have your Colors gone, Crusader?

Creed understood that this "deal" ended in his death. Even if he successfully hunted the three demons, his life would be forfeit in the confrontation that followed. There was no place to run or hide any longer. He was trapped. Feeling numb, Creed turned and looked Rictus in his lifeless iron mask.

"I agree."

Rictus held his gaze for a moment before apparently deciding he was satisfied. "Be warned: I shall brook no attempt at going against our accord. This contest shall end with either the Apostate or Crusader dead."

He fixed his gaze specifically on Joshua. "If I observe any attempt at avoiding this conclusion, I shall call the Preceptor here to reap both of their souls and be done with it."

Joshua just stuck his piece of straw back between his teeth and gave a good-natured smile.

"Thanks for giving us a chance, Boss Man." Despite the words, Creed glimpsed something in Joshua's posture, a slight hint of subterfuge and the promise of mischief that someone as detached as Rictus would never notice.

Creed's eyes narrowed. *That really is Joshua. He looks so different, but it's him.*

Rictus, finally seeming finished with them, uncrossed his arms. "I leave you to your labors. Do not disappoint us."

And with that, he was gone. Once again, there had been nothing to see in his departure; he was simply no longer where he had been. Creed felt a rush of relief as the brand on his back stopped stinging his flesh, and he noticed Joshua do the same.

«Well,» Stryfe intoned in his mind, «*I'd say that worked out rather well, all things considered.*»

Creed let out a long breath and dismissed his clay blade before he decided to stab himself with it. He looked to Joshua, who put on a sardonic grin and clapped his hands together.

"Alright! That bought us some time! Glad to see you two still love making work for me to do! What say we find someplace more comfortable and figure out how I'm gonna get your butts out of the fire this time?"

Chapter V
"You Want it Darker"

If he hadn't been busy seething at his current predicament, Creed might have found some amusement in watching Stella awkwardly circle around the table in the basement, trying to figure out how the ghost of a demon worked.

The withered remains of Stryfe sat upright upon the table, a limbless torso and head propped up like an unfinished marionette. The gaping wounds at his arms, waist, and chest were oozing with the shimmering, ruby-red blood of demons, but whenever the plasma made contact with the table, it dissipated puffs of colorless vapor, as if nothing was there at all.

Stryfe's head hung low, and his ghostly chest heaved slowly with labored breath. Though his eyes remained white and cloudy, he seemed aware of the woman currently observing him.

«You're going to make me blush, my dear.» His ethereal voice bounced off the walls of the room for all of them to hear.

Stella stopped her pacing. "My understanding is that your spiritual essence is contained within Creed, and this is only a projection."

«More or less.»

"Why does a non-physical body bleed and have difficulty breathing?"

Stryfe seemed amused. «*The bodies and souls of demons don't work so simply, I'm afraid. This form is only a shade, but my pain is quite real.*»

"That is unclear and unsatisfying."

The old man drew his lips apart in a toothless smile, which allowed another few drops of blood to spill from his empty mouth and dissipate on the table.

«*Apologies for the unpleasantness.*»

"I find that equally unsatisfying."

Stryfe angled his head slightly in the direction of Joshua, who was currently slouching against a nearby wall. «*I think the sister still doesn't much care for us, baby brother.*»

"Speak for yourself. Stelly and I get along great. Don't we, Stelly?"

Even if Joshua couldn't see the blank, penetrating expression Stella responded with, the utterly empty silence that followed served as answer enough. To his credit, he gave little more than an awkward chuckle at the snub.

"Anyways... the important thing to remember is that the more of Stryfe is on that table, the less of him is in Creed's head."

«*If my visage offends you so, I could always return to my little brother's soul...*»

From where he was sitting cross-legged on the bench, Creed's glare snapped to the back of Stryfe's bald head.

"You keep as much of yourself out of me as possible until this is over."

Stryfe gave a less-than-half turn back over his shoulder. «*At least do me the courtesy of walking around to face me if you're going to speak, brother.*»

Obviously, Creed ignored the request. "I mean it."

He looked to Joshua. "You'd better make sure he stays there. I won't be able to fight properly with him sitting on my soul."

«*No need for empty threats, brother. Lest you forget, I joined myself to you out of desperation. I'm not quite dying to lounge around your mind either. Frankly, all the brooding and self-pity makes for a fine repellant.*»

"Yeah? Fuck you."

«Careful. No matter how much of my essence I put on this table, you and I are still bound. If properly motivated, I could slip back in and do all sorts of snooping if I so please...»

Creed grit his teeth. Irritating as it was, the demon wasn't wrong. So long as most of Stryfe's ghostly energy was focused outside, he wouldn't be able to whisper directly into Creed's thoughts like he'd done in the forest. But that didn't mean they were separate.

Though the strain had been reduced, Creed could still very much feel the disgusting, unwanted weight of Stryfe's soul entwined with his own. They were inextricably tied together and would remain so until the demon's body parts were returned in full. Having the bastard out of his head for now was a relief, but Creed would not feel clean until the foul presence had been shorn from his being.

Ideally with Stryfe's head being shorn from his shoulders right after.

"Jeez," said Joshua. "And here I hoped keeping you two apart for all this time might make things easier the next time we met."

Creed scoffed. "'All this time' doesn't mean anything anymore. Don't expect people to change in a world that can't."

Another silence fell over the room for several moments, only broken when Stella turned to Joshua and finally asked what they'd likely all been thinking.

"On the subject of change: Why do you look like that?"

Creed tried not to visibly perk up at the question, but the truth was he'd been wondering the same thing. He noticed Stryfe give a slight cock of his wrinkled head as well.

"Wow, Stelly. Questions like that sure make a guy feel handsome." Joshua gave another chuckle and paused as if expecting one of them to join in. When no one did, he sighed. "Would you believe I just wanted a new look?"

"*No,*" replied Creed and Stella in unison.

«Perhaps if your eyes weren't missing,» added Stryfe.

Joshua shrank a bit under the joint response, then gave a rueful grin and stopped leaning against the wall.

"Well, it's the truth. Mostly."

He began to pace slowly, as he always did when he had a story to tell. "Had a run-in with Testament some time ago."

"Testament," Stella repeated. "They are the one called the Sacristan?"

"That's right. They have the same job fighting off angels as Creed. Or at least they *did,* until..."

"Rictus said they vanished," Creed recalled. "What does that mean?"

"Just what he said. Boss Man found out they were doing something that wasn't allowed."

"Meaning?"

Joshua waved a dismissive hand. "Won't bore you with the details. Basically, they got caught trying to remove their brand."

Creed balked at the absurdity of the statement. They *what*? Why would they try something that stupid?"

Stryfe sounded equally baffled. *«Not to mention impossible. Even I could not think of anything beyond running. And believe me, I thoroughly explored* all *other options.»*

Joshua gave a shrug. "Couldn't tell you. You guys know how they felt about fighting angels, though. Maybe they just couldn't take killing them anymore." Creed had a feeling Joshua knew more than he was saying—he *always* knew more than he was saying—but something about the man's bearing told him it would be fruitless to continue prying.

"As you can imagine, Boss man figured out what they were doing and sent me in to intervene. First, I asked them to stop. Then I tried to force them. It... went poorly." He tapped a finger against the dark blindfold. "Long story short, they got away."

"And took your fucking *eyes* with him?" Creed asked.

"They *really* wanted to make sure I got the message that they were out out."

«You seem rather unaffected, considering.»

Joshua scoffed. "Please. I can still sense everyone by their auras. I can even feel the shapes of everything around me. Might as well not even be blind. They took them to make a point, not because they thought it would actually hurt me." The plastered grin began to fall away, and his next words he muttered seemed more to himself.

"And here I'd been thinking we were still friends."

He angled his head in Creed's direction. "I guess some people *do* change these days." There was an edge of bitterness to the words that Creed rarely heard in his younger brother's voice.

Apparently realizing that his mask was slipping, Joshua straightened and switched to a more casual tone. "Point is, I haven't seen a hint of them since."

"How is that possible?" Stella inquired. "I was led to believe that you're connected to the other Samaritans at all times."

Joshua gave another shrug. "You're right about that. But somehow, they managed to sever the connection I formed between us all. I can't feel them no matter where I look, and neither can the Boss."

"So they *did* manage to remove the brand?"

Joshua threw up his hands. "I don't know. Don't think so, though. If they had, they'd have gone back to their true form, and we *definitely* would have noticed that. But whatever they did, they've made it impossible to track them."

If this were true, Creed thought, it was quite a dangerous situation. Hiding from the eyes of Rictus was a feat with lots of advantages, and not all of them were good.

In the end, though, Creed decided it had nothing to do with him. He was more than likely going to be dead very soon, and the goings-on of the other Samaritans had no bearing on that.

Joshua was still pacing. "I'll admit, I didn't take the whole thing very well. Guess I had a bit of an identity crisis."

He motioned again to his face, unfamiliar to Creed physically but still bearing familiar mannerisms. "Didn't really see much need to keep up appearances after that."

There was much Joshua wasn't saying, as there often was. But Creed had long since learned it was impossible to draw any information out of the man that he didn't want to give. Deciding to accept it, for now, he asked his next question.

"What about the others?"

Stryfe gasped out a pathetic attempt at a scoff. «*Suddenly interested, are we?*»

Joshua ignored the demon. "Salomé's where she's always been. She finds a new place to drop her castle every once in a while, but doesn't ever leave the walls." He nudged his head in

Stryfe's direction. "Which I'm sure some of us are thankful for." The demon shifted uncomfortably but said nothing.

"And Grendel...well, you know how Grendel is."

Creed nodded, though he couldn't fight a twitch of his scarred eye, and decided to let the conversation die right there; he didn't need to hear anything about Grendel right now.

It was Stryfe, of all people, who changed the subject. *«Not to interrupt, but perhaps we could put aside gossip of our comrades and focus on the task our leader has ever-so-graciously bestowed upon us?»*

Stella's head snapped in the demon's direction. "I don't believe you've earned the right to be impatient when this situation is entirely your fault."

Again, Stryfe seemed more amused than anything by her monotone disdain. *«I suppose you're right, little doll. Once again, you have my deepest apologies for imposing upon your solitude with my brother. I suppose I was just feeling a bit jealous of all the time you've had to spend together.»*

As usual, there was no visible change in Stella's posture, but Creed knew her well enough to see that she was as close to seething as she could be. After a few beats, her gaze went to Creed, sharply enough that he almost flinched.

"I will be upstairs."

With that, the nun turned on her heel and marched up the nearby stairs with heavy steps. At the top, she quickly opened the door, stepped through, and shut it behind her.

«Could it possibly have been something I said?»

"Fucking degenerate," Creed growled as he rose from the bench.

Joshua just sighed again. "Unlike him, I really *am* sorry, Creed. I know she doesn't want anything to do with us."

"She's not the only one."

Joshua set his mouth in a line, but all he said was, "Guess I'll get started, then."

«What a novel idea.»

Ignoring the demon's sarcasm, Joshua took a few steps towards the table until he was standing before Stryfe's limbless form. Raising an arm, he hovered a hand, fingers splayed, over the blood-filled maw that used to hold the demon's tongue.

Creed saw nothing change, but could feel the air shift and thicken as Joshua's power spread out across the room. Stryfe clearly felt it more intensely, seizing slightly as if something had grabbed him.

After a moment, Joshua moved his hand over to the shredded flesh where Stryfe's lower half used to be, and then finally back up to the gaping hole at his chest. He lingered there the longest, brow furrowing. Eventually, he seemed to relax and let the arm fall. Stryfe went slack once more, wheezing from some apparent exertion.

"Well?" Creed asked.

"I used the core of his soul to trace a path to each of his pieces."

"I know how it works. Where are they?"

Joshua looked grim. "I only found two. The third is too well hidden."

«*That would be Belphegor, I imagine.*»

Joshua groaned at the name. "Seriously?"

Stryfe was unfazed by the disapproval. «*He is certainly the slowest of my children, but as you can imagine, none can hide themselves half as well, and so I entrusted him with my heart. Even Rictus would struggle to catch him.*»

"So will *we*, you idiot," Creed spat.

"Two's fine for now," Joshua interjected. "I'll keep looking."

Creed clicked his teeth in annoyance. "The others?"

«*My tongue went to Adrammelech. My limbs to Samael.*»

Creed ran a hand through his white hair, not bothering to see if any more strands fell out. "Picked some real fucking winners."

«*I chose the ones I knew would protect me best. Would you have done differently?*»

"They don't give a damn about protecting you. All they want is to get rid of the crap you forced inside them so they can escape."

Stryfe had not *offered* his body to the demons, Creed knew. Rather, he had *forced* himself into their beings. Despite being let loose, they could only flee so far, as they were still technically bound to their master. This was beneficial to Creed, as it meant they likely couldn't go beyond the surrounding region, but it also meant that all three would be desperate to cast off their chains and fully free themselves.

Stryfe cocked his head once more and looked in Creed's direction. «*You seem uncharacteristically meek, brother. Since when did my children frighten you so?*»

Creed did not respond, which only spurred the demon on. «*Could it be you have some reason to think you may not be able to defeat them?*»

Creed clenched his jaw in frustration at the underlying taunt.

"I was... gonna ask about that, too," Joshua added.

Creed sighed, but was not surprised. Stryfe had seen the truth when he invaded Creed's body, and Joshua's unnatural second sight had undoubtedly picked up on it right away.

"Which Cores do you have left?" his younger brother asked.

Creed considered staying silent out of spite, but muttered, "Malkuth. Just Malkuth."

Joshua drew his lips together in some combination of sadness and pity while Stryfe wheezed out a condescending chuckle.

The concern in Joshua's voice was sickeningly genuine. "What have you done to yourself?"

"Not a damn bit your business. Either of you."

«*I beg to differ, seeing as both our lives currently hang in the balance.*»

Creed's anger flared, and he took several menacing steps towards the ghostly corpse. "I don't want to hear that from the one responsible for this fucking mess."

«*I merely wonder if you are truly a match for my children in your current state.*»

Creed put as much venom into his words as he could. "I'll handle your little bastards, Stryfe. I'll tear them to pieces, and the one solace I can take from all of this is that once I do, I'll be able to kill you, too."

The demon gave a sickening bloody grimace. «*Are you so certain? If you truly are as weak as I felt before, I don't believe I'll have much trouble when the time comes.*»

"That's enough," Joshua declared. His voice was calm, but his words were iron. "Regardless of how we got here, we're on the same side now. If you two can let go of each other's throats for just a little while, we *might* be able to find a way out of this."

Creed stared at Joshua for a moment, and suddenly realized that he was now right back where he started.

This is how it had always been: he and the demon, ever a hair's breadth from tearing each other apart; and the "baby brother," as he so liked to fancy himself, ever eager to play peacemaker and keep their pitiful facsimile of a family together for a bit longer.

This worthless exercise had repeated itself times beyond measure, as cyclical and menial as everything else. And yet, here Creed was, drawn right back into their monotony, the desperate struggle to retain some sense of belonging in a world where nothing belonged.

"You just couldn't help yourselves," he said in a harsh whisper, glaring between his siblings with nothing but contempt. "You knew what I wanted. You could have just left it alone and let me fade away with the rest of it. But you just couldn't let it be, could you?"

"C'mon Creed," Joshua tried to interject, his voice slightly muffled by the straw. "That's a bit unfair, don't you—"

Feeling a surge of irritation, Creed swiped out a hand and ripped the straw from Joshua's mouth. "Knock that shit off!" He crunched the straw in two and tossed it to the floor.

"I bet this went exactly as you hoped!" He motioned to the Stryfe on the table. "He falls right into my lap, the first one of you in ages, and suddenly it's a family reunion!"

Joshua was still for a moment before silently opening up his coat to reveal a bundle of several dozen identical strands of straw tied together inside a pocket. With deliberately slow movements, he pulled out another one and stuck it back between his teeth. Creed felt too exasperated to even sigh.

"I didn't know this would happen, Creed," Joshua said through the straw. Creed knew it was a lie. "I just tried to keep things from going south once it did."

"Really? Because I can't help but notice that even if I *do* live through this, it ends with me right back where I was before all of this, fighting your worthless war."

Joshua's expressions had always been difficult to read, and with a blindfold now obscuring half his face, it was nearly impossible. An empty silence pervaded the room, but Creed refused to speak. He would *make* him admit it. Eventually, Joshua let out a sigh.

"I couldn't let you die like that, brother."

As he'd suspected. Even after all that had happened, it seemed Creed would be granted no say in his own fate. Fight. Don't fight. Live. Die. The outcome didn't matter, nor the means. None of it. He was just as much a corpse as Stryfe at this point, and there was nothing left to do but let the puppeteers make his slack body dance on their strings.

When he spoke next, there was no hint of life in his voice: "Show me where they are."

The statement brooked no further discussion, and to his credit, Joshua didn't try to prolong things. Approaching, he raised a hand and touched two fingers to Creed's temple.

In a flash of invading consciousness, Creed found his mind filled with images, shapes and colors and feelings that weaved together to form a kind of ethereal map.

He saw the two demons Joshua had located, as well as the pieces of Stryfe they bore like unwanted cargo. He saw the paths they had walked thus far and the projected paths they were likely to take.

Joshua withdrew his fingers, and Creed came back to reality, his mind alight with the information he had just acquired. His purpose clear, Creed brushed past his brother and made for the stairs without another word.

«*Good luck*,» came the mocking old voice of the demon on the table.

Creed did not break stride. He made it up the stairs, out the doors, and several steps towards the main entrance before a toneless female voice called out: "Creed."

He turned to see that Stella had been waiting beside the door to the basement. A flush of shame ran through him as he realized he'd actually forgotten her in his anger, but it quickly dissipated against the cold resignation he was currently drowning in.

"You're going," she said. It wasn't a question.

"I am."

She nodded. "Before you go, I—

"You know you can't come. You wouldn't be able to help, anyways; Rictus made it pretty clear I have to do this alone."

"That's not what I was going to say."

"What, then?"

"I wanted to know if you found her?"

Creed blinked, taking a moment to recall what she meant.

Right. She's probably been thinking about that since the moment I left.

The shame returned a second time. Frankly, he hadn't spared a moment's consideration for the girl since leaving the forest. Once again, though, he pushed the guilt back down. There was no point in letting things like that affect him anymore.

"I didn't see her."

"Did you look?"

"A few other things came up."

Stella glanced downwards at his callousness, and Creed sighed. "Look, I'm sure she wasn't there. Rictus would have gone right for her if she was. Wherever she went, I'm sure she's fine. Might as well put it out of mind."

"There are so few left, Creed." She spoke in a soft voice he'd not heard from her in some time. "We have to protect what's left. Don't we?"

There were any number of things he could have said that might have comforted or reassured her, but all Creed could muster was, "I'll be back,"

With that, he turned away and left the church without a backward glance. Stepping into the stagnant chill, he reached into his pocket, pulled out a fresh paper stick and willed another sphere of clay "candy" into existence. Sticking the flavorless sucker into his mouth, he felt a twinge of irritation as he realized he was no better than Joshua.

At least it's more than grass.

Chapter VI
"Imagine"

    Some miles away from the church, the dirt roads tapered off, and the choppy sea of hill-country gave way to plains of dust and rock. Creed stalked across barren flatland, reflecting that his footsteps were probably the first thing to disturb this ground in ages.

    It was a strange feeling, he mused, to be the only force left that could alter a landscape. With no wind and no rain, people had become the only catalysts by which the earth could shift or change.

    A shame there were no longer enough of them left to make a difference.

    As usual, Creed measured the passage of time through the number of false suckers he went through—he was on his sixth now—until he felt the ground begin to slope upwards.

    He followed the incline until it coalesced into one last hill, beyond which the area opened up into the rare sight of a valley still speckled with sparse concentrations of grass. They were ugly, random little patches without a hint of green to be found; certainly a far cry from the colorful flowers back at the church.

    Creed had not seen this part of the region in a long while; it did not lie along the lone path he traveled between his home and the city. He thought briefly that the valley reminded him of a vision he would often have in the center of the crater. It possessed none of the long-lost beauty of that ephemeral field, but its sprawling layout was similar.

It even had its own lone tree serving as a center point, though this one was as dead and bleached as those in the forest. Less impressive to look at, but at least it was real; the one in his visions was something Creed would never see again.

And of course, the tree in his dream hadn't had a young woman kneeling before it.

Creed should have been surprised to see her pale figure in the distance, but somehow, he wasn't, even if the odds of her ending up in this graveyard of a plain just as he arrived were quite vexing.

Regardless, Creed decided to content himself with having fulfilled Stella's wish, even if unintentionally, and began his trek down the hill into the valley.

It took several minutes to reach her, but she never noticed his approach. As he drew near, he could see that she was on her knees, back turned and hunched forward as she performed some task in front of the skeletal tree.

Once he drew within only a few feet, he saw that she was digging into the dirt, bare-handed but with an impressively steady focus. She seemed unperturbed by the brown earth staining her hands and arms as she gouged a small but deep hole into the ground before her.

After several moments, she finally noticed his presence. Unlike their first meeting, she did not freeze, just glancing over her shoulder and slowing in her labor for a moment before looking right back to the dirt and continuing.

"Howdy, Creed."

She sounded a bit winded. Creed didn't think what she was doing was quite so strenuous, but reminded himself that the girl likely hadn't been properly nourished since even before the world had ended.

"Neveah." He thought she might appreciate knowing he had remembered her name, but she gave no such indication as she dug deeper, and Creed wondered if she was wary of him after his callous attitude to her back at the church. "Digging a grave?"

"The opposite."

Creed had to admit he was impressed at how un-rattled she was by his presence. "Decided against going into the forest?"

She still wouldn't look at him. "You didn't mention how absolutely creepy it was. I took one look and went off in the other direction."

Creed very nearly chuckled. "You don't say."

He recalled her mentioning back at the church that she had somehow managed to avoid ever seeing an angel or Samaritan before. He still found that difficult to believe, but evidently the girl's intuition *was* sharper than average. He wondered how she would feel if she knew how close she'd come to death in those woods.

At last, she ceased her digging and pulled her hands from the hole, dusting them off as best she could before reaching into one of the three brown pouches tied at her waist. Creed watched as she rummaged around for a moment before pulling out a single pale-yellow seed.

Though it was tiny and unimpressive, Neveah nonetheless regarded it with a look Creed could only describe as reverence.

Keeping her gaze fixed on the grain, she lowered it into the hole and let it slip from her grasp. Slowly, gently, she took the dirt she had displaced and began filling the hole once more.

She did not rush, nor did she do sloppy work; before long, the gap was filled, dirt smoothed down so expertly that Creed might never have known anything had been disturbed. Her chore complete, Neveah rose, grimacing as she stood on legs stiff from kneeling.

"What kind was it?" he asked, then wondered why he'd bothered.

"Not sure." She wiped the remaining dirt from her hands on the front of her dress, totally unconcerned with the grimy stains she left behind on the thin cloth.

"You don't bother to check?"

"Just because I plant the things doesn't mean I know which is which. The guy who gave them to me skipped the course on telling them apart."

This wit was new as well. Creed wondered if the girl had decided she just plain didn't like him. He wouldn't blame her.

"How do you know it's something that would even grow here if it could?"

"I don't." She strolled up to the dead tree and leaned against it like a post, hands clasped behind her back. "All I do is find a pretty place and bury them deep."

Creed glanced up at the unsightly tree she was lounging upon. "'Pretty place?'"

She shrugged. "Relatively. If it ever greens again, it'll look nice with a new friend growing in front of it." She said it so casually, as if she wasn't describing something that simply couldn't happen. "Besides, it's not as if I—"

She cut herself off, and Creed looked down from the tree to see her staring at him as if he'd grown a third arm. He puzzled for a moment, then realized she was looking at the artificial sucker he was still holding in his mouth.

"What is that?" Her voice barely above a bewildered whisper.

Crap. He hadn't thought about that. With an inward sigh, he pulled the lollipop from his mouth. "It's... just a sucker."

"Oh yeah?" she asked, unable— or unwilling— to hide the naked envy in her tone.

"It's not what you think. I promise."

"Uh-huh."

The intensity with which she was staring at the "candy," lips parted ever so slightly, filled Creed with guilt. The pitiful thing probably hadn't even *seen* food in an exceptionally long time, and even if what he had wasn't remotely real, he was still more or less dangling it before her.

He decided to throw her a bone before she started drooling. "Would you... like one?"

She blinked and finally tore her gaze away to look at him like he'd just offered her all the riches of the world. "Really?"

Creed nodded. "You'll be disappointed."

"Yeah sure fine," came the rapid-fire response.

With another sigh, Creed reached into his coat and grabbed one of the several paper sticks from an inside pocket. He was about to materialize the "candy" from behind the jacket, away from the girl's view, but paused. Feeling an uncharacteristic urge, he pulled the empty stick out into full view.

Neveah's puzzlement turned to wide-eyed amazement as Creed willed the dull, grey-brown material into existence around the tip of the stick. When it had formed, he held the miraculous sucker towards the girl as if nothing unusual had happened.

The wonder on her face was blatant, but she numbly took the proffered item, her eyes flicking back and forth between it and Creed.

"Enjoy," he deadpanned.

Neveah continued to stare for a few more moments before her surely-ravenous hunger overtook the confusion and she stuck the sucker into her mouth with pathetic urgency. She looked enthralled for a handful of seconds before her brow furrowed and she glanced back at Creed with a questioning gaze.

"Sorry, but it's not exactly real. No ingredients. No flavor. Basically just candy-shaped clay. Won't even ease the hunger." He felt another small sting of guilt. "Like I said, disappoi—"

"It's fine," she interjected, returning her focus to the sucker as if nothing was off. Evidently, she was more enthralled with the novelty of feeling like she was eating something than she was with whether or not it was real.

"If you say so." He placed his own sucker back into his mouth. "I just use it to pretend. Helps pass the 'time', such as it—"

Crunch.

The sharp sound cut Creed's words short. He gaped in mild disbelief as Neveah fixed him with a guilty stare, swallowed, and took a bare stick out of her mouth.

"Really?"

"I couldn't help it."

So it *had* been the first thing she'd eaten in a long time. A shame it was worthless as anything nutritional.

Leaning forward, Creed brought his pointer finger to the tip of the stick in Neveah's hand and willed yet another round glob of false candy into existence. The girl's eyes went wide again as if she'd forgotten that was how he'd done it the first time.

"Try to make this one last."

Looking dazed, she nodded and placed the sucker back into her mouth, much less ravenously this time. She fixed Creed with another look of wonder as she "savored" the flavorless material.

"You *are* one of them. A Samaritan..."

Creed wondered when it was he had become so lax about such things. There was a time not long ago—or maybe it was eons ago—where he would have never let anyone realize what he was if he could avoid it. But seeing as how nothing he did mattered, he saw no harm in giving this inconsequential girl a glimpse into a world beyond her own.

Besides, he couldn't deny a tiny bit of amusement watching her eyes widen even further as his silence answered her question. If the girl was overwhelmed, she did an excellent job hiding it.

"I knew it."

"Did you, now?"

She nodded, idly fiddling with the sucker. "You said yourself there was nothing out here or in the city. But somehow your clothes are spotless, and you're the healthiest-looking person I've ever seen."

Creed supposed she had a point. Unlike most of the Lambs, he hadn't been stuck in an emaciated body when time had ended. He supposed it *was* a dead giveaway.

"And that pretty lady. Stella? She's one, too?"

Creed wondered for a moment how best to answer that, and settled on a simple, "No."

"She looks even better than you."

"We take care of each other."

She threw her brow up at that. "I'll bet. Two prettiest people left on Earth, 'taking care' of each other in the church."

Creed balked. "Not even close."

He was surprised to hear the inappropriate implication coming from such a young girl, but quickly reminded himself that she was far older than her body would suggest. Strange how easy it was to forget that even after so long.

Neveah pushed off of the tree and took a few slow steps past Creed, head down in deep thought as she worked on her "candy."

"Something wrong?" he asked.

"No... it's just...." She clenched and unclenched her dirty fists a few times, pondering something.

Suddenly, she whipped around to face him and extended an arm, whole body tense. Creed stared at the outstretched hand, wondering what exactly she thought she was doing.

"I want to thank you." She spoke stiffly, as if she were meeting some celebrity. "And the others, too. Like I said back at the church, I've never seen an angel before. But I know they're out there, and I know you all are too, so... thank you for keeping us safe, I guess."

Creed could only stare. Did this girl *actually* think she was meeting someone important? Could she be so foolish?

"Put your hand down."

She blinked at the bluntness of his tone but complied, seeming more embarrassed at herself than stung by his rejection.

"Sorry. I've just always wanted to meet you. Any of you."

Right, Creed reminded himself, sucking more harshly on his lollipop from the growing frustration.

She'd never seen a Samaritan before, nor the things they fought. She hadn't seen the reality of their war. She had likely painted a picture for herself of seven otherworldly warriors standing gallantly against the mad forces of Heaven in defense of those precious few humans that remained.

"Sorry to disappoint."

"Not at all." She gave a soft smile through her sucker, one so genuine that Creed forced himself to pretend he hadn't seen it. "I mean, you're a bit surly, but you're still a hero."

There it was: the one fucking word he'd known was coming.

Creed couldn't stop himself from gritting his teeth so hard that his sucker cracked to pieces. Letting the paper stick fall from his mouth, he felt the acid sting of disgust well up in his stomach and had to bite his tongue to keep from snapping at the girl.

It doesn't matter.

There would be no use flinging contempt at the girl just for being ignorant. Trying to keep his tone neutral, he calmly stated, "Hate to burst your bubble, Neveah, but you've got the wrong idea."

"I do?"

He began to pace, looking at the black sun in the sky as he continued to address her. "What do you know about the Final War?"

"Not much. Something really bad happened right at the end. Something that made time stop moving and the angels go crazy."

"More or less," he said. Telling her the whole grisly truth would serve no purpose.

"But that's why the Samaritans came, right? You were the survivors, and you've been fighting off the angels to keep them from killing everyone who was left."

Creed once again marveled at how disconnected the girl was. She really hadn't been lying when she said she'd had no contact with this conflict.

He turned back to look at her. "I don't know what idea you've built up in your head, but the Samaritans are *not* heroes. We're not even the good guys."

"Seems like it to me." There was such certainty in her voice, and it only made Creed's blood boil further.

"We're not fighting out of the goodness of our hearts. One of us just happened to be stronger than the rest, and It roped us into this. Only reason we listened was to save our own skins."

That last bit was only partially true; Joshua and Testament's desire to protect the Lambs had always been genuine, and Grendel was more than happy to kill as many angels as he could. But none of that amounted to what Neveah clearly wanted them to be.

"Truth is," he continued, "most of us would happily kill each other if *It* wasn't keeping us from doing so." The girl's expression remained inscrutable, and Creed wondered if any of this was getting through to her. "If you thought we were 'comrades' or something, you're sorely mistaken."

The girl looked down at her feet, fiddling with her lollipop again. She was quiet for a few more moments, then looked back up at him. "I guess that's alright."

"What?"

"It doesn't matter *why* you're doing it. It's been so long, and you're still fighting. You're still keeping people safe. That's worth something, yeah?"

"Wrong again," he shot back. "Haven't fought in a long time."

Neveah took in a small breath at that. "Did they... stop showing up?"

"They haven't gone anywhere. I just don't care to bother with them anymore. I... 'retired,' I guess you could say. Haven't left this region in ages."

"Oh...," she said, her voice only a whisper now. She seemed to mull his words over for several seconds but apparently couldn't find whatever she was looking for. Instead, she just asked, "What have you been doing?"

"Nothing."

It was the honest answer, in every sense. He'd come here to waste away among painful memories, nothing more. He'd been so close to doing so before those bastards had shown up and he'd been dragged back into—

Creed's thoughts came to a crashing halt. What in the hell was he doing? Had his mind rotted so badly that he actually allowed himself to get drawn into a pointless conversation over candy?

In his shock, he hadn't noticed that Neveah was speaking. "I suppose I can understand needing a break, but—"

Creed wasn't listening, growing colder as he continued to remember his purpose. He had come to this valley because the information Joshua imparted upon him showed that his target would make its way there before long. He'd come in advance so as to catch it unawares. It had to nearly be there by now.

He turned his gaze on the girl, who had failed to notice his shift in mood and was still talking. "I haven't seen anybody in a long time, but they're still out there, right?"

She had to leave. He had to be rid of her. There was a horror coming. It would swallow her up. Hell, it would probably swallow Creed in his current state. She *had* to leave.

"There's only seven of you, right? Can you really afford to just—"

He finally held up a hand to interrupt, and tried to sound unaffected when he spoke. "Look, it doesn't matter. You should—"

"It *does* matter." Her tone was still calm, but there was a quickness to her words, a tiny bit of forcefulness that made him realize she was... what? Angry? Concerned? It didn't matter. He no longer had time to puzzle the girl out.

He forced a sharpness into his words. "Nothing matters anymore. And frankly, it's not your business either way." He motioned to the freshly shifted patch of dirt in front of the tree. "You've planted your seed, right? Don't you need to be moving on?"

The girl still didn't seem especially put out by his tone, but he noticed a slight clenching of her jaw around her sucker and wondered if his rudeness was achieving the opposite effect of chasing her away. "What's wrong?"

Creed cursed her bluntness. "What's wrong is that I don't have any more time to waste on pointless conversation. Glad to see you're not dead, but I've got work to do, so I'd appreciate it if you—"

"I thought you were retired." Her tone now carried just the barest hint of attitude one might associate with her physical age. "What work is there all the way out here?"

Again, Creed saw the spark of intuition in her eyes, a kind of awareness and intelligence he had thought lost to the Lambs that remained.

Stubborn fool. There was no time to explain the situation, nor did he particularly want to. "It's none of your damn business. All you need to know is that if you don't get out of here, you're going to get hurt."

His words just seemed to further stoke the girl's curiosity. She glanced around at the wide empty field in which they stood. "You *are* fighting something. Aren't you?"

Was she *immune* to taking a hint? "It doesn't matter what I'm doing. You've got no place here, so get going."

"No way." Her words came out in a near-whisper, tinged with both fear and anticipation. "I've missed everything since the end of time. Let me stay. Let me see."

Creed was taken aback. Of all the Lambs left in the world, he had to across the one who *wanted* to see a demon.

"You're out of your mind," he said, unable to keep the astonishment from his tone. "Whatever you think is about to happen, I promise you; it's not. If you stay here, you die."

"You'll protect me." She said it with such confidence that Creed could have been sick.

"No. I won't."

"I think you will. It's been a long time, but I've met people who have seen the Samaritans. You should hear the stories they tell. You may not think so, but I promise they still see you as heroes—"

Creed could bear it no longer. He held his pointer finger up right in front of Neveah's face in silent threat. When he spoke, his voice was low and dangerous.

"Do not. Say that word. Again."

Stupid girl. Stubborn girl. Ignorant girl. She didn't understand. By some sort of fluke, odds so long they defied reason, she hadn't been broken, hadn't been forced to witness all the horrors of a genuinely dead world. Creed had to make her understand, to send her away from him before he cracked under the weight of her naiveté.

Perhaps the grisly truth would serve a purpose after all.

"Do you want to know what happened at the end? The real reason the world stopped turning?"

She didn't respond, but that was fine. Even if she'd begged him not to, he wouldn't have listened. He was feeling cruel now, and he *would* lift the veil from this pitiful Lamb's eyes.

"God is dead, girl. And the sun died with Him."

A trite statement; the height of cliché. But no less keen a blade to pierce what remained of hope. Creed had not told this laughable story in so long, but now that he had started, he could not stop the flood of words that fell from his mouth:

"Your maker was torn down from the Heavens. Grabbed like a stone and erased from creation by a Beast that shouldn't have been able to touch Him. It shouldn't have been possible, but it happened. He faded away, and everything that mattered went with Him.

"*That* is why the sun turned black. It's why fire can still burn but gives off no warmth. Why the winds went still and rain stopped falling. Why plants stopped growing and landscapes stopped changing. Why food will never sate your hunger and water will never quench your thirst.

"It's why you still look like a girl even though you've been alive for a thousand, thousand lifetimes. Why your body is still as emaciated and starved as it was the day time froze. Why your shape will never change no matter how much you eat, if there was anything *to* eat. It's why new life can never be born, and no one will ever again hear a baby's cry.

"And of course, it's why the angels who once watched over you like shepherds now burn you to ash. They were pieces of Him. He gave them their minds, and once He was torn from them, those minds were lost. In their madness, they decided the only thing left to do was finish His work.

"Now they fall upon the earth again and again and *again*, until every one of you Lambs gets washed away by their light. It won't accomplish anything, but they have no rational thought left. Creation's first children, nothing more than raving, idiotic monsters who believe the world never ended and that they'll somehow be able to see their Maker again if everything burns like it was supposed to."

Creed heard his words echoing in his mind, and part of him knew how terrible they were. This was no longer about chasing the girl away from danger. He was trying to hurt her now, break whatever strength was hiding behind those eyes. But another part of him didn't care, and that part always seemed to win in the end.

"The Samaritans aren't your heroes, girl. We were never 'survivors' of The End; we were *leftovers*. All that happened is that we were forced by a *different* monster to fight a worthless battle in some desperate attempt to keep you all alive just a little bit longer.

"But there was never a chance of winning that fight. Our task had been failed since before it began. I don't even know where most of you are at this point because there aren't enough of you left to *find*. I don't know how it is you managed to stay blind to it all for so long. I'd say it was a miracle, but as I've just told you, those don't exist anymore."

He pointed again to the spot where Neveah had planted her seeds. "Those things you bury will never grow. They will sit in the dirt for an eternity. One day, your sacks will be empty, and you'll have nothing to do but keep walking. And sooner or later, even your unnatural luck will run out.

"Maybe you'll run into a bramble and cut your arms. Maybe you'll fall down a hill and break a bone. Maybe you'll finally give up and try to slit your own wrists. But you won't die. You *can't* die. Any wound you take, no matter how minor or terrible, will never heal, and their ache will never fade. The injuries will add up, and the pain will compound until your mind can't take it any longer. You'll fall to the ground, stop thinking, and never move again.

"Maybe some rare wanderer will happen by and be kind enough to burn your husk. That will stop the *physical* pain, at least. But even once your ashes are scattered, your *soul* will go nowhere. It will be stuck right where you were burned, left to float screaming and tormented in the aether for the rest of eternity.

"And if *all* of that sounds too horrible to bear, then all you have to do is *pray*. The angels can still hear you if you want them to! Any time you choose, you just have to close your eyes and call out to God; He won't come, but *they* will! The sky will tear open above your head, and one of them will show up like your own personal savior. They'll sear you away like all the rest, and that will be the end of it."

Creed felt tired; this impotent display of rage had left him spent. But he wasn't quite done. He needed one last push to get the girl away from this place. Away from him.

"These are the only endings left to us, Neveah: rotting or burning. Having fought enough angels for one eternity, I choose rotting. And I choose to do it alone."

He pointed into the distance. "Leave. And whatever you choose to do, don't let our paths cross again. The world's moved on from people like you. And so have I."

With that, he relented, allowing empty silence to take over once more.

To her credit, the girl had taken his every word without flinching. Now, at the end of his slavering, her gaze finally left his own. It went nowhere, trailing off into the distance past him, past the valley, past the edges of the world.

"I understand." Her voice was neutral but tight, audibly strained by the effort of holding something back. "I get it." For a moment, Creed thought she'd meet his gaze again, but she just turned her back to him, head low. "I'm sorry for making you say those things. I'll go."

She took a few steps past him, then paused. Reaching up, she pulled the paper stick from her mouth. It was bare once again.

"Thanks for the candy. It was nice."

She dropped the stick into the dirt and left him behind, marching back the way he'd come across the valley. Her walk wasn't fast enough to be seen as running away, but not slow enough to seem calm either. Creed watched her travel the whole way until she finally crested the line of hills in the distance and winked out of view.

I suppose that'll do.

In the end, it seemed he hadn't fooled her; she'd noticed what he was doing. He told himself he had done what needed to be done, that it would have all come crashing down around her sooner or later and that this would ultimately benefit her in the long run.

But he knew that was bullshit. The truth was, he had just seen something that was still holding itself together and decided to finish breaking it. Because that was all he could ever seem to accomplish.

For what felt like the hundredth time in a short while, Creed shut himself off. There was nothing more to be done in thinking about what had just happened. He was here for a purpose, even if it was one that made him sick.

Turning, he took a few slow steps over to the pale tree and sat down, back against the trunk. He could not rest, but he could still focus himself for what would be coming. There he remained, staring at the patch of disturbed soil in front of him as he waited for a monster to arrive and distract him from his own loathing.

Chapter VII
"The Devil and the Huntsman"

The demon's approach was signaled by a shift in the air, a thickening around Creed's throat and a phantasmal tremor in the dirt. He wasn't sure how long he'd been waiting by that point, but supposed it made no difference. Turning, he drew his gaze west towards the source of the sensation just in time to see an arm breach from beyond the edge of the hillside.

Deep-blood red and larger than the tree Creed was resting against, the appendage seemed to cast a pallor across the whole of the valley. Creed felt only revulsion as the creature pulled itself over the lip of the hill and clambered down into the valley.

Its naked upper body was shaped like that of a man, but any resemblance to humanity ended there. It was a giant, built like a mountain and taller than three of Creed put together. It shambled on all fours, occasionally dipping its massive head to pointlessly sniff the ground with a snorting muzzle.

Its face resembled a horse in the way a corpse resembled a man; no flesh, nose, or eyes to be found, only deep black hollows that gave it the visage of a terrible equine skull. A ragged mane of black bristle wove its way from the top of the creature's head down to its tailbone, where it met with a wild plume of black-and-red feathers, fanning out several feet in all directions like a bouquet. Its massive legs ended in powerful-looking hooves.

Adrammelech: an amalgamation of man, horse, peacock, and monster. The combination have seemed comical were it not so abhorrent.

Once, Creed vaguely recalled, it had been worshipped by some ancient peoples as a dark and terrible god, and through their fearful belief, it had, for a time, truly become such a thing.

Now it was simply an animal, loping about with hardly a semblance of thought left in its eroded mind. Creed imagined it was instinctively trying to escape the surrounding region, but so long as it held a piece of Stryfe within its soul, it would never be able to venture far enough to be truly free.

The beast had crossed much of the valley now, but had yet to notice Creed even as it approached the tree under which he sat. With a sigh, he picked himself off the ground, dusted the seat of his coat, and took several reluctant steps directly into Adrammelech's path.

The demon halted its movement when Creed came into its eyeless view, which at least confirmed it wasn't *completely* mindless. It seemed unsure what to make of him; he was likely the first living thing it had seen since Stryfe ate it so very long ago.

It simply stood, balancing on meaty fists and heaving vile, confused breaths. Creed supposed that now would be the time to shout something clever and daring at the thing, but seeing as how it was bereft of sapience, there didn't seem much point. Instead, he simply held out a hand and once again called upon the last Core of power within his soul.

Deciding reach would be most useful against an enemy of this size, Creed willed the mass of brown clay that appeared in his hand to shape itself into a spear, although unlike the simple pike he'd made in the forest, this one was a fully-fledged jousting lance, long and heavy with a massive spiraling tip that took up the majority of its length. Despite being made of clay, its ability to pierce flesh would surpass that of tempered steel.

The sight of Creed's unnatural weapon finally seemed to trigger a reaction in the demon. Its breath began to increase in pace, its brutish shoulders pulsating up and down in agitation. Breaths turned to grunts, which turned to growls. Yes, the monster saw him, and it knew to hate him, even if it could no longer recall why.

That's right. You know me. It's been a long time since I last hunted you, but you know me.

Reaching up to the high collar of his coat, Creed grabbed its zipper with his free hand and slowly pulled it downwards to where it ended at his waist. It came apart with a *snap*, allowing the heavy coat to fall open. Creed's bare chest—he never bothered to wear another layer beneath the thick leather—was exposed to the chill air, but he paid it no mind. He would need the extra movement that opening his coat would provide.

Adrammelech gnashed its vicious teeth and bashed its fists into the earth beneath it, making small craters with just the bare amount of force. Mindless or not, the creature was still strong.

Then, unable to contain its source-less fury any longer, the demon opened its equine maw and let loose the madness that had been ravaging its mind for eons.

RRRREEEEEEEEEIGGHGHGHGHG!!!!!!!!!!!

To say it sounded like a horse's *neigh* would be like saying the shattering of a thousand mirrors sounded like a fork on a wine glass. The wretched sound cut through the valley like a tidal wave, threatening to rend Creed's flesh and bone before the battle even began.

Once it faded, so too did what little sound had been left in the valley. The demon continued to stare Creed down, and he tightened his grip on his lance in anticipation.

Finally lifting its hands from the earth, Adrammelech charged with the suddenness and ferocity of a peerless sprinter, covering ground so quickly that Creed was hardly able to look up before one of its titanic fists was bearing down on him.

Summoning all the strength he could into his legs, Creed leaped to the right. The fist landed right where he'd been standing. It pierced into the earth like a small comet, and the resulting shockwave threatened to knock Creed off his feet. He noted that Adrammelech's fist remained stuck in the crater.

Taking advantage, he readied his lance and thrust it with all his might into his opponent's meaty neck. The blow was executed perfectly. But Creed felt that he had not even scuffed

Adrammelech's hide. Its flesh was rigid with the tautness of leather so thick it could never be torn.

With another screech, Adrammelech's head snapped towards Creed as it *wrenched* its trapped hand out of the ground. The wild grasping didn't reach him, nor the subsequent wave of dirt and. Leaping back as far as his supernaturally strong muscles would carry him, Creed's world became a maelstrom of dust and stone.

By the time he landed, Adrammelech was already charging again, empowered by the fathomless determination that came from lunacy.

As he braced himself, Creed began to wonder: did his failure to wound the demon mean it was more powerful than he'd expected? Or had he truly grown as weak as the others had claimed?

Neveah might have admitted to herself that she really *was* as stupid as Creed thought she was, but at the moment was more concerned with the fact that she'd wet herself.

As soon as she'd crested the hill out of the valley and reached the bottom, the Dove had reared its irritating head again, flying over her shoulder right back the way she had come into the valley.

She had groaned and pulled at her hair in frustration, but the fact was that she had most likely been planning to turn around anyways just to spite that chalk-haired jackass. With a sigh, she had promptly dropped to her stomach and stealthily clambered back up to the top of the hill.

Unfortunately, she could no longer recall the childish indignation she'd felt as she reached her vantage point. Nor the petty satisfaction as she lay flat in the dead grass looking down at an oblivious Creed sitting against the tree. Nor the sickening terror when the unholy abomination had scrambled into the valley. Nor the awful thrill in her stomach at having finally, *finally*, borne witness to one of the unnatural creatures that had ruined the world.

She'd expected an angel, but whatever this creature was proved more than enough to finally confirm for Neveah that the world truly had gone as mad as everyone claimed.

Then it screamed.

The myriad emotions she'd been feeling were wiped away in an instant. She'd immediately regretted every choice she'd ever made that had led to this moment, certain that she would drown in this sound forever, losing herself in the insanity until she stopped thinking.

Eventually, the pathetic sensation of something warm running between her legs brought her crashing back to reality, and by the time she remembered where she was, the battle had already begun.

The first thing she registered was Creed's form being obscured by a rain of dirt before he emerged with an inhumanly long leap. Neveah clasped hands over her mouth to try and stifle her pathetic, involuntary gasps.

She would have loved to get up, sprint back down the hill, and run until her feet bled. She would have even settled for shifting aside from the embarrassing puddle she'd created. But there was absolutely no strength in her legs at the moment, and all she could do was wallow in her filth and keep her gaze on the terrible things occurring down below.

The horse-headed abomination chased Creed with abandon, its plumage of feathers swaying behind it like a wild living shadow. It seemed to have learned its lesson and did not allow its fists to get stuck in the earth again as it swiped over and over in an attempt to claw or catch its prey. Every so often, it let out quick shrieks, each sending an involuntary tremor down Neveah's spine.

Creed, for what little it seemed to be worth, was deftly avoiding the thing's attacks. He moved with speed and agility that erased any remaining doubts that he wasn't human.

Whenever he dodged, her eyes would briefly lose sight of him until he came to a stop; when he leaped to avoid a swing, he cleared his opponent's head despite it towering over him. Every so often, Neveah could see a flash of brown that signaled him taking a swipe at the beast with the giant spear he'd seemingly pulled from nowhere.

How can he even hold *something like that?*

It was hard to tell from so far away, but the lance Creed was using seemed to be even longer than the man himself. Yet he wielded it so effortlessly that it couldn't *possibly* weigh as much as it looked, could it?

Regardless, Neveah gathered that whatever hits Creed was landing were not having much effect. If anything, the beast looked to be getting *stronger* as the fight dragged on. Wild swings became focused and more practiced. The occasional kick was incorporated into the string of blows. Creed continued to evade, but Neveah couldn't fight the cold lump of anxiety in her throat.

After several minutes of this mad dance, the monster finally broke the pattern. Rather than follow up one of its swipes that Creed had flipped backward to avoid, it instead crouched and twisted its lower body out in front of itself. Its massive tail of feathers drew in tight, bending up towards its opposite shoulder. Neveah realized what was happening just as the tail whipped back outwards in Creed's direction.

Despite being nowhere near the mass of feathers, he was somehow sent rocketing backward. He rolled and skipped violently across the ground, as if he'd been pitched.

Before Neveah could process what had happened, she was hit with a gust of wind that flung her hair about and shook the ground beneath her. Through her shock, she realized that the monster had swung its plumage with such force that Creed had been battered by nothing more than the resulting shockwave.

Creed himself came to a stop some ways away from the demon. He had kept ahold of his weapon and quickly rose to his knees, but Neveah could tell that damage had been dealt.

The creature gave no time for a reprieve, letting loose another appalling shriek before resuming its berserk charge. Neveah wanted to close her eyes, but couldn't even force them shut as she watched the monster close in. She lay motionless, mouth covered and soaking in her own urine as she waited for Creed to be rendered a distant red stain by the next attack.

It never came.

Just as the monster came so close that Neveah could no longer see Creed, it seemed to be launched back by some kind of force. It sailed away faster than it had approached, and to Neveah's confusion, she saw that there was something physical connecting Creed's kneeling form to the screaming monster.

His lance. The weapon had somehow grown past its initial length and was now extending at an unfathomable pace, pushing the demon like a battering ram.

Long, longer, yet longer it grew, carrying Creed's foe back until it dug its hooves into the earth and forced itself to a stop. By then, it was dozens of feet away. Creed's lance filled the entire span between them.

Neveah's mouth fell open behind the mask of her hands. The massive spear retracted itself as fast as it had emerged, shrinking until it returned to its original form in Creed's grasp. Standing, he leveled its point towards the beast once again. If he still felt the effects of the damage he had taken, it did not show in his rigid battle stance.

Neveah felt something begin to break through the sheet of white terror she'd been draped in. The ice in her veins did not quite melt, but the cold did not sting so sharply anymore. Her muscles, sore from how taut they had been, began to unclench.

She looked at the white-haired man. He seemed small at the bottom of the valley. And yet somehow gigantic as well. Neveah forced herself to remember that this man—this harsh, broken man who seemed to have nothing but despair inside him—was not really a man at all.

No matter how much it seemed to disgust him, he *was* one of those special few that Neveah had heard spoken of in hushed whispers reserved only for the most awe-inspiring forces.

He was a Samaritan.

They'd come from the ruins, people said. The ruins of the old world. Humanity had already scattered by then, chased to all corners of the earth by the mad angels. God's messengers would appear without warning, falling from the sky wherever too many people gathered. Broken as they were, the people could only flee in despair from a power they could not hope to match.

But *they* could.

Supposedly they had been champions who participated in the Final War, though none were certain as to who exactly they had once been or which side they had fought for. Still possessed of their unearthly powers, it was they—and *only* they—who were now capable of matching the angels in combat.

They numbered seven in total, though it took quite some time for the survivors to realize this. Despite being grouped together in people's minds, the truth was they were almost never seen together. To spy even two of them in the same place was considered the rarest of occurrences.

One was a protector, seeking out whatever pockets of survivors he could find and leading them to places of safety. Whenever an angel appeared, he would place himself in their path. It was said that none who stood behind them ever had cause to fear death.

One was a warrior, a being of such incomparable strength that he could tear the destroyers from heaven apart with his bare hands. Despite his power, no survivors flocked to him for protection as they did the protector, for his battles were just as likely to claim the lives of humans as they were the angels.

One was a captain, referred to as such because of the miraculous boat in which they sailed across the starless sky. They possessed sacred weapons and relics of the old world, whose terrible power they used to strike down their enemies the moment they appeared.

One was a hunter, tasked with the killing of demons. In addition to the angels, all the devils of Hell had been left behind in The End, cursed to wander the dead earth as they slowly lost their minds and devolved into little more than violent animals. The hunter would chase them down, taking their heads without hesitation or mercy. Though he rarely approached any humans, the few who had glimpsed him declared him to be even more frightening than the monsters he pursued.

One was a queen, beautiful and terrible. She lived secluded in a glorious castle that could travel anywhere in the world and whose shape was different each time it appeared. Even in a dark and empty world, her citadel was always lit, and the sounds of revelry and pleasure could be heard from behind its walls. Despite the allure, most never dared approach the queen's abode, as it was also said that her castle was truly a prison, meant to contain something even darker and more dangerous than the angels themselves.

One was a traveler, an odd fellow who seemed to appear where he pleased, often in the wake of one of his comrades. He would spend time amongst the survivors, telling them stories of the old world and smiling even in the hopelessness of the new one. It was through he that the scattered remains of humanity learned the most about the seven strangers and their powers.

One was a ghost, or so it was claimed. More than any of the others, this one was a mystery; not even the wandering traveler would speak much of it. Yet somehow, each and every person who yet lived knew of its existence. They could feel it, somewhere in the furthest corners of their perception, watching and waiting with some unknowable purpose.

These stories had been passed from person to person, and many more besides. Even as humanity was broken down to the point that the smallest of civilizations could not flourish, one might hear whispers of the Samaritans' deeds on the rare occasions when they came across others.

Many spoke with awe and admiration for the brave heroes who kept humanity safe from the wrath of the angels, while some spoke with fear and condemnation of inhuman beings who struggled pointlessly in a world where nothing would ever again be created.

None spoke with anything less than deepest reverence.

It had never quite been explained to Neveah *why* the strangers did what they did, but in the end, she didn't care. As someone who was also carrying out her own seemingly pointless task, the knowledge that there were others still fighting somewhere under the black sun was to her a comfort no one else could understand.

She didn't care where they came from. She didn't care why they fought. All that mattered was that they were *there*.

Just seven Samaritans, keeping watch over what was left.

Slowly, almost unconsciously, Neveah's hands lowered from her mouth to rest on the ground. The Dove fluttered down from above and sat beside her, its cocking its head in curiosity at the spectacle. For once, its presence gave Neveah a sense of comfort rather than annoyance. Setting her jaw, she fixed her gaze on nothing but the lone figure in the blue coat below. Her eyes would not leave him for the rest of the battle.

The next time the creature screamed, she did not flinch.

Creed did not outwardly tremble, but his insides were ravaged. To think that even the aftershocks of one of his foe's strikes could do so much damage. Despite having extended his lance with enough force to crush a mountain, Creed could tell that he still hadn't penetrated Adrammelech's flesh. It seemed he *had* grown as weak as Stryfe mocked him to be.

Curiously, Adrammelech did not immediately resume its assault. Instead, it crouched and stared across the field at Creed with its void sockets before letting out another furious screech.

The scream was accompanied by a sudden flaring of the beast's plumage, feathers fanning out in a dark semicircle behind it. As Creed had suspected, it seemed his opponent was growing more intelligent as their battle progressed.

Fine. I can get creative, too.

Summoning his power, Creed called upon his Core yet again, feeling his internal energy decrease as the more advanced technique unfolded. Keeping his eyes on Adrammelech, he felt rather than saw the disc that formed from nothing above his head.

About ten feet across, the circular plate faced the demon like a shield, though this was not how Creed intended to use it. Shifting focus from his body to sharpen his mind, he waited for his enemy to strike.

It did not take long. The demon gave a barely perceptible flick of its plumage, and Creed was just able to make out a black shaft flying towards him at a speed outpacing sound. With a twitch of his will, Creed met the incoming projectile with one of his own.

The clay disc above his head shot off a portion of its body, a small mass that shaped itself into a long, diamond-shaped sliver of earth. Streaking across the field, it narrowly managed to intercept the incoming attack.

The demon's projectile burst Creed's arrow apart, but the sharp diamond had been launched with enough force to stop its momentum. It fell to the ground, and Creed saw that it was one of Adrammelech's many feathers. He had no time to inspect any further, as by then the next plume was already sailing towards him.

Once again, he fired his own missile to meet it and was satisfied that he stopped this one sooner than he had the first.

That brief flash of confidence was quickly forgotten as the onslaught began in earnest.

The feathers came with ever-increasing frequency, each one fired so quickly it should not have been possible for Creed to perceive them. Sometimes they came alone, sometimes in pairs, sometimes in trios and quintets, and they did not all come at him straight on; some were launched at odd angles before veering to come at him from a variety of directions.

From the left, from the right, from above and behind, he deflected them all. For every fringe the demon loosed at him, Creed sent a piece of his disc to meet it. No matter how many diamond shafts flew from the shape above, it never lost any of its volume as Creed willed an endless flood of clay into the construct.

His mind felt more alive than it had been in a long time. Neurons flared, each one a shot of his clay. Each one deflecting a feather. He could not let even a single one through. Despite their appearance, these missiles were *not* feathers, and even being grazed once would break his rhythm. He would be skewered by the rest. And that would be it.

With all of his focus on matching the demon's attacks, Creed could not take the chance to try and get one of his own attacks through. Not that it would help. His daggers weren't sharp enough. Wouldn't pierce the demon's flesh.

Creed didn't know how many feathers had been sent his way, but could see that the dark curtain behind Adrammelech was beginning to shrink; the beast's ammunition was not infinite. Adrammelech would be capable of re-growing its feathers with only a moment's effort, but in that moment lay Creed's one chance. He had to land a blow in that brief opening, and it had to be lethal.

Knowing that he would be unable to effectively land such a strike at this distance, Creed made the foolish but inevitable choice of advancing. Slowly, carefully, he began to walk forward, ensuring above all else that he continued matching the volley blow-for-blow.

One step. Another. Again. Slowly. Another. Keep focused. Four steps now. Deflection became only more difficult as the distance lessened.

Adrammelech's plume grew ever smaller, the frequency of its attacks slowing in an attempt to preserve its dwindling supply. Taking advantage, Creed increased his pace. He'd halved the distance now, but it wasn't close enough. He kicked himself into a jog, earthen plate following overhead like a sentinel.

Twenty steps later, Creed saw it. The final feather. He deflected it like any other, and the black shaft fell to the earth, leaving Adrammelech bereft of weapons.

Creed was still perhaps twenty feet away. He broke into a full sprint, dispelling the disc above him and choosing instead to focus all his will into sharpening his clay lance. Twenty feet. Fifteen. Ten. Five. Creed reeled an arm back as he prepared to leap and bring his weapon down into the beast's heart.

An eruption of what felt like of molten flame pierced into the small of Creed's back, pushing through his body until it exploded from his stomach. He gave a shout and fell to his knees in front of Adrammelech. The demon wasted no time, raising a red fist and bringing it down towards Creed's skull.

Only an eternity of lessons learned in battle saved him. Instinct took over, forcing him backward in a desperate hop. He narrowly avoided the crushing blow. Skittered back several more steps like a bug. Then the pain overwhelmed even his instincts, and he collapsed onto his rear.

The agony intensified, fire in his abdomen lancing through his body like brambles. He looked down to an almost alien sight: his own shimmering blood, like liquid sapphire mixed with starlight, oozing from the hole that now passed through his belly.

Gritting his teeth, Creed watched Adrammelech rise from its missed attack, and could see a small black object floating in the air beside its head, shining in the dimness with his cerulean blood.

Creed cursed himself a fool; just because the demon had fired its plumes did not mean it no longer held sway over them. Glancing around, he realized the utter stupidity of having closed the gap between him and his opponent, as he now stood right in the center of a field littered with countless fallen feathers: his own self-made graveyard.

Sure enough, another of the strewn quills suddenly came alive and sailed toward him. Summoning all of his superhuman reflexes, he leaped up from the ground and somehow managed to move his jugular out of the missile's path, but was unable to reverse his momentum before another ripped into his left shoulder. Another flash of hot pain. Another splash of azure blood. He had no time to agonize over it.

Unable to summon more clay in such a harried state, Creed had only his lance to protect him. He managed to narrowly bring it up and deflect a single feather, only to have another one slice through a tendon in his right leg.

He fell to one knee as another one spun end-over-end like a buzz saw towards his chest, and wrenched his torso to the side. The spinning feather whizzed past, but this only carried him into yet another. It ripped into the right side of his coat, rending a chunk of flesh from his ribs.

No longer able to react, Creed was helpless as multiple harsh stabbing sensations lanced through his body in rapid succession. In his long life, he had felt all manner of pain the world could inflict. The sensation did not debilitate him. But he could still feel it, as well as the increasingly quick drain on his energy as the wounds took their toll.

Just when he was sure he would not be able to avoid another strike, Creed realized the barrage had stopped. He was on both knees now, and numerous black feathers were pierced along his body, making him look like a shining blue pin-cushion.

Creed raised his head to see Adrammelech standing tall, arms crossed along its massive chest. The field of quills had gone still. Creed wondered why. Surely the demon realized that he would have been dead in just a few more moments.

His answer came in a twisting of the demon's features, a warping of its equine mouth as a set of white, jagged teeth bared themselves in his direction. A series of small snorts sounded from the monster's hollow snout, and Creed realized that Adrammelech was sneering at him.

Adrammelech was *laughing* at him.

He let out a grunt as the myriad feathers mercilessly ripped themselves out from his flesh, practically coating the ground in blue. Moving several feet away, they hovered in the air around him. At the same time, the other quills scattered about the ground began to move, rising into the air and arranging themselves around Creed's body.

They formed the pattern of a unified dome, encasing Creed in a sphere of arrows that would descend all at once and tear him to shreds. Outside the sphere, Adrammelech stood, still snorting at Creed with that terrible grimace.

When the demon had first clambered into the valley, it had been mindless, barely even an animal. But by engaging it in combat, Creed had stirred something within its broken soul. He had awakened old feelings, the sensations and thrills of war that had once been the creature's source of power. Long-lost intelligence had been reclaimed, and the flames of cruelty had been lit for the first time in ages. Adrammelech had not regained its sanity, but its rabid mind could at least recall that it had once loved to play with its food.

Creed calmly regarded the cage of feathers hanging in the air, ready to end him. The moment stretched into its own short eternity. He closed his eyes, and realized to his mild surprise that he was not afraid. Rather, having finally understood the nature of the monster in front of him, he now understood himself as well.

I'm no different.

Just like this demon, Creed too had forgotten his old ways, allowing decay to wipe away the warrior he had once been. He had let it happen. He had *wanted* it to happen.

But that was no longer an option. He was a puppet again, and his puppeteers did not care if his joints were damaged or his strings tangled. They would make him dance, and if he wanted to remain on the stage, he could not give a dull performance.

Creed felt the pain drain from him along with his blood as he rose to his feet. As he did, he felt something inside himself, and looked inward to see that alongside the Malkuth Core—which he had thought to be all that remained— there was now the barest flicker of something that had not been there for quite some time.

He grimaced; for so long, he had worked to erase his other Cores, and had nearly finished off Malkuth as well, but now it seemed his battle with the demon had forcibly drawn one of the cursed colors back to the surface. The power was growing steadily, but for now was still too weak to be called upon.

Creed turned his attention back to what he could make use of. The earth he produced from his soul was not some shapeless mass that could only be molded into swords and spears. It was Malkuth—the Umber Core—which held power over the primal clay from which all the earth had been molded.

He reached into the reservoir of power he had tried to abandon, focusing on the weapon in his hand and imparting his will upon it with greater creativity. The lance began to warp, thinning out and elongating. In seconds, it had morphed into a flexible whip of unknowable length. Creed stood tall and calm, the lash extending from his hand to coil around his body like a protective serpent.

Adrammelech watched him, its gruesome laughter ceasing. Creed imagined it was confused as to why the prey it tormented no longer writhed.

Having been robbed of its fun, the demon uncrossed its arms and gave an irritated snort. Creed returned not a single twitch in response, regarding his opponent like one would regard a child throwing a tantrum.

Adrammelech recognized the insult, and that made it angry. No longer wishing to savor Creed's pain, the creature gave a short, sharp shriek. Creed sensed a half-second of pressure ripple across the cage of feathers before the beast's final onslaught began.

They did not all come at once. A flurry of dozens came from his left. With the barest twitch of his fingers, Creed sent his whip slicing through the air. This time, when his clay made contact with the quills, he let loose a small burst of willpower to enhance its sharpness. Each feather was cloven in twain, falling to the ground in useless halves.

From the right, another volley followed. Creed simply had a second lash of the whip split off and slash the attack away. Two more volleys. One coming down above his head. One heading for his legs. Leaping, Creed cut aside the missiles in the air, and by the time they had been deflected, he was able to repeat the process for the ones flying up to meet him from below.

No sooner did he land than a long stream of projectiles come flying directly at his chest. Extending an arm, he willed his whip to grow straight forward before snapping it back and forth, each twitch batting a feather aside.

As he did, Creed was vaguely aware of the remaining dozen or so plumes forming a tight ring around him, ready to carve through his midsection all at once. He quickly pulled his body in on itself, willing the whip to retract to a fraction of its length. The world slowed. His mind's eye took in the ring of quills preparing to skewer him.

He would be faster.

He sensed them rocket toward him at sonic speeds and propelled his inhuman body into a spin with every ounce of strength he had left, telling his whip to extend as he did so.

His vision became a washed-out mass of motion, and the sound of stone carving into something filled his ears. Once it ceased, he came to a stop.

When his sight returned, he was facing down Adrammelech with no feathers between them; his whip had spun through them all faster than they could reach him.

The entire assault had taken mere moments.

Adrammelech did not possess the features on its horsehead to look stunned, but Creed could feel the sensation from where he stood. He would not be so kind as to let it recover. Extending an arm again with fingers splayed wide, he sent his whip towards the monster like a snake leaping to sink in its fangs.

Indeed, the whip encircled Adrammelech's neck like a noose and tightened with intense crushing force. The beast choked out a scream, pathetic compared to the previous ones, and lifted its arms to pry the strangling rope away. The moment it did so, Creed elongated the whip and split it into two tendrils, each of which coiled around the meaty arms and locked them in place.

He did not stop there. As long as his Malkuth Core had energy in reserve, the whip's length was infinite. He willed it to grow, crisscrossing across the demon's entire body. They snaked down its legs like inescapable braces. Creed wrenched an arm downwards, pulling on the whip and forcing Adrammelech to its knees with a crash. The devil continued to let loose its inane screeching, so Creed sent a tendril coiling along its elongated face and wrenched its muzzle shut.

Before long, Adrammelech was bound in a net of clay. Creed could feel the beast straining with every ounce of its unholy rage to break free, but there would be no escape at this point. Instead, Creed took his outstretched fingers and began to close them, willing his web to contract around his foe as he did so.

The demon's thrashings grew desperate and panicked. He drew the earthen net tighter and tighter upon its mountainous body, but knew that Malkuth could not produce a material strong enough to crush his foe.

Looking back into his soul, Creed saw that the flicker of rediscovered power he'd felt before had just barely grown to the point where he could recognize it: Netzach, the Silver Core. He yet again cursed the return of such an old sensation but could not deny that it would serve his current needs.

I remember now.

Unlike Malkuth, which could produce any physical matter, Netzach was one of the Cores whose power was conceptual. Creed could not physically sharpen his clay any further, but with Netzach's power, he would be able to impose the *concept* of sharpness without limit. The energy held within the newly reawakened Silver Core was barely a drop in the ocean it had once been, but there was enough that Creed could grab hold of it.

With a thought, he flared Netzach and willed it into the clay net still holding Adrammelech in place. The winding brown rope began to take on a darker, dull-grey hue, as if it were now made of weathered, flexible iron.

The physical change was meaningless; it was the *conceptual* change that mattered. Netzach held sway over the properties of metal, and Creed made sure to impart these upon his clay as strongly as he could. The now-iron net became imbued with the very idea of the word "sharp," the very notion of "cutting," and the very abstraction that was "keenness." In this state, the word "resistance" became irrelevant. The ability of Creed's weapon to cleave through anything was now a law of physics, immutable and inevitable.

Creed contracted his fingers into a fist as forcefully as he could, and his web followed suit. With one last muffled cry, Adrammelech was rent asunder. Its body erupted in a gratuitous shower of flesh and bright ruby blood, shredded into what barely amounted to chunks.

Creed did not flinch at the gruesome sight, even when a particularly large piece landed at his feet: Adrammelech's head, now a motionless bronco skull that briefly stared up at Creed with empty eyes before crumbling and evaporating in a wisp of black smoke.

The rest of the creature's flesh, blood, and cloven feathers followed suit, pluming into an ebony cloud before dissipating entirely. Creed was once again alone in the silent valley, as if all the horrors that had just occurred had been nothing but a bad dream.

He let out a long breath and dispelled his silver whip, allowing both of his Cores to dim within him. While Malkuth returned to the level it had been before, Creed noticed that Netzach seemed to completely dissipate from his soul, vanishing as if it had never been there.

As he'd suspected, the Grey Core's reappearance had been a fluke. A momentary recollection of something long since abandoned. Perhaps it would return to him the next time he fought, but for now, it was as silent as when he'd first allowed it to die.

At the same time, Creed felt a distinct change in the unpleasant weight that sat upon his soul; not quite a lightening, but more a... shifting, as if his unwanted burden was making itself more comfortable. Whatever piece of Stryfe's body Adrammelech had been holding was likely back in its master's possession.

Creed began to feel the pain of his wounds creeping back in, and even more so the lack of strength in his body. Using the conceptual Cores was far more taxing on his energy than the physical kind, and the backlash of using such power after so long had caught up to him.

With a limping gait, Creed hobbled his way over to the dead tree, untouched by the battle. As he did, he drew his coat together, reconnected the zipper, and drew it upwards to close his garment once again. The jacket had been torn by numerous holes from where the demon's feathers had pierced into him, but Creed was not concerned. Among other things, Elizabeth was an expert seamstress. She could easily repair the coat when he saw her again.

If he saw her again.

Finally reaching the tree, Creed turned and leaned his back against it. He gave a small groan and slid down the trunk, falling onto his behind with legs splayed out and hands limp in his lap. Looking up, he briefly regarded the grey ring of the black sun in the sky, utterly unmoved by what he had just done.

He glanced down at his body, still leaking unnatural sapphire blood, and figured it would be a short while before he could move again. He could have healed the wounds in an instant had he still possessed the Tiferet Core, but his inhuman body would repair itself well enough given time.

With nothing to do but wait, Creed closed his eyes and steadied his breathing. The gesture was purely symbolic, of course; he had never truly been capable of sleep.

Puppets could not dream, after all.

Chapter VIII
"Broken Crown"

When he finally noticed that the pain wracking his body had subsided, all Creed felt was disappointment.

Still too strong to die.

The wounds he'd sustained in the fight had stitched themselves shut, and his blood had evaporated from his body. Even his clothes had repaired themselves, leaving his scar and brand—two wounds that would never heal—as the only things out of place.

Part of him had wondered if the chaotic energy Adrammelech had forced into his body with its attacks would be enough to break his weakened soul apart, but it seemed there was enough damnable life left in him yet.

It was then that Creed realized he was not alone. Raising his head, he beheld Neveah standing a few cautious feet away. Her expression told him she was only just now realizing he wasn't dead.

He wasn't especially startled to see her, but did perhaps feel a twinge of pity. He had only to look into her eyes for a moment to confirm she had seen everything. There was a new lack of focus to her gaze, a near-imperceptible hollowness that hadn't been there before. And though he certainly wouldn't comment on it, his nose picked up an acrid scent that told him she had finally gotten a glimpse into the terrifying world that had passed her by for so long.

Yet there she stood. Creed watched the girl for several seconds, wondering just what it would take for him to be rid of her.

"You know," he finally spoke, voice thick with exhaustion, "When you said you'd never seen an angel, I thought you might just be the last person left who was still sane. But I get it now. You're just as crazy as the rest of us."

The girl hadn't seemed it before, but that was because he'd been looking for the wrong signs. The truth was that she had her own madness; a different kind, perhaps, but madness all the same.

"Sorry." Her voice was surprisingly calm, and she didn't sound particularly apologetic. "I had to see it."

"No. You didn't."

"You're strong."

"I assure you, I'm not."

"Not from where I was watching."

He supposed he couldn't blame her for not believing him. She hadn't seen the wonders he could once perform, and thus did not understand how pathetic a display that had been.

"So, you... make mud?"

Creed was so unprepared for the simplicity of the question that he couldn't do anything but answer it honestly. "It's... more like clay."

"I've never seen clay do that."

"It's not actually clay. It's older than that. It has power."

"Ah. Old magic super clay. I see."

"Show some respect. You were born from it."

"Excuse me?"

"Forget it." Creed wasn't remotely in the mood to give this girl a crash course on the esoteric mechanics of his powers, nor impart upon her the details of how humanity was created. "Why are you still here? You stayed. You saw. I hope it was everything you imagined."

The weight of steel was in her words. "I need to know. I need to know why you gave up. Even though you're so strong."

"All the strength in creation doesn't mean shit when your enemy can't be beaten."

"What does that mean?"

"It doesn't matter."

"That thing looked pretty beaten to me just now."

"That was nothing. A ghost that forgot it was dead."

"Then what are we talking about?"

"It doesn't *matter*." His own voice sounded so raspy in his own ears. "And I see no reason to explain anything to you."

"I won't leave until you do."

Fuck, but he was so tired of it all. "Why do you even care?"

"Because—" she began forcefully before catching herself. When she continued, her voice was calmer, but her stare had hardened, and Creed realized that, for the first time, she was truly angry at him.

"Because even though I haven't seen anyone in a very long time, that doesn't mean they're not still out there. I know I can't do anything to help them. I can't fight angels and monsters and whatever else is hiding in the dark. But you can. Even if what you say is true, and the Samaritans were all just forced to fight, is that really so bad?"

Her gaze softened, turning again to that sickeningly honest look that told him she was trying so very hard to understand him.

"I can't pretend that I know the first thing about what it is you do. I know you've been doing it for longer than I can fathom. I can understand needing a break, but just... giving up? Can someone as strong as you really afford to waste away in some church while people die? Even if you didn't ask for it, don't you think you have a responsibility to at least try and keep them safe?"

Creed just sat and stared for a moment as she finished. The girl was clearly not aware that her heroic speeches were having the opposite effect she had intended. She didn't realize that everything she said was the wrong thing to say, that her every word did nothing but engorge the growing pit of spite within him.

His next words dripped with venom. "So... that's how you see it?"

"Yes."

"You really believe I should still be fighting? That it's my... 'responsibility'?"

"I know it's not fair. But if you're one of the only ones who can do it...."

Creed regarded her for another long moment, his mind going to a dark place.

"Fine," he declared, and the girl couldn't hide her surprise at the sudden concession.

"What?"

"You're right. There are still people out there who want their hero. Who am I to let them suffer? If you wish it, I'll fight the angels again." He raised a single finger. "But I have one condition."

Neveah's expression grew suspicious. She wasn't naïve enough to be immediately trust his apparent turnabout, at least. "What?"

Creed finally picked himself off the ground and stood at his full height, towering over the tiny girl like a grim specter. "If you mean what you say, if you truly believe that what I do is so important, then you need to prove it."

Neveah did not flinch as Creed approached her, but it felt as if she grew smaller under his gaze. He wondered how something so tiny could be causing him such frustration. Slowly, he extended an arm, reaching out with a hand cupped as if to receive a gift.

"The seeds. Give them to me."

To her credit, the girl didn't overreact, though her eyes widened slightly and her whole body tensed, hand moving protectively to the small pouches at her waist.

When she spoke, her voice was tight. "Why?"

"So I can destroy them."

She drew in a shaky breath. "What will that prove?"

"That you *care*," he said, his tone just a hair's breadth away from mocking. "If it pains you so much to know there are people out there dying because of me, surely you're prepared to sacrifice a few handfuls of seed to save them, right? If that's the case, I'll do it. I'll protect those little Lambs until the angels burn the last of them away. All you have to do is show a little conviction."

Neveah's hand was shaking slightly at her waist, and she looked down to her feet. For once, Creed couldn't read the exact emotions on her face, but he could see conflict, just as he'd expected.

He'd neglected to mention the fact that he was bound for this fate regardless. Even should he survive the coming battles, resuming his endless war against the angels was the only fate left to him. But she didn't need to know that. Not now, when he was finally breaking through that stubborn cloak of naiveté she blanketed herself with.

"Unless, of course, you're not as selfless as you believe? Maybe you don't actually think that the lives of a few scattered people too stupid to die aren't that important. Maybe you're wondering if saving them is really worth losing the only thing that makes you feel like you matter."

His gaze left the girl and shifted to the black sun hanging uselessly in the sky behind her. He stared into the endless tunnel of shadow at its core, the gluttonous void that took a little more from him every time he looked at it.

"Maybe... you realize there's no difference between living and dying in a world like—"

A light weight dropped into his hand.

Looking down, Creed stared uncomprehendingly at the three pouches resting in his palm. It took his mind several seconds to even register what they were, and when it did, he raised his head to look at the girl standing before him.

For the first time, he truly saw her.

She stood straight and stiff, arms at her sides with fists clenched. Her small, emaciated body, so frail it seemed a slight breeze could whisk it away, did not tremble. Stringy blonde hair fell in front of a hollow-cheeked face. Behind the loose strands, lake-green eyes glinted in the dimness. Before, they had seemed too large for her head, too open and revealing of every emotion. Now they were iron. Twin walls of pure, verdant will.

"Well?"

Her words were hoarse, but they were clear. Looking closer, Creed could see the unmistakable glint of tears welling in her eyes. But they did not fall.

For the barest instant, an image flashed through Creed's mind of another woman who had once looked at him with that exact same expression. Her words rang clearly in his head even after an eternity:

You are not to blame for this.

Creed was unmade. How could this be real? This strength? This resolve? Such things should have all been drawn into the black sun a thousand lifetimes ago, but here they were, each a single wave in the ocean of will contained in the small Lamb before him.

No. Not small. How had he ever thought she was small?

At last, Creed managed to regain feeling in his limbs. Slowly, he reached his free hand to take one of the girl's wrists. Pulling her arm upwards, he placed the pouches back into her hand with trembling fingers. He looked to the ground, sure he would crumble away if he met her eyes.

"I'm sorry." His voice was so pathetically quiet that she couldn't have heard him. Gathering what little strength he could, he repeated more loudly, "I'm sorry."

Neveah's hand slowly withdrew, seeds in her weak grasp once again. "It's... it's okay."

Creed could not see her expression, but her tone was filled with equal parts relief, confusion, and concern. He wished she would strike him, scream at him, curse him, do anything he would have expected. But of course, she didn't. The girl simply refused to act in a manner he could predict, and in doing so, she had defeated him utterly.

"Please," he begged, the word containing more emotion than he had felt within himself for a long time, "leave this behind. This story you've wandered into is meaningless. It is a *farce*."

"I... don't believe that," came the quiet reply.

"It doesn't matter what you believe. Nothing that happens here will change anything. If you stay, you'll be washed away by the madness like everything else." Finally able to move his legs again, Creed stepped past the girl and began to walk away, noting the laughable reversal from their previous conversation.

"I want to help you."

Creed stopped but did not turn, fearing that the slightest movement would send him crumbling to the ground. Why could she not consider the weight of her words before she spoke them?

"You frighten me," he finally said. "More than any angel. More than any demon. If you're there, I'll never be able to fight."

"Do you have to fight?"

"It's all that's left to me. Every other choice was taken. If you really want to help, then leave. And live."

Neveah didn't respond right away, so Creed moved to take his leave, but he'd only made it a few steps when her voice called out.

"Hey!"

Against his better judgment, he halted once again, just barely turning his head over his shoulder.

"What does the world look like to you right now?"

The same question she'd asked him when they'd first met. If she was hoping for a different answer, she was going to be disappointed.

"It's dark," he repeated.

With that, he resumed his endless walk, trudging away from the dead valley and the unbreakable thing at its center.

I never realized that someone like you could still exist. Thank you, Neveah. And damn you, too.

Chapter IX
"Wayfaring Stranger"

Joshua sat upon the flimsy bench in the corner of the church basement, fingers steepled in a pyramid at his mouth. As always, his mind was alive with a universe's worth of thought.

It was both blessing and curse, he believed, to possess the awareness he had. While it was nearly impossible for anything to surprise him, so too was it impossible for his mind to rest. Always his thoughts were flitting back and forth across the world, consciousness sailing along the mental connections he'd formed with those he'd met.

Currently, Joshua was observing the whereabouts of his "comrades"; as the chain that bound the Samaritans together, he could never look away for too long. Putting aside Stryfe, still wheezing on the table mere feet away, he chose first to look upon their imperious leader.

Rictus remained where he always did when not being forced to intervene, floating in that twilight realm between life and death that only he could reach. He wandered amongst the stranded souls of lost Lambs, plucking them from the aether and bringing them into his being. Or rather, that of the entity which slept *within* his being.

The dark man's attention was focused solely on his work, but Joshua knew that would not last. As soon as the true Preceptor awoke, Rictus would descend as swiftly as a thought to render Its judgment.

Shifting focus, Joshua saw that Grendel was a great many continents away and, in a rare occurrence, was not currently in the middle of slaughtering something. The Prodigal stalked across a snow-covered mountainside, his soul the same unrestrained maelstrom of violence and rage it had always been.

Joshua could tell by its intensity that Grendel had not whet his appetite in some time. Feeling sweat begin to bead on his neck from the heat of such fiery insanity, Joshua decided to look away before the madman started smashing the mountain just to have something to hit.

Salomé, as always, took the longest to find; Joshua wished she would at least *try* to keep herself in one place. Eventually, he felt the Anchoress' presence across the vast western ocean at Joshua's back, amid an extensive collection of islands. The demonic city over which she presided loomed in a vast valley somewhere on the largest of the islands.

It appeared that Gogmagog had altered itself to take on characteristics once associated with the land, its spires in the shape of elaborate pagodas. As always, Salomé's exact presence was difficult to pinpoint amid the swirling darkness that Gogmagog and the other Beasts exuded, but Joshua did not feel the need to bring his mind any closer to find her. He knew she was there, and he would only feel pity if he observed her further.

Despite what he knew would be the result, Joshua did spare a few moments to try and see if he could feel the presence of Testament's soul anywhere. Of course, there was nothing, and Joshua chose not to dwell on the fact; wallowing in the shame of his failure had long since lost any appeal. The Sacristan would reveal themselves again one day, and Joshua would deal with the reckoning that would follow when it was time.

Perhaps he'd be able to take his eyes back then.

Turning from such bitter thoughts, Joshua finally focused his attention to Creed, and the image that came to his mind was of the Crusader wandering back in the direction he had come, the valley where he had battled Adrammelech left far behind. That was good. Joshua had not looked at his brother since he'd stopped to rest after besting the first demon and was glad to see him heading towards his next foe so soon.

The burst of power Creed had regained during the fight appeared to have left him. Unfortunate, but Joshua decided to take solace in the fact that one of the lost Cores had shown itself at all; perhaps things were not wholly unsalvageable just yet.

At that moment, a whisper of sensation flickered at the edge of Joshua's mental image, and he realized that there was another presence in the vicinity. Focusing, Joshua was able to find a thread of life so thin and fragile it could only belong to a Lamb.

Tracing the line, he followed the connection several hundred feet behind Creed's position, where a small figure was currently clambering up a hillside. Closing in, Joshua felt the outline of what seemed to be a girl, albeit a small and emaciated one. He sharpened his senses and evoked a clearer image of the girl's movements, a determined stride that belied her apparent frailty as she followed a—

Joshua's thoughts stopped. It was just for a moment, an instance so small it might not have actually occurred, but the unmistakable, if alien, sensation of his mind being pushed back had halted his observations; he hadn't thought there was anything left that was capable of keeping him out, but it almost felt as if something was—

Oh.

Oh.

Now what are the odds of that? Joshua thought.

His mouth felt dry as he struggled to put the possibilities running through his head aside and focus on the girl from a less intrusive distance.

She was moving at an impressive clip, clearly doing her best to follow the same path Creed was beating. For his part, Creed gave no indication that he was aware of being followed. Whatever had happened when Joshua wasn't looking, it appeared his brother had now acquired a companion, albeit one he hadn't noticed.

Oh yes. This was *very* interesting.

Joshua's attention was pulled from his inner vision by the sudden shifting of Stryfe's ruined torso upon the table, for which Joshua was glad; his thoughts had been starting to spiral away from him, and he always hated when his "curiosity" got the better of him.

Joshua felt rather than saw Stryfe raise his withered head, seeming as if he was trying to listen to some far-off sound. The demon's aura felt slightly more substantial than before; as expected, his tongue had returned after Creed's battle with Adrammelech.

"Odd..." Stryfe's voice was now physical as opposed to projected, but it was no less rasping and unpleasant to hear.

"What is it?"

"Our brother's soul. It has... changed. Shifted. It seems almost... lighter... than before...".

Joshua stood from the bench, using his senses to guide his steps as he began to pace about the room he couldn't see.

He did not need to observe Creed to know what Stryfe said was true; their souls were bound together, and thus the demon would be even keener to such things than Joshua himself. Stryfe could not see the Lamb that currently trailed behind their brother, but Joshua would keep that part to himself.

"Is that so?" he asked aloud, feigning just a bit of ignorance as usual. "Maybe beating Adrammelech gave him some confidence?"

"Perhaps." Stryfe's tone implied uncertainty, but Joshua decided not to elaborate any further and risk arousing suspicion. "If so, I do not think it will be enough. His power remains barely a flicker."

"You realize that if he loses to any of the strays, you go with him, right?"

"Oh, I believe he will be able to overcome my children. But do not forget, our wonderful Preceptor has seen fit to declare a blood sport between the two of us. Once my power has been returned, do you truly think he will last as he is now?"

"You don't have to fight him. There *is* a way for all of us to get out of this alive."

Stryfe gave a few hacking chuckles at that. "Yes, yes, I'm sure your intricate little mind is working out a scheme as we speak. But have you perhaps considered that our Creed is positively spoiling for a fight? And that the feeling may be *quite* mutual?"

This time, Joshua could not hold back a pleading tone. "We're all that's left, Stryfe. All we *have* left. Do you really hate him that much?"

"It is not a matter of hate, baby brother. You have done such an admirable job over the ages keeping our natures at bay, but you must have always known the day would come when this delicate balance was undone. There is too much to settle between us. Too great a reckoning."

Joshua set his mouth in a line and felt his neck muscles clench. How stubborn his brothers could be. But Joshua knew this conversation would go nowhere, and decided his thinking would be better done away from the demon for now.

Reaching into an inside pocket of his jacket, he grabbed one of his many strands of hay and placed one between his teeth before giving his final word on the matter.

"Don't be so sure."

With that, he left Stryfe behind and plodded up the staircase to the ground floor. Opening and closing the door behind him, he entered the main hall of the church. The air was cooler up here, and he drew his wool-lined jacket a bit tighter around his exposed torso; sometimes he wished he wasn't so much more comfortable going bare-chested.

He sensed his way over to the flowerbed in the hall's center, at the edge of which he could feel Stella was currently kneeling. She was motionless, regarding the colorful (he assumed) menagerie of plant life. From what Joshua could understand, if the nun wasn't "resting" in her room at the back of the church, this is what she did with her time when Creed was not present.

Coming to a stop next to her, Joshua waited several moments for his presence to be acknowledged. He tried bouncing his straw up and down with his teeth a few times to see if that might irritate her enough to speak, but in the end, it seemed he would have to be the one to break the silence.

"Does the view ever get old?"

"No," came the response, with bluntness allowing absolutely no room for further conversation. That was fine. Joshua knew how to be a nuisance.

"Think I could take one with me when I leave?"

"No."

"You really *don't* like me very much, do you?"

"No."

Joshua supposed he couldn't blame her. He had met Stella before, of course, the same time that Creed had so very long ago. Or had that been rather recently? Time was so hard to tell when it no longer existed.

Stella had apparently seen something in Creed that she hadn't in Joshua or Stryfe, and when he left them behind, she followed. The result was Joshua still finding himself at a loss when it came to understanding the odd workings of the nun's mind. He often wondered how Creed managed it so well.

"For what it's worth, I *am* sorry this happened."

"A false truth."

"You think I'm lying?"

"No. I understand you to be incapable of lying. So you hide behind misleading facts instead. I believe that you're sorry, but not for the reasons you claim. A false truth."

Joshua didn't bother arguing the point. He had long grown accustomed to his every word being suspect. Given that his role in the Covenant required him to always know more about the others than they knew about themselves, it was only natural for trust to be difficult.

"You hate us for disrupting his solitude?"

"You didn't disrupt his solitude. Only his work."

"You realize that work was more than just making graves, right?"

"Yes."

Joshua was mildly surprised to hear that. "And you were okay with it?"

"It's what he wished."

"That's not what I asked."

"It was my answer."

"Don't you care for him?"

"We are lovers."

The sheer bluntness of that statement hit Joshua like a bottle to the head. "O-oh? How, uh... how does *that* work?"

"He's teaching me. Helping me to better myself. In turn, I'm supporting him as well. I think the relationship is comparable to lovers."

"Ah." That's what she'd meant. Thank goodness. "Is Creed... *aware* of this relationship?"

"He pretends not to be."

"Oh."

"But he is."

"Sure."

"He is."

"I got it."

This was not the turn Joshua had expected this conversation to take. Perhaps he *had* left them out here for too long. "But, if you are, uh... in love... then why would you be okay with—"

"Lovers support each other," she interjected. "They devote themselves wholly to one another and do everything in their power to help each other achieve their desires. I have none of my own, and so I devote my efforts towards helping him achieve his wish."

"And what happens when that wish is granted? Are you sure you won't have any desires, then?"

For the first time, there was a few beats between responses. Which, by Stella's standards, Joshua knew was rare.

"He wishes for peace," she finally said. "I can't give that to him, and so I can't stop him from seeking it out."

Joshua realized that whatever relationship had developed between her and Creed during their long exile was one he was likely not capable of comprehending. If nothing else, he could tell that one way or another, it was not going to end fairly for her.

"I'm sorry," he said. This time, he was not accused of false truths. "But you know, if you're willing to be just a *little* selfish, you can take some comfort in the fact that he won't be going anywhere, now. Coming back to us may not be what he wants, but—"

"He will never find peace with you."

"—but *at least* he'll be alive. I think that means more to you than you'd like to admit."

"You act as if this trial you forced onto him has already ended."

Joshua put on as laid-back a tone as he could. "Oh, I don't think you need to worry about him biting it before the end, Stelly. He may like to wallow, but my big brother is strong."

"No. He is not."

At last, he felt the motion of the nun turning her head from the flowers to look at him. As always, he found it somewhat disconcerting not to be able to sense any emotions through her aura, though for once, he felt as if he didn't have to.

"He is weak," she declared. "And that is why you should have left him alone...."

Chapter X
"The Rust"

 Ducking carefully through a hole in the broken chain fence, Creed stepped into what he assumed had once been a train yard. He'd glimpsed it many times on his trips into the city, but seeing as it was located on the outskirts about a mile away from where he typically traveled, he'd never bothered to pass through it.
 Evidently, he hadn't been missing much. The yard was occupied by a large central building, hollow and decrepit as the rest, with a sizable garage attached to its side into which several of the tracks flowed.
 Creed could picture the parade of train cars which had once passed in and out, mechanics scurrying about to complete their repairs before sending them back into the world. It was silent now, little more than a graveyard of rusted steel boxes that hardly resembled the locomotives they'd once been.
 Creed surmised that most of the city's trains had been stored here sometime before the rails had been shut down. The yard was positively crammed with their husks, crisscrossing across the yard in sizes ranging from a single car to a chain of dozens. Some still stood on worn-down wheels, but most sat uselessly on the ground.
 The result was a veritable maze of decayed metal in which Creed struggled not to lose himself. Keeping the central building in sight, he made his way in that direction to avoid being

swallowed by the scenery. The web of tracks would lead him back into the city if he followed them in the right direction, but Creed hoped he wouldn't have to do so.

Although he was far enough away from the crater that his powers would not weaken significantly, he could still feel a slight tug on his soul, the mild throb of the void at the city's center trying to consume what little was left of him.

The vision Joshua had imparted to him showed that, unlike Adrammelech, Samael had not taken to aimlessly shuffling across the wasteland; instead, it had taken up residence somewhere in this graveyard of metal and did not seem keen on departing. Whereas Adrammelech's instincts as a warrior told it to wander in search of a fight, Samael had been a hunter; its nature would compel it to find a suitable hiding spot where it could lie in wait for any who dared approach.

With that in mind, Creed's senses were on full alert as he finally broke through the walls of train cars and into the yard where the central building loomed before him. Like the church, it was impossible to tell what color it had originally been painted; everything was a dull grey under the black sun.

The exterior wasn't quite dirty or stained—even decay was something no longer allowed in the timeless world—but the building's husk seemed decrepit all the same. There were open spaces where large windows had once been; Creed wondered if it was the shockwave of him burning an angel into the city's center so long ago which had destroyed them.

The main garage was open, yawning before Creed like a dank cavern. He could see almost nothing inside, as the whole interior was veiled in shadow, but could feel a sense of instinctual dread and foreboding emanating from what should have been a completely empty building.

His enemy was inside.

Holding out a hand, Creed flared the Core of Malkuth within him and called a new mass of clay into his grasp, this time shaping it into a long, thin katana whose blade appeared wickedly sharp despite not being made of steel. Unlike Adrammelech, Samael's body would be more vulnerable to slashing attacks, and he'd always found the katana to be one of the Lambs' best-suited tools for such a task.

Creed noted that the clay had come to his hand with less effort than it had taken before, and had shaped itself more quickly. It seemed that his advanced use of Malkuth during the last battle had revitalized the once-dull core to some extent, not unlike an atrophied muscle regaining some strength after finally seeing use. Creed grimaced at the unwanted sensation of increased potency, but hoped that it would at least mean this second hunt would be less of an ordeal than the last.

Holding the katana straight out at his side, he went still and tense. Samael was a patient hunter, but it was still insane. It would not be able to abide Creed's presence for long, and he expected it would be only a short while before the demon sprung from the shadows of the empty building.

Which is why he was surprised when he felt a surge of murderous intent swell directly beneath his feet.

Once again, only an eternity of fighting instinct compelled Creed to leap high into the air just before the ground erupted in a shower of stone. He glimpsed a flash of clawed hands grasping at empty air before his leap became a back-flip that carried him onto the roof of one of the train cars ringing the area. The ancient metal shifted beneath him, and he was surprised that it actually held.

A dark figure emerged from the new hole where Creed had been standing, obscured by the dust cloud. The sounds of slithering and hissing grew louder as the creature he'd been hunting drug itself to the surface, and by the time the cloud cleared, it had fully crawled into view.

Its torso vaguely resembled that of a pale, bald man, not entirely unlike the form Stryfe was currently trapped in, though this one was far less old and withered. Its eyes, by contrast, were altogether inhuman, blood-red with yellow pupils slit like a serpent's.

Its upper arms appeared relatively normal until they were gradually overtaken by purple scales and black spines at the elbows, culminating in hands adorned with vicious draconic claws. Each talon was such a bright red they appeared to glow amongst the dark surroundings of the train yard.

At the waist, any resemblance to humanity ceased. Pale flesh turned again to deep purple scales, coalescing into a long, thick reptilian tail. It was massive, though its exact length was difficult to tell half-coiled upon the ground as it was. It resembled the halfway point between snake and dragon, and the deep purple scales were accented by patches of bright red fringe.

The sickening appendage brought to Creed's mind images of half-human snake-folk from various primitive myths. Fitting, seeing as the Lambs' belief in such creatures had been directly inspired by Samael itself.

By far the most disconcerting feature, however, was the large crystal embedded in the center of the monster's chest. It resembled a diamond in the recognizable shape of a heart, and glowed with a faint but vivid violet light emanating from deep within its core.

To those who did not know, the crystal might have appeared brilliant and beautiful. But Creed was well aware of the power that shimmering crystal contained, and it made the hair on his neck bristle in instinctive fear.

Samael had been one of God's oldest angels before devolving into an abomination when it chose to fall alongside its master at the dawn of time. Unlike with Adrammelech, there was already a flicker of dangerous intelligence in its serpentine gaze. It had possessed enough remaining guile to hide its presence, striking while Creed was focused on the remnants of its aura still left in the building.

Gripping his weapon tighter, Creed had the sinking feeling that, despite what he'd hoped, this hunt would test him more than the last. As before, he reached up and unzipped his heavy coat once again.

Samael had yet to move from its position, balancing on its massive tail and regarding Creed with that unsettling stare. The light within its crystal heart pulsed at a slow, even rhythm. After a moment, it opened its mouth wide to reveal a set of lethal-looking fangs and a forked tongue, letting out a hiss so cold it seemed to peel Creed's flesh away.

"IIIIIIII knooooooow yoooooooooooooou..."

Creed had thought Stryfe's voice to be unpleasant, but it was nothing compared to that of the demon in front of him, somehow both a high-pitched hiss and bone-deep rumble all at once.

"Patriaaaaarch... Firstboooooorn..."

Steeling himself against the sound, Creed responded, "I don't suppose you remember how this went the last time I hunted you?"

"*Noooo... passsst... noooo... faaaate...*"

Creed could sense a shift in the demon's aura, and it was clear that despite being capable of speech, there was no rationality left in its addled mind.

"*Oooone... lasssst... huuunt...*"

With that, Samael's mouth opened further, jaw unhinging to an unnatural length. As it did, the dim violet light of its crystal heart flared to a bright, vivid hue. Creed had just enough time to leap backward off the train car as a stream of concentrated purple liquid spewed from the serpent's maw.

He hit the ground just as it made contact with the car. The sounds of hissing and boiling filled his ears. By the time he looked up, the entire car had melted away, dissolved so thoroughly that it might well have never existed.

There it was: The Venom of God from which the demon derived its name. At the dawn of time, it had been a valuable tool in shaping the primordial world, used to carve mountains and valleys and the vast canyons which became oceans. Now it was little more than a mad devil's deadly weapon.

Creed had known from the start that he would need to overcome it but had yet to muster up a single idea as to how. Samael's poison did not merely melt or corrode; it outright *erased* whatever it touched, wiping it from existence like a dream upon waking.

So far as Creed knew, there were only two things in all of Creation that were immune to its effects: the crystal heart in which it was contained, and Samael's own body into which it was embedded.

He broke off this line of thought as the hissing form of Samael leaped over the destroyed train car, launched into the air by its own coiled tail. Creed scurried out of the way as the demon lanced downward to tear him to pieces with its claws. It landed with an angry hiss and, with a speed that belied its large size, lashed its tail towards Creed like a whip.

He was ready, and brought the katana up to meet the attack. Blade met scaly flesh, and the weapon carved through the demon's tail as if it were butter. The appendage split in twain, and Samael let out a pained shriek as the severed chunk was carried by the remaining momentum into a nearby train.

The demon writhed, stump-tail flinging ruby-red blood everywhere. To Creed's disappointment, the gaping wound began to close almost immediately. Samael did not possess the impenetrable flesh Adrammelech had, but its regenerative capabilities were far greater. Creed glanced behind to see the severed part of the demon's tail dissolve into black smoke while the main body was already in the process of regenerating.

Samael stopped screaming and regained its posture. The crystal heart flared purple once more, and the beast unhinged its jaw to spit another volley of poison in Creed's direction.

Flaring Malkuth again, Creed willed a large, rectangular shield of clay into being before himself. He tried to will as much strength and solidity into the construct as he could, but Samael's venom did not abide by physical laws.

As soon it made contact, the barrier bubbled and warped before bursting apart. Creed was glad to know he could at least stop the poison in its tracks, but this strategy would not remain viable for long; creating such strong shields would quickly drain what little energy he had.

Samael finished regenerating its tail and fixed its fierce red eyes on Creed. Deciding he needed to escape the tight quarters, Creed threw up another clay shield to catch the next volley of venom. By the time he heard the attack impact his shield, he was already sprinting away, leaping through a gap between two linked train cars and making his way deeper into the metal maze.

He dodged and weaved through rusted locomotive husks, searching for anywhere with enough room to maneuver. Behind him, he could hear hissing and the smashing of metal; Samael was likely just flinging train cars out of the way with its tail as it pursued him.

A new whistling sizzle filled his ears, closing in from above, and he leaped to the side just as a stream of poison arced downward like an arrow, boring a sizable hole in the earth as it evaporated from existence.

Deciding it was at least worth a shot, Creed glimpsed inside himself to see if, by chance, this battle was compelling his

Netzach core to stir as it had before. Alas, it appeared that burst of power had indeed been a fluke; Creed felt not a single glimmer of power in his soul beyond Malkuth, and somehow he knew the grey Core would not miraculously come to him this time.

Eventually, Creed used his shoulder to burst through the weakened door of one car and out the other side, emerging at last into a decently open area. It was still ringed with dead trains, but not choked with them. He turned and readied himself for Samael to arrive.

To his surprise, what came flying towards him was not the demon itself, but rather a lone train car sent hurtling through the sky like a stone from a catapult.

Creed willed his katana to extend itself to an immense length, shooting high into the sky like a beacon. With a swing, Creed used the now-massive sword to carve through the rusted metal missile, cleaving it into two halves that flew off in separate directions.

No sooner had he done so when a second car flung into the air, this one from a much closer distance. In the span of a handclap, Creed retracted the long blade before immediately re-extending it, swiping upwards as it did so to cleave the second train just as he had the first.

Suddenly, the car he had burst through to enter the clearing launched towards him, rolling and skipping along the ground. Drawing his blade into a smaller— if still absurd—length, Creed raised the weapon over his head before chopping downward. With a shriek of metal, the train car bisected, two halves rocketing past Creed's body before crashing to a stop some ways behind him.

But the thrown debris had merely been cover for Samael itself. Creed was unable to react quickly enough as a purple-red tail lashed into his view the instant he cut through the car, and his body was gripped and bound by the powerful appendage.

He failed to keep hold of his weapon, which clattered uselessly to the ground. The long tail coiled itself around his body, cutting off his breath. Samael's upper body came into view, fangs bared and bloody eyes filled with hate.

The demon brought its head close to Creed, observing as his bones were snapped and crushed. The crystal heart flared yet again, so close that Creed could almost feel the thrumming of energy within. Samael's jaw began to unhinge, ready to melt Creed's immobile form away.

Blackness began to encroach at the corners of his vision, but before it could fade away entirely, Creed summoned the last ounce of his will and shaped a small but deadly diamond of clay into the air beside his head; the same kind he had used to deflect Adrammelech's feathers. The dagger shot forward like a bullet, and Samael had brought itself too close to dodge in time.

Another shriek tore through the air as the projectile pierced through Samael's eye and lodged itself deep into its skull. Creed felt the vice-grip of the tail loosen ever so slightly, just enough of a relief for him to gather his strength and break away as the demon once again began to whip its body about in pain.

Creed's broken bones did not carry him a sufficient distance from his opponent, and he crumpled to his knees as Samael reached up and tore the blade from its eye. As soon as it did so, the wound began to repair itself.

Turning his attention to the katana still laying on the ground, Creed extended an arm. As if pulled by a magnet, the weapon flew a short distance into Creed's waiting hand.

Unfortunately, the creature had already turned to face him again. As before, the crystal heart flared, its jaw unhinged, and the Venom of God rocketed towards him.

Too close!

Creed's battered body was unable to leap backward in time to fully escape the attack. His senses went shock-white for a moment before he felt his back slam roughly into the ground some ways away.

On instinct, he turned himself over on his stomach, propped himself up on his arms, and attempted to stand but found himself falling back into the dirt.

Looking down at himself, he was somewhat surprised to see his entire left leg gone from just above the knee. Not because he didn't understand what had happened, but because he had expected more pain.

It didn't take long to hit him.

The numbness retreated in a rush, replaced with the sensation of magma filling the space where his leg had once been. Creed could not hold back the roar that tore itself from his throat as he watched a copious amount of sapphire blood glob from the wound and paint the stone below. He grit his teeth, but his screams weren't muffled in the slightest.

Fighting as hard as he could through the pain, Creed took the katana still in his grasp and pierced it into the dirt, using it to prop himself up. He took a hand and placed it on the oozing stump of his leg, ignoring the flash of agony it caused. With a thought, he created a coating of tightly packed clay to encase the wound. The pain only stung that much more sharply, but at least the blood flow was staunched.

He could hear the sound of Samael slithering closer and closer from behind. In seconds, a second volley of venom would fall upon him. With no time to think, Creed allowed reflex alone to take over.

Whipping around, he yanked the katana from the ground and swung it in a desperate upward slash. As he did, he once again willed the blade to lengthen tenfold in an instant. He was moving too fast for his own eyes to see anything more than a blur, and he prayed that his warrior's instincts would be enough to carry his blow where it needed to land.

The blade struck true. Creed's vision focused just in time to see the long katana slicing through Samael's neck. Its jaw had just begun to unhinge. The creature made no hiss or shriek as its bald head flew from its shoulders before landing in the dirt like a boulder. Its bloody eyes had already rolled back, and a long, forked tongue lolled from its slack, open maw.

The main body stood balanced on the rigid snake tail for a short while longer, but eventually collapsed under its own weight. It crashed to the ground with a loud rumble, sending up a plume of dust that briefly enveloped Creed's form.

He didn't move a muscle even as the dust settled around him. The katana was still gripped tightly in his fist, its ludicrously long blade knifing into the air where it had narrowly decapitated the demon.

After several beats, Creed allowed himself a few shaking breaths. Somehow—whether by instinct or sheer luck—he had just barely managed to buy himself a reprieve, but he knew it would not last. Losing its head was a serious wound, but so long as the crystal heart in its chest remained intact, Samael had more than enough energy to heal itself indefinitely.

He looked at where the demon's body had fallen. It remained still for now, but would begin to move as soon as Samael's mind recovered from the shock of losing its head.

Thinking quickly, Creed shrunk his katana back down to its normal length. He sat up on his one remaining knee, ignoring the unending burning in his poorly staunched stump. Taking his sword's hilt in both hands, he held it facing downwards, ready to stab into the earth—

All thought spiraled away as a high-pitched voice filled his ears from behind: "Creed!"

No. No, this couldn't be happening. It could *not*. Warmth drained from Creed's body as he turned to look over his shoulder. Against all manner of logic and reason, he beheld Neveah emerging from behind one of the pieces of train car he'd sliced.

Creed didn't know where she'd come from, and he didn't care. He was too busy questioning if the girl was even human. No ordinary person could possibly be this stubborn and foolish. Surely she was a ghost, some specter that had chosen to hound him wherever he went as punishment.

But that was not the case. She was real. And despite all he had said to her, the girl had followed him. Snuck behind him as he crossed miles of barren hills. Watched his battle with Samael just as she had with Adrammelech.

Now, upon seeing Creed behead the demon, she was rushing out to meet him, a look of deepest distress on her pale features. Perhaps she was too worried about his wound to continue hiding. She didn't realize that such an injury meant little to someone like him. Didn't realize that the fight was not over. Didn't realize that a demon was not beaten if its body had not disappeared.

"Are you okay!?" she was calling. Even from this distance, her lake-green eyes shone.

A foolish question, brought on by foolish concern. But before Creed could overcome his stupor and call out to her, the sound of a low hiss building from behind caused him to whip back around.

Samael's head, still lying on the ground where it had fallen, was moving again. Its yellow irises rolled back into view, its tongue slithered back inside its mouth, and its jaw was already unhinging. Creed wasn't sure whether or not the severed head could actually see or hear, but it didn't have to. The demon could sense its surroundings well enough.

Panic filled Creed's throat like a vial of poison, and he turned back to Neveah, who was too focused on him to notice Samael's movement.

"GET BACK!!!"

It was beyond too late. He heard the sound of sizzling venom zooming through the air, and part of him expected everything to go dark as the terrible fluid erased his flesh, but it was not he whom Samael was aiming for. It had instead focused on the new presence it felt, the little mouse that had scurried by and interrupted its hunt.

For what little it was worth, the stream of venom did not strike the girl. Samael's head was lying on its side in the dirt, and it had attacked on pure, psychotic reflex. Combined with the fact that Neveah had been sprinting towards Creed, the result was a poorly aimed shot. The blast impacted just behind Neveah's fleeing form instead of directly upon her, and for a moment, Creed thought she had escaped.

Then, to his horror, his enhanced vision caught sight of a lone droplet—a single, violet bead—that splashed far enough outwards to make contact with the girl's dress. The drop touched just below her ribs, and Creed was powerless to stop it.

In an instant, most of the girl's lower right side was erased, opening up like a plastic bag before erupting in a starburst of blood. Her body jerked sideways as she was knocked to the ground by the force of her own innards splattering outward. She dropped like a rag doll and rolled several feet before coming to a stop, a motionless heap of white and red.

"NOOOOOOOOOOO!!!!!"

Every ounce of Creed's pain vanished as he picked himself off the ground, bracing on his single leg. Summoning strength even *he* had forgotten he possessed, Creed felt the stone beneath him crack from the force as he propelled himself like a rocket with the lone limb.

Just as he left the ground, he summoned two clay darts in the air and, without looking, sent them sailing towards Samael's severed head. Though he didn't see it happen, the sound of a furious shriek told him the two darts had embedded themselves in each of the demon's eyes, hopefully buying him a few precious seconds.

Creed's empowered leap carried him the entire distance to Neveah's limp form. Landing beside her, he scooped her into his arms.

She was even paler than before, her skin tight and waxy. Her dress was barely hanging on after so much cloth had been erased, though Creed noted that by some infinitesimally small odds, her seed pouches and the rope they were tied to had not been destroyed by the venom.

They were, however, painted in her blood. Her entire right side was an utter mess of red, and Creed caught glimpses of something soft and fleshy that he didn't want to think about.

"No," he muttered. "No, no, no, no, *no...*"

Creed managed to wrench his gaze away from the girl to look behind himself, and found that Samael's body had finally begun to pick itself off the ground. It moved like a marionette with tangled strings, jerking and twitching as it struggled to rise without the use of its brain. At its chest, the crystal heart shone like it was filled with violet fire. Its talons were grasping and clawing in the direction of its fallen head, which still shrieked and hissed with Creed's darts sticking out of its eyes.

Creed watched the abhorrent display, feeling his hands growing slicker with the blood and viscera of the girl in his arms, and felt a long-abandoned sensation boil up inside him: rage. Pure. Hot. Unquenching. All of it focused solely on the abomination groping about before him.

With a snarl that barely sounded human, Creed whipped a hand out towards the katana he'd dropped when he'd leaped towards Neveah. Once again, the clay construct flew through the air and into Creed's grasp. Flipping it downwards, Creed stabbed it into the earth with a shout, as he'd intended to do before the girl had arrived.

Imitating Samael's earlier tactic, Creed flared Malkuth and pushed its power underground, sending it across the gap between him and the demon. Several long cracks in the earth began to web outward, carving jagged trails that marked where the buried clay was moving below.

When the fissures had reached Samael's groping form and coalesced beneath it, Creed took a moment to gather Malkuth's energy into a small, dense bubble beneath the earth. With another furious yell, he commanded the power to burst upwards like a breaking dam.

Ten clay spires, shaped like giant needles, exploded from the ground beneath Samael's body. They pierced its flesh like a pincushion and lanced its headless form high into the air. The head on the ground let out its loudest shriek yet, but its body could do nothing but writhe in agony as it hung suspended, trapped by the earthen spears stabbing through every joint. Ruby-red blood rained down the spires like waterfalls.

One had stabbed through each of its elbows, leaving its arms splayed wide. Two more had gone through the creature's pectorals, one on either side of the crystal heart. Another had drilled right through its stomach and out the back. The rest were pierced along its long serpent tail, raising most of it into the air but still leaving several feet coiled on the ground.

The beast continued to thrash about, but was unable to move from its crucified position. The crystal heart glowed more brightly than ever, and the severed head was now launching volley after volley of its venom in-between screams.

Blinded and panicked as it was, the attacks were random and thoughtless. They sailed far over Creed's head to impact the ring of train cars around them. The sounds of metal bursting and dissolving filled the air, joining the cacophony of Samael's wailing.

Creed was far from finished. His gaze zeroed in on the diamond heart, now fully exposed by Samael's suspension. Taking his hand from the hilt of his katana, he turned his palm upwards, fingers contorted into a claw-like half-fist. He grit his teeth so hard they could have broken, then jerked his hand upwards like a conductor signaling the crescendo of an opera.

From beneath Samael's dangling body, three final spires of clay shot up from the dirt, faster and sharper than the others. The trio of spears converged to a single point, colliding in the direct center of Samael's purple heart with greater force than all of the trains in this yard could have produced.

The diamond core was more solid than any earthly material; at any other time, Creed could not have created anything strong enough to break it. But right now, his fury was the sharpest knife in all of Creation.

In less than a second, Samael's heart shattered.

Creed was briefly blinded as the violet light contained within the crystal was released all at once, and his ears went deaf from the crack of an explosion. He resided in this whited-out purgatory for a short while, part of him wishing it would never clear and bring him back to dreaded reality.

By the time his senses returned, Samael's body had gone completely still, hanging limp on Creed's spires. The three which had pierced its heart now sprouted from its back, crisscrossing each other like blood-drenched spears.

Creed looked down to see the severed head letting out one long, final death rattle. A last bit of venom spilled from its jaw, dripping onto the earth below.

Having erased just a bit more of the world before it left, Samael's head and body finally burst apart into clouds of blackened ash. They dispersed quickly, leaving behind only the spires as evidence of the battle that had just taken place.

Creed did not allow himself even a moment to savor the meaningless victory. All of his wrath dissipated in an instant, replaced only with sheer, cold panic. Thoughts of the demon left him entirely as he turned his attention back to the bloody, broken girl he held. She hadn't budged an inch since he'd taken her into his arms.

"Hey!" he barked. He grabbed her shoulders and gave them a light shake, completely at a loss for what he could possibly do. "Come on! Come on, girl, give me something!"

To his shock, her eyes actually twitched, opening to just the barest slits.

He felt breathless. "Neveah!?"

"C...Creed..."

Her voice was hardly more than a whisper, and he couldn't even tell if she was feeling the pain. A wound this great might have gone past such things.

"I... can't see..."

"You idiot!" His words were harsh, but his voice was so choked that they carried no bite. "What the hell is wrong with you? Why would you come here? Why couldn't you just *stay away!?*"

He didn't expect the girl to answer, since any breath she let out could be her last, but she again surprised him by choking out another weak response. "Don't know... couldn't... stop myself...."

"You couldn't possibly be *that* curious!"

"No..." She winced and drew in a long, rasping breath. It sounded like a death rattle. "Just... too much... pain...."

"Don't focus on the pain. Just listen to my voice."

"Not... mine...."

At this, her eyes closed once again. Creed couldn't move, frozen by her words until he noticed her face going slack. Panic spiked through him sharper than ever. Laying her fully on the ground, his hands hovered uselessly over Neveah's body, unable to find anything they could possibly do.

It wasn't as if the girl was dying. Even a wound as terrible as this would not kill in their forsaken world. Rather than a corpse, Neveah would become a husk, her mind no longer capable of thought beneath the weight of unimaginable pain that would never fade. There was a time when Creed could have healed her wounds, but that power was long since lost to him. As he was now, he couldn't even summon a fire to burn her flesh.

Not that it would matter; if released from her body, her spirit would be in even more agony that she was now. At that point, the only recourse left would be to call upon Rictus and allow the true Preceptor to take her screaming soul into Its being. Creed personally detested the very idea of being trapped within that *thing* for all eternity, but for Neveah it would at least be preferable to any other fate.

Creed didn't want that for her, though. He didn't want *any* of this for her.

"Please!" he hissed in vain over her bloody form. "Please don't. You can't do this. You *can't*."

Part of him was surprised to realize how emphatically he meant it. Creed thought he had *finally* come to terms with the way the world had turned. He had accepted the emptiness and silent cruelty of it all.

But now this tiny, malnourished thing had come along and blown it all away. She'd shattered every notion he'd had, beating him down with the realization that someone like her could still eke out some kind of purpose.

And now he was watching her drown in her own blood.

The Colors. If I just had the other Cores!

It was a vain hope. He had abandoned his power so long ago that he hardly recalled what it felt like anymore. Even the last bit of Malkuth left to him was hanging by the barest thread.

But that was what he'd wanted, right? He had only himself to blame for this impotency, this sense of utter helplessness to keep even a single spark of life from being snuffed out.

In sheer desperation, Creed placed his hands over the crimson mess at Neveah's right side, his breath coming in pathetic gasps as he wet his fingers with her insides. He raised his head to the starless sky above.

"JOSHUA!!!"

Only his own echo answered him at first, bouncing off the husks of train cars.

Creed would not be toyed with. "I know you hear me! I know you see me! Get out here, Joshua!"

"I'm sorry, brother," came the reply, and suddenly the disheveled man was there.

He hadn't appeared from nothing like Rictus did; Creed had felt the warping of space beside him as his brother shifted his body from one location to another. The man stood with arms crossed, and his blind gaze was focused solely on the girl, mouth drawn into a mournful frown.

"Do something!" Creed didn't care in the slightest how his voice faltered like a boy's.

"I can't."

"Bullshit!"

"I *can't* help her, Creed. You know those kinds of things are beyond me. The power I have now can soothe her soul, but not her body. Only you could have done that."

There was no condemnation in his words, but Creed grit his teeth and lowered his head nonetheless. His hands were sticky with the girl's gore.

"I'm surprised." Joshua's tone was just a hair's breadth away from cold. "I thought you'd moved past caring."

"Not her... I didn't know...." Creed's voice trailed off as he closed his eyes tightly.

He'd failed. Like always, he'd failed. No sooner had he found something bright left in the world than he had let the blackness snuff it out again. After all this time, he had thought himself numb to such pain, but that had been a delusion. It was still there. It was sharp. It was empty. It was torturous. It was–

–warm?

Creed opened his eyes at the sudden sensation and felt his mouth go dry at what he saw; a glint, too small to be called a glow, outlining his hands that still clutched at the girl's ruined side.

As Creed stared, the light grew brighter, more solid, and he could see that it was... pink? As the intensity of the light increased, so too did the deepness of the color, turning hot and flushed like solid rose quartz.

Stunned as he was, Creed would recognize this power anywhere: that of Tiferet, the Rose Core. He watched, mouth slightly agape, as a sensation filled his body the likes of which he had not felt in ages beyond ages.

Light began to coil off of his hands and arms like clouds of neon, growing yet brighter as it enveloped the girl's side. The trainyard, dark and lifeless since the end of time, was now illuminated with brilliant pink energy so radiant that it briefly obscured both Neveah and Creed entirely.

The warmth filling Creed reached its peak, and he let out a gasping shout before feeling it vanish entirely. The yard was swallowed in shadow once again, as if nothing had occurred. But as Creed slowly pulled his hands away from where they had been, he could see that was not the case.

Neveah's dress was still tattered, exposing a significant amount of flesh, but there *was* flesh! Where had once been a mass of sticky red plasma, there was now fresh skin, pale and smooth like a newborn's. Creed trembled as he took in the sight, then blinked as he felt a new sensation that hadn't been there before.

Looking down at himself, he was startled to see that Tiferet's light had healed *him* as well. His left leg, erased by the Venom of God, had miraculously returned. The limb was now bare, as his pant leg and boot remained destroyed, but such a concern was far from his mind at this point.

Creed marveled at the healed appendage for another moment, then returned his attention to Neveah. Leaning down, he brought his ear as close to the girl's mouth as he could. Words could not adequately express the emotion he felt when he heard small, weak exhalations and felt the barest breath tickle his ear.

"Very... *very*... interesting..." came Joshua's whisper. The unkempt man had observed the entire thing without moving an inch, thoughts inscrutable behind that blindfold of his. He finally turned his head to look at Creed, who was now gaping at his own hands. "Is it—?"

"No." Creed's own voice sounded numb in his ears. "It's gone...." Just like Netzach, the Tiferet Core's power had vanished just as suddenly as it had appeared.

"That's too bad." Joshua's usual irreverent tone was slipping back in. "Would have been useful...."

His head moved around the area they were in, unnatural senses probably taking in the clay spires that still rose from the ground.

"You sure seemed to fight well enough without it, though. I'll be honest, I thought Sammy had you there for a minute." He looked back down to Creed, the barest ghost of a grin on his lips. "I forgot how scary you get when you have something to protect."

Creed was barely listening, looking back and forth between his hands and Neveah's healed form. With a small sigh, Joshua knelt.

"Alright, now."

He took the girl's limp body into his arms. This finally shook Creed from his stupor, and as Joshua lifted the girl from the ground, he reflexively rose with them. For a moment, his hands reached out as if to grab Neveah away, but he stopped himself. Joshua noticed the attempt, and gave another sigh.

"As curious as I am to learn what the story is here, I'd say this isn't quite the place."

His gaze went to Neveah in his arms, and Creed's followed. She still had yet to stir, but her face had regained a bit of color, and she now looked to be sleeping rather than unconscious, not unlike how she'd looked when he'd first found her in the flowerbed.

Creed glanced up at Joshua, who was watching the girl with an expression he couldn't fathom. Was that... awe on his features?

Joshua finally seemed to notice Creed's gaze and raised a quizzical brow. "First things first: what do we do with this one?"

Creed took a moment to answer. The things he had just said and done here could not be ignored. He wouldn't quite say something had *changed*. He still didn't believe in that. But the fact was that he *had* recalled a power he'd never expected to feel again. Joshua had borne witness to it all, which meant Creed couldn't dare try and claim the girl wasn't involved in their pathetic little game now.

"We bring her to the church," he declared with a sigh. "Not like we can leave her half-naked in the dirt."

He looked to the sleeping girl one last time, and couldn't fight a slight twinge of irritation.

She'd just find me again anyways, wouldn't she?

Chapter XI
"Talk in Circles"

For some reason, Neveah dreamt of the day she got her seeds.

The images were just as hazy as her actual memories; she couldn't make out her surroundings enough to determine where she'd been that day.

Even her recollection of the man himself was hazy, though she could still recall a few details: a seamless robe, perhaps once white but now sullied with dirt and ash; a fluffy brown beard that hid a fatherly smile; rough, weathered hands marred with ugly scars that were nonetheless gentle as they placed the first small bag into her palm and closed her fingers around it.

She remembered feeling hot tears falling down her cheeks without knowing why. She remembered the feeling of her heart suddenly unburdened by a crushing weight she hadn't realized was there.

She remembered looking up at the man who had just given her purpose, meeting a pair of kindly brown eyes that almost seemed to have a white glint in the darkness. She remembered the words he'd spoken to her, his voice soft and calm but filled with pure, unconditional belief:

Why not make the bet? What's left to lose?

"Rook to E8."
"Knight to D6."

Distorted voices invaded Neveah's senses, and the images faded away to blackness. As further awareness worked its way into her, she forced open heavy eyes and was greeted with the view of a tattered wood ceiling. Combined with the firm feeling of wood pressing against her back, she knew precisely where she was.

Taking note of another, softer sensation, she realized she was draped in a cloth blanket. It was old, thin and scratchy, but might have very well been the first luxury of any sort she'd known in recent memory. Looking to her right, she saw the high back of the pew on which she was currently resting.

"Rook to E1. Check."

"King to H2."

Following the pair of voices to her left, Neveah first saw the small set of stairs leading up to the central dais, where she recalled that beautifully ugly collection of flowers would be. Her gaze never reached them, drawn instead to the two figures at the steps only a few feet away from her.

The first was familiar: Stella, just as gorgeous as before. She stood atop the steps, eyes on the ground as if lost in thought.

At her feet was a face new to Neveah. He lounged lazily on the steps, slouched as if he might fall asleep. Shaggy, wild hair and scruffy stubble obscured much of his face, as did a tattered cloth that encased his eyes. He was currently twiddling a strand of hay in-between his teeth.

Over his torso, he wore only a thick, wool-lined black jacket that left his—fairly impressive, Neveah had to admit—chest on display. A pair of baggy, olive-green pants and simple black shoes completed the basic, unkempt look. All in all, Neveah thought he cut the perfect image of a bum.

Then again, wasn't *everyone* technically a bum these days?

"Knight to F2," the man was saying. "Knight takes Pawn."

Stella responded less than a second later. "Knight to F7. Knight takes Pawn. Check."

It appeared Neveah had awoken in the middle of some sort of game. Based on the man's grimace, he wasn't doing well.

"You could at least *pretend* like you're being forced to put effort into this. King to G7."

"Knight to G5. Check."

"Uhhh... King to H6." As soon as the last word left his mouth, though, the man winced. "Uh, no, wait, I—"

"Rook to H7. Rook takes Pawn. Check."

With a groan, the man dropped his head in defeat.

"Stupid of me," he muttered, then raised a hand. "I resign. Man, I *really* thought oh-and-twelve was where I'd make my comeback!"

He then raised his head back up and, to Neveah's surprise, looked right in her direction. She wasn't quite sure how someone with a blindfold could *do* that, but there was no doubt in her mind he was staring directly at her. He flashed her a smile so genuine that it almost unnerved her and called out in a surprisingly kind tone.

"Welcome back."

At his words, Stella's head snapped up from the floor and fixed Neveah with the same inscrutable, slightly-too-wide-eyed stare that she had in their first meeting. The nun took a step forward but seemed to think better of it and stopped herself.

In contrast, the unkempt man stood from his undignified position and sauntered over to Neveah while the other woman stayed stock still.

She pulled herself up into a sitting position, the rough blanket clinging to her. Her body felt incredibly stiff, both from a series of dull aches and her immediate suspicion of the stranger, who plodded over and stopped before her as if he knew right where she was. He extended a hand covered by a fingerless glove.

"My name is Joshua."

Bewildered as she was by the sheer blunt friendliness, Neveah somehow had the gut feeling that the shaggy stranger before her meant no harm. She reached out a cautious hand from behind the blanket and clasped his own. His grip was firm and warm, and she felt her apprehension drain away almost immediately; no one threatening had a handshake that nice.

She *did* wonder how many times she was going to wake up with mysterious, rugged men looming over her, though.

The man, Joshua, looked to his left and called, "Creed."

Neveah followed his "gaze" to see the original loomer himself. He sat hunched forward in the pew across the aisle from her own, facing the pulpit with elbows propped on his knees. His head was lowered as if in thought, and he did not turn to look at either of them.

"I see her."

Before Neveah could think of any kind of response, her attention was pulled to the sudden arrival of Stella. Having apparently overcome her hesitation, the nun was now brushing aside Joshua like one might an especially irritating dust bunny and leaning forward to regard her with wide, violet eyes.

As before, her voice was fairly toneless, but the words came out rather quickly. "Hello again, Neveah."

"H-hey there, Stella."

"I'm happy to see you're awake. How are you feeling? Do you have any pain? Is there anything that you need? Please tell me if there is because I'll be happy to—"

"I-I'm alright." Neveah held up a hand to cut off the stream of questions. And also to keep the nun from leaning any further forward into her personal space. Stella cocked her head, and Neveah wondered if the nun had *wanted* there to be something wrong for her to fix. "Really, I feel fi—"

Wait a minute. She cut herself off as hazy memories flicked through her mind: horrible yellow eyes, a flash of something violet, and the sudden sensation of something wet and hot bursting out from inside her.

With a gasp, Neveah loosened her grip on the blanket and looked down at herself. Based on what little she could recall, her entire right side should have been a mass of blood and viscera, but instead, there was only smooth, unblemished skin.

She was fine. *How* was she fine? She looked up at Stella, who seemed to understand.

"Creed was able to heal your wound. I'm afraid he wasn't able to preserve your dress, though."

Looking down again, Neveah realized the woman was right: her dress was technically still there, but most of the entire right half was gone, and what was left clung to her body in what could only be described as "tatters."

Suddenly aware of the two men in the room and realizing that *someone* had to have carried her here, Neveah pulled the blanket tighter around her form, unable to fight a juvenile flush that filled her cheeks.

She looked at Joshua, who gave a good-natured chuckle before quickly silencing himself and glancing away when Stella turned her head in his direction. Neveah found herself again wondering how someone with his eyes covered seemed to know precisely what was happening.

"If you'd like," Stella said, turning back to face her, "we have lots of scavenged cloth that we have no use for. I'm sure that I can stitch you a new one."

"Oh." For some reason, the notion made Neveah feel sheepish. "That's okay. I don't need...."

She trailed off as she realized how stupid the protest sounded. Was she just going to wear the blanket from now on? "Well... I guess I do, actually."

She looked up at Stella, suddenly feeling self-conscious before the woman's immaculate features. "Um... thank you."

The nun's eyes widened slightly further at Neveah's words. "You are... welcome. I am happy to help. I'll do my best. The materials are downstairs if would you like to—"

Stella cut herself off abruptly, going still, and out of the corner of her eye Neveah saw Creed look up in the nun's direction.

"On second thought," Stella resumed, "would you mind waiting here with Creed? It won't take very long, and I'm sure you have lots of questions."

Neveah pretended not to notice the back-pedaling and just gave a slight nod. "Sure."

Stella returned the gesture. "Thank... you..." She said it in a stilted manner, as if she'd never said the words before.

With that, the nun turned and marched off to the door at the back of the hall, disappearing down the stairs into the darkness below. Joshua watched her go before turning back to Neveah with a half-cocked grin.

"I wish she liked *me* that much...."

"Is that what that is?"

"Don't hold it against her." Neveah looked to see Creed finally rising from his pew. "Her social skills aren't the best, but you're the first person besides me she's known in a long time. I think she wants to impress you."

Neveah almost chuckled at the notion as Creed took several steps across the room.

As he neared, she saw that he had yet another of those flavorless lollipops in his mouth. Glancing down, she also noticed that he somehow had both legs again, even though she *distinctly* remembered him having been short at least one. Evidently, he had healed himself by whatever means he'd healed her, though she noted that the vicious scar running down the left side of his face still remained.

Creed's miraculous abilities clearly didn't extend to clothes, because while his large leather coat was the same, she saw the man's leggings had changed. His pants were the same style, but were now colored a light grey as opposed to the black they'd been before. His new shoes were another pair of leather combats that were similar to the ones he'd had before, only a bit more faded and worn out.

Looking more closely, Neveah could also see that his coat had several new stitch marks scattered across it. She recalled that Creed had suffered a fair bit of damaged from the flying feathers of that horse-headed demon he'd fought back in the valley. Perhaps Stella's alleged sewing skills had already been put to use?

Setting that aside for now, she tried to think of something clever to say, but memories of their last couple of encounters flitted through her head, and she realized that she had no idea where to begin. Eventually, she settled on stating the obvious.

"You saved me?" Her hand unconsciously went to her side beneath the blanket.

"Against my better judgment," Creed responded, though the words didn't carry the same sting they had back in the valley. Perhaps he was just acting surly to keep up appearances.

"Why bring me back here?"

He seemed irritated at the question. "You thought I'd leave you passed out in a dead train yard?"

"Um... yeah?"

"Wouldn't be out of character," Joshua chimed in.

Creed glanced at the blind-folded man. "Shut up." To Neveah, he said, "Luckily for you, I've decided you're a problem."

She blinked, not quite sure what to make of that. "Okay?"

"And like all of my problems, I realize that trying to get rid of you is pointless."

He proceeded to seat himself again, this time on the same steps across from Neveah where Joshua had been. "So congratulations. Since you're too foolish to leave well enough alone, I've decided to entertain you until you're satisfied."

Neveah was too surprised to be put off by how much of an ass he was being. "Really?"

His response was utterly devoid of mirth. "Yep."

"Not bad," said Joshua, giving her a nod of approval. "Took me ages to wear him down like that. You did it in a few conversations!"

Neveah didn't feel accomplished. She didn't really know what to feel. She hadn't been trying to wear anybody down; frankly, she didn't understand why she couldn't leave well enough alone, either. Maybe she *was* just a problem. Regardless, she had found herself here now, so why not go with it?

"How long was I out?" she asked, then winced at what a silly thing that was to ask in a world without time. "Sorry, I guess that's a pointless—"

"Just about four hours or so," Joshua declared.

Neveah started. "What?"

"Yep. Four hours and twenty-six minutes, to be exact."

Minutes? *Hours*? Neveah had not heard these terms in so long that they felt foreign to her ears. "Wha... I don't... how could you possibly know that?"

He just gave a small shrug. "Telling time isn't so hard if you're just talking about numbers. It's frozen in the esoteric sense; nothing can grow or age, and the sun certainly never moves. But in the *numerical* sense—hours and minutes and seconds and such—there's no reason you can't still keep track."

Neveah was flabbergasted at how casual he made the idea sound. She looked him up and down, and there wasn't any sort of timekeeping device on his person that she could see. "How can you keep track of stuff like that when there's no way to measure?"

"Easy!" He tapped a finger on his temple. "I've had a small part of my brain counting each second since everything froze."

Neveah's natural instinct was to call bullshit, but something in the blind man's tone kept her from doing so. As impossible as it seemed, she somehow couldn't bring herself to call him a liar.

Her stunned silence was apparently amusing to him. "A little out there, huh? But it's true." He gave a devious grin, and his next words almost sounded like a threat.

"You wanna know *exactly* how long it's been since the end of the world?"

The concept was so existentially horrifying to Neveah that she responded with zero hesitation: "No."

Joshua gave a rueful chuckle. "Right answer."

Creed finally chose to chime in. "That's enough of that."

Neveah agreed. She'd thought Joshua had seemed pretty normal aside from the blindfold. But if he'd really been counting the seconds since the end of world, then he was as crazy as anyone else. Maybe crazier.

Eager to move on from such abstract topics, she turned to Creed. "What happens next?"

Creed gave a shrug. "Where do you want to start?"

Down in the basement of the church, a monster lay in pain.

His tongue had been returned, but he had nothing to speak but groans of discomfort; his limbs had regrown, but they throbbed at the slightest movement.

All the while, the hole where his heart should have been continued to bleed, though even this had slowed to a crawl by now. The pain would not stop until this void was filled and all of his useless parts were connected to the source of their strength.

And yet, for all this pain, Stryfe did not cry out, nor did he lament his situation. He had known pain. He had *created* pain. And if there was one thing he knew about pain, it was that no matter how vicious or intense it seemed, it was always fleeting. This current torment he suffered was little more to him than a nail in the foot on the path he walked.

He would be patient. And it would pass.

His musings were interrupted when he heard the door to the ground floor open. Though his useless eyes saw nothing, the lack of any presence he felt told him it was the "nun" who had appeared in the doorway. Stella, Creed had called her. An adorable farce.

He heard the door close behind her and the sound of quick steps descending the staircase. He followed the sound until he heard a door opening, followed by a bit of rummaging. Perhaps the basement had some storage room that Stryfe had been unaware of in his blindness.

Whatever she was searching for, it was clear that the doll had no intention of acknowledging Stryfe's presence. He decided not to be so accommodating to her lack of manners.

"I take it the little Lamb is awake?"

He cursed the weakness in his withered voice; taunting others was so tricky when it took energy just to form the words. Judging by the halting of the rummaging sounds, though, the doll had at least heard him.

"You will not see her. She will not see you."

"What's the matter, dear sister? Afraid I'll eat the poor thing's soul?"

The tone of her response was identical, but felt somehow heavier. "You will not speak to her. She will not speak to you."

With that, he heard the sound of whatever door she had just opened slamming shut on anything else he might have said.

Stryfe lay back on the table, unperturbed by the treatment. His presence would always inspire scorn, even from one such as her. It was only natural; the death of God could not free him from that fate.

Putting such thoughts aside, he turned his focus instead to the curious little creature his brothers had brought home. Pained as he was, Stryfe could not deny an interest in what manner of Lamb could have so strongly affected Creed in such a short time.

Expanding his will ever so slightly, Stryfe reached out through the spiritual link he had forced upon his brother and connected his consciousness as lightly as he could, just enough so that he would be able to hear the words spoken upstairs.

He had, of course, given his word not to enlarge his presence in Creed's mind beyond the barest minimum, but when had such a thing ever been worth anything from him? Creed would surely notice the intrusion and try to punish him for it, but Stryfe was not concerned by anything his brother could do to him in their conjoined state.

He would be patient. And it would pass.

Neveah had not spoken for some time by this point. She had started the discussion by quickly retelling her story, such as it was, to Joshua. Unlike Creed, he had not scoffed at her notion of planting seeds in dead dirt. Quite the contrary, he'd seemed positively amused by the idea, smiling like it was the most fascinating thing he'd ever heard.

Frankly, she had found Creed's reaction less strange.

At some point, she noticed Stella emerge from the church basement. The nun had been carrying a box in her hands, presumably filled with whatever materials she was going to use to stitch Neveah a new dress. She had not joined in on Neveah's story time, simply shooting them all a nod before heading to her own room at the back of the church to begin her task.

After concluding her story, Neveah had finally asked for Creed to explain the nature of whatever insanity he was a part of. As promised, he did, and Neveah went silent as the tale washed over her: a demon torn to pieces in the forest, stray fiends that roamed the region with said pieces in hand, and a dark man who had tasked Creed with retrieving them under threat of death.

She listened to all of these impossible things with a neutral expression, trying not to let on how utterly enthralled she was. Creed spoke with his usual gruffness, always being vague on the details when he could afford to be. As if every bit of information he gave her irritated him. But even so, what little he *did* tell Neveah were the most amazing things she'd ever heard.

Alas, it wasn't an exceptionally long story. Soon, Creed was explaining that the demon which had so grievously wounded her was dead and that they'd simply been waiting for her to awaken since they'd returned.

"So..." she finally said, mouth dry from so long spent silent, "that means there's just one left?"

Creed nodded. "That's right."

"And... what happens then?"

"Well," said Joshua, "the boss man says that once Stryfe is back to normal, he and Creed get to duke it out to see who stays and... who goes..."

"'Boss man'. That's... Rictus, right?"

"That's what he calls himself," said Creed.

"It's not his real name?"

"None of us use our real names" said Joshua. "We're not allowed to. Not normally. It's against the rules."

"What rules?"

"We call it the Covenant."

"Joshua." Creed's voice took on a warning tone, but the disheveled man gave a dismissive wave of his hand and ignored him.

"When the Boss first gathered us all up, we weren't exactly... 'team players,' you could say. He had to lay down some ground rules to get us cooperating."

"How'd he do that?" It wasn't as if Neveah knew the first thing about the other Samaritans, but if they could all do the kind of things she'd seen Creed do, she couldn't imagine the monster that would be capable of keeping them all in line.

"Good question."

Standing from his pew, Joshua opened the right side of his jacket and turned to give her a view of his side. She saw what she thought was a white scar halfway between his waist and his armpit, but realized it had too defined a shape to be such a thing.

The mark resembled three symbols, reminding her of hooks, interlocked with each other to create a type of twisting design. Neveah understood what she was seeing and nearly felt sick.

"Holy crap. He *branded* you?"

"Branded all of us," came the casual response.

"Seriously?" She glanced at Creed, who was still clearly uncomfortable with what was being shared, and asked, "Where's yours?"

He glowered for a moment, visibly clenching his jaw around his sucker, but eventually sighed and hooked a thumb over his shoulder to point directly at his upper back.

Neveah let out a long breath. "Wow. No offense, but your boss seems like kind of a dick."

Joshua chuckled. "None taken. He can do a lotta nasty stuff with these things. It's a good way to make sure we follow the rules, though; no fighting each other, no harming the people, no deviating from our roles, et cetera...."

"What roles?"

"We each had a title assigned to us, and a task to go with it. Our own little part in trying to hold everything together."

"Really? What's yours?"

"Me?" He sounded sheepish, but Neveah got the sense he was just pretending. "Nothing too glamorous. I just go back and forth between the others, keep everyone up to date, make sure they're doing what they're doing, and report back to the Boss when he gets too antsy."

"And your... title?"

"He named me the Crucifer. I guess because I 'bear the cross' of dealing with six weirdos who are all *way* stronger than I am." He shrugged. "I think it's supposed to be his idea of a joke?"

Neveah couldn't fight a small grin. "So, you're an errand boy?"

"Why so surprised?" he responded in mock offense, motioning to his own disheveled appearance. "Clearly I'm a lover, not a fighter."

Neveah gave a small giggle and decided she liked the guy, even if it *was* creepy how he saw her without eyes and had apparently been counting in his head for an eternity. He clearly wasn't as laid back as he tried to look, but she could feel the sincerity in his mannerisms and a genuine warmth behind his grins. It was rather refreshing next to Creed's permanent sourpuss.

Turning to said sourpuss, she asked, "And you?"

He shifted uncomfortably. "It named me the Crusader. I fought. That's all."

"Fought the angels?"

He nodded. She waited for more, but evidently, that was the long and short of it. It was just as well. They'd already discussed how he thought "fighting" had turned out, and Neveah wasn't eager to return to the topic quite yet.

"And this 'Stryfe'... his was catching those monsters?"

Joshua threw his eyebrows up—though it was hard to tell behind the hair and blindfold—and turned to Creed. "She's a good listener." He looked back to her. "Yeah, that was his job. The Apostate, they called him. He actually managed to *finish* his role, but... you see where that got him."

Neveah found her gaze drawn behind Joshua to the door at the rear of the hall, still shut tightly. "He's... down there?"

"Don't worry about it," Creed said a bit too quickly. "It's not anything you need to be concerned with."

"I mean, if I'm gonna be here—"

"It doesn't matter. He stays down there. You stay up here. Understood?"

Joshua gave her an apologetic half-grin. "I'd listen to him on that one. Our brother's not exactly in the greatest shape right now. He can also be a bit... difficult when it comes to Lambs."

"'Lambs'?"

Joshua winced. "Sorry. It's what the Boss calls you."

"Humans?"

Joshua nodded. Neveah wasn't quite sure what to think of that, but returned the nod, sparing one more glance to the shut door and deciding to drop the subject. For now.

"Why can't you use your real names?" she asked.

"Right. That's another part of the Covenant. The Boss decided it wouldn't be safe if all of us were able to be at full strength whenever we wanted, so he decided to 'lock' most of it away behind false names."

"How does *that* work?"

"Names have power," Creed interjected. He sounded bitter.

"And the Boss has his ways," said Joshua. "The rule is that we can only call our true names when an angel's involved. It's the only time we can go all out."

"Wait." Neveah held up a hand and almost let the blanket fall. Almost. She pointed a finger at Creed. "You're saying that all that crazy shit you were tossing around was the *weak* stuff?"

Creed just shrugged, and Neveah rolled her eyes. "Think you could maybe explain that, by the way? You said back in the valley that it was some kind of clay?"

If she didn't know any better, Neveah would have thought Creed looked almost sheepish at the question. He glanced aside, fiddling with his sucker. His white pupils shimmered. "It's... a little high-concept."

"Try me."

With a sigh, Creed took a moment as if trying to puzzle out how best to explain it. After a moment, he began: "First off, it's not really clay. It's older, more primal; the original earth that everything in the world was made from."

"Whoa." She certainly hadn't been expecting *that*. "And... what, you just *happen* to be the guy that makes that?"

"It's not me. It's my Cores." Upon seeing her blank expression, he elaborated, "They're like... wells of power inside me. Each one has a color. The one that lets me make the clay is called Malkuth. The Umber Core."

"So you have other colors too, then?" Creed grew quiet at the question, and Neveah mentally kicked herself. What had she done *now?*

"Creed..." Joshua said with a hint admonishment in his tone.

Creed shot the man an irritated look before sighing. "I *had* other colors. There was a Core for each one, but... there's just the one now."

Something about that seemed off to Neveah. "But wait. What about when you were fighting in the valley? It looked like you turned that whip into metal? And what about when you healed me back at the—"

"Those were flukes. Don't count on them again."

"Okay," she responded quickly, not wanting to turn him off from his new sharing mood. "So, what could the other colors do?"

"They were more... conceptual," Creed said, still uncomfortable with the topic. "Malkuth lets me take the clay and shape it however I want, but the rest of the Cores let me take their colors and use concepts associated with them to enhance the clay."

"How does that work?"

"Like I said, it's hard to explain. The short version is: Malkuth lets me make whatever I want, and the other Cores let me make it *how* I want."

"When you put it like that, it sounds like you can make anything."

His expression darkened a bit once again, and his gaze went to the floor. "Never enough,"

Desperate not to let the conversation get derailed by brooding, Neveah turned to Joshua. "What about you? What can you do?"

He seemed to notice what she was doing and kept his tone light. "Me? Nothing *that* fancy. I'm just a leftover Esper."

"Esper?"

"Yeah. You know, ESP?"

Neveah cocked her head in confusion, and he pursed his lips as if trying to find the right words. "You ever hear of a 'Jedi'?"

Neveah's stare just grew blanker, and Joshua dropped his head with a sigh. "Alright."

Turning his head, he promptly spat the straw he'd been holding in his mouth away. It fluttered towards the ground, but just as it was about to hit, Joshua held up a gloved hand, and the straw halted its fall just a few inches above the ground.

Gripped by some invisible force, it was pulled back into the air, coming to a stop just before it reached Joshua's hand. It hovered in the air above his palm, rotating end-over-end like a tiny propeller. Neveah's eyes went wide at the display, and Joshua fixed her with an almost cocky grin.

«*Pretty cool, huh?*»

The voice was his, but his lips hadn't moved. Instead, it had resounded within Neveah's head, startling her and almost making her drop the blanket again as she grabbed at her temple.

"Don't show off," Creed deadpanned.

Joshua grinned again. "He's jealous."

He let the hay drop into his hand and placed it back in his mouth. "But don't be too impressed. Compared to the others, it basically just amounts to parlor tricks."

"Oh yeah?" Neveah decided to address the elephant in the room. "What 'trick' are you using to see through that blindfold?"

"Oh, I can't see through anything." He tapped a finger against the cloth over his eyes. "I really need it, trust me. I've just got a sixth or seventh sense that helps make up for it. But all they tell me is where things are, how they're shaped, and what kind of aura they give off. I can't actually tell what you look like." He grinned a little wider. "I'm sure you're adorable, though."

Ignoring the tease, Neveah lowered her head and let out a shaky breath as everything she'd been hearing started to overwhelm her.

Joshua sounded concerned. "You alright?"

"Y-yeah. It's just... so amazing."

She meant it. Despite the casual way in which everything had just been explained to her, the weight of what Neveah had been told was not lost on her. She had glimpsed a world far beyond what she was meant to, and though she considered herself resilient, even she had to admit that her head was beginning to spin.

After several moments, she decided she'd learned enough impossible things for one day and that it was time to cut to the chase.

"Alright. Where do we go from here?"

The question hung in the air for a long while before Creed eventually stood from the stairs, fixing Neveah with his sharp blue gaze.

"Look—" he began but was interrupted by the sound of a door creaking open.

Everyone's eyes went to the back of the hall, where Stella was finally emerging from the back room, hands behind her back. She approached calmly but quickly, covering the ground between them in only a few long strides.

"Already!?" Neveah asked in surprise. It hadn't been long at all since the nun had gone downstairs.

The woman seemed oblivious to Neveah's befuddlement. "I'm sorry for the wait. We only had so much white cloth, so I'm afraid that it's somewhat of a patchwork."

Stella took her hands from behind her back and showed Neveah her work. The dress looked remarkably similar to her current ruined one, and she could tell it would somehow fit her perfectly.

As the nun had said, it was a patchwork; though most of it was a similar faded white to her own, there were several stray patches of grey and brown near the hem of the skirt. They clashed horribly with the rest of the dress, although the stitching itself was quite well done. All in all, it was quite the mishmash of a dress.

And it might have been the most amazing thing she had ever seen.

Unable to control herself, Neveah shot up from her seat and beheld the garment, the only gift she'd received since her seeds so very long ago.

"It's perfect," she whispered, voice thick with emotion.

It was then she realized that upon standing, her blanket *had* fallen away this time. Coming back to herself, she let out an embarrassing yelp and swiftly retrieved the cloth from the ground, covering herself as blood rushed to her face.

Joshua had the manners to glance away (seriously, how could he tell what had happened!?), though the grin was certainly still present. Creed, meanwhile, just gave an exasperated roll of his eyes.

Noting her embarrassment, Stella stepped in front of Neveah and turned to face the two men. "The two of you will go downstairs now."

Creed balked. "Seriously?"

"I will not have a girl be ogled while she makes herself presentable."

Joshua tilted his head in befuddlement. "Yeeaah... I don't think you need to worry about that with us."

And just what does that *mean?* Neveah thought. Joshua was blind, but what was Creed's excuse? Just as she was contemplating whether she should be offended, Stella pointed in the direction of the door in the back of the church.

"Go. This is Ladies Time now."

Joshua threw up his eyebrows and looked to Creed. "'Ladies Time,' she says."

Regardless, he turned and began to head towards the rear of the hall. Creed stayed behind another moment, fixing Neveah with an expression that almost looked like pity.

"Good luck," he said before turning to follow Joshua.

Neveah wondered what he meant by that when Stella turned around, now standing *very* close. Holding the new dress in one hand, she reached into a pocket of her habit and pulled out a small, white cloth.

"Before we can put this on, I think you could do with a bit of cleaning."

The nun motioned to Neveah's body, which was admittedly caked in a fair layer of dirt and grime save for the spot where Creed had healed her. "I would also like to do something about your hair. But before anything, we'll need to get your current dress out of the way."

Stella stepped forward, destroying the very last of Neveah's personal space, and she understood what Creed had meant.

"She's certainly a breath of fresh air, isn't she?"

Joshua sighed. He had been hoping there would be at least a few moments for him to cut to the chase before his brothers started up again, but Stryfe was speaking not a moment after Creed shut the door behind them.

Resigned, Joshua sensed his way down the stairs and propped himself against a wall, waiting for Creed to follow and inevitably begin yet another argument.

To his surprise, though, his brother simply walked past the table to his usual bench in the corner and said, "Not nice to eavesdrop."

Joshua turned towards his brother's aura with a raised brow. Even Stryfe seemed intrigued at the response. Joshua could sense the demon was currently sitting cross-legged on the table. He had regained his tongue and limbs now (his lower body had, at Creed's *emphatic* insistence, apparently been wrapped in a spare sheet Stella had lying around), but without his heart, his aura still felt to Joshua like little more than a half-dead mass of fading willpower.

"Come now, brother," Stryfe said in a rasping voice dripping with condescension, "it's no fun if you don't try to impotently bite my head off at every turn. Could it be that you're starting to grow accustomed to my presence inside that head of yours?"

Creed took his seat and propped up a leg on the opposite knee. "I've grown accustomed to the fact that I can't kill you right now. But I can wait until this is over."

Stryfe gave an impressed-sounding chuckle at the barb, though it sounded more like a sickening cough. Deciding to head the conversation off while it was still less than heated, Joshua pushed off the wall and clapped his hands together.

"Anyways, what say we get back to business? The Boss isn't gonna wait around forever. We've still got one stray left to find, and I gotta be honest, I haven't the foggiest clue where it is."

When he hadn't been getting his butt handed to him in mental chess, most of the time they'd spent waiting for Neveah to awaken had seen Joshua expanding his consciousness over and across the surrounding region. Unfortunately, there was not a single hint as to the whereabouts of Stryfe's final demon.

"Belphegor was never my strongest child, but he was certainly the laziest. Which eventually made him the best at hiding from his duties. Even I struggled to find him at times."

"It," Creed interjected. "Not 'him.'"

Joshua noticed a slight twinge of anger in the demon's aura; even Stryfe, it seemed, did not like to have his "children" insulted.

"*His* capture was a relatively recent occurrence; his mind has likely not devolved to the same extent as his siblings. I assure you that wherever he is hiding, he has been observing your progress. You will not find him until he shows himself, and he will not do so until he is certain he knows the method of beating you which exerts the least amount of effort."

"If it's so well-hidden," Creed countered, "how exactly were *you* planning to find it if we hadn't come along?"

"Cowardly as he is, Belphegor is still bound to me by my heart. Sooner or later, he would have come to me in an effort to bargain for his freedom."

"And now?"

"Now there is a game afoot. And he never likes to play."

"Excellent plan."

"Regardless," Joshua interrupted, "I don't think I'm gonna be able to find him by hanging around here."

Creed's aura turned curious. "Meaning?"

"When you leave, take me with you. The way I see it, our only option now is to cover as much ground as we can as quickly as we can. However well Belphegor can hide, if I get close enough, I'll feel him."

"Are you certain our illustrious leader will abide by such interference?" asked Stryfe.

Joshua shrugged. "He didn't seem to have a problem with me showing Creed where the first two were. Long as I don't help him fight, I think we're okay."

The truth was, Joshua was confident that Rictus was allowing his little "interferences" because, for all of his foreboding words, the Preceptor didn't want to lose two Samaritans any more than Joshua did. As long as it wasn't *too* blatant, Joshua figured his assistance would be tolerated if it brought about a final contest between his brothers.

Not that he was going to allow it to come to that.

Creed was silent a moment before responding: "Alright."

Joshua couldn't hide his surprise at the concession. "Really? Just like that? You're not gonna tell me you're better off alone or that you don't need my help?"

He felt Creed rise from the bench, and once again, Joshua noticed his aura seemed much less distressed than before.

"I've given up trying to get people to do what I want." Joshua could feel his attention being drawn away from the conversation. "I'm gonna go make sure Stella hasn't violated her too badly." With that, he made for the staircase.

As he passed Stryfe on the table, the shade asked, "Anything *I* can do to help?"

Creed didn't break stride. "Keep out of my head."

Joshua's senses followed him up the stairs and back out the door, not quite sure what to make of his new behavior. After a moment, he went to follow his brother out but had only taken a single step when—

"Joshua."

He stopped at Stryfe's withered voice and turned over his shoulder. The decrepit demon's aura was tinged with disdain.

"I know why you really want to go with him. If you can't convince me, you'll never convince him."

"I don't know," Joshua turned back to where Creed had gone. "Something's different. You feel it, right? He's getting... better."

"Oh yes. This girl is having the most interesting effect on our brother. Such a deep bond in such a short time, but it nonetheless seems to have made him stronger... *and* weaker."

The words hung ominously in the air, and Joshua felt the prickle of foreboding across the back of his neck. The statement wasn't exactly wrong, he supposed. Nonetheless, he resumed his walk and followed Creed up the stairs.

Despite having just been cleaned, Neveah couldn't help but feel stained by something else now. With no water available, Stella had gotten rather *forceful* with her cloths, and though she had done an excellent job of wiping away the grime that covered Neveah's body, the girl wasn't quite sure she'd ever really be clean again.

Regardless, the "pampering" had concluded, and Neveah now sat cross-legged in front of the flowerbed, clothed in her new patchwork dress and feeling more comfortable than she had been in a long time. Behind her knelt Stella, running her fingers through Neveah's hair like a brush.

Neveah had expected a great deal of tugging and yanking as the nun tried to fix her rat's-nest of hair, but the woman's fingers moved with shocking dexterity, untangling knots in such a way that Neveah hardly felt a thing.

"How are you so good at this?"

"A lady should always be presentable."

That didn't really answer Neveah's question, but she let it drop.

"I don't know how much things like that matter anymore," she said, hiding the fact that she was actually trying not to cry from the attention. She couldn't remember the last time anyone had treated her with such tenderness; frankly, she couldn't remember the last time anyone had treated her any way at all.

Those morose thoughts were interrupted when the rear door opened, and Creed emerged once again. He wandered over and regarded them with a look of befuddlement, and perhaps even mild concern.

"Ladies' Time is not over," Stella deadpanned. Neveah found it amusing how juvenile the woman could come across sometimes.

"Settle down," Creed responded. "We'll be out of here soon enough." He turned to Neveah. "You alright?"

She shrugged. "A little violated, but I'll make it."

Creed gave an awkward nod, and for some reason, Neveah felt compelled to stand. She motioned to herself, the new dress and fresh skin. She tried not to sound *too* expectant.

"Well?"

Creed did a poor job of pretending he had any idea what to say. "Uh... not bad?"

"Wrong," Stella stated as she rose.

"Oh. I mean... amazing?"

There was absolutely zero confidence in the response, but it seemed to placate the nun. "Better."

Neveah tried not to smile. Seeing as he was the first person she'd seen after lifetimes of solitude, it felt a little satisfying to prove she could actually be made presentable. Not that she cared what the melancholy jerk thought of her.

Moving past the forced compliments, Neveah thought about what Creed had just said. "You're leaving?"

He nodded, and as if on cue, the rear door opened again to reveal Joshua's shaggy form. He sauntered up to the group and slapped Creed on the back.

"Whenever you're ready!" he barked, ignoring Creed's look of annoyance and strolling across the hall into the open doorway of the church. He halted there, facing the dark sun outside while he waited for Creed to follow.

Creed, however, was busy trying to avoid Stella's gaze, who Neveah could tell was expressing disapproval; she was slowly getting better reading the nun's subdued expressions, it seemed.

"He's going with you?" she asked.

"We're out of options. We've got to find the third stray, and he's not gonna be able to do it from here."

"If he's able to accompany you, then I should also—"

"He's not helping in that way, Stella. He's just gonna find it, not fight it."

"Even still, I can be of—"

"*No.*"

It came out a bit more firmly than Neveah assumed he'd intended. Stella did not flinch, but glanced down at the floor.

Creed's gaze softened a little, and he continued, "You know I can't let you involve yourself in this." His tone turned slightly admonishing. "Have you gotten *any* rest since all of this started?"

The nun did not answer the question, and Creed fixed her with a look like an exasperated parent. Neveah said nothing, but wondered at the words. Was Creed saying she hadn't slept since this whole monster-hunting business had begun? That didn't seem possible.

Creed motioned in Neveah's direction. "What I need you to do is stay here, get some rest, and keep this one out of trouble. It's harder than it looks, trust me."

Neveah personally took that as a compliment but said nothing as Stella gave a short nod, still looking at the floor. With a nod of his own, Creed moved to follow Joshua out of the church. But Neveah wouldn't let him go that easily.

"Speaking of 'this one'..." Her voice halted him in his tracks. "You still haven't answered my question. What happens to me next?"

Creed didn't answer right away, so she continued, "Look, I get what's going on now, and I know I don't exactly fit into any of this. So... what's the plan? Why bring me here?"

Creed sighed but turned around halfway to look at her. "The reason I brought you here is because it's less of a hassle than trying to make you stay out of this. And the 'plan,'" he pointed to Stella, "is for you to stay here and do what she tells you."

"And what about when this is over?"

Creed let his arm drop. "When it's over..." he whispered, more to himself, it seemed. To her, he said, "Listen, Neveah. You heard our story, right? You get that in the best-case scenario, it still comes down to a fight between me and Stryfe?"

Neveah nodded, and he continued, "That means this all ends one of two ways: either I lose, in which case it's finished... or I win, in which case I get the *honor* of going back to fighting angels like a good Samaritan. Either way, I won't be coming back to this church."

He motioned to Neveah's waist, where she'd tied her precious seed-bags. "And sooner or later, you'll have to move on, too."

Neveah's response sounded small in her own ears. "One of those outcomes still sounds better than the other...."

Truthfully, she hadn't wanted to bring the subject up again. Creed had made his opinion on fighting the angels very clear back in that valley, and Neveah braced herself for another round of harsh words decrying how foolish and naive she was.

To her surprise, his expression didn't turn cold or cruel; instead, it was overcome by equal parts resignation and pity, coming together to paint a picture of deep sorrow that nearly broke Neveah's heart in half.

"I'm sorry, girl," he said, in perhaps the kindest tone she'd heard from him yet, "but I can't be whatever it is you need me to be. Please... just stay here until the danger's passed."

As if to punctuate his words, the stupid Dove flew into the church through its doorway, obviously unnoticed by Joshua at the threshold. Neveah had nearly forgotten about the annoying thing in light of everything that had happened and grimaced as she followed its path. It sailed right past her to flutter down in the center of the flowerbed, snuggling up to itself in a clear message that this was *right* where she should be.

Smartass, she thought.

If Creed was confused as to why she had just turned to follow something he couldn't see, he didn't express it. Taking her lack of response as an end to the discussion, he turned and moved to follow Joshua out of the building. Neveah nearly let him go, but found herself overcome by a compulsion she couldn't fight down.

"Wait!"

Not quite sure what she was doing, she took several long strides to catch up to Creed, fiddling around inside one of her pouches as she did so. By the time she reached him, she had pulled out a single, tiny seed from the pouch.

Reaching out, she grabbed Creed's wrist with her free hand and placed the grain into his grasp, forcing his fingers closed around it. He seemed too surprised to resist.

"What are you doing?"

"You're going to live!"

She said it as emphatically as she could, not thinking about what she was saying but instead letting it come on its own. "You're going to live, and even if you have to leave afterwards, you're going to come here first and plant this with me."

"I already told you—"

"I know what you said. You're going to do it anyways."

Creed looked at his closed fist as if he were afraid to open it. "It... would be a waste."

"I don't care if it's a waste. And I don't care if you think it's pointless. If it doesn't matter either way, what's the harm in doing it?"

She forced herself to look more deeply into his sharp blue eyes than she ever had before, meeting his unnatural glowing pupils without hesitation.

"Please. Just one. Just one, and you'll see...."

A small eternity passed between them, but in the end, there must have been *something* in her gaze that finally got through, because Creed slowly opened his fist and looked at the seed in his palm before locking eyes with her again.

"Fine."

Gently pulling his arm from Neveah's grasp, he opened one of the several pockets on his silly coat and placed the seed inside. When he looked at her again, it was with the same expression he'd worn back in the valley upon handing her pouches back to her: almost as if he was *afraid* of her.

That was fine, Neveah decided. Being able to frighten a Samaritan was quite the impressive feat, wasn't it?

"Good luck," she said. She hoped he knew how much she meant it.

"Yeah," was all he said. He spared one last look at Stella, who had watched their entire exchange in silence, and finally turned again to leave.

This time, Neveah let him.

Chapter XII
"Everything in Its Right Place"

Although he was immune to pain, Stryfe could not deny a particular weakness to boredom. He could be patient when needed, of course; he'd stood by for eons prior to the end of time, waiting for destiny to remember he existed.

Back then, at least, he'd had his games to content himself with in the meantime, the sport of whispers and manipulations that served to satiate his need for discord while the world came closer and closer to cracking under the weight of its own design.

Now, down in the dark little box beneath a decrepit church, Stryfe was not only alone, but ignored, and while he could weather the former, he would never abide the latter. His brothers and the false nun had thrown his ghost into this makeshift prison and proceeded to neglect him as best they could.

It was not as if he didn't understand the treatment; for as long as Stryfe could remember, those who thought themselves on higher ground had wished nothing more than to pretend he didn't exist, going about their lives giving him as little recognition as possible. Even so, Stryfe would admit to a certain level of childishness: he would not be denied his fun for much longer.

In a desperate attempt to pass the time—not that there existed any real time to pass—he was currently detaching his spirit from the husk in which he was trapped. It was an old trick, a mechanism he had developed in the old days when the looming of fate sometimes overwhelmed him.

He couldn't project himself quite as expertly as Joshua, but Stryfe could allow his consciousness to briefly drift away from reality to a state where silly things like thought and desire no longer existed, where he did not have to wonder as to what the world had in store for him. It took a substantial amount of effort in his weakened form, but soon enough he began to feel the familiar sensation of his surroundings blurring and the physical world falling away.

For a brief moment, as his consciousness drifted from the withered form on the table, he was hyper-aware. He could feel every inch of the room around him, every fleck of dust on the neglected floor, and every crack in the decaying walls.

His mind drifted up and out of the basement, and he could feel the hall above, where the nun and the girl sat together in comfortable silence, observing that gaudy collection of weeds they so admired. Even this image began to darken and fade as Stryfe's perception flew further and further away.

Then, just as his soul reached the razor-thin edge between reality and beyond, he saw it: a presence, slick like oil and transient as a dream, doing everything in its power not to be seen. But Stryfe saw it. For the briefest of moments, he beheld a gleam of emotions, a mixture of disdain, boredom, patience, and above all, cunning.

Stryfe's attempt at detachment was forgotten, and he came back to himself in such a rush that he instinctively shot up as if woken from a nightmare. This action sent a wave of agony through his shriveled body and resulted in several seconds of convulsions, but by the time he had stilled himself, Stryfe could not have cared less about the discomfort. His thoughts were only on the presence he had felt, that transient whisper of a being so well-hidden that it was only through sheer chance he had found it.

Clever child. Hiding right in the threshold.

A hideous smile spread across his wrinkled face, bloody gums staining the room around him. The desire for detachment was gone, replaced by the craving for chaos.

Perhaps his hunger for attention would be sated sooner than he thought...

Neveah had long since stopped caring what she looked like; vanity had no place in a world devoid of luxury. At the moment, though, she would have killed for a mirror. For the first time that she could remember, she was *clean,* skin free of grime and hair untangled.

Unfortunately, with nary a reflective surface to be found, Neveah had to content herself with Stella's promise that she looked "exceptionally better" than she had before. Insensitive phrasing aside, the nun had seemed to be telling the truth, and that would need to be enough for now.

Neveah was currently sitting in front of the flowerbed, but her attention was focused more on Stella kneeling opposite her than the flowers themselves.

The older woman was observing the flowers as usual, but Neveah noticed a lack of sharpness that had been there before. Her gaze often drifted, sometimes to Neveah herself, sometimes to the open door of the church, and sometimes to a place Neveah couldn't see, some distance too great for her to fathom. It was an odd thing to observe in someone who didn't seem to display much emotion, but Neveah could only describe her behavior as "fidgety."

After enough glances at the door, Neveah asked, "You're really worried about him, aren't you?"

"Creed is capable of protecting himself." Her tone was even more inscrutable than usual, as if she were reading from a script. "We've all been forbidden from interfering directly in the task his leader has given him."

A pause, then she continued in a less rehearsed-sounding tone, "But even so, I would have... liked to help him, if I could."

Neveah once again took note of the fact that the nun seemed to believe she could be of assistance to a man who could make swords and shields and who-knows-what-else out of thin air.

"Stella... I know what Creed said, but... you're *really* not a Samaritan?"

Stella took several seconds to answer, which by her standards was impressively slow. Her gaze returned to the flowers and began to run her fingers across the tips of their petals.

"No. I am not a Samaritan."

Then why do you think you can go help fight monsters?

Neveah was going to verbalize the thought but stopped when she saw Stella freeze again, fingers halting in place over the flowers.

The nun's entire body went still in the most severe sense of the word. There wasn't an ounce of movement to be seen, not the twitch of a muscle nor the flicker of an eye. The odd phenomenon lasted for perhaps five seconds before she moved again, continuing her brush along the flowers as if nothing had happened.

Neveah couldn't swallow her concern any longer; it had taken her a while to notice, but these short bouts of stillness had been occurring intermittently, sometimes separated by long stretches and sometimes by what felt like only brief interludes. Neveah had wondered at first if she was only imagining them, but by now, she was certain.

"Creed mentioned something about you needing rest, didn't he?" Stella didn't look at her. "Have you really not slept since all of this started?"

"A lot has happened since we met you."

"Well, no offense, but I think it's taking a toll. You're not looking so good."

"I will be alright."

"I don't know about that. Time may not exist anymore, but that doesn't mean you can go without sleep forever. Everyone's got a limit, right?"

Stella finally looked at her again. "I've been asked to keep you safe."

Neveah forced a lighter tone into her voice. "Hey, I'm fine. I could probably use a nap myself, actually." She motioned to the mound of dirt at the center of the flowerbed. "I think you've seen that I can sleep just about anywhere, right?"

Stella somehow didn't seem amused, and Neveah sighed. "Look, I still don't really get Creed, but you seem to be the only thing he actually cares about. If you can't help him by going with him, maybe you can help by taking care of yourself like he asked?"

It seemed a flimsy argument to Neveah, but it did seem to give Stella pause. Her violet gaze drifted towards the door in the back right of the church, where Neveah had deduced her bedroom was.

She briefly wondered why the nun couldn't just grab some shut-eye on one of the pews if she was so concerned about leaving her alone, but then supposed if there was an actual *bed* back there, she wouldn't want to sleep anywhere else either.

Stella turned back to Neveah, who got the sense that she was currently debating with herself behind the emotionless mask.

"You won't leave the church?"

"Hey, Creed may think I'm a dummy, but I *do* know how to do what I'm told." She paused. "Well, most of the time. Besides, I've got no plans to get caught up in another crazy demon fight."

She really meant it, but Stella still looked her up and down as if gauging her trustworthiness.

"You will stay here?" the nun asked again. "You promise to stay right here?"

Neveah raised her right hand. "I swear."

Stella stared at her hand as if she didn't understand the gesture and was quiet for so long that Neveah almost thought she had frozen again, but eventually she stood and clasped her own hands in front of her waist.

"I'm sorry. I thought I was stronger than this. It's... embarrassing?" She said the word as if she wasn't sure it was the correct one.

Neveah found the pseudo-bashful behavior to be almost endearing. "Don't be. Like I said, everyone's got a limit. Go get some rest."

Another brief pause, then a nod. "Alright. I promise it will only be a short while." With that, Stella turned and began making her way to the back of the hall.

"Take all the time you need," Neveah called after her. When the nun opened the door to her room, however, she couldn't help but be drawn to the *other* door at the back of the church. The one leading down to the basement.

"All the time you need..." she repeated.

Joshua tried not to sigh as he drew his awareness back to a normal range. Unrelenting negativity was Creed's specialty, so someone had to remain positive, but seeing as this was the dozenth time Joshua had put out a pulse without feeling a hint of demonic energy in return, he couldn't deny a sense of frustration.

Standing, he turned to Creed, who had been waiting patiently beside him.

"Nothing," he declared.

From what Joshua could sense, the two of them were currently standing at the peak of a particularly steep hill, which gave Creed a decent enough view of the surrounding plains and Joshua a solid focal point from which to expand his clairvoyance.

Even if he'd still had his eyes, there was obviously not a thing to be seen for miles, but Joshua's powers weren't being used to see; wherever the final stray was, it would be incorporeal, hidden somewhere between the material and immaterial.

"This doesn't make sense," Creed was saying. His words were slightly muffled by one of those artificial lollipops he always seemed to be sucking on. "Demon or not, it's the only thing with a soul in this region aside from us. Its power should stand out no matter how well it's hidden."

"There's some trick," Joshua stated, though that much was obvious by now. "I don't know how, but it's masking its aura. And Belphegor's the demon of Sloth, so I'm sure it's something simple, which just makes it more frustrating."

When Creed spoke next, there was reluctance in his tone. "Let's head closer to the city."

Joshua hadn't expected that. "You sure?"

"Stryfe said that wherever the stray is, it's probably been watching and listening. If that's true, it might know that I grow weaker the closer I get to the void. It'd be the best spot to hide."

Joshua was glad his brother was at least not bothering to try and hide the truth. "Even if so, are you sure you can risk it?"

"Malkuth is the only Core I have left, but it was never very lively to begin with. It works well enough even near the void, and Belphegor isn't a fighter. If we can flush it out without letting it pull any tricks, killing it shouldn't be a problem." His aura turned a tad bitter. "Besides, it's not as if I have a choice in the matter."

Joshua couldn't argue. Rictus hadn't given an actual limit for Creed to accomplish his task, but that didn't mean there wasn't one. As soon as the Preceptor looked up from Its work long enough to remember, their chances would be gone, and Joshua had a gut feeling that moment was fast approaching.

"Speaking of Stryfe," he said, trying to sound casual. "Have you given any thought to maybe—"

"No," came the response, blunt as a hammer.

"You *have* to realize that there are other options besides some deathmatch, Creed."

"Pretty sure Rictus made it clear that there aren't."

"Don't give me that. You know how the Preceptor is. It likes the scary ultimatums, but It needs us. *All* of us. There *is* a way out of this, but you two would rather kill each other than try."

He felt a wave of disdain roll off of Creed, just as it had from Stryfe. "How long are you going to keep playing at this? You've been keeping him from getting what he deserves since The End. I get that you're big on mercy, but at some point, even you have to admit there's a limit."

Joshua felt himself frowning. He couldn't keep the darkness out of his voice. "He'll get what he deserves. We all will. But not until we've fixed this mess."

Creed's aura sobered a bit at Joshua's tone, but the indignance remained. "And how do you propose we do that? Even once we put Stryfe back together, the Preceptor doesn't exactly bargain."

Joshua tensed. He'd been waiting for a chance to bring this up. "You know, I've been giving that some thought. The only reason that's true is because we don't have anything to bargain *with*."

He felt Creed's aura turn curious. "The hell does that mean?"

Joshua considered tiptoeing around the point a bit longer, but decided bluntness would get through to Creed the fastest. "What if we brought It the Nephilim?"

As expected, Creed came to an abrupt stop, and Joshua followed suit. Even without his senses, Joshua could have felt the gaze his brother was giving him right now.

Creed was silent for a moment, then declared, "Even after so long, you still find new ways to surprise me with your bullshit."

"You know it would work, Creed. Rictus wants it more than anything. It's the *one* thing the Preceptor fears, and if we managed to find it, everything would be square."

He heard Creed let out a disgusted sigh. "Un-fucking-believable. The Nephilim is *gone,* Joshua. Even Rictus gave up on ever finding it again."

Joshua wouldn't let himself be deterred. "Only because none of the Samaritans have ever been able to devote all their time and effort into locating it. We were too busy with our roles. But Stryfe's is finished now! Once he's whole and Rictus comes, the three of us just have to convince the Boss to assign him a new role of finding the Nephilim."

"Just that simple, huh? And how receptive do you think Stryfe will be to this little proposal?"

"Of course he'll hate it. But I bet he'll find it preferable to dying. And you and I can offer to help him search as a way to square away our own debts with the Boss."

Creed's aura wasn't growing any more receptive. "That's seriously your best plan? Throw ourselves at Rictus' feet and promise that we can somehow catch a creature that's literally impossible to find?"

"It's not impossible," Joshua insisted. "We never put forth the effort to find one Beast when Salomé already had the other six. Frankly, finding it is something *all* the Samaritans should have done a long time ago."

"'*All* of the Samaritans?' Joshua, the seven of us aren't even *allowed* to be in the same place because we'll fucking kill each other! You may spend your time bouncing back and forth between us, but aside from you and Stryfe, I barely recall the last time I even saw the others. Even *you* don't know where Testament is anymore!"

Joshua couldn't hold back a flinch at the words, and he felt Creed's aura soften just a hair in response.

In a calmer tone, he continued, "You were always the only one who believed in the idea of the Samaritans, Crucifer. But there *are* no Samaritans. There never really were. Offering to go on some bullshit quest to find the Nephilim just so you can postpone our deaths won't change that."

"Is it so wrong for me to try and keep the only family I have left alive?"

The question caused the anger to flare back up in Creed's aura.

"When are you gonna cut that shit out? We were never a family. I was Stryfe's replacement, and *your* prototype. That doesn't make us real brothers!"

Silence filled the air between them, old and familiar. That always seemed to be how these arguments ended. Without another word, Creed began wandering down the hill in the direction of the city, which was close enough that Joshua's senses could just make out the distant shapes of its ruined skyscrapers.

"You still don't have to do this!" he called out one last time. "Neither of you do. Nothing will change if we all just stay slaves to our natures."

Creed's aura no longer felt angry. Just tired. "Nothing will change regardless, Joshua. Nothing can. Now get moving."

Joshua obeyed, following behind his brother in what felt like a death march. He wouldn't bring up the Nephilim again for the time being, but he had no intention of giving up. The one good thing about how stubborn his brothers could be was that it made it easier for him to disregard them and do what was needed to keep them alive.

Joshua didn't plan on letting them off easy by allowing them to kill each other, and he didn't much care for their thoughts on the matter. He would find them—*all* of them—a way out of this nightmare, even if he had to drag them kicking and screaming behind him.

The fact was, he could be pretty stubborn too.

It took Neveah a fair while to figure out that what she was feeling was, in fact, boredom. This befuddled her, because she had spent the equivalent of several lifetimes doing nothing but walking and placing seeds in the dirt without ever once feeling that particular sentiment. She had thought the very concept one that no longer existed; in a world where nothing happened, there was no excitement present for boredom to dampen.

Evidently, she had only forgotten the feeling, and now that she had experienced stimulation for the first time in ages, her body was already rejecting the return of empty silence.

Part of her was irritated at this; Neveah had thought herself long-since accustomed to being alone, only for a handful of conversations with a nihilistic jerk and an emotionally-stunted nun to leave her positively desperate for more. It was rather sobering to find she wasn't nearly as self-sufficient as she'd believed.

It was in this state of mind that Neveah was currently lounging on one of the wooden pews in the main hall, staring up at the frail-looking ceiling and wondering how she was going to resolve this long-forgotten conundrum.

She *could* have left and tried to go find Creed, but she wasn't nearly so deceitful as to break her promise so flagrantly. Besides, she had meant what she said: even someone like her only needed *one* experience with their insides being liquified by demonic poison to dissuade them from any further spying.

For perhaps the hundredth time since Stella had gone to rest, her gaze went from the ceiling to the wood door at the rear of the hall, and her mind to what she had been told was down there.

Naturally, she had been wanting at least a *glimpse* of this "Stryfe" character since the moment Creed forbade her to. He'd been especially adamant that she never so much as breathe the same air as his "fellow" Samaritan, and even the laid-back Joshua seemed to agree. She had intended to be patient and hassle Creed for a look when he returned, but being left alone had made the temptation increasingly difficult to resist.

Neveah bounced her leg in restless contemplation, and glanced over at the flowerbed. At its center, the Dove still lay sleeping in the dirt. It hadn't budged since it had first laid down.

As much as the delusion often annoyed her, Neveah couldn't deny the sobering feeling it gave her. Clenching her jaw, she made a decision.

No. Don't be stupid. Stay here

She admitted that part of her decision was motivated by a desire to prove Creed wrong about her. He clearly thought she was just a foolish little girl, despite the fact that she'd been alive for at *least* a thousand lifetimes. And sure, she *had* ignored his orders several times already, but that was only because he'd been such an asshole about them! Once he'd stopped trying so hard to get rid of her, his requests had seemed far more reasonable.

Besides, at the end of the day—a rather pointless phrase, she mused—Neveah *was* smart enough to realize what a bad idea going down there would be. She had seen two demons by this point, and regretted every second of it.

They had been little more than ravenous animals, but the sheer heinousness of their existence was something even she could instinctively feel. And although Stryfe was supposedly too weak to be a threat, Neveah wasn't foolish enough to assume he'd be harmless. Anything that could hunt and command those horrible creatures could *never* be harmless.

For once, Neveah was able to fight down her curiosity, and resolved to remain where she was. Going down there now would not only be dangerous for herself, but it could also mean causing trouble for Creed, and she would *not* let that happen. She had already brought him enough grief. For once, she was going to listen.

"No one ever achieved anything by doing what they were told, Little Lamb."

Neveah's eyes widened, and her resolve turned to ice as the horrible words whispered their way into her ear. Suddenly unable to move anything but her head, she turned to her left to find the demon had come to *her*.

Stryfe could not see the girl, but he could feel her gaze boring into him the moment he'd apparated beside her in the pew on which she sat. He expected the sharp sensation of fear to spike from her aura, or perhaps to hear her scrambling away in horror. He'd hoped she wouldn't scream, lest the doll in the adjacent room awaken.

But he felt no terror, and heard only a soft gasp. He'd certainly surprised the girl by appearing so suddenly, but she didn't seem inclined to flee. The emotions he felt stream from her presence were so unexpected that it took Stryfe a moment to place them.

Was that... concern? Yes, there was genuine distress in her feelings, and empathy as well. The girl beheld his wretched form, and she actually pitied him.

He decided right away that he did not like this one.

But alas, he had a role to play, and made sure not to let his distaste show. Even in this weakened state, Stryfe was a master of masks, and was confident he could charm the girl despite his wretched visage. She had yet to verbally respond to his appearance, and Stryfe chose to claim the initiative.

He held out a hand and willed what paltry wisp of power he yet retained into his palm. A small amount of mist curled, molded, and colored itself into the shape of an apple. It was illusory, of course, but Stryfe ensured that it was a deep, fresh red the likes of which he knew the Lamb had not seen in her life, even before The End.

He felt the girl behold the fruit but sensed little shift in her emotions aside from a mild increase in confusion. Seems he had made the wrong choice; the apple was an old favorite, but perhaps too cliché, even after so long. And as Stryfe recalled, the girl's fascinations lied elsewhere.

With yet another burst of concentration that should have been less than a thought to him, he shifted the apple back into mist before reshaping it into a long-stemmed rose, the same shade of red and decorated with beautiful, deadly thorns. The girl *did* seem more intrigued by this form, but did not feel any more at ease than before.

"Do I frighten you, little Lamb?"

Stryfe made sure to sound as weak and frail as he could when he spoke. It was not as difficult as he would have liked.

"Yes," came the reply, which perplexed him. Nothing he sensed indicated fear. He attempted to look beyond the emotions projected on the surface, peering deeper into her heart.

To his surprise, he could not see it; it was *there*, to be sure, but his attempts to focus were met with a blurring of his view, like a still lake whose reflection was distorted whenever one tried to touch it. Stryfe was perturbed; surely even in this state, his ability to perceive the souls of Lambs had not diminished so greatly?

The girl was speaking again. "You're Stryfe."

"And you are Neveah," he responded, allowing the false rose in his fingers to dissipate. He had failed to lower her guard right away, but he was satisfied that she wasn't going to leap up and run for the sleeping doll in the back room. He felt apprehension begin to grow in her spirit, and decided to assuage it.

"Apologies if I startled you, my dear. To be honest, I had been hoping you might come see me, and I suppose I grew a tad impatient."

He heard the girl swallow before she spoke. "I was told to stay away from you."

Stryfe nodded. "Yes, I know you were. And you were wise to heed that advice. Unfortunately, they seem to have forgotten that despite appearances, I am not the crippled old man I appear to be. A staircase and a door is not quite enough to keep me away, especially when I have become rather starved for conversation."

The girl still felt tense, and Stryfe felt her attention go to rear of the church. "No need to worry about disturbing the dear sister. She is a profoundly deep sleeper these days. If you would like to talk, we have some time before she awakens."

The girl still did not seem to relax, and Stryfe had to admit that he was impressed. She was obviously a fool for not immediately fleeing his presence, but at least she was not so ignorant as to lower her guard. At the very least, though, he needed to get her talking.

"You need not be so frightened. Despite what my brothers may have told you, I've no desire to harm you. Even if I did, I am little more than a shade at the moment. I could not lay a hand upon you if I tried."

He smiled as best he could without parting his withered lips, lest the sight of his bloody gums disturb her further. "And besides, I could feel you debating with yourself on whether to meet with me or not. Seeing as I wished to meet you as well, I merely made the decision for us."

At that, he finally seemed to have peaked the girl's curiosity. "Why would you want to meet me?"

Stryfe allowed his aching shade to sink further into the pew, trying to appear relaxed and non-threatening. As non-threatening as a skeletal old man with a gaping chest wound could appear, at least.

"Why would I not be eager to meet the Lamb to which my brother has become so attached?"

At the mention of Creed, the girl's attention seemed to shift away from her apprehension. Predictable.

"You really are his brother?"

"Of a sort. We are rather far apart in age, but we did share a father. The truth is, we once numbered among many siblings, but alas, only three remain: I the eldest, Creed the middle, and Joshua youngest."

"Haven't been the best big brother, from what I hear."

Straight to the point. Amusing. "My brothers do like to exaggerate my more negative qualities. What have you heard of me?"

"That you're forcing Creed to do your dirty work and this entire situation is your fault?"

"Well... I suppose, in this case, there wasn't *much* room for exaggeration." He motioned to his shriveled body, ignoring the aches that shot through his bones. "But truly, can you disparage me for wishing to be rid of *this*?"

He felt her gaze flit across his decrepit form. "I'm not really qualified to judge." She sounded remarkably more causal than someone talking to the shade of a demon should have been able to. "Creed definitely seems to be holding it against you."

Stryfe couldn't help but choke out a weak excuse for a laugh. "Quite true," he conceded. "But this is always how such things have gone between us."

"This has happened before?"

"Nothing quite this dire, I suppose, but don't let them fool you. We may be estranged now, but there was a time when my brothers and I traveled this dead world together, playing our parts as good little Samaritans and fulfilling our roles. Of course, mine and Creed's natures have often resulted in... friction. I admit there *would* be a spat every so often."

He felt skepticism roll off of the girl, and admitted, "Alright, *perhaps* one of us tried to occasionally kill the other. Joshua was always there to make peace."

"Sounds like a healthy relationship."

"In a world such as this, one can only be so particular about family."

"What happened?"

"Who can say? Perhaps one day I pushed him a bit too far, or perhaps he just finally made a mistake that he couldn't blame me for...."

She didn't bite at the vague, leading words, and Stryfe again felt impressed; he had expected the girl to wither in his presence, but here she was keeping pace with him, if just barely. It made him dislike her all the more, but he kept such thoughts to himself.

Out loud, he said, "You're quite the interesting little Lamb, taking all of this in stride. Is it that fortitude which affects my brother so?"

"'Affects'?"

"Oh yes. Recall that our souls are connected. Though I have been forbidden from accompanying him directly, I still feel Creed's spirit as if it were my own. The ebbs and flows of his heart. When I first bound myself to him, I was shocked at how weak he had become, but when it comes to you, I find myself amazed at what I see stir within.

"He saved your life in the battle against Samael, correct? When he did so, I felt a surge of power I could have sworn was lost to him. For a moment, he was just as I'd known him before this melancholy took hold of him. I know not how, but you inspired in him such strength as to briefly surpass how small he had become."

He felt the barest twinge of bashfulness flush across the girl's aura.

"You think... that was because of *me*?"

Stryfe had to keep from rolling his blinded eyes at the pathetic sense of attachment. A mere handful of conversations with Creed, and already this girl desperately wanted to believe she was important to him. Such desire was so typical of Lambs, even in a dead world. Stryfe was more than willing to feed that desire.

"That's right. I cannot begin to fathom why, but you have become a source of great strength for my dear brother."

He felt a sensation of comfort the girl exuded at the notion, but it was quickly followed by a surge of guilt. Perhaps this one was a bit *too* aware of how unnatural her standing was in this scenario. Stryfe could use that too.

"Of course, strength can become a weakness as well." He felt the question in her soul at his words, and elaborated:

"In a hopeless situation such as this, my brother's greatest advantage is his lack of self-preservation; my demons feed on fear above all else, and his ennui served to starve them. But your presence has changed things. For the first time in a *very* long while, my brother has something he wants to protect. Such bonds can be a source of power, but so too can they become a vulnerability, one which more devious enemies would be all too eager to exploit. You see the contradiction, yes? My brother may have been weak, but he did not *have* any weaknesses. Now, he does."

The girl's mind became distant while she contemplated Stryfe's words, but after a long moment, her spirit hardened. When she spoke, there was strength in her quiet words, and Stryfe realized he had miscalculated.

"He's not as weak as you think."

There it was. That riotous human arrogance. That iron-clad belief that their understanding of things was the only truth, no matter how narrow and simplistic it was.

It would have been enough to churn bile in Stryfe's stomach had he been capable of such things. He did not blame the girl for her foolishness, of course; even after so long in a dead world, a Lamb was still a Lamb, as much a slave to their defective natures as they ever were.

"Such certainty!" he rasped. "What a treasure it must be to know the heart of another after so short a time!"

He felt the girl chafe under his patronizing. In a less mocking tone, he continued, "Do not presume to understand my brother so quickly, little Lamb. You may have lived many lifetimes more than your appearance would suggest, but he was old even before time ceased to flow. You may believe yourself capable of comprehending the depths of his being after a few emotional meetings, but *I* have known him since his first days."

The girl was silent, which showed she at least had the sense not to argue such an obvious point. Stryfe leaned in her direction ever so slightly, ignoring the throbbing in his false bones.

"Would you like to know something? The truth is that despite how he may seem now, our dear Creed was once the most devoted Samaritan of us all! He protected you Lambs with such a fervor that you could have sworn he was *born* for a world like this! So don't be fooled, child. My brother may have convinced himself that he has grown numb to the cries of those few that remain, but the fact is that the moment the first stray Lamb came to his doorstep, he *had* to protect it."

He grinned inwardly at the flush of abashment from the girl's soul at the implication of his words.

"I'm sorry if you believed yourself special, but the truth is that any one of you would have served to stir his old spirit once again." He was going to say more, but the girl spoke first.

"That's okay."

For the first time, Stryfe didn't have an immediate response, which unfortunately prompted her to continue speaking.

"I mean, it would be nice if that was the case, but... I guess it's good to hear that he just needed a little push. He suddenly felt sure she was staring into his blinded eyes directly, and her soul was awash with conviction. "Like I said: stronger than you think."

Oh yes. Stryfe *very* much did not like this one.

"I think I like you," he said aloud. "Apologies if I offended you, Little Lamb. All I meant to say is that I am most curious to see where this fascinating bond the two of you have forged will take us."

It seemed Stryfe truly *had* lost his touch at manipulation after so long without a worthy subject. Perhaps it was time for a change in approach. If the girl was going to let her guard down, it wouldn't be through the breaking of her confidence. No, it would have to be through kindness.

"But enough of my whispers," he said, shaping his tone as kindly as he could while still sounding genuine. "As I have said, I wish to know your nature. Please stay, and perhaps tell me your story?"

Neveah had assumed that coming face to face with the monster the others so despised would fill her with dread and make her sick to her stomach. Instead, she had beheld a shriveled old man who, despite the abhorrent appearance and bloody chest wound, seemed far too pathetic to be some kind of supreme demon.

She was sure he'd been dangerous back when he was whole, but in this state, even she didn't feel especially threatened. When he said he couldn't harm her if he tried, she could somehow tell he wasn't lying.

It was because of this that she was willing to remain where she sat and tell Stryfe her story, such as it was. She had started off quietly, still nervous about whether or not Stella would emerge from her bedroom, but as time passed, she had to agree with the old man's assertion that the nun wasn't going to wake any time soon.

Neveah had gradually become more comfortable as she recounted the endless doldrums that had been her life since time had ceased. She felt it strange that she still found enjoyment in telling the tale despite it being the third time in a very short while. Perhaps talking about oneself took a while to get old when you hadn't done it in a few lifetimes?

It helped that Stryfe, once he had stopped trying to sound ominous and otherworldly, was a rather good listener. He absorbed her story with no interruption and little reaction, save for a thoughtful look when she mentioned the robed man who had first given her the seeds.

When she saw that, she decided to ask, "Do you have any idea who it was?"

An absurd question, but Stryfe *was* a Samaritan; perhaps he had more knowledge of the other few humans who had survived The End?

"I could venture a guess," Stryfe said, "but such things would be pointless. I assure you that whoever it was, they are no longer with us."

Neveah was unable to hide her disappointment. "Oh."

Stryfe's wrinkled features contorted in what she guessed was supposed to be sympathy. "I fear knowing would give you nothing worthwhile, my dear. Better to let it stay a heartening memory."

Neveah had reluctantly dropped the subject, and Stryfe said nothing more as she continued the tale. Her timeline caught up to the present before long, and when she had finished, Stryfe merely gave a slow nod, as if everything she said added up.

"An interesting story, to be sure. I look forward to seeing how it ends." He stared at Neveah for a moment with those blank white eyes before continuing, "Thank you for the company, my dear. You are the only one who has been willing to speak with me in any meaningful capacity since this whole affair began."

He spoke with such vulnerability, as if Neveah were the only friend he had in the whole world. It would have been almost touching, if she hadn't already caught on to the fact that every last bit of the demon's attitude was horseshit.

She had to admit, he'd *almost* had her at the start. Between his pathetic appearance and the weakness in his voice, she'd almost let herself believe that the spectre really just wanted someone to talk to.

It was only when she'd argued against his declaration of Creed being weak that she'd seen through the façade. He'd taunted her, tried to make her feel like a fool for thinking she knew anything about the man. He'd backpedaled quickly, but it was enough for Neveah to glimpse the truth beneath his polite words.

Whatever this creature wanted from her, Neveah was certain of one thing: it *hated* her. In light of this, she decided it was about time for both of them to drop the act.

"Hey Stryfe," she began, "why don't we cut the bullshit?"

The old man didn't react very strongly. He went still, mouth setting in a thin line and head cocking to side. She couldn't tell if he was surprised by her statement.

"Beg pardon?"

She rolled her eyes. "You know, you and Creed really are brothers. You both keep treating me like a kid just because I look like one. I get that I'm still way younger than whoever the two of you are, but I've been around long enough. I know that you're trying to sweet-talk me, and I know you don't actually give a rat's ass about my life story. So why don't you tell me what it is you really want?"

Several beats of silence passed, and Neveah couldn't deny a twinge of anxiety. She felt confident that Stryfe really was incapable of harming her in this state, but on the off chance that she was wrong, it wouldn't end well for her.

Oh well. She'd lain down the gauntlet herself, so all she could do now was wait to see if the demon picked it up and cracked her head open with it.

To her surprise, Stryfe did not appear to take offense. In fact, he seemed downright amused, letting out a series of chuffing wheezes that Neveah took to be some sick imitation of laughter.

The act seemed to pain the old man, and the laughter quickly turned to a series of hacking coughs. His body seized and writhed as he calmed himself, but he didn't seem to mind whatever pain he was in.

After finally getting himself under control, the old man let out a sigh and took a far more casual lounging position, draping his arms over the back of the pew. He angled his cloudy white eyes towards her and gave her a wide smile, exposing yellow teeth and bloody gums. Ruby-red blood began to trickle from his lips, as well as from the wound on his chest. Neveah wondered if the demon had somehow been staunching his own wounds in order to look less threatening.

If so, he was certainly letting the illusion drop now. When he finally spoke, his voice had morphed from that of a weak and harmless grandfather to that of a vile old lecher.

"Honestly, this wretched form makes it *so* hard to be charming. If I were able to wear my prettier faces, I could have made you a pet in no time at all."

Neveah felt her stomach churn, but did not outwardly react. She wouldn't give him the satisfaction. "Is that what you wanted? A pet?"

He scoffed. "Hardly. Violating you Lambs lost any appeal for me long before The End."

Neveah couldn't resist asking the question. "Who are you? Who are you really?"

Stryfe licked his lips and fixed his blind eyes firmly on her own. Neveah felt like icy fingers were tickling their way up her spine.

"You know who I am."

Once he said it, Neveah realized that she did. Unconsciously, instinctively, she knew who and what this creature lounging before her was.

In an instant, she resolved not to acknowledge it. She wouldn't say it aloud. She wouldn't even say it in her head. If she did, she knew she'd vomit.

She struggled to speak around the lump of tension in her throat. "What do you want?"

"An answer. Nothing more. Just an honest answer to an honest question."

"Then ask it."

Neveah wasn't able to keep the urgency from her tone. She was fully terrified now, and the old man could hear it. She could see the amusement on his wrinkled features.

"Do you believe in him?"

The question hung over her like a guillotine, and didn't need to ask who Stryfe meant. "Do you really, truly believe that he has not abandoned the Lambs? That he would protect you, despite how broken he has become?"

Neveah ruminated on the question for a moment. She thought of every conversation she'd had with Creed up to now; in reality, there hadn't been very many. How long had it been since she'd awoken in that flowerbed to find him looking down at her? It probably hadn't been very long at all, but she had seen and heard so much since then that it felt like a lifetime ago.

He'd been cold to her. He'd been cruel. He'd been spiteful. But there was always something there beneath the surface. Something deep and dark behind his scowls that told her the harsh words weren't directed at her. Not really.

Creed didn't hate her; he hated the pain she caused just by being around him. She hadn't yet learned the source of that pain, but whenever she looked down at her side to where a mortal wound had somehow been healed, she knew it hadn't broken him entirely.

"He would," she declared. The words came easy, and her voice was clear.

Something in her tone caused Stryfe's blank eyes to widen slightly, but beyond that the demon didn't react other than by giving a slow nod.

"I see..." He bowed his head and closed his eyes, as if her answer had given him some sort of relief. When he spoke next, he once again sounded like the kind old man he'd pretended to be before, albeit with a more exaggerated, mocking lilt to his voice.

"Thank you, my dear. I am glad to hear you say as much. For what it's worth, I believe your answer is correct: he *would* protect you. At all costs. As I said, you have become both a weakness and a strength."

His blind eyes opened again, slowly and deliberately.

"Luckily, I can make use of both."

Before Neveah could ask what he meant, the old man leaned his head back and looked to the ceiling. He called out to something Neveah couldn't see, speaking more loudly than she thought him capable of.

"No need to hide any longer! I think you'll agree this one serves your purposes well enough!"

Neveah tried to say something, but found that she couldn't speak around the sudden dread that rose in her throat. Dread turned to silent panic as some sort of bubbling sound filled her ears from behind.

She became intensely aware of *something* rising behind her, crawling its way up out of the floor. Neveah thought to turn and see, but found that her nerves had gone numb from fear.

"Oh, father..." came a new voice, slow and groggy and dripping with boredom. "What cruel games... you play with them...."

A shadow passed over her, and she felt that something tall was looming behind her, casting her form into shadow. She felt as if oil was being spilled down her neck, and couldn't stop a single, icy tear from spilling down her cheek.

"Don't cry, Little Lamb," Stryfe spoke beside her. His rasping voice carved at her mind like a blade on stone. "If what you said was true, then you should have no reason to fear."

Neveah felt something cold and slick coil itself around her head, and she didn't even have time to lament what an utter fool she was before everything turned to shadow.

Chapter XIII
"Lazarus"

Despite his efforts to ignore it, Joshua found himself unable to keep from analyzing Creed's aura as the two of them neared the city.

The changes had been subtle at first: a shift in his gait and the occasional too-sharp intake of breath. Now, as they approached the outskirts of the ruined metropolis, the void's effect on Creed were clear as day.

He was hobbling along as best he could, but his breath came in short, stifled bursts, and Joshua could "see" that his spirit was significantly dimmer than it had been a short while ago.

And yet, despite how fatigued he looked, Creed did not seem particularly bothered. His forward progress was steady, and he certainly didn't act like someone whose very soul was being drained away.

Joshua couldn't imagine the full effect the void was having on Creed, but he knew it was far worse than what he saw on the surface. If Creed could bear that pain as if he was simply winded, Joshua could only conclude one thing:

"You've come here a lot, haven't you?"

Creed huffed out a reply between breaths. "Don't pretend... you don't know what I've been doing."

"There are easier ways to go about it, you know."

"Not like this. Not for good."

Joshua didn't have a response for something like that. All he could do was lament.

Those thoughts were interrupted when Creed doubled over and gave a guttural shout. His brother's aura went berserk, fluctuating in shock and pain. He heard Creed growl through clenched teeth, and for a moment, Joshua worried the void was having a more significant effect than expected, but quickly realized that was not the case/

Expanding his consciousness, he probed into Creed's mind, where his suspicions were confirmed by the presence he felt. The prickle of tension spread across the back of his neck once again.

"Stryfe?"

«*Brothers,*» came the hissing voice into both his and Creed's minds. «*There is trouble.*»

"Get out!" Creed demanded through gritted teeth.

«*The girl has been taken.*»

Creed's writhing ceased. "What?"

«*Belphegor. He was there, in the church, all along.*»

"Impossible," Joshua asserted. "I've been keeping a third eye inside the church since this all started. The second someone set foot inside, I'd know."

«*It seems he made a perilous gamble. He deliberately unbound his soul and withdrew into the aether between life and death. So deeply that it nearly killed him. But it kept him hidden.*»

Joshua wanted to reject such a possibility on principle, but couldn't deny that it made a ludicrous sort of sense. He could detect many things without effort, but would have needed to focus intensely on a small area in order to feel a presence that had reduced itself to such an extent.

He cursed himself the fool for not searching thoroughly enough around the church, but then again, he would not have expected such a suicidal move; for Belphegor to have spread its soul so thin that he couldn't feel it, the demon had to have placed itself unfathomably close to the edge of death, a point where the slightest lapse in focus would result in the unraveling of its being.

«*He was among us the entire time. Watching. Listening. The girl stepped outside for only a moment, and he took her.*»

Creed eyes were wide, darting back and forth in blatant panic. "Stella—"

«*The sister was regaining her strength in darkness at the girl's behest. I believe she had been planning all along to escape and follow you as she had before. I was observing her from below but could not stop her from leaving.*»

"Bullshit," Creed spat. His aura had stopped fluctuating so violently, but he still felt like a powder keg ready to blow. "What have you done?"

«*Be sensible, brother. I am an invalid made of whispers. What could I have* possibly *done in such a state?*»

Creed seethed but did not continue to argue. His furious aura turned on Joshua.

"Find them."

Joshua complied without argument. Allowing the straw in his mouth to drop to the ground, he turned from the city ruins and faced the wasteland behind him, then sent his consciousness outward in a single massive wave that pulsed across the entire region.

Such a broad scouring resulted in a shallow level of detection, but Joshua had a feeling his search would not have to be thorough; wherever their quarry was, it wouldn't be hiding anymore.

Indeed, it took only a moment for him to come across the devil's presence, sticky and black like oil. At its side was a second, smaller spirit, almost invisible next to the choking vastness of the other. Focusing his mind, Joshua saw images flash into his mind of dead white trees with twisted limbs.

"I see it. In the forest where you found Stryfe."

Joshua could feel Creed trembling in place, practically panting in his distress.

«*What will you do, brother?*»

Creed was silent for a few seconds, but Joshua already knew what his answer would be.

He fixed Joshua with a hard stare. "Take us."

Joshua was still very much aware of the uneasy feeling crawling down his back. In a cautious tone, he began, "We need to be careful here...."

Creed took several steps in Joshua's direction, though in his weakened state, it wasn't especially threatening.

"Wasn't asking. Take us *now*."

"The boss might see this as interference, Creed."

"I don't care!"

For just an instant, the other man's voice broke. Joshua could hear the panic in his tone, and he realized that Creed had become far more attached to the girl than he'd let on.

Haven't sensed this in him since before Michael, Joshua thought.

Joshua accepted that there would be no reasoning with his brother right now. With a sigh, he lifted one of his arms, crooked as if attempting to link elbows. Creed clutched the proffered forearm without hesitation, his grip tight and angry.

"You'd better have a plan," Joshua cautioned, "because Belphegor sure will."

"I'll think of something."

Such a response provided little reassurance, but Joshua returned his thoughts to the twisted presence in the forest, drawing a metaphysical line between it and himself. Tracing the line, Joshua willed space to shift and warp around the two of them.

As everything fell away and their bodies sped along the traced line at the speed of thought, his feeling of unease began to flower into full-on dread. Whatever came next, Joshua knew it ended badly.

Although it had been ages, the sensation of warping across space was still familiar to Creed; a bizarre sense of weightlessness where the world turned to a blur and direction became meaningless.

It lasted for only the briefest of moments before his surroundings sharpened back into focus, and he found himself again surrounded by an endless graveyard of white hands clawing towards an uncaring sky. The feeling of dirt road beneath his feet turned to the crunching dust of long-fallen leaves.

Creed took not a second longer to observe the area before turning to face Joshua, who had appeared alongside him.

"Where to?"

Joshua tilted his head as if listening for something before fixing his blind gaze in a specific direction and pointing.

"That way. It's not far."

Creed was walking away before the man's words were finished, his stride long and steps quick. He heard Joshua's voice call from behind.

"You need to think, Creed!"

«*He's right, brother,*» came the sickening voice he couldn't ignore. «*This will not end well if you aren't careful.*»

"Shut up." He had no time to deal with the demon. "You delivered your message. Now get out of my head."

«*I think not. One way or another, the game ends here, and I will be there to see how it unfolds.*»

Creed gritted his teeth, but at this point, he was too preoccupied with a maelstrom of thought to bother arguing anymore.

Stupid girl. Stubborn girl. Idiot girl. Creed had actually believed her this time when she'd said she wouldn't try and follow him. Had he been a fool? His thoughts went to his coat pocket, where the tiny, insignificant seed rested.

She'd made him promise, hadn't she? He'd agreed reluctantly, but he *had* agreed! What reason would she have had to step outside? Should he be angry with Stella? He'd told her to rest as well, hadn't he? Could he blame her? What about Stryfe? Was he really uninvolved? Should Joshua have been paying closer attention? Who was to blame here? Who could—?

The whirlwind in his mind went still when, after walking only a short distance, he became aware of a figure to his right, some twenty feet away, where the concentration of dead trees was lighter.

There, in the middle of a small clearing, was the final abomination.

The creature was hunched over, but still loomed around ten feet tall, which made it smaller than the previous two demons. It's body was completely obscured by a massive, thick cloak of silver fur that shimmered in the pale sun's light. Atop the cloak sat the large white skull of a deer, sharp and smooth, with a set of large, multi-pointed horns adding several feet to its height.

At a glance, Creed might have thought this demon had a similar head to Adrammelech, but upon closer inspection, he saw that unlike the horse-beast's black hollows, he could actually see through the sockets of the deer skull. Furthermore, the skull itself was completely still, and it's bony jaw hung open and slack. The only irregularity, to his disgust, was the slow and steady stream of what appeared to be drool pouring from the orifice onto the dirt below.

In terms of appearance, the demon seemed overall less imposing than Adrammelech or Samael, but Creed was not fooled. Rather than size, it was the creature's presence which instilled an instinctual dread within him. There was a force radiating from the thing, a feeling of filth and foreboding which seemed to choke the stagnant air around them. It pressed down upon Creed from all sides, as if it was attempting to force its way down his throat and suffocate him.

Despite the empty skull looking into nothing, Creed could tell that the demon's attention was fixed squarely on him, and he could not fight down a tension that far outweighed what he had felt against the previous strays. Even from here, he could feel a dangerous intelligence in this new foe; Belphegor was not remotely as mindless and broken as the others had been.

"Greetings... Crusader..."

To Creed's surprise, the demon's voice sounded remarkably human. There was no deep reverberation, hissing echo, or other distortions, but rather the simple sound of a completely normal man, which only made it all the more unsettling. Its tone was calm, but also listless and tired. The words came slow, as if every syllable was a chore.

"That is... what they call you now... yes? Or... was it Creed? I find it... so bothersome... to keep track..."

Creed also noted that, although the voice was physical and clearly coming from the creature, the drooling deer-skull did not move with the words, lending credence to his theory that it was merely a disturbing decoration.

"I suppose... I prefer either... to your true name...."

With every word, Creed could feel the smothering presence grow even heavier around him. The edges of his vision seemed to darken slightly, and against all logic, his eyes began to feel heavy.

Of all things, it was Stryfe's wretched voice that pierced through the spell. *«Do not let him speak, brother. Every word he utters compels you to an eternal slumber.»*

Creed grit his teeth in habitual irritation at the voice, but as he did, the fog in his thoughts dissipated as well, and his eyes snapped back open. For once, the demon's unwanted presence had come in handy. Steeling his mind, he whipped a hand out, preparing to flare Malkuth.

"I would advise... against it."

There was enough implication in Belphegor' unsettling voice to make Creed hesitate. "There will be... no need... for your wrath today... Firstborn. I fear that... not all who are present... could withstand it."

At that, the demon's body began to shift for the first time. The fur cloak enveloping its form pulled open, drawing apart slowly like a curtain. Absolutely nothing but sheer blackness could be seen within, but the sickening squelching sounds of *something* slithering around could be heard.

After a moment, two perfectly round orbs of pale yellow light materialized from within the darkness, and Creed could tell by their position that he was looking at a pair of demonic eyes. As he'd thought, the cloak and drooling skull were nothing but adornments to hide Belphegor's true shape, whatever it was.

"Don't worry.... I kept her... quite safe..."

Creed's whole body tensed as Neveah's body slowly emerged from the darkness, slack and still. She hung several feet off the ground, suspended only by a thin black arm that gripped the back of her neck. The limb barely looked human, emaciated and withered to the point of mummification, with inhumanly-long fingers encasing the girl's throat. The hand held her just off-center, ensuring that the drool still falling from the deer-skull above was barely missing her.

«There she is. How will you save her?»

Be quiet, Creed thought in response.

«Belphegor's true body cannot be harmed by physical means. Your clay will be useless here. What other power is left to you?»

"Be *quiet!*" he hissed aloud.

By this point, he had become aware of Joshua standing a few paces behind him near one of the trees. He was silent, as Creed expected; there could be no interference in this standoff now that the demon had shown itself. The fact that he had warped them to this location might have already forfeited Creed's life in the eyes of their leader, but he was wholly unconcerned with that at the moment.

Belphegor's round yellow eyes continued to bore into Creed from within the void of its cloak. "I take it my father... is here with us?" It's words were infuriatingly calm as it dangled Neveah like a doll. "Hiding... in the corners... of your mind?"

«You won't have long. Think. How can you defeat him in a single stroke?»

Creed did all that he could to ignore the whispers, even as small pit began to form in what a normal human would call their stomach.

Belphegor was still droning. "The three brothers... gathered before me. I suppose... I should not hope to escape... unscathed...."

Creed finally forced himself to call out, if only to stop the demon's speech from weakening him any further.

"Belphegor!" His mouth was dry and his throat tight, but he did a sufficient job of keeping his tone intense and leveled. "What is it you want from this?"

«Don't try and trade words," Stryfe whispered. *"Only in strength do you outmatch him.»*

The creature's eyes seemed to warble slightly at his words. "Always so direct... you warrior types. I appreciate that. Negotiations... are so tiring... but I suppose... I can make it simple enough..."

The yellow globes shifted slightly, angling towards the unconscious girl in its grasp. "Even one... as dull as you... can follow the thread. This girl... she is important to you. And you are... so very noble. She is in my grasp now... and there are so many ways... I could snuff out her light. If you wish to avoid this... you will hear my words."

Stryfe's words remained unrelenting. *«He knows your weakness, but not what it is you're hiding. Use it!»*

The pit was growing more noticeable now, and Creed felt his breath begin to come more difficultly, as if he were still near the vicinity of the void within the ruined city. He looked at Neveah's small, defenseless form and forced himself to remain as composed as he could.

"I already asked you what you want!"

"It is not such... a puzzling thing. I have been forced... into a game... whose rules I did not agree to. I do not... wish to play. I am sorry to say... you will never... meet this girl again... but if you do as I say... you can ensure her survival... if nothing else."

The yellow eyes bored into Creed again, and he felt them like fangs at his throat.

"You know my nature... 'Creed'. I will not... struggle with you. The only way out... is to make a deal...."

«You cannot play his game,» Stryfe warned. *«Killing him is the only way.»*

"You will force my father... to sever the chain... that he has bound me with," Belphegor declared. "Of course... I will not... return the heart... he so lovingly... 'entrusted' to me. But even so... I *will* be... permitted to leave...."

«He means to force a loss for us both. You cannot allow this.»

"I understand... that this game will not... last forever. Once your master... has grown bored... he will come... to punish you. You will stand before him... and you will forfeit your life to him... as well as my father's. I shall be... far from here... when that time comes. The girl... will still be with me... but as soon as your souls... have been reaped... and father's heart.... fades from within me... I will have... no more use for her. I will let her go... leave her to her fate... and be on my way...."

«You cannot trust his words.»

As if Creed needed to be told as much. "I'm supposed to just take your word on that?"

"Come now... Crusader. As I said... you know my nature. I do not lie. Deception is... so very tiresome. And as far as deals go... this one is... quite simple. Your and father's lives... for my freedom... and the child's safety...."

Stryfe's whispers dug into his mind like claws. *«He thinks he holds the cards. But you still have another power left, don't you?*

"Creed," Joshua finally spoke, and Creed realized that he had been listening to Stryfe's words as well. "You need to stay calm."

"I don't need you to tell me that."

«*It is the only way. You know this!*»

"There's a way out of this," Joshua insisted. "We just have to use our heads."

"Both of you, be quiet! Let me think!"

"Oh...?" came Belphegor' voice. For the first time, there was a twinge of amusement alongside the lethargy. The yellow eyes seemed to shine a bit brighter in the blackness. "If you need time to think... I suppose... we can go elsewhere..."

From within the cloak, Creed saw an additional five arms slowly slink out of nothing. The sickening limbs reached for Neveah's dangling body, two each gripping her arms and legs. The fifth reached for her pale face, gently cupping her chin in its overly-long fingers.

"I think she finds it... rather comforting... inside me...."

The hand angled her lolling head, bringing it closer to where the deer skull's drool was still spilling. It dripped mere inches from her face now.

"Stop!" Creed yelled, holding up a desperate hand.

His mind was racing, flailing to come up with some way to alter the deal. "You don't have to do this. If you hand over the heart, the bond will be severed all the same! You can go wherever you want!"

"And allow Father... to regain his power? I think not...."

"You know the rules of the game, right? Once he's back to full strength, we fight. I'll kill him, and you won't have to worry anymore!"

"You really... think me a fool... don't you? I have observed your weakness... Crusader. I think we both know... how your silly duel... will end...."

Creed clenched his jaw, but could not find it in him to deny to claim.

«*He doesn't know. He doesn't know that the power you've been using all this time was borrowed from another. Show him the strength that belonged to you before* she *hid it away!*»

"That's enough, Stryfe." Joshua spoke with unusual forcefulness, but Creed wished *he* would stop talking as well. The pit was impossible to ignore now, gnawing at his insides.

"And of course..." Belphegor continued, "even if you were... to survive... I imagine your first task... would be to hunt me down... in father's place. Once again... I think not. This game ends... with both of you gone... or stained... with innocent blood. The time has come... Firstborn. Do you... accept my terms? Or do I... embrace this Lamb... forever...?"

The demon's six arms shifted all at once, receding slightly as if to begin pulling Neveah back into the fathomless shadows within the open cloak.

"It's bluffing," Joshua declared, though the quickness of his tone gave away his desperation. "If it kills her, nothing keeps you from tearing it to shreds."

"True enough..." Belphegor replied. "But you know... I have always found living... the most tiring thing of all. At this point... seeing the despair in your eyes... as you destroy me... would feel just as nice... as freedom...."

A bold claim, but Creed could hear the truth in its words. There was no path to victory laid before him; all that was left to be determined now was whether Neveah lived or died.

«*There is a way,*» Stryfe continued to prod. «*You can kill him and save the girl!*»

"Stop it!" Joshua's voice had a hint of panic to it now. To Creed, he said, "Listen to me. You know what he's doing. Shut him out."

«*Belphegor is not Michael. Only a fraction of power is needed compared to before!*»

The pit began to churn inside Creed. His thoughts grew hazier, and it was no longer due to Belphegor's voice.

"Both of you be quiet," he commanded, though his own voice sounded distant in his ears. "I can't think...."

"No more thinking..." Belphegor called.

«*He's right. You know what to do!*»

"Stryfe!" Joshua shouted.

But even the Demon of Sloth's patience appeared to have reached it limit. "If you choose... to squabble like children... I will treat you... as such. I shall count down... from Five.... If the bond with my father... is not severed..."

It didn't finish the sentence, but Neveah's body was only a few feet from being pulled back into the demon's hidden insides at this point, and the threat was beyond clear.

"Don't worry..." it drawled. "I'll count sloooow..."

Joshua had a dangerous edge in his voice now. "Stryfe, get out of Creed's head *now*."

«*I will not. You know how this ends!*»

"Fiiiiive...." Belphegor began, drawing out the word to a positively mocking length.

"Stop," Creed begged, but his voice was too hoarse to be heard. He couldn't move, and even the fear he felt was slowly being swallowed by the yawning of the pit.

«*You want to save her, don't you? If you do nothing, she dies. If you listen to him, we all die!*»

"Fooooour..."

«*The girl thinks you're a hero! She told me she believes you'll protect her! Will you prove her wrong?*»

"Creed, listen to me! You have to calm down!"

Part of him tried to listen to Joshua's pleas, but he just felt so fucking *weak*. "I... I don't..."

«*You gave away the power your wife gifted to you! All you have left is that with which you were born! There is only one way out now, and you've no one but yourself to blame!*»

"Stop it!" Joshua's voice sounded like it was underwater.

"Threeeee..."

"Please..." Creed gasped, though he could no longer even hear himself. He didn't know who he was begging anymore. His balance faltered, and he felt himself stumble. The pit reached his mind, and he clutched at his head in desperation.

«*Will you fail again? Will you stand by while your children suffer until it's too late?*»

"Creed, please! You'll kill her, too! It's what he wants!"

"Twooooo..."

These bastards. Why had they forced themselves back into his life? Why couldn't they have just left him alone? Why did he have to find the girl? Why did a part of him have to feel again?

«*You've been holding it back. Let it out!*»

He had been so close. It had almost been over. Now everything was so goddamned *loud*.

"OOOOONE..."

«LET IT OUT!»

A single sound broke through the cacophony whirling in Creed's head: a weak, childish groan, a whimper so soft that he shouldn't have been unable to hear it. His vision sharpened for an instant, and he could see the girl in Belphegor's grasp.

Her pale face twitched, soft features contorting in pain. Slowly, her eyes drew open. Her gaze was bleary and unfocused, but somehow, perhaps by sheer coincidence, her lake-green eyes met his own for a single instant.

Creed unraveled.

He was vaguely aware of Joshua shouting something and saw him leap towards Belphegor just as everything faded to sheer, impenetrable blackness. Stryfe's presence in his head shrank to nothing, and for the first time in what seemed like forever, everything was quiet.

Creed was in a universe of silence and darkness, alone save for Belphegor' disgusting form, sharper and clearer than ever before. Creed could see nothing else. Nothing but his enemy. His insides felt heavy and sluggish with the blackness that had gathered within, and there was only one way to relieve the pressure:

He let it out.

Neveah felt as if she were floating yet again; she wondered how many more times this was going to happen.

Whereas the ocean she'd dreamed of as she slept in the flowerbed had been vast and ephemeral, the space in which she now resided was utterly oppressive and far more physical. It was as if she was submerged in a sea of mud and muck, a torrent of filth pressing down upon her from every direction. It crushed her bones, burned her eyes, and clogged her throat as if trying to entomb her.

After an unknowable stretch of time, she felt the oppression recede just as suddenly as it had consumed her. She did not regain full awareness, but her dulled senses began to recognize the familiar touch of the dead, chill air to which she was accustomed. She experienced the unpleasant feeling of her body being gripped by some unseen force, holding her in place as if to pose her like a doll. Reality blurred around her, incomprehensible save for the sounds of voices so muffled they may as well have been white noise.

Cognizance gradually began to return, and the voices became sharper. When Neveah was finally able to feel her heavy eyes again, she forced them open with no small amount of effort.

Then everything vanished.

It was difficult to properly describe, but for a handful of moments, everything simply ceased to *be*. All sensation, all thought, all awareness stopped wholly and completely. Neveah forgot who she was, forgot what it was like to think or feel; there was nothing inside her or around her. Nothing anywhere.

It passed. Her senses came back to her in such a rush that she woke up *too* quickly, eyes snapping open wide as she let out a sharp gasp. Air filled her lungs with too much force, causing her to cough and spam for several seconds before she managed to get control of herself.

Steadying her breath, she blinked several times to clear her vision, but nothing came into view. She nearly panicked, but quickly realized she was simply lying on her back, and the blackness she saw was simply the starless sky above.

But there was something else; the scraggly face of Joshua came into view. He seemed to be crouched down, and Neveah realized she was lying in his arms. The blind man was panting, head darting around with a worried expression before looking down at her.

"Hey! You still there?"

Neveah felt compelled to answer the man, but all she could muster when she opened her mouth was a weak groan.

"Good enough." He gently set her down onto the cold ground. "Whatever you do, do *not* move from this spot!"

Neveah wasn't quite sure what he meant by that, but didn't get a chance to ask before he rose and rushed off somewhere she couldn't see.

Finding the sharp crunching of dirt beneath her to be uncomfortable, she rolled onto her side to try and see just where she was. She was met with a line of dead white trees.

The forest she'd avoided entering before? They seemed somewhat distant. Was she outside the tree line? Lowering her gaze, Neveah started and pushed herself up by her hands in shock.

All around her, extending in a perfect circle for about fifty feet in every direction, was... water? No. Not water. It looked more like ink, pitch black and bubbling as if the earth itself had been melted down into hot sludge. The mysterious substance gave off a sense of sheer, absolute revulsion, and some instinctual part deep inside Neveah told her that she would die if it touched her.

She herself appeared to have been spared that fate, as beneath her was a small patch of regular dry earth. The island was barely large enough for her to fit, but the tar did not seem as if it was going to encroach any further. Looking around, she could see that the area was ringed on all sides by the bleached trees.

Confused as she was, Neveah was able to piece together what had happened: someone—or something—had cut a swathe through the part of the forest they'd been in and reduced everything to this terrifying liquid. She surmised that Joshua must have somehow protected her from being caught in whatever power had done this, and that she would certainly be dead otherwise.

Just as she was pondering what could have possibly resulted in such a horrific scene, Neveah became aware of two figures directly in the center of the black lake.

One was a man with short white hair in a blue coat: Creed. To her shock, he seemed unaffected by the vile fluid, as he was currently soaking in it on hands and knees, head down and panting like he'd just been sick.

Behind him was Joshua, who had one hand placed on Creed's back. At first, Neveah thought he was standing in the tar as well, but a closer look showed her that he was actually *floating*, feet hovering just a few inches above the bubbling ground. Recalling how he had made the piece of straw float back at the church, Neveah figured he must have been using his strange powers to avoid touching the muck.

Joshua's posture was stiff and cautious. Neveah thought she could make out some sort of distortion where Joshua's hand met

Creed's back, and she could swear something was *moving* from the kneeling man's body into his own.

Befuddled as she was, the fact that Joshua was avoiding the mud while Creed wallowed in it told Neveah all she needed to know: whatever this horrible substance was, Creed had been its source. Just as she was about to call out to the two men, her attention was stolen by a light coming into her peripheral vision.

Turning, she gaped at a bright flame sputtering into existence some dozen feet away from Creed and Joshua. Neveah might have been awed at the first source of natural light she had seen since the sun went dark, if the flame hadn't looked anything *but* natural.

It gave off no warmth, and flickered in violent motions, as if something inside was trying to escape. Its color seemed wrong to her as well, appearing as a deep, harsh red rather than the comforting orange a flame should be.

Glancing back to the others, she saw that only Joshua was reacting to the bizarre sight; his head was turned towards the spectacle, whereas Creed's still faced the ground.

Her attention was drawn back to the flame when, with the sharp *pop* of a small explosion, a burning arm burst forth from its center. Unpleasant crackling sounds filled the air, and Neveah watched as an unknown figure clawed its way out of the fire in some heinous mockery of birth.

Eventually, the figure fell from the floating corona into the tar below, which promptly lit up with more crimson flames as if to cushion the landing. The viscous substance began to rapidly cook and solidify beneath the fire, allowing the figure to slowly rise and stand.

It appeared to be some kind of walking corpse, its flesh seared and charred black by the very fire that had birthed it. Burnt skin flaked off its body like paper, exposing red muscle and sinew beneath.

Neveah watched, hardly able to think, as the figure turned its head in her direction. It had no face—just a broken, hollow hole where one should have been—but Neveah knew it saw her. Then, slowly and deliberately, the singed body began to march in her direction. With each step, a small burst of flame spread outwards from its feet, burning the black liquid into a solid surface it could walk upon.

Even had she the wherewithal to run, Neveah wouldn't have been able to; all strength left her frozen limbs as the disgusting thing approached in a slow, searing march. She wondered if Joshua and Creed were watching what was happening, but if they were, they weren't moving to help, and Neveah couldn't tear her eyes away long enough to check.

The creature finally came to a stop only a few steps away and regarded her with its shattered face. Neveah stared back, eyes wide and jaw clenched, swearing she could feel its charred fingers closing around her neck

«*Afraid of me after all, Little Lamb?*»

The voice resounded in her head like Joshua's had when he'd demonstrated his powers, though this one was far more unpleasant. It was legion, a chorus of tones speaking all at once: some were deep, some were soft; some harsh, some kind; some young, some old; some male, some female; some imperious, some fearful. The resulting cacophony was so debilitating that Neveah thought it might drive her insane.

Abruptly, the creature's form began to shift and warp, like it was molding itself into a more definitive shape. Seared skin shifted to flesh, hair, and cloth before Neveah's eyes, and the empty hole in its head was filled in with a human-looking face.

When it was over, the horrific thing was gone, replaced by a tall, thin man with pale skin. His clothing was simple but elegant: immaculate dress shoes, black trousers, white dress shirt, dark waistcoat, and a perfectly ironed black tie.

His face could have been handsome, but hollow cheekbones and sunken eyes gave his features a sharp, skeletal quality. His dirty blond hair was neatly slicked-back, exposing a mark on his forehead: three hook-like symbols linked together in a sort of spiral pattern. It was identical to the one Neveah had seen on Joshua's ribs back at the church.

The man's right eye was a frighteningly bright shade of red, like an ember that wouldn't cool. Neveah thought the left one was a different color, but upon a second glance, she realized it was red as well, only far more dilated than its counterpart for some reason. Both pupils, like Creed's, were white rather than black, giving his gaze an eerie, otherworldly glint. Conversely, his sclerae were pitch black rather than white, which only emphasized the crimson glow of his irises.

The thin pale man looked down upon her with those frightening eyes, regarding her for what seemed like ages before fixing her with a stunning grin, bright and inviting and just the right amount of arrogant, a smile so perfect that Neveah could have melted into his arms had she not seen the horror he'd been just moments before.

The man raised a hand, and she noticed that the tips of each finger were black, as if they had been coated in soot. In his grasp was a cigarette, acquired from nowhere. He placed the stick in his teeth, where it somehow lit itself, and took a long draw. When he finally spoke, his voice was now physical and singular, dripping with a cultured accent that hit her ear like music.

"I had a feeling you'd be small...."

"Stryfe," came Joshua's grim voice, and Neveah was finally able to tear her gaze away to the other two Samaritans. Joshua was regarding the well-dressed man with a deep frown while Creed still knelt where he had been. He was no longer panting, but had yet to raise his head.

Neveah looked back to the man—Stryfe, as she had feared—just in time to see him give her a wink of his over-dilated eye before turning to face Joshua and Creed. Throwing up his hands, the reborn demon called out.

"Hallo, spaceboys!"

Creed finally lifted his head. He said nothing but looked disgusted at what he saw.

Stryfe looked perplexed and motioned to his face. "Not a fan?"

"Great," Joshua muttered. "Who's he wearing this time?"

The demon gave an exaggerated shrug. "What can I say? I love a little oddity."

Joshua seemed wholly unamused. "It's disrespectful."

Stryfe rolled his glowing eyes. "Come now. The strays are caught, the girl is unharmed, and all my pretty faces have been returned. Surely there's no cause for such bitterness?"

"It didn't have to be this way."

The demon's grin only widened, and his eyes narrowed slightly. "Actually, baby brother, I believe we both know it *did*."

This finally seemed to prompt Creed to speak. He glared at Stryfe with a rage that would have been frightening had he not seemed so utterly broken. "*Why?*"

"Oh, Creed, you know *precisely* why. You were never going to find Belphegor, and he wasn't going to show himself until he was perfectly sure he had our backs against a wall. All that I did was give him a last bit of incentive to wander into the open!" The cocky smirk widened, and he motioned to the lake of black liquid all around them. "Of course, it certainly didn't work out for him, did it?"

Looking down at the boiling tar, Neveah realized she hadn't paid a single thought to the whereabouts of the demon that had taken her hostage. She immediately realized where the thing had ended up, and felt sick to her stomach.

Stryfe began to pace, taking another drag on his miraculous cigarette as his footsteps continued to burn the blackened surface beneath him. Creed's eyes followed his steps as he continued.

"And let us not forget that you've only yourself to blame for this! If you hadn't done such an excellent job killing yourself, you might have still had a few tricks left to use! But seeing as all that's left is your worthless clay, I'd say it was clear you weren't going to contend with my cleverest child unless you stopped holding back!"

He tapped a finger against his temple. "Don't forget, I've been in your head; I know *precisely* where your limits lie. But I have also seen that for whatever reason, that little Lamb over there," he jerked a blackened thumb in Neveah's direction, "has a remarkable capacity for bringing out the best in you!

"True, it was a *terribly* rotten thing to do. But I told you from the start that I had no intention of leaving this world a shriveled-up invalid in a church basement! I plan to play around up here for a while longer, and if that means you needed a push to break through your pathetic little bout of melancholy, I was more than happy to provide one!" He stopped pacing and fixed Creed with another sickening smile. "Just like with Michael."

Creed snapped. With a growl, he whipped out an arm, and a diamond-shaped clay missile shot from his hand in a blur, embedding itself into the brand on Stryfe's forehead before Neveah could blink.

The demon's head snapped back but he remained standing, smile frozen on his face and cigarette stuck in his teeth. After only a moment, he leveled his head again, the barb extending from his skull like a horn.

"Fair enough."

Reaching up, Stryfe gripped the blade and ripped it from his forehead. Bright ruby-red blood spilled out of the wound before time seemed to reverse and it was drawn back up into the gash, which promptly sealed itself as if nothing had happened.

Stryfe dropped the blade into the black tar, whereupon it disappeared from sight in an instant, as if it had been dropped into a fathomless ocean. There was no sound or sight to indicate what had happened, but somehow Neveah could tell that the clay barb had just been utterly erased from the world.

With a smirk, Stryfe continued. "I suppose there's no use standing around chatting when we're supposed to be settling things."

The air seemed to shift, and a feeling of dread struck every one of Neveah's senses. It reminded her of the terror she'd felt when she'd seen that horse-headed demon in the valley, only dozens of magnitudes greater. Everything she thought and felt seemed to be drawn into the malicious maw of Stryfe's being, and she briefly wondered if he was going to tear out her soul without even trying.

The other two Samaritans reacted to the display of power as well; Joshua braced himself, while Creed just seemed to wince under the pressure and grit his teeth. This reaction seemed to disappoint Stryfe more than anything else.

"What's the matter? This is what you wanted, isn't it? What happened to all that proud talk of killing me when this was over?"

Creed finally rose from the ground, but his back was hunched and his stance fragile, like his body was filled with glass that tore at his insides when he tried to stand.

Stryfe was growing visibly irritated, and his voice rose as he spoke. "Could it be that was all bluster? Could it be that you know you haven't the slightest chance at even scratching me as you are now? Could it be that you're too weak to properly *stand* in my presence, little brother!?"

Creed continued to glare, but even Neveah could see it was a farce. His clenched fists shook at his sides, and his shoulders heaved with heavy breaths. Despite Neveah's silent plea, his blue eyes finally lowered to ground ever-so-slightly.

The suffocating pressure immediately abated, and Neveah found she could breathe again. Stryfe's shoulders slumped, and he sighed as if all his energy had left him.

"How terribly disappointing."

For the first time, Neveah finally understood how out of her depth she was. The three men in front of her were beyond her ken, demigods among ants. Looking at Creed's broken face, she cursed her weakness but couldn't deny that she had absolutely no place among the madness unfolding before her.

"The truth is," Stryfe continued, "I was looking forward to settling things just as much as you were. I've a thousand children inside me that wish nothing more than to rip you to pieces, but if this is all the sport you're capable of offering, I'd sooner let them starve."

Joshua finally chimed in, sounding like a parent standing up for a child that couldn't speak for themselves. "It's your own fault, Stryfe. You took things too far, like you always do!"

"He's just weak! Like he always was!"

"You want a good fight? You're not gonna get it here. Not now. Leave, and give him time!"

"And just how much time do you imagine he *has*, baby brother? A fight is all we have left to us in this game, and our dear Preceptor surely will not wait much longer before It decides to end things Itself."

"Rictus wants the strongest Samaritan to come out of this. You fight now, and it proves nothing. Give him a chance to recover. The Boss will understand, and you'll get your fight."

Even Neveah could tell it was a desperate last-ditch effort to keep Creed from being slaughtered right then and there. Creed, for his part, had let the discussion over his fate proceed in silence, his downcast expression making it clear he no longer cared what decision was reached.

Stryfe, however, seemed at least a little contemplative, taking a long drag on his cigarette and eyeing his brothers up and down. After a moment, he exhaled the smoke through his nose, took the stick from his mouth, and dropped into the black mud, where it too vanished faster than Neveah could process.

"Why not give *him* the choice?"

He fixed his red eyes on Creed. "I suppose I won't kill you here, brother. I personally think you're well and truly spent, but *he* seems to think you might just have something left. I'll leave it up to you; if I'm right, and you're ready to be done with it all, then save me the trouble and call Rictus yourself. Tell him you surrender and let him put you out of our collective misery."

He held up a black-stained finger. "However, if you think you can still give me a decent fight, then prove it! Come find me once you've woken from your foolish little dream. I'll still kill you, of course, but at least then you can die like the king you once pretended to be!"

Creed finally looked up from the ground, and Neveah couldn't determine which way he was leaning; there seemed to be equal parts rage and despair in his eyes. Stryfe seemed to notice this and gave a mocking chuckle.

"Don't worry. I'll give you time to mull it over. If you decide you want to finish things, I shall be waiting." He pointed a pale hand to somewhere beyond the horizon. "You know where."

With that, the man turned back and looked to Neveah, raising his eyebrows as if he'd forgotten she was here. He gave her another stomach-churning grin and, with a mischievous glint in his crimson eyes, called out:

"⟩ℇ⏋⊤⏋, Stolas!"

The words sounded utterly alien to Neveah's ears, and reverberated across the clearing as if they were loaded with some form of unnatural power. From the wide swathe of earth beneath Stryfe's feet that had now been burned solid, a black and red shadow seemed to expand outward before rising from beneath the earth, lifting the demon into the air as it did so.

The dark mass grew about a dozen feet high before molding and shaping itself into a recognizable form: an enormous bird, some unholy cross between an owl and a dragon. It was covered in rippling black feathers and armed with massive talons. Its face was snow-white with glowing red eyes, and it let out a soul-splitting shriek before expanding two massive wings that cast Neveah in shade.

Stryfe stood tall on the creature's back, looking down at her like she was an amusing animal to play with. Glancing over his shoulder, he shot one last look to the other two Samaritans, who had barely reacted to the sudden appearance of the demonic bird.

"Don't take too long, Creed! In a world like this, getting to choose how we die might just be the only luxury we have left!"

With that, the monstrous owl flapped its massive wings and lifted off the ground, creating a gust of air that knocked Neveah roughly onto her rear. With Stryfe still standing atop it, the bird flew off into the sky in the direction its master had pointed earlier. In moments, it was out of sight, and the desolate forest was silent once more.

Finally feeling like she wasn't going to die at any moment, Neveah picked herself off the ground, looking around at the corruption surrounding her tiny patch of ground and wondering how on earth she was going to get away from it.

Joshua's urgent voice called to her. "Stay there, Neveah! We're coming to get you!" As if she had *any* intention of moving.

At Joshua's side, Creed had closed his eyes, head bowed as if in prayer. Neveah thought he was probably cursing himself. Joshua grabbed him by the shoulder and, to Neveah's great surprise, the duo suddenly seemed to fold in on themselves and vanish. Not an instant later, they reappeared in a similar warping of space, now only a handful of feet away from her on the island of safety. She yelped but managed to keep from leaping back into the mud.

Joshua winced. "Sorry. Forgot to mention I could do that." Turning to Creed, he said, "Get that stuff off of you."

Neveah looked and realized that Creeds hands and feet were still caked in the black tar, which dripped to the ground like sizzling acid. Creed looked at his own hands as if he wanted to vomit, but merely clenched his fists with a small breath of exertion.

In an instant, the substance transformed from the pitch-black fluid to the familiar brown clay Neveah had seen Creed use before, which in turn began to dry and flake off of his clothing like harmless dust.

Turning, Creed knelt at the surrounding lake of mud and placed a single finger upon its surface, at which point a wave of the clay radiated outward to overtake the darker substance. In just a few seconds, the entire area had shifted from tar to earth, which cracked and broke into a field of dust before wisping away into nothing, presumably at Creed's command.

When it was gone, the ground had been left grey, featureless, and impossibly smooth; anything that was there before had been completely and utterly erased.

As she gaped at the sight, Neveah's attention was pulled to a large dark mark on the ground, the only spot that wasn't like the others. Upon closer inspection, what she thought was a formless stain was actually a definite shape: that of a tall, horned figure with numerous long limbs splayed out in all directions.

The black shape was imprinted on the ground like a shadow, as if it had been there since the dawn of time. Feeling sick, Neveah quickly turned from the image and the horrible fate it implied. Looking at Creed, she saw him too staring at the shape with a look of utter disgust. After a long silence, Joshua finally spoke.

"Well, I... suppose that could have gone worse."

Without hesitation, Creed wheeled around and struck his brother in the face. Hard. Neveah flinched as the unkempt man stumbled back a few steps. Had the dark liquid not been cleared away, he would have stepped right into it.

Clutching his jaw, Joshua straightened almost immediately, seeming more caught off-guard by the blow than actually hurt.

"I'm sorry."

"No. You're not."

"I didn't think he'd go that far."

"Joshua." Creed didn't even sound angry. Just tired. "If you pretend one more time that this isn't going exactly how you thought it would, I'm gonna rip your fucking head off."

At that, Joshua's expression seemed to fall away, replaced with some unknowable look Neveah couldn't describe.

"We can talk about it back at the church." He lifted a crooked arm, presenting his wrist to Creed as if for the other man to grab it. "Let's head back and get our heads straight."

Creed looked at the proffered arm like it was a knife. "I'll walk."

He turned his back on Joshua without a second thought and began to march away, only stopping when he came within a few steps of Neveah. It was the first time he'd even acknowledged her presence since she'd awoken. He said nothing, just staring with a look of abject shame.

Neveah desperately wished she could think of something, anything to say. But all she could picture in her mind was the shape of that demon seared into the ground and the feeling of cold nothingness that had consumed her before she'd awoken. Try as she might, her mouth wouldn't form the words.

Creed seemed to take her silence as an answer, lowering his gaze to the ground and continuing past her. She turned to follow his path, watching as he wandered into the line of unharmed trees without once looking back. She briefly considered following after him, as pointless as that would be, but Joshua stepped up beside her.

"Don't worry. I promise he's stronger than he looks. This won't break him. He just needs time."

"Was he right?" Neveah asked. "Did you know everything was going to end up like this?"

The shaggy man stared at her for a moment, then fixed her with a sad-looking smile and said, "I wasn't going to let anything happen to you."

It both did and didn't answer her question.

He offered his forearm to her just as he had done to Creed. "C'mon. Stella's probably worried sick about you."

Neveah was reminded yet again at that moment that she was never going to understand any of these people, and there was nothing she could do about it. Nevertheless, she reached out a hand to clasp Joshua's wrist and was only mildly surprised when she was sent hurtling across space.

Stryfe had to admit that the atmosphere of the city was indeed oppressive. He stood atop Stolas' back, unmoving in spite of the speed at which the beast flew, and took in the desolate husk of the once-thriving metropolis he and his brothers had destroyed.

It wasn't the blasted landscape and ruined buildings which unnerved him, but rather the soul-rending pull of the void radiating from the center of the massive crater which now made up most of the city's mass. A veritable maelstrom of nothingness that threatened to drain away everything Stryfe held within, leaving behind a husk no different than any of the empty buildings.

From so high up, Stryfe could make out the ashen shape that still stained the crater: an enormous, inhumanly shaped body from which the imprint of six giant wings extended.

Proud Michael, now just a shadow in the dirt.

Stolas reacted negatively to the void below, instinctively shifting itself to avoid the spot Stryfe wanted him to land upon. In response, he stomped a heel into the demon's back and flexed his power. Incapable of resisting, Stolas began its descent, circling around the crater twice before finally coming in and landing at its center.

Stryfe leaped down from the demon's back, landing softly despite it being at least ten feet to the ground. As soon as his feet touched the earth, Stolas let out a series of hisses and chirps, a plea to leave the cursed space in which they stood. Seeing no point in berating the creature for its cowardice, Stryfe gave a dismissive wave of his hand, at which point the owl burst into a cloud of black mist and feathers.

Stryfe felt the twinge of the demon's spirit returning inside his soul and allowed himself a moment of satisfaction; he was far from recovered from his time spent torn apart, but the monsters within him were subservient to his dominance as before. This was good. Stryfe would need adequate control over his children in the coming battle with Creed.

If the coward bothered to show.

Looking around at the blasted landscape, Stryfe could see what appeared to be a large number of clay stakes arranged all throughout the crater, embedded into the ground wherever the black stain of Michael's corpse was not present. He didn't need to wonder as to their purpose; he'd seen into Creed's memories when they were bonded, and knew of the pathetic ritual he'd performed during his visits to this place.

So transparent of you, little brother. Acting as if you're dead inside, yet so eagerly seeking out your own punishment.

Stryfe allowed the sensation of the void to touch the edges of his spirit. He could understand perfectly why his brother had chosen this method of suicide. To someone like Stryfe, already stained with madness and the evils of the world, the void was unpleasant but harmless. To Creed, whose very strength had been the lives of his children, the vacuum created by the annihilation of this city would have been the deadliest of poisons.

Craven a method as it was, Stryfe had to give him credit for somehow finding a way out of their farcical world that wouldn't result in his soul being handed over to the Preceptor for eternity.

Of course, Stryfe had successfully deprived his brother of that particular means of escape, and all that remained now was to settle things between them. He had made sure to push Creed as far as he could, but with as weak as the man had become, it was possible Stryfe had simply broken him instead. He hoped that wasn't the case; if this story didn't end in blood, everything up to now would have been pointless.

Stryfe regarded the dirt at his feet, permanently blackened with Michael's ashes. Feeling petty, he gave the ground a kick of his heel.

I suppose you get the last laugh in the end, my poor, mad twin. Is that why you left your shadow here? So you could watch us finish tearing each other apart after all this time?

An amusing thought, but Stryfe didn't much care whether he was right or not. With a snap of his blackened fingers, he willed a small pillar of red flame to appear behind him, from which formed a smooth, high-backed throne made of solid obsidian.

Stryfe approached the throne, turned, and slumped down as if he was tired from a long day's work. Flourishing his fingers, he called another cigarette into his grasp, lit it with his mind, and placed it between his teeth.

As comfortable as something like him could be, Stryfe propped one leg atop the other and resigned himself to wait for whatever result would come his way.

Come, little brother. Come and put an end to all of this.

Chapter XIV
"Good People"

For once, Neveah hadn't needed to guess what Stella was feeling. The moment she and Joshua appeared in the church, the nun had been there. In stark contrast to before, she would not come within ten feet of Neveah. Hands clasped and head bowed, the apologies had come without pause, and nothing Neveah tried was capable of assuaging the guilt.

"It wasn't your fault."
"It was."
"You needed rest."
"I could have waited."
"Stryfe tricked us."
"I knew that he would try."
"I brought it on myself."
"I should have been there to help you."

So things had gone until Joshua mercifully interjected, explaining to Stella what had happened in the forest and why Creed was not currently with them.

Stella all but ignored the man, claiming she was aware of what had happened. Neveah wasn't sure how that was possible but chose not to speak up lest she send the woman into another spiral of remorse.

At that point, the only thing left was to wait until Creed made his way back. Neveah seated herself on a pew, as did Stella, though hers was far from Neveah's own. Joshua had once again sprawled out on the stairs leading to the pulpit, though the way he kept fiddling with his newest piece of straw belied how he really felt.

He briefly tried to coax Stella into another game of chess, but the nun had gone utterly silent, so still in her seat that Neveah could have thought she was dead.

As "time" passed, Neveah replayed the events in the forest over and over again in her head, and each time grew angrier with herself as she recalled the broken look in Creed's eyes. Why hadn't she spoken up? Why hadn't she told him it was okay, that she wasn't afraid of him?

Perhaps because that hadn't been entirely true at that moment?

If that was the case, even screaming at him to stay back or running away would have been preferable to her cowardly silence. Steeling herself, Neveah swore that whatever she said to Creed when he returned, she *would* say something.

She didn't know how long it had been when the Dove appeared at her feet, the first time it had deigned to show itself in quite a while. She glared, wondering if it was curious why she'd had the gall to get kidnapped by demons when it had told her to stay put in the church.

But her delusion just gazed back with its unknowable expression before flapping its wings and lifting off the ground. At the same time, Joshua's head perked up. For a startling moment, Neveah thought he could actually *see* the bird, but realized he was just reacting to what was behind her.

Turning, she followed the Dove as it flew to the entrance of the church, where Creed had finally arrived. It circled the white-haired man's head before landing on his shoulder, unseen as always.

Neveah and Stella stood together as he approached. While he didn't seem quite as utterly miserable as he had been in the forest, his posture was slouched, and his footfalls were heavy as he plodded his way into the church. Neveah wasted no time, marching forward and placing herself in the man's path. Nary a second later, Stella was there was well, and the two of them began in near-unison:

"I'm sor–"

"Creed, I–"

But he held up a gloved hand to silence them, which prompted the Dove to flutter off his shoulder and out of sight.

"Don't."

He looked even wearier than Neveah had feared. His gaze seemed to pass through them as if he couldn't actually see where they were. "This is my fault," he declared. "All of it."

As exhausted as he sounded, there was an iron-clad certainty in his voice that broke Neveah's heart. For the first time, she finally understood that as much as Creed claimed to hate the angels, the other Samaritans, and their whole broken world, he hated nothing half so much as himself. Remembering her vow, Neveah hardened her expression.

"Fine, it's your fault. How do we fix it?"

"We don't."

"Is that supposed to be your answer?" came Joshua's voice from behind.

Neveah turned to see him regarding Creed with a deep frown, seeming truly angry for the first time since she'd met him.

"That what you decided on your little walk? Stryfe gets one over on us for the millionth time, and you decide it's the one he gets away with?"

Creed didn't seem as angry with Joshua as he had before, but there was no small amount of scorn in his response. "And what do you think I should do? Face him down with all the strength I don't have?"

Joshua clicked his teeth, and probably would have rolled his eyes if he'd had any. "Oh, for the love of—"

He spat his strand of hay out in irritation. "Enough with the self-pity! You're only weak because you *want* to be! If you actually chose to try—"

"I *did* choose. Stryfe said it himself, didn't he? Choosing how we die is the only freedom we've got left. I made my choice a long time ago, but you all decided to show up and take it away from me. If my only options now are letting Stryfe's monsters tear me to shreds, or waiting for Rictus to come do it himself, I'll take the latter."

Joshua was openly furious now. "Those *aren't* your only options, you nihilistic fool! Why do you and Stryfe think you're both trapped in some kind of horrible cycle where death is the only way out!? If you'd both just *try* and take a stand, we'd be able to get out of this!"

Creed just shook his head, as if he pitied the other man's outlook.

"Why get out when there's nowhere to go, Joshua?" The resignation in his voice left no room for the other man to offer a rebuttal. "I know you thought that if you played your cards right you'd be able to bring out whatever fight was left in me, but you miscalculated."

Joshua clenched both his jaw and his fists, meeting Creed's empty stare with a grimace.

"You're both just so selfish, you know that? Too busy wallowing in your pain that you haven't even noticed there's still a world left to fight for."

"World's already dead, little brother. You're the only one of us left who won't let it go."

Neveah found herself flashing back to her argument with Creed in the valley at the base of the dead tree. He had been so harsh to her then, saying what he knew would hurt her to drive her away. Now he was doing the same thing to Joshua.

She was tempted to call him out on it, but chose not to when she saw that Joshua's expression hadn't budged an inch at the words.

In an unshaken tone, he declared, "Maybe the world has a stronger hold on us than you'd like to believe."

With that, he walked forward and pushed past the other man, making for the entrance.

"Where are you going?" Creed called after him.

"To talk to Stryfe. At this point, I've got a better chance with him than with your stubborn ass."

He stopped just outside the church doors, waiting under the grey light of the black sun.

"If you decide you're tired of letting him and the Boss have their way, come find us so we can settle things the way brothers are supposed to."

Creed let out another sigh that seemed to deflate him even further. "We're not worth it."

Joshua threw his hands up in an animated shrug without turning. "What can I say? I take care of my family!"

With that, space warped and folded around the Samaritan's body, and he vanished without a trace. Creed stared at where he'd been with an expression not dissimilar to a dead man.

"Creed..." Neveah began.

"You should leave."

She wasn't surprised to hear it, but the bluntness still hurt.

"It's for your own good. Rictus will be here before too long. He'll be here for *my* soul, but you don't want to be around when that happens. He won't kill a Lamb without their permission, but he'll do his best to convince you that you should let him put you out of your misery. He can be very persuasive, so if you want to avoid it, I'd suggest taking your seeds and being on your way."

Swallowing her frustration, Neveah asked, "And what'll you do?"

"Exactly what I said."

Without another word or a single look back, Creed plodded his way to the front of the church, right where Joshua had vanished, and sat down atop the wooden steps at the entrance.

Neveah watched him for a long while, shoulders slumped and unmoving, and in the end could do nothing but close her eyes and turn away.

Upon arriving at the ruined city, Joshua allowed himself to reappear at the edge of the giant crater rather than its center, as he would need a few moments to adjust to the painful atmosphere. The sheer emptiness that permeated every inch of space around him nearly compelled him to fall to his knees and weep for all the lives lost, but he stood firm and simply allowed the chill of the void to pass through him.

Taking a full breath, Joshua found his composure. Though it was still a ways off, he could feel the demented presence at the crater's center as if it were inches from his face.

Steeling himself, he contorted space once more and closed the remaining distance in an instant. When he reappeared, his senses outlined the shape of a sharp, solid throne upon which Stryfe lounged.

"Just you?" the demon called in that fake charming accent. Joshua assumed he was still wearing the same disrespectfully stolen face, and was glad he couldn't see it.

"He'll be here," Joshua declared, hoping he sounded more confident than he felt. "And when he arrives, I'd like us to at least *try* and talk about another way out of this mess."

Stryfe's aura flared with disdain. "Ah, yes. How could I forget your clever idea regarding the Nephilim?" Joshua started, and he could practically feel the demon rolling his eyes. "Yes, I'm aware, baby brother. I was listening in when you told Creed your clever plan to keep us alive a bit longer. Honestly, the desperation is almost embarrassing."

Joshua didn't rise to the obvious bait. "If you already heard, then I don't need to bother explaining how it's the only option that even gives you both a chance at surviving this."

Stryfe let out a weary sigh, and Joshua sensed him slouch further in his throne. "Round and round we go. How long are you going to try and keep our world spinning before you realize that it came crashing to a stop long ago?"

"I'll never stop. Not when the alternative is you two idiots killing each other just because he's tired of living and you're bored with the world."

Stryfe's aura flared with some vague emotion Joshua couldn't place. "Bored, you say? Is that how you see it?"

"It's my best guess. Why else would you be trying so hard for a fight?"

"Who can say? You could always try taking a look into my thoughts to see if you're right. Or are you too polite to go poking around in big brother's head without permission?"

Joshua scoffed. "Please. I've been trying to read your mind since I showed up, but you've got all of your demons swirling around your thoughts."

"Clever trick, yes? But you needn't bother. My thoughts are not so unknowable if you'd just listen."

He leaned forward, then declared slowly and deliberately: "We don't. Fucking. Like each other."

Joshua grit his teeth. "Only because neither of you knows how to let go of the past!"

"I'm afraid there was never a chance of that, Crucifer! Enemies was all we could ever be, since the very beginning. It's simply the natural order of things!"

"That's an excuse, and you know it! There *is* no natural order anymore! We've all been free of our destinies for a long time, and the only reason you still hate each other is because you *choose* to!"

"Then I suppose even after all this time, we're still just not as forgiving as you, baby brother. But who could blame us?"

Stryfe's tone was still taunting, but Joshua noticed a hint of ruefulness as well. "How could he be expected to forgive the monster who stole the world he was promised? And how could I forgive him for turning me into that monster in the first place?"

Joshua grimaced. "Is that what it all comes back to? Everyone needs to pay for sins that can't be paid for?"

"*That's right!!!!*" Stryfe roared, bolting up from his chair. For a moment, his true voice rang out, a thousand shouts resounding across the crater.

Joshua felt Stryfe's gaze upon him like molten lead, and the sound of an utterly inhuman snarl filled his ears.

He wasn't impressed. "It won't matter. Regardless of who lives or dies, it won't solve anything for anyone. Neither of you will find peace through killing the other."

He felt Stryfe's aura slowly regain its composure, and the snarling stopped. For a moment, the demon seemed just as tired as Creed.

"I don't think I feel like talking anymore, baby brother. Either he comes here and fights, or stays there and dies. Nothing left to discuss."

"That all depends on what the two of you choose,"

Stryfe let out one more spiteful chuckle. "You know, I never understood why it was *my* voice the world was so frightened of..."

Joshua sensed Stryfe raise an arm and make a finger-gun with his hand, putting it against his own head.

"I swear, listening to you is enough to make someone—"

The sound of blood and viscera splattering all over the throne filled Joshua's ears, and g=he sensed Stryfe's body go limp and flop down in its seat..

He sighed. "Stryfe...." The demon remained unresponsive. "Stryfe!"

His irritation flared to maximum. "Seriously? You're gonna be petty about this?"

The only response was the sound of dripping blood.

"Fine! Be that way! But I'm not leaving, so you can just sit there being a baby until he shows up!"

Exasperated, Joshua allowed himself to drop backward, using his power to form an invisible platform on which to sit. There he remained, hovering a few feet above the ground across from his idiot brother bleeding all over his fancy chair.

Angrily resting his chin on one hand, Joshua decided that all he could do now was wait to see if his other brother would be strong enough to show.

Alright, Neveah, he thought. *Your turn.*

As she once again sat in a pew staring aimlessly at the ceiling, Neveah wondered why it was she felt so ashamed of how useless she was.

Creed and his brothers were beings of a sort far beyond what she could fathom. They were powerful enough to destroy the world and knew things about its workings that ordinary minds couldn't handle. Even in a world without time or fate, they were on another plane of existence from mere mortals like herself.

Besides, she was just one person. Even when the greatest minds of humanity came together to build the Eidolons—the final culmination of man's capacity for creation— they had still failed to reach the unnatural heights in which Creed and the others lived. What role could one useless Lamb such as Neveah play in a story this fantastic?

Knowing this, when Neveah looked outside to see Creed sitting on the front steps in the black sunlight waiting for death, she shouldn't have felt like there was something she should be doing. These people were unknowable to her. She couldn't understand them, couldn't help them, and certainly couldn't save them... right?

Her unchanging view of the rotted wood ceiling was interrupted by the appearance of the Dove fluttering into view. Neveah felt more irritated by its presence than ever, but followed it as it fluttered down to the ground and settled on the dirt mound at the center of the flowerbed.

Currently, Stella was crouched before the blossoms, softly running her fingers across their vibrant petals as she had before. Her head hung low, and she wouldn't so much as look at Neveah, which hurt more than expected. She would have taken a hundred of the woman's invasive grooming sessions over watching her wither under self-loathing.

Neveah could see the Dove was lying down in the dirt again, right where she'd been sleeping when Creed first found her. Drawing its soft wings in close and curling its head in tight, it seemed to relax, and Neveah was startled to realize that it was going to sleep. As if to emphasize this, the Dove proceeded to fade from view, disappearing before Neveah's eyes.

She felt a brief flash of panic; the bird had always flown off out of sight before, but never outright *vanished* in front of her. What did that mean? *Did* it even mean anything? The bird was just a hallucination, so would anything it did actually matter?

Yes, she told herself. It did.

No matter how random its actions, Neveah had always somehow known what the Dove was telling her: where to travel, where not; who to trust, who to avoid; when to stay, when to go.

This time was no different: by settling to the ground, it was saying this is where she should be; by going to sleep, it was saying this is where she should stay; by vanishing from her sight, it was saying the rest was up to her.

Looking again to Stella, Neveah observed the nun's expression, unchanged since the moment they met. But Neveah knew the mask was just that: a mask. There was sadness and helplessness behind it. Neveah hadn't been able to perceive such things at first, but after only a short time with the woman, she knew there was far more to her than a pretty face.

Neveah had assumed she could not understand Creed and the other Samaritans. But who had told her that? No one. It was just something she'd assumed when she realized they weren't human. Was that truly the case?

Stella may not have been a Samaritan, but she was just as much of an enigma. And yet, Neveah was able to perceive her thoughts and feelings more accurately now than when they had first met. There was still much to learn, perhaps more than Neveah would ever be capable of, but that didn't mean it was impossible.

These people were not unknowable. Not unless she believed them to be.

Tired of sitting around and allowing impossible things to overwhelm her, Neveah gathered her courage, stood from the pew, and walked over to where Stella was crouched.

The nun didn't shy away or attempt to apologize again, which was a start. Neveah glanced over her shoulder to where Creed still remained slouched outside the Church walls, then set her jaw and turned back to the nun.

"Who is he? Who is he, really?"

Stella blinked at the question but did not meet her gaze. Did she seem... uncomfortable? Bashful? Neveah couldn't quite tell yet.

"I don't think he would want me to tell you that without his permission."

"Who cares what he wants? He's moping around like a baby."

She knelt to Stella's level, wishing the nun would look her in the eye. She didn't.

"I'm sorry. It's not my place."

Neveah sighed, thinking of how she could convince the older woman to open up. After a moment's rumination, a thought came to her.

"Could you at least tell me who Michael is?"

At long last, Stella turned to look at her, and Neveah could see surprise behind the mask. "Where did you hear that name?"

"Stryfe mentioned it. In the forest. He said he had to give Creed a 'push' to save me from that demon, and that he'd done it before with someone named Michael."

Looking into the nun's vibrant violet eyes, Neveah implored, "Please, Stella. He's sitting outside waiting to die. I need to know what happened to make him like this."

A long silence followed, possibly the longest she'd seen Stella take to come up with a response to something. Eventually, however, the nun turned her gaze back to the flowers.

"Michael was an angel," she began. "The strongest angel aside from their master, or so Creed tells me. It's descended many times since The End, and while the Samaritans have repelled it each time, it always took many lives with it in the process."

That gave Neveah pause. "What do you mean 'descended many times?' They never managed to kill it?"

Stella shook her head. "You misunderstand. Once an angel appears, it will not stop its attack until it has erased every human in its path. Destroying it is the only way to gain a reprieve."

"'A reprieve,'" Neveah parroted, trying to make sense of the nun's words. At that moment, she recalled something Creed said to her during their talk in the valley:

But there was never a chance of winning that battle! Our task had been failed since before it began!

As if to confirm her suspicion, Stella continued, "The truth is that the angels cannot be defeated. Not permanently. They can be destroyed, but in time, they will always return."

Neveah felt as if the dark sky outside were pressing down upon her. The nun's words horrified her, but something inside her knew they weren't wrong.

"How is that possible?" she asked, unable to bring her voice above a whisper.

"It is the power of the one who commands them: The Metatron."

"The fucking *what*?"

"The Voice of God. From what I've been told, it was the highest of all angels. After the death of God, the angels were driven mad and lost their minds. The Metatron, as the Voice of God, was able to retain its sentience, but not its sanity. In its delirium, it took command of the other angels and locked itself away in Heaven, where not even the Samaritans are capable of reaching. It is the Metatron that allows the angels to descend to the Earth, and when one is destroyed, it is the Metatron that brings their soul back to the Heavens and gives it life once again."

Neveah had no way to respond to such an existentially horrifying concept, so she fell back on her standard, "...Oh."

"I don't fully understand the process, but I've gathered that the Metatron seems unable to allow more than a single angel to descend at a time, and that the more powerful angels take significantly longer to return from death than the others."

"Like Michael?" Neveah asked, returning to the initial subject so she could distract herself from the frightening truth she'd just learned.

"Yes. At the time of Michael's most recent descent, it hadn't been seen in a very long time." Her gaze shifted past Neveah to something beyond their current surroundings. "It wasn't very far from here."

"That ruined city?"

Stella gave another nod. "At the time, it wasn't ruined. Not completely. It was considered the last bastion for humanity left in the world. Such a large gathering of humans naturally drew attention. The angels came many times, but they were always repelled."

"By Creed?"

"And his brothers."

That caught Neveah off-guard. "Wait, Joshua and Stryfe? They fought *together*?"

Another nod. "It may seem difficult to believe, but they were comrades, once. Although their roles as Samaritans were different, they often worked together to achieve them. Joshua and Stryfe's roles often took them away from the city, but Creed's duty was to defend the people from the angels, so he was nearly always present. Word of the city and its protector spread, drawing in many other survivors. In time, it became the only place left in the world that could be called a civilization."

"And you were there?" Neveah realized she still wasn't aware of how the nun knew all of this. "How did you two even meet?"

"We were... aware of each other for some time, but it was only a short while before the city's destruction that I first met him. I thought perhaps I could join the community that Creed was building, but in the end, I... couldn't find a place for myself."

She motioned to the inside of the church around them. "It was Creed who led me to this church. He let me stay here, away from the crowds."

"You don't like crowds?" Neveah almost laughed. In a world where most everyone was gone, the idea of agoraphobia seemed downright comical.

"I have always found it difficult to be around people. I wish I could have been stronger, but Creed visited me often, telling me stories of how things were within the city. I was content to watch from afar. Until the day I watched it fall."

"What happened?"

"Michael descended. All three of the Samaritans were present, but the angel was strong. In the end, they were able to destroy it, but the toll it took..."

"It destroyed the city," Neveah guessed. "And he feels guilty that he couldn't stop it."

Stella shook her head again. "That's not entirely correct. Michael took many lives, yes, but it didn't destroy the city. Creed did."

Neveah felt a chill run through her. She was going to ask how but suddenly remembered what had happened in the forest.

"That power," she whispered. "That... whatever it was...."

"Yes."

"What is it?"

"I don't fully understand it myself. It's not something he's ever shared with me."

The nun's gaze seemed to drift even further away, and though her tone still did not change, Neveah could somehow feel a dull anger in the following words:

"I'm told it was Stryfe's doing. Against Michael, even the three of them together were pushed back. The longer the fight dragged on, the more lives were being lost."

Neveah finally began to understand. "So Stryfe goaded him. Like in the forest."

"Yes. I don't know the full details, but I understand that Stryfe forcibly drew this power from Creed in the hopes that it would turn the tide. It did, but in the process, Creed lost control. He destroyed not only Michael but the city as well. By the time the angel was defeated, every life within had been snuffed out."

Neveah drew in a shaky breath, unsure of what she could possibly say to such a thing. She noticed her hands had clenched into nervous fists, and she couldn't will them to relax.

"Creed couldn't recover from the loss. He tried to kill Stryfe, and it's my understanding that he would have done so if Joshua hadn't intervened. The two of them left this place, and Creed didn't follow. We've been here ever since."

"Why would he stay? Wouldn't it be too... painful?"

"That is *why* he stays. And why he visits the ruins as often as he can."

"He still goes back there?"

"Yes. I think he would always be there if it weren't for my presence. He only comes back to make sure I'm not alone for too long."

Neveah noticed that, at some point, Stella's hand had also curled into a fist. The nun's gaze was laser-focused on the flowers in front of her. In that moment, Neveah came to a rather obvious conclusion.

"You love him. Don't you?"

"Love isn't something I've ever been able to feel properly. Concepts like that evade me, no matter how much I pretend."

Neveah nodded. If nothing else, she'd gathered that the nun wasn't quite on the same page emotionally as most people. "But you do care about him?"

"He's the only thing left for me. Nothing is waiting anywhere else."

"And what are you to him?"

"A distraction." She said it without hesitation, making Neveah want to hug her and cry. "He would have accomplished his goal long ago if not for me."

"What goal, Stella? What is he doing in that city?"

A slight hesitation, then, "He is planting graves. A new one for every visit."

Neveah recalled certain things Stryfe had said back in the woods, and knew that wasn't the whole truth. "That's not all he's doing, though, is it? What's his real plan?"

Another long pause. When Stella finally answered, the bitterness was finally audible. "I believe that's something he should tell you himself."

Neveah sighed inwardly but decided it was best to leave it at that. She had learned much from this discussion, all of it painful. But that was precisely what was needed.

In the end, she'd been right; these people were not unknowable. They were weak and broken, just like her. Just like the whole world around them. Neveah wasn't sure she could fix them, but they weren't necessarily in need of fixing.

Just understanding.

"Alright, then" she declared. "Guess I'll go ask him. Thank you, Stella."

She moved to rise but stopped herself. Reaching out, she took one of Stella's hands in her own. Her flawless skin felt cold, but Neveah gripped it tight. "And for the record, you are *not* just a distraction to him. I think you're the only reason he's been able to hold on this long."

Stella regarded her with wide eyes, and Neveah could not read the emotion behind the mask this time.

"Thank you," the nun eventually said, voice softer than it had ever been before.

Neveah smiled and gave her hand one last squeeze before rising, turning, and marching toward the front door.

Chapter XV
"Don't Give Up"

There had been a fair number of times since the end of the world when Creed had wondered if he could fly into the black sun. His body had been built from a star, after all. Why not return to the sky and see if anything lay beyond?

Maybe it was a path into the heavens. Maybe it led to an entirely different world. Maybe it would just kill him.

He always ended up scoffing at the idea. The sun was the same celestial body it had always been, just warped into an unnatural black hole that somehow loomed in the same position no matter where on the planet you were. A symbolic transformation of a scientific object; he found the juxtaposition poignant, if nothing else.

Regardless, as he sat on the front steps of the church, chewing on what would be his last piece of tasteless clay candy, Creed found himself ruminating on the impossible idea once again.

Should have let the Old Man turn me into a star when He first offered.

Creed wondered offhandedly if he'd gone insane, but decided it wasn't anything quite so dramatic. This must just be what happened to someone when they truly resigned themselves.

Death would be coming for him as soon as It bothered to look, but the fact was he felt more at peace now than he had in a very long time, and the only thing on his mind at that moment was how badly he missed being able to fly.

These meaningless ruminations were interrupted by the arrival of the small pale girl who never seemed to leave him be.

Neveah approached without a word and gently down sat to his left, close enough that it felt uncomfortably familiar for someone who was still technically a stranger.

No. Not quite strangers anymore, I suppose. She's seen more of me than anyone but Stella and the other Samaritans by this point.

"Gimme one."

Creed blinked at the brusque command. He wondered what she was talking about before realizing she could only be referring to his fake candy.

"Could I get a 'please?'"

"Do you really care?" She had yet to look at him.

Creed gave it some thought, then decided he didn't. With a shrug, he reached into his coat, pulled one of the paper sticks from his dwindling supply, and willed a sphere of artificial candy into being. He held it up to the girl, who took it without a word and popped it into her mouth.

"You were right," she said after a few seconds. "These are pretty disappointing."

"Sorry."

"Could you give them flavor if you had those other Colors you told me about?"

"Not really. Even when I had them all, my powers were based around creating things, but I could only give them shape. I wasn't the one who gave them life."

"Who was?"

"God."

"Ah." She sounded far less impressed by such a concept than he would have thought. "Didn't realize you'd had a working relationship with the guy."

Creed almost chuckled. "That's one way to put it."

"Creed... are you an angel?"

Again, the sheer bluntness of her words caught him off guard, but after a moment, he couldn't help letting out a single mirthless chuckle at the question.

"I can see why you might think that. But no. I'm not too far off from one compared to the rest of you, but I don't really count."

"Then who the hell are you?"

For a brief moment, Creed honestly considered telling her who he'd been before The End, but frankly, it seemed like too much trouble at this point. He would be dead soon, and knowing his true identity would do nothing for the girl.

"Sorry," he said aloud. "I'm keeping that to myself. No use complicating things right at the end."

Neveah obviously wasn't satisfied, but didn't push the matter any further, so Creed returned to the original topic.

"That aside, yes, you could say I 'worked' with the Old Man. I couldn't make anything that was fully realized without His power behind it. Once He was gone, that was it."

He pulled the half-finished sucker from his mouth and held it up to his eyeline. "I could make water, but it wouldn't hydrate you. I could make food, but you wouldn't taste it."

"You're telling me we could be eating flavorless pizza instead of flavorless lollipops right now?"

"It's not as appealing as it sounds. The candy works best."

"Fair enough."

Creed wondered at her apparent indifference as he put the sucker back in his mouth. A few run-ins with some demons, and suddenly nothing seemed to impress the girl anymore.

"Truth is," he said, not sure why he was about to share this, "I wasn't even the one who provided the color. The Cores weren't mine originally."

"Whose were they?"

"My wife's."

The confession seemed to hang about him like a specter. Creed had hoped his current resignation might have dulled the pain caused by mention of her, but it still stung as fresh as ever, and he immediately regretted having mentioned.

"Oh," Neveah responded. He couldn't tell if she was surprised to hear that. "Is she—"

"Gone," he interjected quickly. "And that's all I have to say on the subject."

To her credit, the girl was smart enough not to pursue the matter any further, nodding and allowing another silence to overtake them.

She stared up at the black sun as if trying to figure out what he'd been looking for. Creed appreciated the courtesy of not forcing more discussion, but it did occur to him that he owed the girl one last fair warning.

"You really shouldn't be here when the Boss shows up."

"Oh yeah?"

"I mean it. Unless you want your soul taken. If you'd really rather keep on living, letting him meet you is the last thing you want."

"Hm," she mused in a tone that told him she didn't think much of his opinion on that matter. Oh well. She could do what she wanted, he supposed. Her fate was no longer any concern of his.

"What's he want with my soul so badly?" she asked.

"It's his role. Without an afterlife, the souls of Lambs whose bodies get destroyed are left to suffer in the aether. Rictus gathers and holds them inside his being."

"What for?"

"No reason at all. He's got nowhere to put them and no way to help them. It's just all he knows how to do. Joshua says that if ever we manage to bring life back into the world, we'll be glad to have saved them because we can reintroduce them back into the cycle of life, but you already know my opinion on that subject. I suppose it beats getting killed by an angel, at least."

"How so?"

"They aren't concerned with souls. When they kill you, they burn it all away: body, mind, and spirit. No coming back. Ever."

"And that's why your Boss has you fight them? So he can get the souls instead?"

"More or less."

Her brow furrowed in thought. "I don't get it. If he's so powerful that he can force you all to work for him, why not just fight them himself?"

"You noticed that, huh? Truth is, he can't do a thing against angels."

"Why not?"

"Long story. Short version is that when it comes to humans and demons, the Boss has absolute power; nothing with a mortal or corrupted soul can harm It, but *Ii* can do whatever It wants with them."

"And angels don't have souls?"

"Not mortal ones. He can't be killed, but he can't do anything to affect them either. So, he decided to rope in the rest of us to use as meat shields and keep the angels from burning you all away before he can get his hands on you."

She gave another slow nod, taking a moment to mull over his words. "Gotta say, it sounds like there are a lot more ways out of this mess than I thought." She side-eyed him. "So why are you going to that city all the time?"

Of course, he thought. Stella had never been great at keeping secrets.

"Just... paying my respects to the dead." It wasn't a *total* lie, as the grave stakes he'd planted could attest to. But Neveah narrowed her eyes at him, and he realized she'd already caught on to the truth. All she was waiting for was to hear him to say it. He sighed.

Oh well. Why bother hiding things at this point?

He glanced away from her. "Actually... I've been trying to kill myself."

Even Creed was surprised at how easily the admission had come. He looked to the girl for a reaction, but her head was lowered, bangs shifted to cover her eyes. The sucker was motionless in her mouth. Seeing no reason to stop now, he continued:

"Everyone in that city died all at once. No souls left behind. That much death, so much life erased in a single instant, created a... void, I guess you could call it. A concentration of non-existence. To all the other Samaritans, it would be painful, but with the way my powers work, it's a lot more dangerous."

"Is that where all your other colors went?"

Creed nodded at her perceptiveness. "Eight gone in total. My—" he took a moment to get the word out, "my wife gave them to me a long time ago. So that I wouldn't have to use the power I was born with."

"That stuff in the forest."

He clenched his jaw. "Best to forget about that. When I die, it dies too."

An unsatisfying answer, to be sure, but it was all he would give her on that subject. She seemed to understand, and didn't ask after it any further, so he continued:

"Those Cores weren't just my power; they became my soul, and that void in the city is the antithesis of their color. The longer I stayed, the more they drained away, and the weaker I became. By the time you and I met, Malkuth was all I had left. Even that's just about gone now."

Neveah was quiet for some time, deep in thought. Eventually, she said, "Well, that's definitely a creative method of suicide. But why go to all the trouble? It sounds like there's plenty of easier ways to die."

Creed was slightly unnerved by how unaffected she seemed by his confession, but now was the time to lay it all on the table, and if she wanted to make it easier for him, who was he to complain? "It's the only way I can make sure a soul doesn't get left behind."

"What about the angels? You just said they burn everything away."

"Not for Samaritans. Our souls are bound to Rictus. Or the thing *inside* Rictus."

"Meaning?"

"The Preceptor. Once upon a time, Rictus was just a man. The *real* Samaritan used his body as a host. Whenever the rest of us call our true names, we're reverting to our original forms. When Rictus does it, he's just letting *It* take control."

"Spooky."

"The difference is irrelevant at this point; they've been stuck together so long, I don't think they can tell where one ends and the other begins. Point is, we're all tied to It, so unless It's destroyed, there's no killing us. And seeing as that will never happen, we're effectively immortal."

"What about the angels? You said they don't leave anything behind."

"Samaritans are the exceptions. Our souls might as well just be on loan; they don't really belong to us. An angel could burn me to ash, but my spirit would just be drawn into the Preceptor's being like all the rest."

"And you don't want that."

"What I 'want' is a way out. A real one. Spending all of eternity swirling around in that thing's body is just about the worst thing I can think of. By letting the void drain my being away, I could have had a death that was real. Final."

Her voice was barely a whisper now. "Why?"

"Because in a world without time, or death, or change, it was the only choice I could make that would really matter."

The girl still didn't seem inclined to give her thoughts yet, so he decided to finish his confession:

"It's all a moot point now. My idiot brothers came along and took that choice away. There's no version of this story that doesn't end with Rictus getting my soul, so all that's left now is to wait for it."

Finally done, Creed leaned back onto his palms, waiting for whatever the girl had to say. After several long moments, she let out a long breath. She pulled her sucker from her mouth, and Creed saw that she had finished it off.

Tossing the stick to the ground, she declared, "Alright. I've got one more question."

"Shoot."

"Is there anybody left out there?"

"What?" How did that have anything to do with what he'd just told her?

"People," she specified. "Are there any people still out there?"

Creed felt anxious without knowing why, and spoke cautiously.

"There are. Not many, and not in any in numbers that would qualify as civilization. It's mostly lone wanderers like you. Maybe a few scattered groups here and there. Honestly, I have no idea where any of them are anymore. The last time Joshua took a tally, there was about one percent of one percent of you left. And even *that* was a long while ago."

Neveah nodded at his response, still seeming totally inscrutable.

"I see. That's good. To be honest, it's been so long since I've seen anyone that I was afraid I might actually be the last." She gave a humorless chuckle and finally turned to face him with a sad smile. "Pretty full of myself, huh?"

Creed was thinking of a response, but then Neveah stood.

She walked down the steps.

She turned to stand before him.

She punched him in the jaw.

It was quite possibly the weakest blow that had ever struck him. The girl was puny and emaciated, and her bony hand had essentially no force behind it. Even had Creed not been a supernatural entity, he wouldn't have felt a thing.

And yet somehow, he found his head jerking to the side involuntarily, sucker flying from his mouth onto the ground, and the sharp sound of her hand against his cheek echoed so loud that it cut straight down to the core of his being.

The blanket of calm resignation that had enveloped him shattered in an instant, and when he jerked his head back to look at the girl, he was met with a pair of green eyes burning with such a fire that he thought he might ignite on the spot.

"Your brother was right," Neveah declared, her voice like iron in a forge. "You are selfish."

Still reeling from a punch he shouldn't have been reeling from, Creed could only stare as the girl began to berate him.

"One percent of one percent. I don't remember much math anymore, but I'm pretty sure that's at least a few thousand; a few thousand people left in the *whole* world. And only seven who can actually fight. Seven shepherds for a few thousand 'Lambs,' and one of them says he wants to die because it's *too hard*?"

Creed's anger flared. "Who the hell are *you*?" he seethed. "A girl who's never even *seen* an angel, and you think you can stand there and judge me? You have no idea—"

"What? That you can't really beat the angels? That they can't die? Neither can you!"

"But *you* can!" Creed shot back. "And you *do*! Every time! The angels come down, and we beat them back, but they always take a few more of you with them! This was *never* a war we could win! No matter how many of us fight, no matter how often, sooner or later, you'll all be gone!"

"Then why not keep fighting until we are!? We're weak, Creed! Powerless! We can't protect ourselves against God's psycho children! You're one of the only ones who can! Maybe it's useless, but if you have the power to fight, then you have to fight!"

"*I DID FIGHT!!!*"

Creed leaped to his feet and towered over the girl, who shrank back a step beneath his anger. Creed had thought himself beyond such rage, that he had finally resigned himself once and for all. Evidently, he had been wrong.

"I fought, girl! I fought for so long that I couldn't remember a time in my life where I *wasn't* fighting! I played the role I was given! I played the hero! No matter how many of you died, I kept telling the ones who were left to stand behind me, that I would keep them safe! I gathered them in that city and told them I would protect them. I swore I would keep the monsters out so they could at least *pretend* they were living a life with any sort of meaning!

"But it was all a fucking lie! They knew it! I knew it! And when the time came, I couldn't protect a single thing! I made myself out to be some kind of warrior, a champion for the poor remnants of humanity, but in the end, I was just another monster! And now you dare to stand there and call me a coward because you think I didn't *try* hard enough!?"

His voice was breaking. He wasn't capable of crying, but somehow it sounded as if he was choked with tears.

"I killed them..." he rasped, his gaze involuntarily leaving the girl and staring into nothing as memories overtook him. "I killed... my children. They trusted me. And I killed every single one of them!"

Coming back to himself, he fixed Neveah with what he hoped was a spiteful gaze, but suspected it was far more pathetic than that.

"This world has no future, Neveah. This story has no end! The last page was ripped out and burned! How long can I be expected to fight against that kind of madness? Huh!? Tell me! What am I supposed to do against that!?"

"*YOU'RE SUPPOSED TO LIVE!!!*"

Her shout was so forceful that Creed found himself taking a step back without meaning to. He had thought the girl cowed by his rage. Once again, he had been wrong; her eyes shone brighter than ever, and her tone grew fiercer with each word.

"You said that in a world without an afterlife, choosing to die is the only choice that matters! But that's wrong! In a world like this, *living* is the only thing that could possibly matter! If everything *is* meaningless, and death is really the end of it all, then how could staying alive not be the single bravest thing someone could do!?"

The girl took a step forward, and again Creed took one back.

"It's the hardest choice anyone could make..." Without looking away, she pointed a finger behind her out into the horizon. "...but *they're* all making it. Thousands of people are choosing to stay alive despite the world itself telling them they should die! Even though it would be easy to let go!

"You said it yourself! If anyone wants to die, all they have to do is pray, and the angels will burn them! All they have to do is find your Boss, and he'll reap their souls! But they haven't! They've been holding on because they know the life they have left is all there is!"

Another step forward. Another step back.

"Stryfe said you were old even before the end of the world. That may be true, but those few thousand people have been living in the dead world just as long as you. Even though they're weak! Even though they're powerless! Even though most of them probably never understood why any of this happened in the first place! If even a *single* one of those people still has the will to live, how can you stand there and say you have *any* right to give up and die? *TELL ME!!!*"

One final step forward. One final step back. Creed felt his heel catch on the bottom stair behind him, and before he even realized it, he had fallen. The wooden steps dug into his back, and he could do nothing but stare up at the girl who now loomed over him.

Try as he might, he could not seem to get his breath under control. Even after all he had seen, Creed found that he feared nothing in the world half as much this slip of a girl whose green eyes pierced down into the very core of his being. He had been utterly defeated. Again.

Watching him on the ground beneath her, Neveah softened her gaze. Righteous anger was replaced not with pity but immense sadness, and not one bit of it was false.

"I'm sorry," she choked out. She had managed to hold back her tears when he threatened to destroy her seeds in the valley, but now they fell freely down her cheeks.

"I would take your role if I could. Any of those thousands of people would, I think. But we can't. It has to be you. I know it's not fair, but it *has* to be you. You *have* to make the choice. You *have* to live!"

Creed's voice trembled as he spoke. "Why do you care? Why do you care about any of us? You're strong. Stronger than any Samaritan. Why can't you just leave it all alone?"

"I don't know," she admitted, and her voice began to break even more so than his own. "I really don't. I don't know why I think I have any place among angels and demons and Samaritans. All I know is that I have done nothing but wander through an empty world with my head down for as long as I can remember. I never looked up to see what was happening, not once. But ever since you found me sleeping in those flowers, I've felt like I'm really awake for the first time! And no matter how pointless it all seems, I just can't leave. I can't go back to what I was before."

"I can't be what you need me to be," Creed declared once again. "It's too much. And I have nothing left... I can't make myself believe anymore...."

The girl was almost unintelligible through her tears now. "That's okay! If you can't go any further, I'll grab your hand and pull you forward! Everyone else will get behind you and push! You say you were pretending to be a hero before, but you don't have to be one again. All you have to do is *choose* to keep living. That's enough. I *promise* that's enough."

Creed's mouth was dry, and speaking was proving to be nearly impossible. "How... how do I know if I can?"

Neveah took a long, shaky breath to calm herself, though the tears still fell.

"It's okay," she repeated. "You don't have to do it all at once. You can start small." Standing up straighter, she held out a hand.

"And if you can't believe in yourself, start by believing in me."

Creed was unable to move for the longest time. At this moment, there was nothing in the entire world but the girl standing before him. She seemed so large that he might be swallowed up, so bright he might burn away.

But eventually, for reasons he couldn't even begin to fathom, Creed realized that he wanted nothing more than to take her hand.

So he did.

As she grasped Creed's leather-gloved hand in her own, Neveah felt confident that even with her foggy memory, this was the most important moment of her life.

As such, she felt incredibly embarrassed when she tried to pull the man to his feet and he didn't budge.

Oh. Right. He's six feet tall and I'm malnourished.

Luckily, Creed seemed to remember that he was a supernatural being after Neveah's second tug and swiftly pulled himself to his feet before she embarrassed herself further.

Choosing to ignore what had just happened so as not to ruin the beautiful moment, Neveah just gave as warm a smile as she could and squeezed Creed's hand tighter, using her free hand to wipe the hot tears that still stained her cheeks.

"So..." she began, before realizing she was still gripping Creed's hand and letting go a bit more quickly than she intended. "What are you gonna do first?"

Creed's breathing had steadied, but he still seemed half-dazed as he spoke. "I, uh... I guess should deal with my brothers."

She noticed a dark cloud come over his face at the very thought. "C'mon," she insisted. "It'll be alright."

"I... don't know." He had mostly composed himself by now, but Neveah could see a new fragility in his eyes. He had been as far to the edge as one could be, only to pull himself back at the very last instant; that wasn't something he would recover from quickly.

"You may not have to fight. Joshua thinks you can avoid it, at least."

"Joshua's thinks he's an optimist. He's just in denial. Things have gone too far between us. One way or another, this ends in a fight." He looked down at his hands, expression downcast. "And Stryfe was right. I don't stand a chance like this."

As much as she disliked it, part of Neveah felt he was right. But even so, if he was going to start over, she'd rather it not be with killing his own brother, even if that brother *was* a lying demon asshole.

"One more try," she declared.

Creed furrowed his brow. "What?"

"One more try. We'll go together. We'll try and talk. And if you *do* have to fight, then you fight. But I think you have to give it one last chance."

Creed regarded her for a moment before looking again in the direction of the city far out of sight. He took several slow steps past Neveah, lost in some kind of thought. He looked again at his hands, then back to the horizon, and finally back over his shoulder to Neveah. For the first time since she'd met him, he looked genuinely determined.

"One more try."

Neveah smiled at his response, then noticed his gaze had shifted to something behind her. Turning, she beheld Stella standing stock-still at the threshold of the church.

Her eyes were fixed on Creed, expression the same as usual save her lips being parted ever so slightly. Perhaps her equivalent of surprise? Neveah felt an immediate rush of shame shoot through her as she realized she had forgotten about the nun entirely.

"Oh!" she called, her voice an octave higher. "Sorry, Stella... Did you, uh... did you catch all that just now?"

The older woman turned to look at her. "Your conversation was thirty feet away, and most of it was shouting."

"Right..." Neveah hoped the dimness of the entire world was enough to hide how red her face was.

Creed walked past her, climbing the steps and standing only a few paces away from Stella. They regarded each other for a time, and Neveah decided to stay silent for now.

"You're going?" Stella asked.

Creed gave a solemn nod. "I have to."

"You'll die. The void will make you even weaker."

"Don't worry. I know what to do now."

Stella's eyes flicked between Creed, Neveah, and the direction of the city a few times. "Creed—"

"Don't."

"I can't stay behind again."

"You have to. Please."

She motioned to Neveah. "You're taking her."

"It's different, and you know it."

"I can at least protect her."

"Joshua will take care of that. You can't intervene in this, Stella."

"I *cannot* stay behind again. You know that I can help, even if I have to—"

"*Stella!*"

Creed quickly closed the distance between them and clasped one of the woman's hands in both of his. Her mouth opened slightly once more, and her eyes grew wider as Creed brought his face in close, his expression deathly serious.

"You told me that you didn't want to be a weapon anymore. It was the first thing you ever wished for yourself. And I promised that I would never let it happen again." He drew her hands closer to his chest, near his heart. "Please. I have to know you're here waiting."

The two of them stayed just like that, almost long enough for Neveah to start feeling uncomfortable, when Stella finally looked to the ground and gave a short nod. Satisfied, Creed released her hand and stepped back. Stella clasped her hands again, still looking down, and Neveah felt a pang of sadness for her.

"Stella!" she called out. "Don't worry! I'll be there to keep him in line! And when we get back, let's make another dress together!"

Neveah couldn't quite read the nun's reaction from where she was, but she did receive a rather emphatic nod in response.

Still atop the steps, Creed turned around to look down at Neveah.

"For the record, I'd rather you stay behind, too."

"Oh yeah?" Neveah replied in a mockingly high-pitched voice.

Creed's shoulders slumped. "That's what I thought. Don't blame me when a demon eats your heart."

"Fair enough."

Turning around, Creed regarded Stella one last time. "I swear we'll be back."

The nun was still for a long moment but eventually unclasped her hands. "I know you will."

There was more emotion behind the words than Neveah had yet heard from the strange woman. Returning the nod, Creed finally turned and made his way down the steps, shooting Neveah an aside glance as he passed her.

"Let's get this over with."

Not quite the confidence she'd hoped for, but it would have to do. She moved to follow him but was briefly distracted as a small, white shape flashed past her head from behind. Blinking in surprise, she caught sight of the Dove sailing away over a hill towards the city. She scoffed, and fell into step behind Creed as they began their trek along the dirt path.

Like I needed you to tell me that, bird.

Chapter XVI
"The Man Who Sold the World"

The one good thing about a world where time didn't matter, Joshua mused, was that it was difficult to notice how long you had to wait for certain things. As he allowed his consciousness to drift across the world, he had no earthly idea how much time had passed.

At the moment, he was observing Rictus in his realm between worlds, still wandering the endless twilight in search of lost souls. But Joshua had noticed a slowing in the Boss' steps, an occasional twitch that indicated a distraction with other things. It wouldn't be long before the Preceptor sleeping inside him remembered the game It had initiated and turned Its gaze to observe their progress.

If It looked now, the results would not be pleasant for anyone.

When a twitch at the back of his mind finally alerted him to the arrival of someone else, Joshua was exceptionally grateful. Snapping back to the physical plane, he rose from his psychically-created chair and turned to detect the shape of Creed leaping down from the edge crater far in the distance. The smaller aura close to his chest told Joshua that Neveah was in his brother's arms.

"How lovely," came a voice from behind, and Joshua sensed Stryfe sitting up in his chair, his illusory head-wound presumably gone without a trace.

Ignoring the childish demon, Joshua continued to observe Creed's distant aura drawing ever closer, as well as that of Neveah now walking alongside him. He wasn't quite sure why Creed had thought it was a good idea to bring her along, but had a feeling it would end up being the right call.

At the moment, the girl's aura was a mix of anticipation and curiosity. Joshua could feel her looking around, and he supposed she was looking at the large field of clay stakes they were navigating.

Joshua had felt the graves earlier as he'd entered the crater, and once he'd realized what they were, he'd been overwhelmed by a profound combination of both pride and sorrow for his brother who had placed them.

Unable to avoid prying, Joshua psychically enhanced his hearing such that even at so great a distance, he could hear the approaching duo speak as if they were right next to him.

"You... placed all of these yourself?" Neveah was asking.

Creed's voice responded, "I did."

"They don't have names on them."

"I know whose is whose. Didn't think anyone else would ever see them."

"Why do it at all?"

"Someone had to remember."

"Wow," there was a beat, then Neveah's tone turned teasing, "So you're telling me that after all that grief you gave me about how pointless my seeds were, you've been out here planting graves?"

There was a pause. "It's... different."

"Putting things in the ground even though you think there's no point?"

"The difference is that unlike you, I don't expect anything to come of it someday."

A small silence fell between them, and Joshua felt a quick flush of emotion in Creed's aura. Was that... shame?

"Sorry," his brother finally said. "Guess you can add 'hypocrite' to my list."

"It's okay," Neveah responded, and her aura felt genuinely unbothered. "It's very human of you."

Creed's aura flashed with surprise, and Joshua heard him actually let out a dry chuckle, which nearly caused him to fall over in shock.

Their conversation ended there, and once Joshua got over his surprise, a grin tugged at the corner of his mouth. When he'd left Creed back at the church, the man's spirit had been so small and tattered that he might as well have already been dead. His aura didn't necessarily feel stronger now—it still flickered and wavered against the pervasive pull of the void sleeping beneath the crater—but there was most certainly *something* there that hadn't been before.

Good work, Neveah. I knew you could do it.

Trying his hardest to look confident, Joshua waited as Creed and Neveah finished crossing the blasted landscape. When they drew near enough, he jogged the remaining distance to greet them, fixing Creed with what he hoped was a brotherly smile.

"Glad you could make it." He thumbed over his shoulder to Stryfe behind him. "You'll never believe it, but this one's been a pain."

"It's about to get worse," was all Creed said. In addition to his aura, Joshua could also hear the change in Creed's voice. A firmness that he hadn't heard in quite some time.

Before he could comment on it, Creed was stepping past him, marching towards the place where Stryfe lounged, presumably smirking. Joshua glanced down at Neveah, whose aura was shining like fire as always. He felt her look up at him, and he tried to give her a smile he hoped wasn't too nervous.

"Good to see you. Think you might regret tagging along, though."

"Maybe."

He admired her bravery, if not her survival instincts. "What did you say to him?"

"Nothing much. Just asked him to try one last time."

Joshua nodded. He was sure there'd been more to it than that, but whatever she'd done had probably meant far more than she realized.

"Let's hope he makes it a good one."

Creed met Stryfe's mocking crimson eyes and sickening smile without flinching. However this was going to end, he would not give this monster the satisfaction of seeing his weakness ever again. The demon, for his part, looked thrilled to see him.

"I just *knew* you wouldn't let me down, brother!"

Glancing behind Creed, he gave a wink to Neveah at Joshua's side. "Hello, Little Lamb!"

"Asshole!" the girl called out. Creed was thoroughly impressed, even if she did duck behind Joshua when she said it.

Stryfe seemed to get a kick out of it, a dangerous toothy grin spreading across his features. "Oh my. Could it be I actually *do* like her?"

"Stryfe," Creed stated as plainly as he could. There was no longer time for any games. "Congratulations. You got me here." He gave a casual shrug. "Now what?"

"Must I really explain that again?"

"Why do we have to fight?".

Stryfe's falsely chipper demeanor vanished in an instant, the grin falling away.

"You *must* be joking." The demon seemed positively incensed at Creed's words, and pointed to Joshua behind him. "Did this worthless coward get into your head? Could you *possibly* be trying to weasel your way out of this?"

"I didn't ask *if* we had to fight. Just *why*. What's the reason?"

Stryfe let out a scoff as if it were the most absurd question. He waved his black-stained fingers at the desolate world around them. "Did you *need* more of a reason?"

"You didn't destroy the world, Stryfe. The Beast did."

The demon's hollow-cheeked face clouded over with the first genuine anger Creed had seen, red eyes glowing dangerously against black sclerae.

"Sins of the father, Creed. But fine. If you'd like a more personal reason, why not take in a deep breath of the air around you?"

Creed didn't have to. The void had been grasping at his spirit since the moment he'd entered the city. Neveah had been quite upset when he nearly collapsed at one point, but he'd composed himself since then. It still pained him, but he wouldn't let Stryfe see that.

"All those poor souls," the demon continued. "Not a piece left behind, save for their stains upon the ground. In fact—" he lazily tapped a heel on the ash-black soil beneath them, "—there's more left of Michael here than any of them, isn't there? And at least his soul got to fly back into the heavens after you seared his flesh into the earth!"

He bared his teeth at Creed, and they were shaped like fangs. "You nearly killed me after what happened then, you know. Haven't you been dying for a chance to finish the job?"

Creed was impressed at how well he was keeping his own temper in check thus far. "Alright. That's why *I* have to kill *you*. Why do *you* have to kill *me*?"

"I tire of whatever game this is you're playing, brother."

"Answer the fucking question."

The demon glared for another moment. "Fine."

He rose from the black throne and held out his arms, palms up.

"I want a fair fight."

There it was. The worst answer he could have given. The pettiest, most banal response Creed possibly could have expected.

"'A fair fight,'" he parroted, unable to keep the disgust from his voice.

Stryfe sneered. "Do not be so quick to judge! It matters more than you think!"

With hate in his gaze, Stryfe began to pace back and forth, like a preacher delivering a sermon.

"There was a reckoning to be had at The End! All were to be judged; all made to account. But it was a farce! While all the Lambs were to be cleansed by the fire, my sentence had already been passed! I was destined to be weighed and found wanting! Defeat was the only reckoning allowed to me! The deck was stacked against me from the very start, and the moment I tried leveling the playing field, it all buckled under the weight! But do you want to know something?"

He stopped pacing and fixed them all with a manic stare, eyes practically glowing in the dimness. "I *love* this world!"

The declaration was so insane that nobody present was capable of responding to it, so the demon continued unabated:

"You see a world with no future? I see one where my fate hasn't been decided since the dawn of time! I see a world where I can be whatever I choose to be, not what others decide that I am *meant* to be! A world where I am not propped up as the scapegoat for all mankind's evil just so my Father can justify the salvation of *His* flawed creations!"

"Holy shit," Creed heard Neveah's stunned whisper from behind. "It really *is* him…"

Stryfe hissed like a serpent at the girl's words. "Oh, she *is* a bright one!"

"Keep talking," Creed ordered. He didn't want one iota of the demon's attention on the girl in this increasingly rabid state. Luckily, Stryfe seemed more than inclined to continue ranting.

"In this world, there *are* no reckonings! No justice! No damnation! No judgment! No resolutions," he held up a single blackened finger, "save one! There's still one last story you and I can write, brother. One last ending we can reach! I have been your enemy since the day you were born, but only *now* can our feud be settled!"

Stryfe placed a hand over his heart, looking down at himself. "I've finally gathered all of my children together again. After so very, *very* long, I have earned the fight that was denied to me: a *real* fight, a *fair* fight! One I haven't already been ordained to lose!"

His grimace expanded into a psychotic smile that sent a chill down Creed's spine.

"And you know something? If killing you is half as fun as I think it's going to be, why stop there? Perhaps I'll take on Joshua next? Perhaps *all* the Samaritans! Or perhaps I'll just let these monsters inside me loose again to finish off what's left out there! The Preceptor will tear me to pieces, of course, but how many of Its precious little Lambs will pay the price?"

He lifted his head to the sky and raised his arms as if to embrace the black sun above.

"AND WHY SHOULDN'T THEY!?" he screamed, his true legion voice breaking through. "This world was made for something like me, so why not *ENJOY IT*!?"

With that, the tirade came to an end, and all any of them could do was gape at the sheer depths of the Devil's madness.

Taking a few quiet breaths to steady himself, Creed turned over his shoulder to his companions. Joshua stood in place, head bowed and face obscured by blindfold and hair. At his side was Neveah, wide-eyed and almost as pale as when Samael had nearly destroyed her.

"Joshua," Creed called. "Is that enough for you?"

His little brother raised his head slowly, and Creed saw nothing but regret and sorrow. He gave a slow nod, granting his long-overdue assent; Creed felt not an ounce of satisfaction in receiving it.

Turning back to Stryfe, he set his jaw and looked directly into the demon's asymmetrical eyes. "I guess that's that."

Stryfe's insane disposition seemed to reel itself in slightly at Creed's words, his smile reverting from insane back to smug, his eyes from manic to mocking.

"Just wanted to make sure I got the point across."

Holding out his right hand, Creed flared his Malkuth Core and molded a clay spear into his grasp. He did not level it at his opponent, instead holding it straight like a staff. Stryfe regarded the weapon with amusement.

"That reminds me. I'm still wondering how precisely it is you think you're going to be putting up any sort of a fight as you are now? Even if we weren't right in the middle of your greatest weakness, I don't quite see you standing a chance with stone and dust!"

Creed wasn't listening to the taunts. He had already closed his eyes, head bowed and freehand clenched. He proceeded to reach deep into his own soul, further than he could ever remember going.

Even now, he was shocked at how little was left; he had indeed been at the furthest end of his rope. But there was still something there: eight shells, each one so dull and cold that they seemed like they might not even exist.

But the truth was they had never really been gone. He had simply allowed them to be drained from his soul by void he himself had created through his failure. The colors were still there, hidden in the abyss and smothered by the unrelenting mire of death he'd left behind.

Opening his eyes, Creed turned over his shoulder to look at Neveah. The girl was still pale, but when she met Creed's gaze with her own, there was no fear in her eyes. She gave him an encouraging nod, which he returned before turning back.

This time, when he felt the brittle shells, he took a firm grasp upon them, no longer afraid that they would shatter. The gifts his wife had given him could never be so fragile.

At the same time, he turned his consciousness to face the unrelenting presence that permeated the crater. Its energy yawned before him like the black hole sun itself, begging him to give up and fall into its depths forevermore. Creed stared back, forcing himself not to blink, and reached his will into the darkness to grab hold of what he'd let it take from him.

With all of his might, Creed wrenched his lost Cores out from the depths of the void. As they broke the surface, he implored them to return to the shells that had been left behind within him. He felt their myriad flames ignite, and opened his eyes wide as the Colors burst forth.

One last try.

Neveah was unprepared for the brilliant light that burst from Creed's person, and instinctively averted her gaze. Recovering her bearings, she forced her eyes open.

A whirlwind of myriad colors now flowed off of Creed's form, twisting around and about him like ribbons of iridescent paint. After a few moments, the ribbons focused and coalesced in the air behind Creed, condensing into a total of nine small spheres, each a different color: red, blue, green, yellow, orange, pink, purple, grey, and brown. They hung suspended in a perfect circle just behind his back like a small, colorful solar system.

In his hand, Creed still grasped the clay spear, which now seemed to be cleaner and brighter than it had before. Creed himself looked far more vibrant as well; his white hair, once sickly-looking, was now pure as the driven snow, and his faded navy coat was as deep a blue as flawless sapphire.

The saturation of color seemed to extend outwards from Creed's body to enliven the world around him; even the dirt stained by the ashen imprint of the dead angel beneath his feet was a deeper and darker shade of black.

Looking down at herself, Neveah was startled to see that even *she* was affected. Her normally pallid skin looked flushed and healthy, her patchwork dress was stainless and bright, and her stringy pale hair practically shimmered.

Turning, she saw that the landscape far behind them was still as dull as always, and realized that only the space around Creed had been enriched; he was literally *radiating* color.

To her right, Joshua—just as bright and brilliant as herself—beheld his brother with unseeing eyes, a truly joyous smile across his features.

"It was still there," he whispered, as if he hadn't truly believed it until now.

A psychotic laugh ripped through the air and tore the beautiful moment to pieces. Neveah narrowed her eyes as Stryfe reeled back in delight, cackling like a madman.

"I KNEW IT! I knew you still had it in you, brother! Oh, it's just as beautiful as I remember!"

The devil hunched forward, panting like a dog in heat.

"I don't think I can wait a second longer!"

With that, Stryfe took several steps back towards his obsidian throne. As he did, his body appeared to blacken and burn as it had back in the forest, the charred flesh cracking and falling away to reveal another body underneath. By the time he settled back into his throne, his appearance was a distorted version of what it had been.

His facial features seemed mostly unchanged, but the rest of his appearance was far more demented. His hair was still swept back, but it was now wilder and more unkempt, changed from dirty blonde to a garishly-bright red. His face was painted with a positively clownish amount of blush, eye-shadow, and ruby-red lipstick.

Despite the changes, Neveah noted that his eyes were still the same bright, asymmetrical crimson they had been before, and that the three-hooked brand remained emblazoned upon his forehead.

His outfit had shifted into an equally showy new form. He now wore a leather jumpsuit, unzipped to expose most of his pale chest. Vertical stripes of bright red and green raced down the length of the suit, stopping at a pair of knee-high red boots with absurd platform soles providing several extra inches of height. A pair of large yellow pads adorned his shoulders, and an equally oversized collar of the same shade completed the ostentatious look.

The jumpsuit was unzipped enough to expose almost all of the demon's pale chest, and Neveah could see several tattoos emblazoned on his flesh, all blood-red and in the shape of a star. She could see similar markings on the back of each of his hands, his left cheek, and an especially large one stamped onto his right eye.

All in all, the demon now resembled some kind of glamorous harlequin. In another context, Neveah might have laughed at how utterly gaudy the demon now looked, but the sheer absurdity of the change made it seem far more frightening than humorous.

Settling into his throne, Stryfe let out a sigh and bared his flawless white teeth in a smile utterly devoid of what little sanity had been present in his previous visage.

"Ready!" he called in a gleeful, almost childlike voice that unnerved something deep inside Neveah's being.

Beside her, Joshua let out an utterly exasperated sigh. "It's Ziggy, isn't it?"

Creed didn't bother to entertain the question, but looked just as repulsed by Stryfe's new form as he had the first.

"Get her out of here," he ordered.

"Fair enough!" Joshua put a hand on Neveah's shoulder and looked at her with a smile, though she could tell he was just as anxious as her. "Let's find better seats!"

Space warped around Neveah, and when she became aware of herself again, she was standing back at the edge of the crater, far from where Creed's fight was beginning.

Looking down, she saw that she was once again as dull as the rest of the world. She felt a pang of regret at the sight, but knew that getting far away from this battle was the right choice.

At the center of the crater, she could still see the large swathe of color and light that Creed was radiating, as well as the vibrant spheres floating behind him. If nothing else, it would make the battle easy to see.

Joshua put a protective hand on her shoulder. "Whatever happens, don't leave my side."

"Wasn't planning to," she responded, keeping her eyes on Creed.

She wouldn't tremble or look away this time. She was stronger now, and so was Creed. She would bear witness to this fight, and she would do it without flinching.

Then the hundred-foot-long fish sprung out of the ground, and Neveah realized she was entirely unprepared for the madness she was about to see.

Chapter XVII
"Black Sabbath"

Despite the severity of the situation, Creed struggled to maintain his composure against the power that now thrummed within him. The familiar sensation of the colors he'd ripped back from the void coursed through his veins like lightning, bringing the world around him into sharp focus and heightening his senses to levels he'd forgotten he possessed. Though he could still feel the presence of the void around him, its icy grip was dulled by the warmth of the nine Cores floating behind him.

For quite possibly the first time since the end of the world, Creed felt strong.

As soon as Joshua and Neveah warped away, Creed took his clay spear in one hand and aimed it in Stryfe's direction. His other hand reached up to the zipper of his coat and pulled the garment open to allow for wider movement, just as he had against the previous devils he'd fought.

Stryfe, sitting across from him in a form just as disrespectful as his first, did not seem the least bit intimidated by Creed's recovered power. In fact, the Devil appeared downright thrilled, scarlet eyes gleaming like a hungry predator.

"Before we begin," he began, posh accent now touched by the uneven trembling of barely-contained lunacy, "should you do something about these little graves of yours?"

Creed spared a glance at the field of clay markers throughout the crater floor. "What do you care?"

The demon gave spiteful smile, emphasized by the crimson lipstick he now wore.

"Come now. I can't have you falling down in tears if I were to *accidentally* break them..."

An obvious taunt, but Creed refused to be goaded. In truth, he'd already considered the graves.

Let's see how much I was able to get back.

Extending an arm, Creed opened his hand and turned his palm to face the ground, then called upon the Malkuth Core. Though he had never lost this particular power, the speed and intensity with which it responded now was entirely different from before. He felt a warmth on his back as the umber sphere behind him flared with newly enhanced strength.

With a thought, Creed expanded his will across the entire breadth of the crater, encompassing the countless clay stakes in his thoughts. Despite their number, Creed could feel each of the markers as if he was grasping them individually.

As he did, familiar names flashed through his head: Elizabeth, Adrian, Zidane, Gideon, and so many others. A mere fraction of all the lives he had failed to save in his eternal life.

Once the graves were in his mental grasp, Creed lowered his outstretched hand towards the ground. As he did, the myriad stakes throughout the crater began to sink into the dirt, pressed by some unseen force. In truth, Creed was *pulling* on them, gently dragging them beneath the earth. Deeper and deeper he sent them, until he had buried them far enough below that he was certain they were at no risk of being harmed by the battle to come.

Relaxing his "grip", Creed allowed Malkuth to dim. The crater floor was devoid of the clay graveyard he had planted, now occupied only by himself, Stryfe, and the ashen remains of the archangel Michael.

Stryfe seemed to recognize the implications of how easily Creed had performed this feat, grinning all the wider.

"Not bad at all, little brother. You really *were* choosing to be weak, weren't you?"

That wasn't entirely correct. It was true that Creed had willingly allowed the void to drain him of most of his power, but it wasn't as if he could have simply called all of his Colors back any time he'd wished. The only reason it happened now was because, thanks to the meddling of one stubborn Lamb, Creed had finally regained the determination to do so.

Of course, he had no desire to explain any of this to Stryfe. Returning his full attention to the demon, all he said was, "Won't know for sure until I cut that stolen face off your neck."

Stryfe barked out a laugh. "Agreed! Show me what this new lust for life of yours is worth!"

The Devil raised his left hand, on the back of which was emblazoned one of the several dark red stars that adorned his body. Using his enhanced vision, Creed saw that the inside of the star was not filled with solid ink, but rather a densely-packed mass of twisted, unintelligible letters. It had been quite some time since Creed had lain eyes on the unholy crimson script of devil-kind, but the sight still filled him with instinctive dread.

The star on Stryfe's hand began to glow a brighter shade of crimson, and Creed felt a spike of dark power so sharp it nearly took his breath away. In a light-hearted tone that belied the monster beneath, Stryfe declared:

"⁊℈⊐⊽⊐, Bahamut!"

In an instant, Creed was leaping backward, his re-found strength carrying him dozens of feet away in a single backflip. The nine spheres at his back followed his every movement.

He landed far from Stryfe just in time to see a vortex of blue flame erupt from the ground behind his obsidian throne. The fire twisted and coiled its way more than a hundred feet in the air before solidifying and coalescing into the shape of an utterly titanic fish.

Its gargantuan body was covered from head-to-tail in flawless blue scales that shimmered in the pale silver light of the black sun. Its massive head resembled that of a dragon more than a fish, sporting three sets of mouths layered one atop the other, each filled with rows of jagged fangs. Six black fins extended from the creature's sides, not entirely unlike the feathered wings which had adorned Michael. A massive, finned tail swished back and forth as it loomed over the crater, suspended as if floating in unseen water.

Bahamut: most powerful of all sea monsters and ruler of the ocean's darkest depths. Stryfe was wasting no time going all out, it seemed.

And yet, despite the absurd stature of this first foe, Creed felt no fear as he faced the beast. For the first time in ages, he was himself again; he had been hunting demons since the world was young, and today would be no different.

Bahamut seemed as eager to begin as Creed. The lowest of its three mouths opened wide and let loose a shriek that shook the earth and rattled Creed's bones. A torrent of tainted black water spilled from the sea serpent's mouth, gathering into a massive sphere before its maw.

From this sphere burst forth dozens of long, thin streams that rocketed their way down to where Creed stood. As they drew closer, he saw that each stream was shaped like a smaller version of Bahamut itself.

He was ready. The storm of watery serpents crashed into the earth like javelins, each seeking to smash Creed into paste. But he was already evading with a series of lightning-fast backflips and cartwheels.

Each attack pierced into the earth with enough force to shatter the rock, but none landed a blow on Creed's form. He was moving too quickly to see where the attacks were coming with his eyes, but his senses told him where each one would land just before it did so.

The water itself seemed to be alive. Each torrent twisted and adjusted its aim, attempting to out-maneuver Creed's agility. They pierced into the earth around him in all directions, trying to close him in and limit his movement. Space to maneuver was quickly disappearing.

Hanging in the air after an exceptionally high leap, Creed swung his spear towards the wall of geysers. His strike clove through them like vines in a jungle. The water burst, and the moment Creed's feet reached the ground, he was dashing through the opening he had made.

In the brief window of time he had, Creed willed his spear to change shape into a large, deadly scythe. Its blade was nearly as long as Creed was tall, and its handle twice that length, but Creed did not find the weapon unwieldy.

Just as he had against Adrammelech, he reached inward and called forth the power of Netzach, the Silver Core. The scythe shifted from clay to a bright, lustrous steel, and Creed imbued it with the ability to cut through any substance on Earth.

He gripped the weapon in both hands and hefted it over his shoulder like an axe. As the rain of serpents fell around him again, he began to cut.

The weight of the massive weapon carried his blows into a series of spins. He carved through the incoming geysers before they could reach him, feeling like a farmer as he scythed through them like a field of wheat. His feet remained planted on the ground, inhuman strength allowing him to dash back and forth at insane speeds to prevent his attackers from getting a bead on him.

The flood seemed never-ending. The water-serpents were coming faster. Their numbers increased, as did the force of their impacts. Before long, Creed was surrounded once again. Deciding he'd had enough, he crouched down and brought his body in as tightly as he could.

The scythe in his arms warped, changing into a whip that coiled around Creed's body like liquid mercury. The whip was far longer and sharper than the one he'd used against Adrammelech, and rather than a single segment, he had split this one off into nine separate lashes. With as much force as he could muster, he brought his body into one last spin.

The nine-pronged whip shot out like a whirlwind, carving through the geysers around him all at once. The wall of water burst outward in all directions, and Creed brought his spin to a stop as the scattered black liquid rained down upon him. The tainted fluid stung his flesh, but otherwise did no harm.

Looking upward, Creed saw Bahamut floating above him. The sphere of water still hung in the air, its volume unchanged despite all the geysers that had sprung from it. Creed noticed the sphere was beginning to rotate, picking up speed until it became a whirling globe.

The monster was about to *launch* the damn thing at him.

Letting go of his whip, Creed willed the weapon to transform once again. It grew in size, elongating and widening into a hollowed, cylindrical shape. When it finished, there was now a colossal cannon floating beside him, its barrel nearly six feet wide and three times as long.

Placing a hand on the floating firearm, Creed reached inside and called upon a third power: Binah, the Amber Core. He felt a sharp warmth as the orange sphere at his back flared with his will.

Creed's hand began to glow with auburn light, which he promptly forced into the cannon beneath his fingertips. In his mind, he saw the image of a small sun, a corona of molten flame so immense in the magnitude of its heat that it would burn anything to less than ashes. This image took physical shape within the barrel of his cannon, which started to glow white-hot from the energy building inside.

By now, Bahamut's sphere of water was spinning so quickly that it appeared to be smooth and still. With a shriek from all three of its mouths, the serpent let loose its attack. The sphere shot toward Creed like a comet, propelled with enough force to turn him and everything behind him into dust. But Creed was not afraid.

Just as it seemed his silver cannon would burst from the gathering heat, Creed allowed the projectile of Binah's flame within to be released. It launched from the weapon's barrel at a speed many times that of sound, rocketing forth to meet the oncoming attack. Bahamut's globe was much greater in size, but Creed had made sure his would be the stronger of the two.

The moment his bullet made contact with the sphere, all of the water vaporized, reduced to a ring of steam that burst outward from the force. The miniature sun continued its path unimpeded, streaking into the air until it collided with its proper target. Bahamut had no time to even make a sound before the missile made contact and its entire head was consumed in an explosion of white light.

For a moment, Creed was blinded. A split second later, he heard the thunderous crack of the blast as it tore through the air with a wave of heat that threatened to peel away his own flesh.

When the light cleared and his vision returned, there was little more than a pillar of ash and smoke where Bahamut's head had been. The rest of its vast body hung suspended in the air for a few moments more, all six fins having gone still. Then, the mighty fish's form wavered and crashed back down to the earth, at which point it burst into a cloud of dust and faded away completely.

If Creed had bothered to count numerical time, it would have been about ninety seconds since the demon had launched its first attack. He allowed himself an exhalation of breath as Binah's sphere cooled behind him, but did not relax his guard.

The ashes of Bahamut dispersed to reveal Stryfe, completely unharmed, awarding him with uproarious applause from upon his throne.

"Marvelous!" The demon called, practically bouncing in his seat. Despite the distance between them, Creed could hear his voice as if it were right in his ear. "You haven't lost a single step!"

The clapping stopped, and Stryfe seemed go limp, letting out a sigh of pleasure as if he were coming down from a high. "But be honest! You're still not at your best, are you?"

Creed didn't bother denying it. His lost Cores were responding once again, but the ever-present sensation of the void was not gone. It choked the air around him, threatening to drain his power just as soon as he had regained it. His colors were keeping it at bay for now, but Creed knew it would only grow worse as the fight dragged on.

"As for myself," Stryfe continued, "I haven't fully recovered either!" He motioned to himself, indicating the stars that scrawled his flesh. "I managed to dress myself with a few of my favorite darlings, but I don't believe I have it in me to call more than this! That being the case, why don't we set up a little game to see that this ends before we both give out?"

Stryfe held up his left hand, showing Creed the star he had used to summon Bahamut; rather than crimson, the letters were now faded and black like dried ink.

"You've already beaten one! Overcome the rest, and I'll have nothing left! Yours for the taking!"

"Or I could just kill you now!"

Stryfe laughed at the taunt. "You know, I thought you might say something like that!" As he spoke, another string of letters on his chest began to glow.

"𐤀𐤁𐤂𐤃, Baphomet!"

In a burst of black fire, a second demon materialized in front of Stryfe's throne. It had the body of a man, emaciated and ugly. Its face was that of a goat's, complete two vicious horns curling from its head. A pair of thin, black wings like those of a rotting crow extended from its back.

The Baphomet sat cross-legged in the dirt before its master, bringing its hands together in a sick imitation of prayer. It began to speak in a horrible, unintelligible language that seemed to tear at the inside of Creed's head. As it did, a dome of demonic energy sprung up to encase both the Baphomet and Stryfe's throne, blocking them from view.

The barrier appeared to be made up of the same lettering that riddled Stryfe's body. The glowing symbols formed a dome that Creed knew would protect those inside from all harm. He gritted his teeth in frustration.

"Alright, brother!" Stryfe's voice resounded, somehow unimpeded by the barrier he cowered behind. "No more preamble! The real fun begins now! 𐤀𐤁𐤂𐤃, Moloch!"

Yet another geyser of flame—this one a sickly golden color— exploded upwards from the ground in front of the barrier, spraying high into the sky. A massive dark form wrenched itself up from the fiery portal and onto the battlefield.

Grimacing, Creed beheld an enormous bull, not quite as titanic as Bahamut, but still colossal enough to dwarf him. Its body was made of pure bronze, and its massive horns were twin pillars of blood-red crystal glowing bright with the heat of hellfire contained within. The bull let out a snort, sending up a veritable maelstrom of dirt.

It was to be a contest of strength, then. With a sigh, Creed willed the cannon at his side to morph back into a spear, which he then proceeded to impale into the ground beside him. He would not need it for this.

Deciding to play along with the foul beast across from him, Creed stomped one of his own feet before lowering himself into a wide fighting stance, one arm clenched at his side and the other raised toward the bronze bull Moloch in challenge.

The mindless beast took expected offense at Creed's boldness. With a furious roar, it charged, bounding across the crater to crush him. Each stomp of its massive hooves caused a small quake.

Bracing himself, Creed reached inside and called upon Yesod, the Golden Core. Rather than expel this power outward, Creed focused it within, allowing it to fill every fiber of his being. His entire body began to glow, lit aflame by noble yellow light.

Moloch was drawing near, lowering its head to impale its prey with its mighty horns. It was already too late. Yesod was the Core that controlled strength and the power of earth itself. Creed had imposed that power upon his own being; he was now a mountain that could not be moved.

As his foe came upon him, Creed dashed forward briefly, just enough to dodge under the glowing horns, and reached out with his hand to clutch the monster's snout.

The beast's charge was halted in an instant, unable to even budge the much smaller man. The sheer momentum of the charge carried Moloch's body upwards, lifting it into the air and threatening to flip it onto its back.

But Creed's grip was unbreakable. With a shout of exertion, he brought his arm down with all the might he'd been granted. The bull's flip was halted, and its enormous body slammed into the ground like a hammer.

The earth shook and threatened to buckle beneath Creed's feet. He both felt and heard the unpleasant sensation of every bone in the demon's body shattering at once. That alone seemed to be enough, and the monster promptly burst into a cloud of black dust as it died.

Creed's vision became a mess of darkness and debris, the demon's essence stinging his eyes and choking his lungs. It dispersed, but Creed was left to hack and cough as the utterly atrocious sensation assaulted him. He was given no time to recover before Stryfe's voice rang out again:

"⁊ℇ˥ᛕ˥, Stolas! ⁊ℇ˥ᛕ˥, Eligor!"

Blinking the pain out of his eyes, Creed watched as two more demons formed from pillars of flame, one red and one violet.

From the red came the beast on which Stryfe had flown away back in the forest: Stolas, a monstrous amalgamation of owl and dragon.

From the violet pillar burst a humanoid knight standing about ten feet tall. Its body was encased head to toe in obsidian plate armor. On one arm, it bore a large rectangular shield nearly as tall as it was, and in the other, it held a sword made of the same purple flame from which it had emerged.

The knight—Eligor—pointed its blade at Creed from across the crater before leaping high into the air to land upon Stolas' back. The monstrous owl let out a screech and took to the air with one mighty flap of its wings. Creed lifted his head to follow the two demons into the sky and was racked with one last series of painful coughs.

Oh yes. This was all proving to be *very* unpleasant.

Neveah wondered if perhaps she had gone insane without noticing.

The things she had seen up until now—the things she was *currently* seeing—should by all logic have left her a drooling invalid on the ground. It defied reason. It defied logic. It went against what every fiber of her understanding told her should be possible.

And yet somehow, here she was, watching it all unfold before her as if she was capable of comprehending it.

"A little scary, isn't it?"

Neveah was unable to tear her gaze away from the madness occurring below, but responded to Joshua's question. "Of course. They're demons."

"I was referring to Creed."

At the moment, Creed was enveloped in a wispy green light, dashing across the crater at such high speeds Neveah had given up trying to follow his movements.

It was much easier to track the horrible black bird zooming around above, high in the air but still low enough let the black knight on its back launch volleys of purple fire from the sword in its hand. The flames rained down all across the crater, but the green blur that was Creed dodged and weaved between them seamlessly.

"He's amazing..." she whispered.

Joshua sounded a bit surprised. "That's a word for it."

"This is how he was before he lost his power?"

He chuckled. "Oh no. This is barely half as strong as he was."

That statement was too unfathomable for Neveah to process, so he continued, "Three Samaritans were given the same role of destroying angels whenever one descended. They wouldn't have been given that task if they were anything less than the strongest."

"Stryfe told me Creed was a warrior," Neveah recalled.

"One of the best. Not that he ever wanted to be." His voice took on a sorrowful note. "Those colors were supposed to be tools of creation. They were made to give life. But all he's ever been forced to use them for is taking it."

Neveah finally tore her gaze from the battle to look at the man. Even with his eyes covered, she could see the regret on his features.

"When this battle is over," he asked without turning to her, "will you still be willing to recognize him? Will you be able to welcome him back and look at him as you did before?"

Neveah was surprised by the question but found herself responding without hesitation: "Yes."

Joshua gave a small, sad smile. "Good. That's good. Until then, don't look away. He's just getting started."

Creed was running. He'd cast off the yellow cloak of Yesod in favor of Chesed, the Laurel Core. Wrapped in ribbons of green light which imbued him with the speed and power of wind, he dashed along at an unnatural clip, covering tens of feet with each stride.

Creed was only vaguely aware of the violet bombs of fire that fell around him from Eligor's attacks high in the sky. He was more concerned with devising how best to bring his airborne foe down. As such, he barely heard the voice of his true enemy calling forth yet another demon:

"⁊ℇ⊐⌐⊐, Reynard!"

Looking up, he saw a gigantic red fox, only slightly smaller than Moloch had been, bearing down on him. The beast had materialized almost immediately. Its crimson fur stood on end, giving it a wild look, and its mad yellow eyes were constantly darting in separate directions. Clenched between its jaws, slick with foam and slobber, was a massive golden sword.

Reynard the Fox whipped its head to swipe the blade at Creed, and he leaped high in the air to avoid it. Unfortunately, he underestimated just how fast his new opponent was. In an instant, the demon effortlessly twisted its body with impossible speed and precision, bringing its sword up to where Creed hung in the air. Unprepared, he could not avoid the giant sword as it carved into his body.

He felt himself spinning through the air. For a brief moment, he panicked, but quickly calmed himself. All he'd lost was an arm, a leg, and most of the left side of his body.

Nothing to be concerned about.

Creed called upon Tiferet, the Rose Core. Pink-tinted light flowed across his wounds, and the relief was instant. All pain faded. His missing limbs and organs shimmered back into existence. This time, even his clothes had repaired themselves; he was never quite sure how that part worked.

Righting himself, Creed landed on his feet with a grunt. He immediately had to begin his Chesed-empowered sprint once again as Reynard bore down on him with frightening agility.

He dashed in a circle around the ring of the crater, making sure to dodge away from the blasts of fire Eligor was still raining down from above. Reynard kept pace, racing alongside him and waiting for another opportunity to swing.

Calling upon Malkuth and Netzach, Creed called a mass of metal clay into his hand and molded it into a silver katana. He swung it upwards, willing it to expand in length until it was fifty feet long.

The massive blade tore a sizable gash into Reynard's side as he passed. Ruby-red blood rained down, and Reynard let out an angry growl, but Creed noticed the wound begin to close itself almost immediately after he made it—a regenerator, like Samael.

Reynard moved in for another attack, and Creed was forced to use his now-massive sword to defend against the fox's own. The blows came fast and hard, each one threatening to send Creed flying once again.

He decided that might be for the best; on Reynard's fourth swing, he allowed the force of the blow to propel him into the air. This time, he made sure to maintain control during his flight. He retracted the sword to half of its current length; still absurd-looking, but more manageable.

He needed something to halt Reynard's impressive regeneration. Upon landing, Creed flared Hod, the Violet Core. He touched his fingers to his blade, and purple energy traced itself down its length. Among other things, Hod was the source all natural toxins and poisons of the world. In an instant, Creed had imbued his blade with the most potent venom he could muster.

Reynard was nearly upon him now. Flaring the golden light of Yesod into just his feet, Creed kicked off the ground with immense strength, propelling himself forward and under the fox's sword.

He managed to land a clean slash into the demon's front left paw before he had to leap to avoid the counterblow. Reynard turned to pursue but stumbled when it tried to take a step. The gash Creed had put in its leg was tinged with Hod's poisonous violet energy. While not as destructive as Samael's Venom, it did its job well as it coursed further into the monster's bloodstream and prevented the wound from healing.

Reynard's constantly flickering gaze finally focused solely on Creed. With a rabid snarl, the fox resumed its charge, ignoring the injury. But its movement was noticeably slower with only three working legs, and Creed was able to leap above its head.

He flipped upside down in the air and swung his lengthy sword in a two-handed chop. The blade carved into Reynard's back, leaving another long purple wound.

He landed behind the fox, which finally let out a yelp of pain and dropped its giant blade. Before it could turn around, Creed dashed toward its hind legs. He delivered a slash to each of its tendons. Another yelp. The beast was unable to support itself any longer, and fell to the ground with a crash.

Creed leaped onto its gouged back and sprinted across. He reached the fox's head, and stabbed his poison blade directly into its skull without hesitation. The fox's ever-twitching eyes went wilder than ever before going still. This time, Creed made sure to leap away before it burst into ash.

No sooner did he land than more volleys of purple fire fell upon him from above. Unable to flee in time, Creed flared Malkuth and morphed his sword into a large domed shield to intercept the flames. They impacted harshly, each one superheating and nearly shattering the barrier, but it held firm.

He heard a wicked screech and moved his shield just in time to see Eligor leap off of Stolas' back and out of sight. The demonic owl itself was now speeding towards Creed like a rocket, deadly beak poised to pierce his flesh.

Flaring the Binah Core once again, Creed raised a hand and let loose a torrent of orange flame just before Stolas reached him. It was not nearly as hot or concentrated as what he had slain Bahamut with, but the sheer force was enough to stop the monster's dive in its tracks.

Shrieks of pain tore through the air as its body was consumed and roasted by the unrelenting stream of Creed's fire. He could just barely make out the owl's silhouette within the inferno and watched as its shape gradually shrank before crumbling away.

Cutting off the stream of fire, Creed allowed himself a single breath—

—only for Eligor to leap forth from the still-present cloud of smoke and ash, flaming blade held overhead. It brought the weapon down in a mighty overhead chop that Creed just barely managed to scamper back from.

Forming his weapon into a metal spear once again, Creed began a short dance with the black knight, dodging the fiery sword's blows while using the extra range of his spear to keep the demon at bay.

Eventually, he found a gap in the knight's defenses and thrust forward directly into its chest where its heart would be. The blow landed, and the force launched Eligor back several feet. It dug its heels in to stop itself, and when it straightened, Creed saw that his strike had left not a single scratch on the knight's impenetrable black plate.

"𝟽𝟾𝟕𝟽, Astaroth!" came Stryfe's voice once again. "𝟽𝟾𝟽𝟽, Astarte!"

Two more torrents of golden flame appeared on either side of Eligor, shaping themselves into a pair of demons, one male and one female.

They looked as if they could be twins: shimmering silver hair, the male's reaching his shoulders and the female's her lower back; flawless aurum-colored bodies, naked but devoid of anatomy; and a pair of glimmering eyes that seemed to be literal emeralds.

The female, Astarte, rode on the back of a large, white-furred lion with ugly scars where its eyes should be. The male, Astaroth, was on foot, and in his right hand, a white viper with ruby eyes hissed and lashed itself about like a whip.

Creed clutched his weapon in both hands before swiftly pulling them apart; one metal-coated spear split seamlessly into two simple longswords, and Creed took up a new defensive stance, waiting for his enemies to make the first move.

He did not have to wait long.

As one, all three demons lunged forward. Creed's world became a whirlwind of purple fire, slashing claws and lashing vipers. He was purely on the defensive, blocking what blows he could with his swords while dodging the ones he couldn't. His opponents were flawless in their skill, never once getting in each other's way. It was as if they had been fighting together all their unnatural lives.

Creed brought both blades up to block a blow from Eligor's sword, but it was a feint. The knight dropped low and swung its black shield upwards, knocking Creed's weapons apart and breaking his guard. He attempted a wild stab with his left sword in response, but felt something halt his movement.

He turned to see Astaroth's viper coiling its way up his arm. When it reached his neck, the serpent sank its long fangs into his jugular. Creed let out a grunt of pain just before Astarte's lion swung a mighty paw into his chest, gouging flesh with its claws.

The force of the blow sent Creed sailing, longswords flying from his hands, though the speed at which he flew did at least wrench him out of the viper's grasp. He skipped and skidded across the ground before rolling to a stop. Gasping for breath, he came up on one knee. Bright blue blood spilled onto the dirt like water.

Putting a hand to his chest, Creed flared Tiferet and allowed rose-colored light to envelop his form once again. The wounds closed themselves, but he did not feel great relief. The Tiferet Core could heal most any injury, but could not restore energy or vitality; he still felt the fatigue and residual pain of the wounds he'd been dealt.

The three demons observed him as he stumbled to his feet, probably with amusement. That was fine—if the monsters were too arrogant to press their advantage, Creed would instead. Although he knew doing so would put a rapid drain on his energy reserves, Creed flared three of his Cores at once.

First came Netzach, whose grey energy he willed to envelop his entire body, transmuting every inch of his skin into solid, nigh-indestructible iron. Next came Yesod, whose golden energy once again raised his physical strength to impossible heights.

Lastly, he called as much of Malkuth's clay as he possibly could to his hands, where he condensed and shaped it into a massive war-hammer. It's appearance was simplistic, but its weight and density were so vast that just holding the weapon would have torn Creed's arms off had they not been enhanced by Yesod's power.

Fully prepared, Creed hefted the hammer in defiance towards the three demons who had arrogantly allowed him to ready himself. Before the trio could renew their charge, he rocketed himself off the ground with Yesod-infused legs, closing the distance with the speed and force of a small meteor.

Eligor was unprepared for the suddenness of the charge, and could do nothing as Creed raised his hammer high before bringing it down upon the black knight's head. The demon's armor cracked and buckled under the titanic strike, and a small earthquake erupted as the ground below split from the seismic impact.

Creed's vision was obscured by the rush of debris for several beats, though he was vaguely aware of Astarte and Astaroth sailing away from the sheer force of his blow. When the dust cleared, Eligor was gone, having burst into ash almost immediately. All that remained was the sizable crater Creed's hammer had left in the earth.

As soon as he righted himself, Creed sensed the bloodlust of one of the remaining demons coming at him from behind. Spinning, he wrenched his hammer in an upward swing just as Astarte leaped from the surrounding dust cloud on her mount.

Creed's blow met its mark with perfect timing, slamming into the lion's chin just as it came within range. The denseness of the hammer caused the beast's head to burst like a balloon, sending ruby-red blood in all directions. Astarte was thrown from her seat by the force, launching forward to bounce along the dirt like a ragdoll.

No sooner had she come to a stop than Creed was upon her again, raising his hammer like an executioner's blade. The golden demon raised a hand in useless defense before the weapon crashed into her prone form and burst her into ash just as it had Eligor.

A metallic roar resounded from nearby, and Creed turned to see Astaroth, emerald eyes ablaze with rage at the loss of its twin. Lashing out a hand, the demon flung its ivory snake in Creed's direction at too great a speed for him to react.

The viper reached his throat in less than a second, but this time, its vicious fangs failed to pierce his new iron skin. Taking one hand off the hammer still embedded in the earth, Creed grabbed the snake's neck and pried it from his own. The rest of its body coiled around his arm in a vain attempt to crush him, but the metal limb was now far too strong for that.

With his free hand, Creed grabbed the handle of his hammer and willed it to change, shrinking and compressing itself until it was a clay sphere no larger than an average ball. With Yesod-enhanced strength, he pitched the earthen globe like in Astaroth's direction.

The golden demon could not react before the projectile—just as dense as when it was a hammer—slammed into its chest and smashed apart its entire upper half. The rest of its form promptly burst into ash as the sphere continued to sail onwards. It eventually crashed into the high wall of the crater, where it impacted with enough force that Creed could feel the tremors beneath his feet.

Whipping around, Creed waited for another demon to be summoned, but it appeared only the dome of glowing script and the Baphomet hiding behind it remained. Looking to the snake still hissing and gnashing in his grasp, Creed had an idea.

Tightening his grip on its throat, Creed called upon Gevurah, the Crimson Core. Red energy traveled from Creed's fingers into the snake, which let out a distressed hiss. It loosened its grip on his arm and struggled to free itself, but there would be no escape. The viper went stiff, then began rapidly expanding. Seconds later, its form burst into a shower of ruby-red blood.

Rather than let it dissipate, Creed further infused Gevurah's energy into the demon's plasma, allowing him to control its shape. He willed the blood to shift and change until it resembled a long, lethal needle. Taking it in his grasp, Creed looked to the glowing barrier far in the distance that stood between him and Stryfe.

He would have one shot.

Enveloping his body in Chesed's green light, Creed began a swift flight towards the barrier. As he approached, a pair of glowing blue pentagrams materialized above the dome. No doubt summoned by the Baphomet within, the unholy stars spun rapidly in place and fired beams of destructive energy. Creed did not slow his sprint, dashing as quickly as he could to avoid the incoming attacks. The blue lights sailed overhead, creating blinding explosions wherever they impacted.

As he drew closer to the barrier, Creed focused Yesod's golden energy into the arm which held the blood-spear. Digging in his heels, Creed reeled back as he skid along the ground. When he had slowed enough to aim properly, he threw the blood like a javelin, sending it sailing into the barrier.

The Baphomet's demonic spell was capable of keeping powers like Creed's at bay, but when struck by a needle infused with the equally demonic blood of Astaroth's viper, the barrier's power was canceled out. The blood-spear pierced into the shell, not stabbing through completely but embedding itself deep enough to create several visible cracks.

Creed resumed his sprint with even greater urgency than before. Still avoiding blasts from the pentagrams, he finally came within range of his target.

With a small leap, Creed brought up a leg and stomped his metal-coated foot into the lance, forcing it the rest of the way through. The sound of shattering glass filled Creed's ears, and he came to a stop as an explosion of light briefly robbed him of sight.

When his vision cleared, Creed was greeted with the sight of the barrier destroyed and the Baphomet impaled. Pinned to the ground by a lance of blood, the goat-headed demon could only pathetically grasp at the intruding weapon before both it and the spear dispersed into black ash.

And with that, all that remained were Creed and the Devil.

Chapter XVIII
"Words That We Couldn't Say"

All the energy Creed had expended and the wounds he had received caught up with him in an instant. To conserve what little energy he had left, he allowed the Cores he was flaring to dim. His body shifted from iron back to flesh, and his enhanced strength left him like an expelled breath.

Unable to support himself, Creed fell to his knees, panting. The void swirled all around him, leeching at his life force. The spheres of color still hovered behind him, but they were dimmer than they had been at the start.

Despite how heavy his eyes felt, Creed refused to take his gaze off the Devil before him. For what little it was worth, Stryfe did not seem to be in better shape than he. All of the hellish stars adorning his body were black and faded, clashing with the bright shades of his absurd costume and makeup. Though he still sat upon his black throne, his posture was slouched and his breathing noticeably labored.

Evidently, Stryfe had not been lying; nearly all of his energy had been placed into summoning that gauntlet of monsters, and now he was left almost as weak as Creed despite having received no wounds. Yet still he wore that same elated grin, as if he couldn't possibly be having more fun.

"You truly are... the best!" he panted. He had placed most of his weight onto the armrest of his throne to stay upright. "This is... everything... I hoped for!"

Creed's anger proved enough to give him strength. Though it was a struggle, he managed to rise to his feet once again. He fixed his brother with a burning stare, but the bastard just responded with a tired-sounding chuckle.

"You slaughtered my children so beautifully! And I'm nothing if not a monster of my word! But I must say, you're looking a bit worse for wear. Are you sure you have anything left?"

"I've got enough."

In truth, quite nearly all of Creed's strength had been spent, but he still had one last trick he could pull. It wouldn't be much, and it wouldn't end the fight quickly, but looking at Stryfe's exhausted stance before him, he believed it would indeed be enough.

Stryfe hissed in excitement. "I'm waiting!"

Reaching within one more time, Creed accessed the one color he had yet to use: Chokmah, the Azure Core. The image he conjured was simple, and materialized with little effort: a globe of pure, blue water, not unlike that which Bahamut had summoned, hovering in the air before him.

Stryfe made no effort to hide how unimpressed he was. "Well... it's better than nothing, I suppose."

Ignoring him, Creed willed the sphere to shift. The water split off into four separate streams, each flowing to one of Creed's limbs and encasing his arms and legs. The water then froze itself instantly, forming into gauntlets and greaves of ice. Prepared as he could be, Creed raised his frozen fists into a boxing stance and glared his opponent down.

"Really?" Stryfe asked, sounding utterly exasperated. "All those theatrics, and you're going to end this by *beating* me to death?"

Creed did not respond, and the devil shrugged. "I'll give you points for enthusiasm, if nothing else. But before you start throwing punches, I have to make one last confession."

His scarlet eyes fixed on Creed, a glimmer of mischief behind them.

"I lied."

With his most dangerous grin yet, the Devil stuck out a long, serpent-like tongue, upon which was scrawled one small crimson star.

A voice rang out in Creed's mind: «⁊ᘿᒣᖌᒣ, *Cerberus!*»

A wall of smoke and flame erupted between the two Samaritans, and from the blackness burst the snarling heads of three hellhounds. Having been summoned with such a small sigil, the beast was not present at its full strength; only the heads appeared from the flames, and their form lacked solidity, as if they were made of little more than fire and ash. But six glowing yellow eyes and three sets of gnashing teeth told Creed that Cerberus, once the most devoted of all Hell's guardians, was still more than capable of defending its master.

"It isn't much," he heard Stryfe's voice jeer from behind the flaming hounds, "but seeing as he's the only one of my children who remains truly loyal to me these days, I simply *had* to give him a chance!" As if in acknowledgment of its father's words, the middle of Cerberus' heads released a small jet of flame.

"Sorry to make you waste your last trick, but if you really believed—!"

Whatever Stryfe was going to say was cut off as Creed rocketed forward, punched through Cerberus' form with a single icy fist, and carried his blow through to crash directly into the Devil's face.

Stryfe's head was rammed into the back of his chair, which promptly burst apart in a shower of ebony stone. The demon was sent flying backward just as his hellhound finished bursting out of existence. Creed was left standing on the remains of the throne, watching Stryfe's jumpsuit-clad form skid and roll about twenty feet away before coming to a stop in the dirt.

The demon lay in a motionless heap for several seconds while Creed looked on, unfeeling. Eventually, Stryfe shot up with a howl of pain, clutching at the right side of his face. The cheek where Creed's fist had struck was burnt black and melted to the point where bone had been exposed. His bright-red hair was now wild and unkempt, flared out in all directions.

Stryfe groaned and growled in agony, but the grievous wound was already beginning to heal itself. In moments, the flesh was unblemished, though Stryfe still looked to be in no small amount of torment. His expression was one of sheer pain and anger, a sharp contrast to his clownish appearance.

"AH!" he seethed, still clutching at his face. "Holy water! *VERY clever*!" He staggered to his feet, body heaving with pain. "I was sure that with Father gone, it wasn't possible anymore! I'd never have guessed *you* were still holy enough to bless anything!"

Creed refused to respond. He merely hopped down from the broken throne and took several steps closer before dropping once more into his fighting stance. His fists remained encased by the blessed ice made solely to destroy the Devil standing across from him.

Against all reason, Stryfe let out another smile, though this one was filled with nothing but spite. Standing upright, he slid a hand through his disheveled hair, slicking it back once again.

"Fine! I'll play along!"

Stryfe clapped his hands together, and both his arms and legs erupted into pitch-black fire. The ebony flames warped and shifted just as Creed's water had, shaping themselves into wicked burning claws and talons. Stryfe dropped onto all fours, taking a wild stance like a beast ready to hunt.

"What say we put an end to this nightmare, brother?"

For once, Creed was in complete agreement. Without another word, he charged forward just as Stryfe pounced for his throat.

"What is he *doing*?"

Neveah turned at Joshua's words. "Who?"

The disheveled man was still "watching" the fight intently, lips taut in apparent confusion. "Stryfe. There's no way he's letting this end in a *fistfight*, of all things."

"Why not?"

"He isn't a fighter. Not compared to Creed, at least. He never bloodies his own hands if he can avoid it, *especially* in his restricted form."

Neveah supposed he was referring to the form forced upon the Samaritans by the mark they'd all been branded with. She recalled Joshua telling her before that their actual names and power could only be used against the angels. Based on the utter absurdity of the things she'd just witnessed, Neveah couldn't rightly fathom the idea that both Creed and Stryfe were still nowhere near their full strength.

Regardless, Joshua seemed baffled at how the battle was progressing. Looking back to the crater, Neveah could tell even at this distance that Creed had the complete upper hand.

Whereas Stryfe's garish red form was leaping and swiping wildly with some sort of claws, Creed's stance was tight and flawless like a champion kickboxer, and he was beating his opponent down with almost embarrassing ease. Even to someone like Neveah, it was evident that Creed's victory was inevitable.

So... why did she share Joshua's unease?

She should have been relieved. Creed was going to survive, and that lunatic who said he was planning to destroy the rest of humanity would be finished. This was the best possible scenario, right? So why was there such a feeling of trepidation in the back of her head?

And why, she realized, had she been feeling this way since the start of the fight? Why did everything about this just seem *wrong*?

"Joshua," she began in a low voice, "Is Stryfe... supposed to be this weak?"

Joshua turned back to her with a look that said how ridiculous he thought the question was. "Excuse me?"

"No," Neveah corrected herself, "not *weak*, just... I know we just saw some *crazy* shit, but..." she struggled to give voice to her nebulous concern. "I mean, come on! He's the fucking *Devil*, right? It's not as if I know what you all are capable of, but shouldn't he be putting up more of a fight, or... something?" She groaned in frustration. "I don't know how to explain it!"

But Joshua seemed to understand what it was she was getting at. He looked back to the battle, and Neveah could almost see his thoughts racing.

"No... You're right. Something's off."

Neveah's own mind was going a mile a minute. She went over everything she had witnessed about Stryfe up to this point: she recalled her conversation with him at the church, and everything the others had told her about him. She thought of what he'd said in the forest and the terrible threats he'd made before this battle began.

Her thoughts were interrupted by movement to her right, and she looked to see the Dove perched on Joshua's shoulder, head twitching and wings flapping about like it was desperately trying to alert her to something. Neveah's breath caught in her throat. What was she missing?

A distant shout called her attention back to the crater. Creed was reeling; it seemed Stryfe had actually landed a blow. She felt a pang of worry, which quickly turned to shock as she saw Creed go berserk, striking back with a flurry of vicious strikes. Neveah watched as Stryfe was pummeled without mercy, the Devil himself unable to raise even hand in defense.

It hit her.

Neveah's heart shot up into her throat, realization striking so hard she felt dizzy. She whipped her head in Joshua's direction just in time to see the Dove leap off his shoulder and zoom off in the direction of the fight.

"We have to stop them!"

As his brother rained blow after blow upon him, each strike searing his flesh and rending apart his very soul, Stryfe realized that he had never been happier.

The sheer exhilaration he felt as he swung his flaming claws at Creed's body was matched only by the elation he felt as each swipe was expertly dodged and countered: a swipe at the throat, missed, repaid with a blow to the temple; a wild stab at the stomach, blocked, rewarded with a kick to the sternum.

Stryfe's healing abilities were in overdrive, repairing the parts of his body that burned away at the touch of the blessed ice that coated Creed's arms, though it did nothing to dull the pain. To Stryfe, it was nothing less than beautiful; every paroxysm was a loving embrace, the sounds of his own screams like music to his ears.

But it wasn't finished yet. There remained a single, final push to give: one blow. He needed to land one blow. Just to prove that he *could*. Stryfe flung himself about like a wild animal, flipping all around Creed while trying to land any strike that he could.

But his dear brother was so much greater a warrior than he; his form was perfect, defense flawless, and reprisals merciless.

Stryfe would not be deterred. Not when his victory was so close. Strong as Creed was, he was just as exhausted as Stryfe, if not more so. He just needed to survive long enough for the opening to present itself.

In the end, it did. Creed attempted a heavy straight blow to the head that Stryfe just barely managed to duck beneath. Having overextended himself, Creed's exhausted body stumbled ever so slightly, and he took just a moment longer to regain his stance.

That moment was all Stryfe needed; with a wild scream, he swiped his black claws upward, carving deep into Creed's chest. Four burning gouges were left diagonally across his torso, and Stryfe was satisfied to feel his brother's bright-blue blood splatter across his face. Creed reeled back, roaring in rage and pain as the black flames licked at his flesh.

Perfect.

His work done, Stryfe could only smile as Creed's head snapped back into position, eyes filled with white-hot hate. When the rain of blows began again, Stryfe hardly bothered to defend himself. His futile guard was broken instantly, and he did not attempt to bring it up again as Creed beat him with all the fury that had been building between them since the dawn of time.

Again and again and again the vicious strikes came. A swift punch to the left eye caused the organ to liquefy with a sharp *pop*. A fist in the stomach left a gaping hole in his gut. A stomping kick to the right knee melted the joint and severed the leg completely. Stryfe had gone numb to the physical pain by now, but the searing of the holy water upon his mind and soul burned as harshly as ever.

At last, with one final uppercut, Creed delivered a blow to Stryfe's chin so fierce that his entire lower jaw melted and burst into viscera. He lost all of his senses and didn't realize he had been sent flying through the air until he crashed upon the dirt.

It was over.

When he regained some semblance of awareness, Stryfe managed to just barely raise his head. He could already feel his jaw beginning to repair itself, not that it mattered; he had no words left to speak. He beheld his brother, standing tall like Stryfe's own personal savior.

Come on.

The ice on three of Creed's limbs began to shift, turning to frost and flowing off his body. They collected around his right arm, combining to form one large, icy spike.

Come on!

He made no move to escape as Creed loaded his arm back and readied the stake.

Do it!

Without an ounce of pity in his gaze, Creed lurched forward, makeshift lance headed straight for Stryfe's heart. Feeling truly at peace for what may have been the first time in his entire existence, the Devil closed his eyes and held his arms out wide, welcoming the end.

I'M READY!

Creed saw himself. He saw Stryfe. He saw the frozen javelin attached to his hand. There was nothing else. There didn't need to *be* anything else. Not until this was over. He was charging forward. He would pierce the bastard's heart. He'd set himself free. He'd—

Joshua was there. Right in his path. Body crouched. Head down. One arm extended toward him, the other towards Stryfe. Creed's body stopped moving. Every muscle tensed at once, joints locking and limbs held in place by some irresistible force.

Joshua turned to look at him. Even with the blindfold, he looked half-terrified, half-furious. A flick of his finger. The ice around Creed's arm shattered and fell away. Yet another force slammed into Creed's chest, and he sailed back before landing with a grunt. He rose immediately, ready to charge again without thinking.

Then he saw Neveah standing at Joshua's side, and his senses came back to him. The rest of the world appeared again, the dark sky and desolate cityscape. His exhaustion, ignored up to this point, returned in full force. He refused to fall to his knees this time, and fixed his younger brother with a hard stare.

"Move."

What was happening? Joshua had given his consent, hadn't he? He had seen the depths of Stryfe's madness and knew there was nothing left to be done. But here he was, placing himself between the two of them as he had so many times before.

"Wait!" Joshua urged. Creed was too angry to listen.

"Damnit, we are *not* doing this again. Get out of the way, or I *will* go through you!"

To Creed's surprise, Stryfe lifted his head behind Joshua, fixing the man with angry red eyes. His melted jaw had healed, though his scarlet hair had once again gone wild.

"You fucking coward. Stay out of this!"

"QUIET!!!"

At the word, Joshua clenched both of his fists. Stryfe was pushed flatter into the ground, while Creed was forced down onto his knees, arms locked at his sides and unable to move a muscle. Joshua looked back and forth between them both, looking angrier than Creed could ever recall seeing him.

"For once in an eternity, the two of you are going to shut up and *listen*!"

"Why!?" Creed begged "What else has to happen for you to let this end!?"

"You don't get it, Creed! Neither of us did!"

"There's nothing to get! You heard him! He's been planning for this all along! As soon as he had all his strays, he came here to kill us!"

"You're wrong!" Neveah declared, stepping from Joshua's side to stand before Creed. "If that's really true, why did he set it up like this? Why would he go on and on about how badly he wanted to fight you, just to throw a few monsters at you when he's supposed to have a whole army inside him?"

Creed's confusion only grew. All of this had been explained already! "Because he's still weak! Hell, he was half-dead by the time I reached him!"

"How do you know that?" Neveah challenged. "Because he *told* you?"

Creed paused, feeling a flash of uncertainty. "What are you saying?"

"Stryfe didn't gather his demons to come kill you, Creed..."

Joshua finished the statement for her, voice thick with anger. "He came here to die."

No one spoke for the longest time. Creed's eyes were wide, breath coming in pants as he tried to process the utter absurdity of what he'd just heard. Why were they saying this? How could they have come to such a ludicrous conclusion? He felt dizzy, as if he might fall over if Joshua's power wasn't holding him upright.

"No..." he whispered. "No, that can't... that's impossible..."

Such a thing couldn't be true. Not for Stryfe. It was unbelievable, unthinkable, absolutely....

Creed looked past Joshua and Neveah to where Stryfe still lay pinned to the ground. He hadn't said a word, and had turned his head away from them all. The look on his painted face was one of indignant fury.

"Stryfe?" Creed called out, barely hearing his own words.

Joshua turned to look down at the demon. "Well?"

Stryfe refused to meet the other man's gaze. "That's absurd."

"Yes," Joshua replied. "It certainly is."

"It didn't make sense," Neveah was saying. "If he really just wanted to kill you, why didn't he do it in the forest? Why set up some kind of grudge match?"

"Because," Creed insisted, still searching for some way to deny what was happening, "he said he wanted—"

"—a fair fight?" Joshua concluded.

"That's right!" Stryfe shouted. "I deserve it. I've *earned* it!"

Joshua looked unimpressed at the rage. "If that's true, why did it have to be Creed? Why not me? You knew where I was. Or Grendel? He's always spoiling for it. What about Salomé and the Beasts?"

"He was the only one who would give me a decent fight!" Stryfe insisted.

"Liar. The way Creed was when we found him, any one of us would have made a better match."

"All those things you said when we got here," Neveah continued, as if she and Joshua were some kind of bizarre detective duo. "All that taunting, all those horrible threats. Creed was already willing to fight you, so why go that far? You were just acting like the Devil we expected!"

If looks could kill, Stryfe's glare would have burst the girl into flames. "I meant every word!"

"Maybe," said Joshua. "Or maybe you knew that Creed had the most personal reason to hate you. Maybe you knew he'd be the one most willing to fight you, so you got him trapped in the Boss' game and goaded him on the whole way to make sure he'd want to kill you. Maybe the reason you gathered all your demons inside you was so that when you died, they all went with you. Maybe this *whole* thing was just a ploy to let Creed get his revenge while killing off every demon left in the world all at once!"

Creed wanted to keep denying it. He wanted to rage and shout that it couldn't be true. But it made sense. Absurd and unbelievable as it was, it made *sense*.

Looking down at himself, Creed saw that the gashes Stryfe had clawed into his chest had healed without him noticing. That shouldn't have been possible. The black fire Stryfe used was an unnatural kind that would burn for all eternity if it was allowed. It should have still been there, searing Creed's skin and preventing the wound from closing. The only way it could have been extinguished was if their caster had willed it.

"Creed!" Stryfe had managed to raise his head and fixed Creed with wild red eyes. "Don't listen to these naive fools! You know! You know more than anyone what I am!"

Creed just stared back, and something in his gaze must have been alarming, because Stryfe's tone grew more desperate. "You're going let them stop you? After all that's happened? After all those people I made you slaughter!?"

"It's true..." Creed whispered, hardly believing his own words.

"No! I came here to kill you! I came here to kill all of you!"

Creed's shock turned to a deep and righteous anger. "After everything you've done...."

"Listen to me. If you don't kill me, I *will* do as I said!"

"After everything you've destroyed...."

"I'll let every demon out of this body. I swear I will!"

"You have the gall to make me put you out of your fucking misery!?"

"They'll tear the girl to pieces, Creed! I'll make them torture her until there's nothing left!"

"Why?" Creed growled. "Why you?"

"I'll send them all across the world! They won't stop until every pathetic little Lamb has been slaughtered! They'll all die if you don't kill me!"

"You've never regretted a single thing you've ever done, so why now...?"

"Just kill me, you coward! You fucking weakling! Kill me, or I'll kill everything that's left!"

"Why?" Creed asked again. "Why, after all this time? *Why—*"

"BECAUSE I DESERVE IT!!!"

The shout was made in the demon's true voice, a chorus of all ages and genders that shook the ground. Neveah stumbled back in surprise but recovered quickly. Stryfe began to breath more heavily, his eyes darting between the three of them.

"I... I didn't want this..." he muttered. Something seemed to have broken inside him. "I didn't want... *any* of this!"

He stared upwards into the sky where the black sun lorded over them all, unmoved by their suffering.

"I just wanted them to see. I wanted to show them I was strong enough to defy the destiny He set for me! I wanted to prove that I wasn't wrong for opposing Him! That I was *more* than He made me to be! I wanted Him to know that He was wrong to say we existed to serve *them!*" He shot a brief spiteful look at Neveah, but the girl just stared back with pity in her eyes.

"I wanted to know if it was even *possible* to choose my own fate! I wanted Him to see that the world He made was a mistake!" Crimson eyes darted across the sky, searching for something that was no longer there, "But *this*... who would ever want *this*? We... *I* never wanted to bring it all down like this..."

He lifted his head once again, and Creed was stunned to see a single stream of ruby-red blood spill from Stryfe's eye and streak down his painted cheek. His brother looked him right in the eye, and when he spoke, his voice was so weak that it couldn't possibly belong to a demon.

"I never wanted my Father to die...."

With that, he was spent. His head fell back down, utterly defeated, and the rest of them were left to soak in the words.

Joshua had turned away, mouth drawn tight. Neveah continued to stare, and the sadness in her eyes was utterly genuine. A little girl, pitying the Devil; Creed might have laughed if it weren't so preposterous.

And yet, somehow, it also told him what he needed to do.

"Joshua. Let me up."

His brother fixed him with a suspicious expression, but evidently there was something in Creed's aura that said he could be trusted. The unseen pressure that had been holding him down released. He nearly fell over without the support, but caught himself and staggered to his feet. Even now, he could still feel the void trying to rob him of his Colors. He limped over to where Stryfe was lying, every step an effort. He loomed over the demon, who looked up at him with dead eyes.

"Why me?" Creed asked.

There was no more anger or hatred in Stryfe's words when he spoke. There was nothing at all. "I've taken everything from you since the day you were born. It was only fair to gather all my children together and let you be the one to finish us."

"You think your life—the life of every demon inside you—is worth even *one* of my children?"

"It's all I have to offer."

"That's it?" Creed couldn't help but scoff. "You think you've earned that? You think you get to just leave it all behind when everyone else—"

The rest caught in Creed's throat as his own words lanced through him. Looking down, he saw that Neveah had come to stand beside him at some point.

She stared up at him, and her expression said, *Well?*

Creed felt light-headed, reeling internally at the sheer weight of his own hypocrisy.

Oh God. He's the same as me.

Staring down at the broken demon in the dirt at his feet, Creed realized that his brother was no different than he had been, waiting on the steps of the church for death to come. He thought this world had broken him, and he hated the other Samaritans who seemed able to keep living.

But he had been wrong. It wasn't just him who was broken. Maybe they *all* had been broken, right from the start. Perhaps the girl beside him and the few thousand people like her were the only ones left who weren't.

Stryfe was looking at him with a beseeching gaze. "It's enough now, isn't it? Just put an end to this. I'm so tired...."

"No..." Creed responded softly, still not quite believing he was saying it.

"*Why?*"

"Because you don't want to die," Joshua interjected. "Not really." He looked down, seemingly unmoved by the weakness he sensed. "What you want is to be forgiven."

Stryfe's eyes went wide as if the very notion terrified him. "There *is* no forgiveness. No atonement."

"But that's not true, is it?" Joshua was standing up straighter than he had before. "There's still one thing left you could do, isn't there?"

Stryfe just stared back in confusion, and Creed had to admit he shared the feeling. He hadn't seen Joshua look or speak like this in a very long time and wondered what he could possibly—

«*ENOUGH.*»

The voice rumbled through Creed's mind, garbled and crackling with the sound of interference. He froze in place while Neveah let out a shocked yelp and clutched at her head. He wanted to reach out to her, but molten pain lanced through his back as his brand began to burn, and he heard Joshua and Stryfe let out identical growls as theirs did the same.

The air became choked with some overpowering presence, pressing down around them from all angles and threatening to swallow them body and soul. Though he could scarcely think, Creed managed to twist his body enough to turn, as did the others.

The figure stood tall and menacing, body enshrouded by pale, tattered robes. Beneath a small hood was a face adorned with a dark, iron mask in the shape of a human skull. No features could be seen behind it, save for the glimmer of two white pupils. They scanned back and forth among the four unfortunate souls that stood before him, gaze as heavy as the sky.

"This farce," Rictus declared in a voice that sounded as if it were coming through an old radio, "is finished."

Chapter XIX
"Pale White Horse"

Neveah clutched at herself and tried desperately to stifle her shivering, but it was futile. She thought the giant horse-headed demon had frightened her. She thought the venom-spewing snake-man had frightened her. She thought all the twisted and horrible things she'd seen thus far had frightened her, to the point that she had become numb to it. But this... *thing* that now stood before her was magnitudes beyond those monsters.

It was like a walking singularity, a vortex of pure will drawing in everything around it. When Neveah managed to shift her gaze long enough to look at Creed, she saw he seemed nearly as incapacitated as she, which erased all remaining doubt in her mind. This overwhelming presence could only belong to the leader of the Samaritans she'd heard so much about.

"Crucifer," the dark man spoke, "explain."

His voice was awful, muffled and crackling like it was coming from a speaker that had been doused in water. Neveah wanted nothing more than to cower behind Creed—or perhaps simply curl into a ball and cry—but frozen in place as she was, all she could do was tremble as Joshua answered the call.

"Hey, Boss..." His voice was surprisingly composed, though it still had a definite edge to it. "I know how this looks, but I'd *really* appreciate it if we all kept our cool here, yeah?"

"I did not ask for supplication. Only explanation."

"Well, as you can see, this... *fun* little game is over." To Neveah's surprise, Joshua managed a weak smile and a shrug. "And if you ask me, it's worked out just *great* for everyone! Stryfe's got his body back, Creed's got his old colors, and frankly, I think we're finally starting to address some very long-standing family issues!"

"I am aware of what has transpired here."

"Really? How, uh, how long were you watching?"

"Do not take me for a fool. My gaze has been upon you since the moment the Apostate and Crusader clashed."

"If that's the case, then you've seen that the situation has changed quite a bit—"

"Has it?" The dark man gave a slight tilt of his head. "I do not recall altering the Preceptor's terms for this contest." Joshua tensed slightly at the rejection, and the Boss continued, "But perhaps you are not the one whom I should be questioning."

Neveah saw the white pinpricks behind the skull mask shift to focus on Creed, who noticeably flinched beneath the gaze.

"Crusader. I confess that I did not expect you to survive this ordeal, but it seems you have emerged victorious. Why, then, does the Apostate still live?"

Creed's voice was strained as if he were carrying an immense weight. "Like Joshua said... things have changed."

The dark man seemed to consider Creed's words. "I cannot deny that you seem quite different from our last encounter. I am pleased to see that you have regained your power. However—"

Whatever he was going to say next was cut off as he finally seemed to take note of Neveah's presence. The gaze of his skeletal mask fell upon her, and the beating of her heart seemed to stop entirely.

"Ah. A stray Lamb. However did you find yourself here?" Neveah, of course, could not even attempt to respond. "You seem tired, child. Perhaps you have come in search of rest?"

Neveah's vision was beginning to grow dark at the edges as her breathing was stifled by the sickening presence. Her skin grew cold, and it felt as if her muscles and bones had turned to water. Just as she feared she might collapse, she saw Creed place himself directly into her path, the first one of them to manage any real movement.

The pressure Neveah had been feeling diminished, and she found herself able to breathe once again. A defensive arm raised in front of her, Creed stared down his leader with a defiant, if still strained, expression.

"You're here for us, Rictus."

"The Preceptor is here for all Lambs, at all times. But this is intriguing. Have you perhaps also regained the affection you once held for them, Crusader?"

"I told you, Boss," Joshua interjected, "this whole mess has been surprisingly good for us, all things considered. Frankly, you'd know that if you'd bothered to watch the entire time instead of just the end."

Rictus' gaze shifted back to Joshua, who seemed to regret his bold words. "Perhaps, Crucifer. But the fact remains that the Preceptor's orders have not changed, and my question remains yet unsatisfied: why does the Apostate still live?"

"Rictus."

Neveah looked down to see Stryfe, having managed to struggle himself into a sitting position. He seemed just as on-edge as the rest of them but spoke defiantly.

"Enough with the dramatics. As you said, I lost. If the Preceptor wants me, I'm right here."

"Shut up, Stryfe," Creed growled.

"Don't be a fool. Let It have me. It will just kill us both if you don't."

"Braver than I thought you capable of, Apostate," Rictus declared. "But the Preceptor's demand was clear. If the Crusader wishes to return to the duties he has abandoned, he must prove his loyalty as a Samaritan once again." His gaze shifted once more to Creed, "It's patience grows thin. I command you one final time: strike the Apostate down."

Everyone was silent as Creed was left to make his choice. Stryfe looked up at the man with pleading eyes, while Joshua's expression was wholly unreadable. Neveah saw the conflict in Creed's eyes, and she couldn't blame him; even she understood that if they defied this man, there would be no fighting back. They would all be killed. Wiped away like stains. But even knowing this, when Neveah saw the despair that was beginning to creep onto Creed's features, she found herself unable to accept it.

"Creed," she managed to say. It was weaker than a whisper, but it nonetheless prompted him to look at her. Straining against the crushing presence all around them, she forced out all that she could:

"One more... try...."

Creed's eyes widened slightly, but he set his jaw at her words. He gave a slight nod, then turned back to face his leader. Against all odds, he managed to stand up straight and spoke in a clear, strong voice.

"No."

Rictus did not visibly react, but Neveah got the sense that he was not used to being openly defied. Even Joshua seemed surprised at his brother's declaration. At their feet, Stryfe was much less impressed.

"You fucking fool. What are you trying to prove?"

Apparently in a mood to show off, Creed actually managed to *turn his back* on Rictus, looking down on Stryfe with an intense glare.

"Who are you?" he demanded. "Are you The Prince of Darkness? The root of all evil?" He shook his head. "Right now, you look like a fucking clown lying in the dirt! You're no Devil. You're just another broken thing waiting for its pieces to be swept up. But if I don't get to lie down and die, you sure as shit don't either!"

Uncertainty tinged Stryfe's features. "We... we'll die anyways."

"No shit. But if so, we do it on our feet. I spent so long hating you, but in the end, I have no right to judge you. We're just two weaklings who can't match the strength of one girl! We don't deserve the luxury of dying before we've had a chance to atone for our weakness, but if this is how it has to end..."

He gave everyone one final shock by actually extending a hand to the demon. "...then the only thing you can do is get up, take off that *ridiculous* fucking outfit, and stand with your brothers!"

His final word echoed into the emptiness of the canyon. Even Rictus did not seem willing to intervene. Stryfe looked at Creed's hand like it was the most frightening thing he'd ever seen, just as Creed had looked at Neveah on the steps of the church.

After a few moments, a look that can only be described as sheer irritation spread across the Devil's features. Gritting his teeth, he slapped the offered hand away.

"Don't get too full of yourself, you child."

Stryfe sneered, though it didn't seem especially convincing while he picked himself off the ground. As he rose, his features turned black and burned once more, and by the time he was on his feet, he had once again taken a new form:

He still wore the same handsome, hollow-cheeked face as before, and the brand remained stamped upon his forehead as always. His eyes were still blood-red and oddly dilated, but the intense amount of makeup had been replaced with simple dark eyeliner that gave his eyes a gothic look. Beyond these subtleties, his style had completely changed again.

His hair was dirty-blonde once more, but was now much longer, reaching down to his upper back. It was styled in an impossibly flamboyant mullet, the top feathered and layered to provide several inches of height with its absurd volume.

He wore a velvet waistcoat shot with blue, black, and silver, embroidered with what appeared to be broken jewels and pieces of shattered glass. Its sleeves flared out at the ends, practically obscuring his hands. Beneath the jacket was a silver silk dress shirt and a fluttery cravat. His legs were covered by form-fitting leather pants, and a pair of flawless high-heeled black boots completed the extravagant outfit.

Combined with the eyeliner and glinting ear-piercings, the ensemble as a whole made him look somewhere between a noble prince and a drag-queen, and Neveah couldn't decide if it was more or less ridiculous than the star-painted harlequin he'd been before.

Creed, for his part, seemed more exasperated than ever. "Are you shitting me?"

"Oh?" Stryfe asked, his voice still velvety-smooth but now far haughtier and more imperious. "You asked for a Prince of Darkness, yes? Well, I hate imitating Ozzy, so this is the closest I can do."

Joshua seemed to realize what form the demon had taken and gave a dry shrug. "I mean, you *were* kind of asking for it..."

"I can't believe I'm going die with you idiots," Creed groaned. Neveah wondered if she was included in that.

Joshua seemed more amused than anything, but added, "I'll never understand how an omniscient demon can have such an awful sense of style."

"Silence, fool!" Stryfe scoffed. Stepping forward, he raised a hand to reveal that another impossibly lit cigarette had appeared in his blackened fingers. Placing it his mouth, he set his fists upon his hips and took up a defiant stance, facing down Rictus across the way. It was, quite possibly, the silliest thing Neveah had ever seen.

"Let us dance this pointless dance and be free of this maddening labyrinth of a world!"

Despite his clear annoyance, Creed gave a resigned nod and pulled a small paper stick from his coat. He willed a sphere of false candy to appear at its tip; unlike the colorless ones from before, this one was bright emerald green. Without a word, he popped the sucker into his mouth and stepped forward to stand at Stryfe's side.

Letting out a sigh, Joshua ran a hand through his shaggy hair and sauntered over to stand beside them as well, pulling out yet another strand of hay and holding it between his teeth.

Neveah beheld the Samaritans standing side-by-side against their invincible foe, respective fixations hanging from their mouths, and for the first time, it felt as if she were really looking at three brothers.

"Well!" Joshua called out. "There you have it, Boss! What next?"

Rictus had watched everything unfold up to now in silent stillness but finally seemed to come alive again, lowering his head as if in deep thought.

"I have always considered myself merciful. Long have I stood between you and the Preceptor, urging restraint when It would prefer discipline. I see now that I have been too lenient."

He raised his hooded head, and the white pupils behind his mask seemed to be glowing brighter than before.

"Hear me. The Preceptor has passed Its judgment: it is time to remind you of your place."

At his words, Neveah began to feel something she had long forgotten: wind. Actual *wind* was starting to swirl about the area, as if some kind of storm was brewing, even though all forms of weather had ceased the day the world died.

"Oh, come on, Boss!" Joshua shouted over the rising gusts. "You're really gonna kill all three of us just to prove a point!? Grendel's insane, Salomé's useless, and Testament is missing! You think you're gonna be able to handle the Adversaries without us?"

"Fear not, Crucifer," Rictus declared. "The Preceptor has given much thought to this dilemma, and has determined that erasing you will not be necessary."

"Beg pardon?" Stryfe demanded.

"We need not snuff your souls out completely when we can simply... grind them down."

"*What!?*" Creed shouted, looking appalled.

"Your memories. Your wills. Your identities. The Preceptor shall erase these things without destroying the whole of your beings. The flames of your souls shall be reduced to the barest flickers, and you shall begin again, pure and untouched by the flaws which have broken you. It shall reforge you into proper Samaritans, devoid of the defiance and doubt which has festered in your hearts. Your fates shall serve as a warning to the others that the Preceptor's Covenant is not to be ignored."

Neveah thought it impossible, but she felt even colder than before. It was perhaps the most horrible thing she had ever heard. The winds were growing fierce now, seeming to whirl about Rictus' form directly. The dark man raised a hand to his face and grabbed at the bottom of his iron mask.

"Let It be awakened."

"Here we go," Neveah heard Creed mutter as Rictus tore the mask from his face.

Before they could glimpse even a hint of the man's face, the swirling winds burst into a full-on gale, and Rictus' form erupted into a pillar of pale-green flame. The four of them were rocked by intense force, and Neveah was sure she would have fallen had the three men not been standing in her path. As the fire swirled, she heard Rictus' voice ring out, suddenly a thousand times stronger than before:

> *I heard a voice amidst the four beasts,*
> *And looked to behold a pale horse.*
> *Its name that sat upon him was Death, and Hell followed with It.*

The chant ended and the flames dispersed, revealing a *much* different being standing before them. Its body seemed to be made of dull grey metal, like some kind of flexible iron. It stood nearly ten feet tall, and Its torso was molded in the shape of well-sculpted muscles without flesh to cover them. Its arms—all *four* of them—ended in long, bony fingers with wicked claws.

Its lower body was wrapped in the same tattered pale cloth as Rictus had been, and a pair of skeletal feet could be seen poking out. Its head was shaped like a humanoid skull, no longer a mask, from the top of which grew a sharp crown of bones. The skull glowed with an eerie pale light, the same shade of bluish green as the flames that had heralded Its appearance. From within Its hollow eye sockets, there were no longer any glimmers of light to be seen.

"We art Maveth, behind this veil. The final Death, The Rider Pale. The last of o'er wrought Horsemen. Preceptor of Samaritans."

"He's *WHAT!?*" Neveah shrieked, her shock at the monster's words overcoming her terror at its appearance.

"Surprised?" Stryfe shouted over the winds, cigarette somehow still held between his teeth. "What manner of creature did you think was capable of holding those like us in check?"

"No path unfolds, nor fate befalls, save chosen doom which We doth call."

Neveah hadn't thought anything could be worse than the artificial radio voice Rictus had used, but it now seemed positively pleasant by comparison. Despite the lyrical way in which it spoke, the eldritch creature's words hit her ear like the sound of a thousand rusted blades scraping together.

"Thy flesh be stripped, thy souls be rent. Anon thou faceth righteous end."

The terrible cyclone continued to buffet the group, but Neveah watched as the three Samaritans dropped into fighting stances: Stryfe raised his fists, again enveloped in black flames; Joshua lifted both arms, palms open, like some kind of wizard ready to cast a spell; and Creed summoned his silver-coated spear into his hands. After a moment, Stryfe looked down at himself and his brothers in confusion.

"What precisely do we think we're doing?"

"Guess we still have some fight left in us!" Joshua responded.

"Joshua," Creed called. "Can you at least get her out of here?"

The blind man shook his head. "I've been trying, but the Boss is veiling the whole crater with his presence. I can't warp."

"I'm not going anywhere!" Neveah shouted. Her words sounded defiant, but that was only because she had *far* passed the point of rational fear by now. Her hand went unconsciously to the bags tied at her waist. Even in the face of something like this, she did not want to die so long as a single seed remained unburied.

Stryfe let out a single haughty laugh. "Brave, Little Lamb, but foolish! Victory is not an option here!"

The creature that now called itself Maveth took a single step forward with one of Its skeletal feet. The ground seemed to groan and creak beneath Its weight, and the three brothers began a slow, measured retreat, forcing Neveah to stumble back in time with them. They backed away slowly, every step forward from their enemy met with a step back from them.

"We don't have to beat him," Joshua declared. "We just have to survive!"

"Oh yes, that's *far* simpler!" Stryfe retorted.

Creed seemed mildly less nihilistic. "You have a plan?"

"Not yet, but give me some time! None of our powers can reach him, but he'll have to get us with the scythe to finish it. We just need to stay out of range until I can think of a way out."

"Like Stryfe said, that's easier said than done."

"Yeah, but frankly, I'm tired of letting the Boss get Its way. Killing us is one thing, but if It thinks It's gonna rebuild us like some busted tools, It's got another thing coming!"

"Struggle if it be thy will," Maveth called in Its agonizing, archaic voice. "A traitor's lot shalt greet thee still."

With that, the creature held up its upper right hand. A grinning skull shimmered into existence within Its grasp. It shone such a clean, stark white that it seemed to have been carved from pure pearl.

Creed looked like he might be sick. "It's not playing around."

Maveth held the alabaster skull aloft. A moment later, the three Samaritan brothers let out simultaneous cries of pain, their bodies seizing up as they instantly fell to their knees. Neveah leaped back in shock, wondering what had happened.

It was Stryfe who gave her the answer; the brand upon his forehead was glowing like molten lead, veins of white energy webbing across his face as he hissed in agony. She looked next to Joshua, whose hands were hovering near the right side of his chest, then to Creed, who was simply arching his back as if he were being stabbed from behind. All three dropped the items they'd been holding in their mouths to the ground as they groaned.

Neveah covered her mouth in horror. Was this the power of the "Covenant" they'd told her about? Creed had said that fighting their leader was impossible, but Neveah hadn't realized that meant they were literally incapable of raising a hand to It!

As her mind whirled, she felt a light weight rest itself upon her. Turning, she saw the Dove perched on her shoulder as if it hadn't a care in the world.

"*You* got any ideas?" she shouted. As if the stupid thing wasn't just an extension of her own mind.

At her words, the Dove promptly flapped its wings and lifted off from her shoulder. It sailed past Maveth and out of the crater at surprising speed, eventually disappearing into the wrecked skyline of the city's buildings

Coward, Neveah thought dryly to herself, not that she could blame the thing—if it was running away, that just meant *she* wanted to.

Just as she was about to turn back, she noticed something: a small blue light had begun to shine from behind the building where the Dove had vanished. And it was steadily growing brighter.

What the hell?

The only one other than her who seemed to notice was Creed. Straining in his vain attempts to break free, his gaze happened to turn upwards and catch sight of the approaching light. His struggle ceased and his eyes, which had been squinting from the effort, went wide as saucers.

Through clenched teeth, he growled, "Oh, you gotta be—"

A bright blue object of some kind burst *through* the skyscraper, rocketing towards the crater like a comet. Neveah heard a high-pitched sound, like the revving of an engine into overdrive, just before the object zoomed over Maveth's head and slammed into the ground between It and them, with an impact that shook the ground beneath their feet.

A cloud of dust and debris shot up to obscure the object, but Neveah could see a dark figure standing from the small crater it had just created. It appeared to be humanoid in shape, wearing some kind of cloak. It stood with its back to the four of them, and Neveah watched as it seemed to raise something in the direction of the monster, who halted Its slow advance.

"Who dares impede this reckoning?"

In apparent response, a shining blue beam the size of a small house shot from the figure's position, deafening Neveah with the roar of exploding energy and launching the four of them back from the force. She landed with an *oomph* but immediately sat herself up, going as wide-eyed as Creed from what she saw.

The beam had dissipated, leaving a trail of black smoke and blue flames that reached all the way to the edge of the crater. Maveth was nowhere to be seen in the destruction, and the dark-robed figure stood tall before turning around to face the others.

As it did, Neveah saw that the right sleeve of its robes had been completely seared away, revealing not an arm underneath but rather a long, intricate-looking rifle that extended from the figure's shoulder. It looked like something from a long-forgotten age, stark white and lined with circuit-like patterns that pulsed with azure energy.

Neveah gaped at the impossible weapon before tearing her gaze away to look at the figure's face. Her jaw promptly hit the floor as she realized she had been wrong about what the figure was wearing: not robes, but the habit of a nun.

"Why?" came the sound of Creed's voice. The burning of his brand kept him locked in place, but the look in his eyes said he was *far* more concerned with this new arrival. "What the hell are you doing!?"

"If I cannot be a weapon," Stella declared, violet eyes glowing like beacons in the dimness of the world, "then I will be a shield."

Chapter XX
"Everybody Wants to Go to Heaven"

Kaleidoscope Unit 01, Designation "Diva": Initiating Combat Mode
Preliminary Assessment: Four non-hostiles present.
First Subject: Creed. Condition: Energy depleted, injured. Likely upset by Unit's arrival. Anger will be disregarded. Protection Priority: High.
Second Subject: Joshua. Condition: Energy level high, but viability for combat assistance is negligible. Protection Priority: Medium, reduced to Low if he attempts to speak.
Third Subject: Stryfe. Condition: Severely wounded, energy level unknown. Current Status: Unclear. Reason for non-hostility to be determined later. Protection priority: Zero.
Fourth Subject: Neveah. Condition: Unharmed, but weakened, distressed, confused. Understandable given current circumstances. Protection Priority: Maximum.
Declaration: This Unit will now attempt to explain its presence to—
Alert: Incoming energy signature.
Analyzing: Evasion unnecessary. Impact detected... no effect. As expected, Universal Authority granted by the skull of Conquest can only affect living creatures.

Observation: Target has now emerged from wreckage of beam cannon explosion. No visible damage. Unfortunate, but not unexpected.

Confirmed: Target identified as Rictus, leader of Samaritans, currently in full-powered form referred to as "Maveth".

Maveth: "An Eidolon we could not see. This battle holds no place for thee."

Response: "Incorrect. I believe I am precisely where I need to be."

Maveth: "Our power slays with but a thought. Thy struggles shalt avail thee not."

Response: "Also incorrect. Your powers will have little effect on me."

Maveth: "If magicks eld will not suffice, then quarrel We with inborn might."

Observation: Target has produced second skull in lower right hand. Composition: pure ruby. Presumably once belonged to Horseman of War.

Warning: Target's physical parameters and destructive potential increasing rapidly. Likely enhanced by power of War.

Threat Level: Immeasurable.

Danger: Target engaging. Speed greater than predicted. Incoming attack. Evading... evasion successful. Generating nano-machines to feet...

Produced: Repulsor boosters. Mobility enhanced.

Engaging: Circling behind target. Routing strength to left arm. Punch strength: 10,000 pounds. Strike delivered to back of target's head... ineffective. Target countering with unexpected flexibility. Dodging low... evasion successful. Generating nano-machines to arms.

Produced: Twin Miniature Beam Rifles. Moving to point blank range. Targeting enemy chest. Reducing output so as to not damage self. Firing.

Observation: Attack successful. Ineffective as expected, but target is stunned.

Engaging: Routing power to left leg. Kick strength: 25,000 pounds. Launching attack...

Danger: Target has recovered faster than predicted. Left leg caught. Crushing force: immeasurable. Enhanced punch incoming. Activating repulsor boosters... target successfully unbalanced. Extricated from target's grasp, but unable to evade attack. Damage received. Withdrawing to safe distance.

Running Diagnostic: Damage to chassis... minimal. Damage to clothing... significant, but acceptable. There are spares at the church.

Observation: Despite Creed's objections, modifying dress to allow for easier leg movement was a beneficial course of action.

Evaluating: As hypothesized, the Skull of War's ability to increase physical strength without limit in response to an enemy's spiritual power does not properly function against Diva Unit's purely mechanical strength. However, Unit's attacks are equally ineffective at current output level. Chances of physical victory... 0%.

Conclusion: Unit will continue to keep target at bay until allies propose viable strategy. Recommend enhancing combat parameters.

(Increasing energy output to Combat Lv. 2)

System Alert: Energy Levels at 45%. Unit will disregard.

Observation: Target producing third skull in upper left hand. Composition: pure obsidian. Presumably once belonged to Horseman of Famine.

Danger: Sudden energy spike detected, makeup unknown. Terrain in front of target is deteriorating and shattering rapidly. Shockwave expanding in Unit's direction. Taking to air... evasion successful.

Observation: Area struck by unknown energy appears to have deteriorated at immensely heightened speed. Power of Famine appears to have forcibly degenerated terrain instantaneously. Unknown if this ability will also affect Diva Unit's chassis. Will not attempt to verify. Unit will now commence aerial combat. Generating nano-machines in space around Unit's body...

Produced: 2 beam rifles, 2 pulse cannons, 2 rapid-fire energy chainguns, 2 heavy-duty cannons.

Engaging: Beginning aerial bombardment... successful. Target off-balance, but attempting to reprise. Repeated volleys of corrosive energy from black skull detected, but target's aim is insufficient. Evasion is simple.

Hypothesis: Target is unaccustomed to battling an opponent that is capable of fighting back.

System Alert: Energy Levels at 40%. Unit will disregard.

Engaging: Continuing bombardment, focusing on target's weapons. Increasing firing rate... successful. Target has lost grip on both red and black skulls. Enhancing thrusters. Initiating dive. Routing power to both arms. Punch strength: 100,000 pounds... strike successful. Target has been launched some distance away. Moving to pursue. Continuing bombardment. Generating nano-machines....

Produced: Graviton Hammer.

Observation: Target is recovering. No visible damage. Moving to intercept.

Engaging: Readying Graviton Hammer. Maximum output. Expected impact strength: 500,000 pounds... overhead strike successful. Target crushed. Significant damage to surrounding terrain confirmed. Acceptable. Retreating to safe distance.

System Alert: Energy levels at 35%. Unit can no longer disregard. Dispelling generated weapons, but maintaining current Combat Le—

Danger: Incoming attack from behind. Evading... successful.

Observation: Target has rapidly closed distance. Red and black skulls have returned to its grasp.

Danger: Target has produced sickle in lower left hand. Presumably target's personal weapon as Horseman of Death. Sickle is small in size, but energy makeup cannot be determined.

Recollection: Creed once mentioned to Diva Unit that the sickle of Death is capable of cutting through any material both physical and spiritual. Generating nano-machines.

Produced: Close-Combat Energy Saber. Initiating dueling protocols. Evasion of sickle is highest priority.

Engaging... Engaging... Engaging.... Engaging...

Observation: Target's physical parameters currently outstrip Unit's. Victory unlik—

Danger: Guard broken. Energy Saber lost. Attempting to eva—

DANGER: Slashing wound delivered to abdomen. Severe internal damage detected. Recommend immediate enhancement and retreat.

(Increasing energy output to Combat Lv. 3)
Emergency Action: Generating nano-machines.
Produced: Chest-Mounted Repulsor Cannon.
Engaging: Concentrating range. Repulsive strength: 1,000,000 pounds. Firing... attack successful. Target launched into crater wall. Unit has been rendered airborne from resulting force. Recovering posture... successful.
Running Diagnostic: Damage to chassis: notable. Internal damage: notable. Loss of artificial blood: notable. Damage to clothing: total. Generating repair nano-machines at damaged area... damage repaired successfully. Lost blood replaced.
Observation: That particular habit was Diva Unit's preferred article of clothing. Unit will now re-engage with increased aggression.

Upon reflection, Creed truly did feel sorry for Neveah. The girl had seen too many things in too short a time. A human mind was never meant to experience something so far beyond its ability to comprehend. All in all, he was impressed at how well she had managed to hold herself together.

But now, as she watched Stella rocketing around Maveth in all directions while bombarding It with the multitude of energy weapons she had generated in the air around her, the girl finally seemed to have reached her limit. She stared blankly, eyes glazed and expression vacant save for her mouth hanging open slightly.

She had been silent for so long that Creed began to fear her mind may have been genuinely broken. Though he was still unable to move from his kneeling position thanks to the searing brand on his back holding him in place, he attempted to call out, "Hey—"

"What the *FUCK* is going on!?" she screamed. Creed flinched back. Maybe she *wasn't* at her limit quite yet.

He struggle to speak though gritted teeth. "Look, it's a very long story. I promise I'll explain if we make it out alive."

Her response was shrill. "You'd better!"

"I must agree with the Little Lamb," came Stryfe's voice to Creed's right. He wondered how the demon could still sound so haughty while his brand was aflame. "I had assumed the doll must be defective for you not to bring her along, but now you're telling me she was perfectly functional all along?" He shot Creed a glare. "What on *Earth* was she dallying about in that church for?"

"Not a damn bit your business."

Stryfe rolled his eyes. "Shocking. I suppose I can't fault her flair for the dramatic, at least. She might very well have saved our souls with that timely entrance."

Creed wished he could argue. His initial reaction to Stella's arrival had been somewhere between fury and terror. He was still far from pleased but couldn't deny that they would certainly be dead already if she hadn't appeared.

Maveth was an avatar of judgment. All mortal and demonic souls had been placed under its power at the outset of The End, and ever since it had integrated the other three Horsemen into its being, it had gotten *much* better at reaping those souls.

The fact was, Stella was more or less the one thing left in the world could resist the Preceptor's powers. The skull of Conquest—which could command and control any being branded with Its Mark—would have no authority over one who lacked a natural soul.

The skull of War—which responded to an opponent's spiritual power and could infinitely heighten its wielder's own to ensure It was always stronger—could not properly measure the nun's purely mechanical strength.

The skull of Famine—with its ability to weather and decay any substance—might be able to damage her body, but she seemed easily capable of outmaneuvering its energy.

And while the Sickle—Maveth's own personal weapon—could instantly take the life of any it so much as grazed, that power was useless against one with no life to take, although its ability to slice through literally anything still presented a genuine danger.

All in all, Creed could have sworn her arrival was fate if such a concept still existed.

Unfortunately, although Stella would not be effortlessly slain like the rest of them, she seemed just as unable to affect Maveth in any meaningful way. Each one of her blows did little more than knock It off balance and dealt no real damage. Seeing as the

Pale Rider's body was not subject to things like the laws of physics, it wasn't surprising.

At the moment, Stella was slamming her Graviton Hammer down upon her foe's head, triggering a massive explosion of rock and dust that caused Neveah to yelp. It looked impressive, but Creed knew it wouldn't be enough.

Too frustrated to keep quiet, he craned his neck as far as he could and growled, "Are you done yet?"

His question was directed at Joshua, who was kneeling in place with his head bowed, silently muttering to himself. He appeared to be having some sort of fit, but this was simply what happened when his brother was utterly racking his brain.

Powering through the burning of his brand, he was currently running through scenario after scenario, possibility after possibility, trying to find any path that would lead them out of this nightmare. Unfortunately, Creed knew it was only a matter of time before Stella was overwhelmed, and couldn't bring himself to wait any longer.

"Joshua!" he shouted, prompting the man to turn towards him in irritation.

"I'm sorry. Am I taking too long to figure out how to stop the unstoppable embodiment of death?"

Creed heard the crashing of metal and energy behind him and looked to see Stella now engaged in a *swordfight* of all things. She had generated a shining white-blue beam saber into her grasp, and was currently wielding it against Maveth's vicious sickle.

The two weapons never clashed against each other, as the scythe would have cleaved through Stella's blade like it were air. Instead, she placed all of her focus on dodging the Horseman's attacks while reprising with her own.

As a machine, Stella moved with little flair as she fought, but nonetheless with absolute precision. Every movement was sharp and flawless, without a single ounce of wasted effort. Each time she evaded Maveth's scythe, it was by the barest of inches. Each time she struck, it was towards a weak point that would have slain any normal being in a single blow.

As skilled a fighter as she appeared to be, Creed knew the situation was dire. If Stella had resorted to such basic close-range tactics, it meant she was already being forced to conserve her energy. Which meant there was no time left for rumination.

"She won't last much longer," he yelled. "Joshua, you've got to—"

They were all silenced by the sound of Neveah's scream cutting through the air. Creed jerked his head towards her to see that her hands had shot up to cover her mouth.

Following her gaze, Creed's alarm grew tenfold as he saw Stella, evidently having made her first misstep, retreating with a long gash carved across her abdomen. Artificial white blood splattered about like paint.

"No!" he cried.

But before his panic could rise any further, an eruption of bright blue light burst from Stella's body, followed by a blast of force so intense it nearly sent him falling onto his backside.

His vision cleared to reveal a plume of dust and debris shooting into the air. He saw no sign of Maveth but was stunned to see Stella, body flipping wildly through the air towards them. Evidently, she had been blown back by her own attack.

Creed's breath caught in his throat, but the nun managed to right herself in the air as she tumbled. She landed roughly on her feet, skidding to a stop not twenty feet from the four of them. Her habit had been completely destroyed in the explosion, leaving her true self laid bare for all to see.

Without the hood, her lustrous hair, long enough to reach her lower back, was free to whip about in the wind, shimmering like gold even in the darkness of the world. Though her body was shapely and feminine, she possessed no anatomy, as the flesh-colored chassis that served as her skin was flawlessly smooth save for several noticeable seams along her joints, neck, and abdomen. Even with the grievous wound from which her white blood still poured, she stood tall and graceful like a beautiful mannequin, the last of her kind left in the world.

Creed watched as the gaping hole in her stomach was quickly sealed and repaired by the mysterious machines she housed within herself, leaving her body stained white but healed. He heard a soft gasp and turned to see Neveah gaping at the woman in awe.

Maveth emerged from the cloud of dust and rubble at the crater's edge, still without a hint of damage on Its form. The moment her wound closed, Stella rocketed forward with the boosters on her feet to engage her foe once more, shaping her arms into cannons again and harrying the Preceptor with energy blasts from a safer distance than before.

"She's... amazing..." came the girl's breathless voice.

"She is," Creed admitted. "But she's not invincible." He turned and glowered at Joshua, who had returned to his muttering. "We need a plan. Now!"

"Precisely what solution is it that you're expecting to hear?" Stryfe taunted. "I've an army of demons inside of me, and even if I *were* capable of summoning them all in this state, not a one would be of any use. We would have better luck fighting an army of angels than this monster!"

"Wait!" came Neveah's voice, and Creed turned along with his brothers to see her in a remarkably similar pose as Joshua, hand-on-chin in wild thought. Without looking at Stryfe, she shouted, "Say that again!"

Stryfe looked irritated at the girl making any sort of demand, but he nonetheless began, "I said we would have—"

"No. Never mind. Shut up! I don't actually need you to!" Stryfe looked ready to murder the girl, but she just let out a gasp and looked up as some apparent epiphany overcame her. "That's it!"

"What?" Creed asked, unable to keep the incredulity out of his voice.

Suddenly, Joshua's head jerked up in alarm. "Crap."

Creed turned, terrified of what he'd see this time, and felt his blood go cold.

Stella was unharmed, but the actual threat was Maveth's sickle, which had burst into a small pillar of pale green flame. When it dispersed, the Horseman's weapon had nearly tripled in size. It's handle now required two hands to grasp—Maveth had dispelled the useless black Famine skull in order to do so—and its sharp crescent blade was probably longer than Neveah was tall.

The reaper, it seemed, had grown tired of holding back. It had unleashed the seal upon Its sickle, and was now brandishing the one, true Death Scythe.

Maveth swung the terrible weapon down towards Stella, who wisely leaped to the side just in time. The Scythe embedded itself cleanly into the ground, but its immense cutting power was such that the scar of its impact burst over a dozen feet past where it hit, cleaving through a much more significant swathe of stone than should have been possible. The searing of Creed's brand suddenly seemed negligible compared to the sheer chill of the Scythe's mortal energies radiating across the crater.

"He's done playing around," Joshua said, voice tight with anxiety. "He's gonna cut right through her and finish us off."

Neveah took a step forward and raised her hands to cup her mouth. "Stella!"

The nun turned her head towards the girl for less than a second before returning her attention to Maveth, who was already delivering another slash of its massive weapon. It was enough to let Neveah know that she had been heard.

"Just hold him back a little longer! We've got a plan!"

"We do?" Creed and Joshua asked in unison.

Stella jumped and flipped over a horizontal swipe that Maveth had aimed at her legs. Once again, a long, crescent-shaped gash tore through the ground below. Stella landed, and turned over her shoulder to look at Neveah once more.

"Understood."

She raised both arms and held her palms towards Maveth as if to block Its path. As she did so, a small square of translucent blue energy appeared before her outstretched hands. The square quickly expanded into a rectangular barrier which stood twice as tall as Stella and thrice as wide.

Creed marveled at the sight. He knew that Stella's nanomachines—the last and greatest achievement of human science before The End—were capable of printing almost any weapon or construct, but the sheer potential of their versatility never failed to amaze him.

Even Maveth briefly halted Its charge at the sight, though the hesitation did not last long. Stepping forward, the Pale Rider swung Its weapon right into Stella's barrier. For a brief second, it seemed the construct might hold, but in the end nothing in all of creation was capable of resisting the Death Scythe's power. The blue shield cracked and shattered like a pane of luminescent glass, and Stella was pushed back several feet in the dirt from the force of the blow.

Undaunted, the nun raised her hands once more and brought up another shield. This time, she generated three at once, each layered close atop one another. Maveth struck again with its scythe, and though it broke through the barrier as easily as before, only a single layer was shattered.

Alas, all this did was delay the Horseman's advance. With frightening speed, Maveth swung the Death Scythe twice more in succession, breaking apart the remaining barriers and sending Stella back another few feet.

She only redoubled her efforts, bringing up shield after shield and layering them together as quickly as she could. Maveth's attacks were swift and merciless, a ceaseless combination where each slash destroyed a single barrier.

Its progress was slowed by the sheer number of shields Stella created, but the meager defense was not enough to halt It entirely. The Pale Rider gained a small step of ground with each handful of barriers it broke, slowly but surely pushing Stella back as It beat her defenses down again and again.

Icy dread stuck in Creed's throat. Stella's efforts were admirable, but those barriers were likely draining her energy reserves at a frightening rate, and it wasn't as if she'd arrived at full strength to begin with. She'd been neglecting her rest for a long while now, and Creed knew it was only a matter of time before what strength she had left would be exhausted.

"Creed," Neveah called to him. He turned to see her fixing him with wild eyes. "Remember what you told me about your Boss back at the church?"

Creed was utterly flabbergasted. "What?"

"If what you said is true, and you really can't beat him, then our only chance is to prove to him that he needs you!"

"What *are* you on about!?" Stryfe barked.

Before the girl could answer, a thunderous crash shook the ground. The four of them turned to see Stella sliding back in the dirt from an especially heavy strike of the Death Scythe that shattered three azure barriers at once.

The nun quickly brought up several more, but was now less than twenty feet away. She turned over her shoulder to look at them all, and the message was clear: in a moment, there would be no further retreat for any of them.

"No time!" Neveah shouted, and when she looked back at Creed, her expression was apologetic. "Please don't hate me for this!"

With that, she turned in the direction of the ongoing fight and abruptly dropped to her knees. She seemed to briefly lock eyes with Stella, then clasped both her hands before her chest.

Every thought in Creed's head turned to static as he realized what was happening. Powerless to reach out and stop the girl, he could only let out a desperate, "WAIT!"

But it was too late. Closing her eyes tightly, Neveah hunched forward, her forehead nearly reaching the ground.

"I'M HERE!!!"

GONG

The thunderous sound echoed through the sky and blanketed the entire area, commanding all other things to be silent. The unnatural winds whipped up by Maveth's appearance ceased in an instant, and the Pale Rider immediately halted Its attack. Its green skull slowly raised towards the sky, utter shock evident in its bearing despite the expressionless skeletal face.

GONG

The cadence of the titanic sound was unmistakable: that of a bell, larger and more powerful than any that had ever existed in the world. Its chime resounded like an earthquake from the heavens, signaling only certain doom.

"What senseless plot hath been commenced?"

Creed wished he could say he wasn't thinking precisely what Maveth had just voiced. Feeling numb, he looked to Neveah, who was still hunched forward with her eyes shut tight, her whole body trembling.

"Why?"

"I'm sorry," she whispered, sounding on the verge of tears. "It's the only way."

Stryfe's mouth hung open. "The girl's lost her mind."

"No," Joshua interjected. His mouth was agape as well, but some apparent realization seemed to come upon him. He looked up to the sky and, to Creed's shock, cracked an actual smile, albeit one tinged with no small amount of fear. "She's exactly right."

"Thou foolish Lamb, by terror yoked." The Preceptor had fixed its fathomless eye-sockets on the still-hunched girl. "'Tis from such fear, bedlam invoked?"

Neveah finally raised her head, and when she opened her eyes, they were filled with fire. To everyone's amazement, she met Maveth's gaze without flinching.

"Y-you think you're pretty hot shit, huh!?" Her voice was trembling, but only slightly. "But I hear there's something even *you* can't fight!"

Creed felt his jaw fall as he finally realized what was the girl was saying. This couldn't *possibly* be her plan, could it?

GONG

The third bell was loud enough to cause Neveah to flinch, but she refused to take her eyes off the monster.

"Let them up! I know you can't beat... whatever it is I just called! You have to let them do their jobs!"

"No doom but thine hath thus been sealed. With but a thought, we quit this field."

"Fine! Then you lose three Samaritans, one Lamb, and..." she motioned uncertainly towards Stella, "*that* whole situation!"

"Thy ends alone is what was sought. By scythe or wing, it matters not."

"Bullshit!" she barked, and Creed grew even more amazed. Speaking in such a manner to the Preceptor shouldn't even have been *possible,* but the girl continued without hesitation:

"What was all that you said about turning them into 'proper Samaritans'? Pretty sure you won't get to do that if we're burned to ashes! And you won't get *my* soul either! Besides—"

GONG

She flinched once more but grimaced and began again. "*Besides,* if you were going to run, you'd have done it by now! The fact that you're still here means you know what has to happen!"

GOOONG

Neveah stumbled as the earth shook with the force of the fifth crash. Quaking groans reverberated across the entire city as if all of the ruined buildings were threatening to collapse under the weight of what was coming.

"Sounds like we don't have much time!" Neveah declared. "What's it gonna be? You gonna give up and let it have us, or are you gonna let these three stand up and remind you why you need them?"

The atmosphere went eerily silent, as if the universe itself was waiting for a response. Maveth's hollow gaze bore into Neveah for what seemed like ages, its thoughts unknowable to all. The girl stood tall, but Creed could see how tightly she clenched her fists, as well as the sweat beading down her face and neck; she wasn't nearly as confident as she looked.

Then, without a word, the pearl skull of Conquest in Maveth's grasp vanished without a trace. Instantly, the terrible weight that had been pressing down on Creed's body from all directions abated, and the searing of the brand at his back cooled.

With a gasp, he fell forward onto his hands and knees, as did Joshua and Stryfe alongside him. He took in several deep breaths, his terror briefly overridden by sheer relief. When he finally looked up, Maveth had fixed its empty black sockets on him alone.

"FIGHT."

With that, the Preceptor was gone, fled to that unseen world only it could reach to watch events from afar.

"Boy," Neveah breathed, the look on her face telling Creed she had *not* expected her gamble to work, "h-he sure runs away fast, doesn't he?"

Joshua was the first to pick himself off the ground and let out something between a laugh and a sob, his terrified smile only growing wider. "Oh man. Never mind, Stryfe. She *is* crazy!"

Stryfe, who had also risen, let loose a dark chuckle of his own as he dusted off his fanciful outfit. "Oh, Little Lamb. I believe you are going to regret this."

GOOONG

Upon the sixth crash, the silver band of light that outlined the dark sun flared several magnitudes more brightly, illuminating the world around them from a dim grey to a frighteningly near-white. Everything seemed to grow sharper, the surrounding shadows heightening in contrast until they looked like solid blotches of ink.

As all of their heads snapped up to the now-gleaming hole in the sky, Stella finally dispelled her barrier and moved to join the group, hovering across the ground on her repulsive boots until she reached them.

"Welcome back!" Joshua called. "Gotta say, you sure know how to make an—ooooookay..."

He trailed off as Stella brushed by him without the barest of glances and approached Neveah. The nun looked down at her with the same muted expression as always, hands clasped in front of her.

"I have... a lot to explain."

"I'll say."

"This was the plan you decided on?"

"Yep."

"You understand that even if we do survive, the Preceptor will probably destroy us anyways."

She gave a shaky nod. "Yeah, I figured."

"This was not a very good plan."

"No it wasn't."

Creed finally picked himself up as well, and Neveah turned to look at him with eyes not unlike those of a dog who knew it had done something wrong.

"You..." he began, his voice shaking from sheer exasperation, "are an idiot."

"We've established that. What happens now?"

Creed racked his brain to think of a proper explanation for what exactly was coming, but in the end, all he could say was, "Now... you're about to see something terrible."

GOOOOOOOOONG

As if to punctuate his words, the loudest crash yet, like a million bolts of lightning shattering a million glass windows, rang out. Creed, Neveah, and his brothers clutched their heads and yelled in pain as their eardrums threatened to burst.

When he was finally able to unclench his eyes, he looked up to see that the yawning black maw of the dark sun was now marred by a long, jagged fissure that extended across the whole of its diameter. The insides of the fissure shined with pulsating golden light, and Creed found himself reminded of a vision he'd seen not so long ago about a burning field.

Then the sky burst open, and a soldier of God descended to destroy them all.

Chapter XXI
"Hallelujah"

Despite how futile a dream it had been, part of Neveah had always hoped she would one day be able to see light—*actual* light—shining in the sky again. Now, as the heavens burst open like a shattered window to reveal a canyon-sized void of sheer, golden brilliance, she regretted having ever wished for such a thing.

The light that now blanketed the city was not the warm, comforting shine of the sun; it was a harsh, imperious radiation, bearing down upon them with a force that threatened to bring them to their knees, demanding their supplication before it seared them away. It was one of the most terrible things Neveah had experienced.

Then the angel appeared.

Having never seen one, Neveah couldn't deny she had maintained a stereotypical image of God's warriors in her mind: great winged folk, beautiful and strong and shining with pure glory.

The thing that descended from the golden light was nothing like this. For one thing, it was roughly the size of a skyscraper; for another, it didn't remotely resemble anything humanoid.

It looked more to Neveah like some kind of floating crystal, wider in the middle and sharpened on both ends. Its "body" was a clear, shining white, like the most flawless stone she had ever laid eyes upon. There was no face or eyes that she could see, and numerous indecipherable symbols, crests, and letters appeared to be carved into its "flesh." The symbols linked together to form several bands of some sort, encircling the massive crystal like a set of glowing golden chains.

The ethereal crystal didn't do much as it finished emerging from the golden portal, just hanging in the sky and slowly rotating in place. She heard Creed click his teeth and looked to see him glaring up at the thing like someone being forced to confront their greatest fear.

"Ah," came Joshua's voice. "That feels like Uriel."

As Stryfe had declared, Neveah couldn't possibly have regretted her rash decision sooner. "How... how bad is that?"

"Could be worse," Creed responded, sounding surprisingly calm despite his glare. "Could be better."

It was then that the angel seemed to truly awaken. A deep, monotonous tone like an army of horns began to ring out, rising in volume and pitch until Neveah felt her teeth rattle. Just above the top of its crystal body, a massive halo of light shimmered into existence. It gleamed white-hot like metal in a forge, and Neveah had a feeling that if the creature drew any closer to the ground, her very flesh would melt from her bones.

"We need to prepare," Joshua declared. "Stryfe, distract them."

"I don't recall ever saying that you could give me orders," the demon huffed, but nonetheless stepped forward and held up a hand to the sky, his flared cuff fluttering dramatically in the wind.

"⁊ℰ⊺ᛋ⊓, Legion!"

Several dozen feet above their heads, what appeared to be a giant mass of some oil-like substance pulsated into existence. It seemed to be made of countless wriggling tentacles, swirling and lashing about into random shapes. Upon closer inspection, Neveah was horrified to see that the tip of each tentacle was marked with the image of a gaping, red-eyed face. The sound of a million voices moaning in agony filled her ears.

"I knew you were still holding back," Creed accused.

Stryfe ignored his brother and raised his other hand. He began to wave his arms as if he were a conductor, and the unholy mass of demons moved in response. It shaped itself into a long, swirling funnel and began to rocket away from the center of the crater at a surprising speed for its massive size.

The appearance of a demon finally seemed to compel the angel into action. A large, circular crest appeared in the air before it, adorned with the same strange symbols as its body, and from its center was fired a laser of bright blue light. The beam arced outwards, aimed right at the fleeing demonic whirlwind.

Stryfe wrenched his hands in a harsh motion, and the cloud twisted to just barely avoid the attack. Several buildings, however, were not so lucky; the beam of light passed through them like a hot knife. Rather than explode or vanish, they seemed to shift and change, becoming stark-white and looking to Neveah like they had been turned to stone.

She let out a gasp as the transformed buildings promptly buckled under their own weight, collapsing to the earth and disintegrating into a storm of white dust. The ground shook from the impact, and a colossal wave of debris spilled into the crater before pluming towards them.

Neveah latched onto Creed's arm, and couldn't hold back a shout of alarm. Just as it threatened to spill into the crater and choke them all, the wave appeared to slam into some kind of invisible wall. Startled, Neveah turned to see Joshua, hand raised and a look of exertion on his face as he somehow managed to keep the dust-storm out of the crater.

"Maybe take it *above* the buildings, Stryfe!" he shouted.

"It needs cover, you fool!" Stryfe shot back, hands still moving erratically.

"It's ignoring us?" Neveah asked.

"Legion may be a demon," Creed explained, "but it's made up of corrupted souls. Angels can't tell the difference. It can't be detected as long as it's hidden inside Stryfe, but bringing it out into the open is like throwing up a beacon."

"That being established...!" Stryfe shouted, "could one of my dearest siblings try making an actual effort to assist?"

Following Joshua's advice, he had commanded Legion to fly higher into the sky, above the cover of the buildings. The crystalline angel continued to fire its beams, and the swirling demonic cloud seemed only barely able to remain untouched.

"I'd prefer we end this before dear Legion is turned to a pillar of salt!"

Salt, Neveah thought numbly. *That light turned those buildings to salt.*

Joshua fixed his brother with a determined stare. "Creed. It's time."

She saw the white-haired man grimace, though he seemed to have been expecting this. When he spoke, she could hear a twinge of the old despair creeping into his words. "I can't. I'm out of energy."

"I'll form a link with you," Joshua responded. "You'll have all the strength I can give!"

Neveah didn't know what that meant, but the idea did not seem to reassure Creed in the least.

"I can go," Stella declared. "I'm not a Samaritan, but I should be able to weaken it enough for you to finish off if I enhance my attack output to the highest level."

Creed balked. "*No!* I don't know how much power you have left, but you're not wasting one more ounce of it!"

"If that's the case," Joshua said, "then there's no other option. You know I can't take the form to fight this thing, and Stryfe has to keep it distracted!"

Creed looked back and forth between Joshua, Stryfe, and the angel, which was still mindlessly firing its light at the demonic cloud swirling through the sky. Stryfe's dramatic gestures were growing tired and erratic, and it was clearly all he could do just to keep up.

Fixing Joshua with a look of honest fear, Creed asked, "What if I lose control again?"

"Then we die. Simple as that."

The words only seemed to further demoralize Creed, and Joshua's mouth softened into a sympathetic line. "I'm sorry, big brother. It's gotta be you."

Looking up at him, Neveah felt her heart break as she saw the trepidation in Creed's eyes. She understood why he hesitated and wished more than anything that she could think of some way to let him avoid this fight.

Unable to think of anything inspiring, she settled for reaching out and squeezing his arm in encouragement. He looked down at her as if he'd forgotten she was there, and she met his eyes with what she hoped was a determined gaze. Creed grimaced yet again but set his expression in stone and turned back to Joshua.

"Just do it."

Joshua gave a firm nod. He stepped over to them, cupping a hand around his mouth as he did so and whispering something Neveah couldn't make out. She realized she was still clinging rather childishly to Creed's arm and let go just as Joshua reached them.

Without warning, the unkempt man lashed his hand outward and gripped Creed roughly on the forehead. Creed reeled, growling through clenched teeth, but Joshua held firm. After a few seconds, he released his hold, and Creed stumbled back, gasping.

Joshua seemed somehow winded by whatever he'd just done. "Well?"

Creed straightened and looked down at his hands, flexing them a few times. "It'll have to do."

"Don't worry. I won't be stingy. You'll have every last drop if you need it."

With that, Joshua slowly lowered himself to his knees before bowing low and resting his hands palm-down on the ground before him. He lowered his head in intense concentration, and Neveah saw Creed straighten up with a jolt. In a moment, all of his exhaustion seemed to fade; somehow, Joshua was apparently sharing his strength with Creed to replenish the energy he'd expended during the fight with Stryfe.

"Neveah," Creed said, and she turned to see him removing his massive coat. He peeled the heavy garment from his body with deliberate motions to reveal his bare, muscular torso beneath.

Neveah let out a small gasp as she observed his back, upon which was branded the design of three hook-like symbols locked together in a spiral. It was much larger than Joshua's and Stryfe's had been.

Creed turned to face her, and she noticed the scar on his face extended far down to his chest as well. Folding his coat, he held it out to her with surprising casualness.

"Hold on to this for me."

Neveah took the garment without question. It was so big that she had to clutch it in both arms. Creed turned next to Stella.

"Joshua won't be able to defend while he's maintaining the link. Keep her safe. And yourself."

"Understood," the nun responded.

Walking over, she placed her hands on both of Neveah's shoulders. With a low hum, a new barrier of blue energy, this one smaller and dome-shaped as opposed to the rectangular one from before, shimmered into existence, encasing Neveah and Stella under its canopy while the three Samaritans remained outside.

Creed gave Stella a firm nod. The two stared at each other for several seconds, and whatever passed between them was something Neveah couldn't see. Eventually, he turned his attention back to her.

"Creed..." she whispered, unable to find any words beyond that. Despite her attempt to encourage him, the truth was that fear had gripped her heart tight and wouldn't let go.

His expression softened ever so slightly. "Don't worry. I'll be back. Whatever happens, don't leave Stella's side."

He turned away from them to face the rampaging angel, which was still aimlessly firing its holy beams as Legion shot back and forth through the air to evade them.

"What are you going to do?" Neveah called after him, even though she already knew the answer.

"Same thing I've always done: Protect my children."

With that, Creed stood taller and prouder than Neveah had yet seen him, holding his arms straight out to the sides and bowing his head. His voice, now carrying a powerful echo, resounded into the air as the brand on his back began to glow:

"When the earth was formless and void, and darkness covered the deep waters..."

At once, all of Creed's colors swelled around his form, enveloping his body and obscuring him from view as they began to swirl about like a vortex of paint.

"The Spirit of God hovered o'er the dark surface..."

The colors swirled faster and faster, mixing and growing brighter as they did so. Their individual pigments became indistinguishable, turning to a font of pure white.

"And the Lord said, 'Let There Be Light.'"

The white pillar flared like a sun, briefly blinding Neveah and forcing her to cover her eyes. To her surprise, the sensation was not unpleasant. Unlike the harmful radiance exuded by the mad angel, this light felt warm and soothing, its mere presence seeming to fill her with vitality. When the shine had faded, Neveah uncovered her eyes to behold the most beautiful sight she had ever seen.

He was still Creed, insofar as he possessed the same frame and build. The pants and boots had vanished; all that adorned him now was a pure white robe covering his lower half. His torso was even more impressively sculpted, tanned skin now devoid of the sinister brand that had been there before.

Pearl-colored energy radiated off every inch of his body, as if his very flesh was exuding starlight. His hair, once cropped short, now flowed long and luxuriously down his back like a lion's mane. It was whiter than ever, so lustrous and bright that it seemed to be formed from light itself.

At his back, the nine colored spheres had reappeared, each more vibrant than ever, but were joined by a tenth as well, this one larger than the rest and white like a dwarf star. The spheres arranged themselves in an intricate formation with the new white globe at its center.

A series of white bands shimmered into the spaces between each sphere, connecting them in a shape that reminded Neveah of a tree and its branches. As if to complete the resplendent look, a flawless alabaster crown materialized atop his head, tall and regal and fitted to adorn him alone.

Neveah found herself unable to do much but gape at the resplendent sight before her. The being turned slowly over his shoulder, and she saw that a smooth, featureless mask now covered his face. It appeared to be made of an opal-like stone, and it too glimmered with a variety of colors.

To her surprise, the large scar could still be seen extending down to his chest past the mask, the only imperfection to be found on his form. It seemed almost wrong to Neveah's eyes; what force could possibly have left such a scar on a being this immaculate?

"My Name is Adam," the being declared in a familiar voice, calm and solid and full of glory. "First King of Man. Father of the Lambs. Crusader of the Samaritans."

"...Oh," was all Neveah could muster.

"Don't be afraid," he intoned, and his words filled her with a strange sort of comfort.

The tree of spheres at his back flared once more and, propelled by some invisible power, the shining man rocketed into the sky like a brilliant comet. Neveah could only clutch the coat in her arms more tightly and try to hold back tears as she followed his ascension.

For just a single moment, the Man called Adam allowed himself to simply revel in the joy of flying once again. His power carried him high into the air, leaving the desolate earth behind him. He soared without effort, warmed by the glow of ten spheres behind him.

Keter, the Alabaster Core, had finally appeared, arranging the other Cores into their true form as the Tree of Life from which his wife had once drawn her power before passing it to him.

As he drew closer to the ongoing battle in the sky, Adam could see that his arrival had come not a moment too soon, as Legion had finally been cornered. Dodging away from one of Uriel's purifying lights, it was unable to avoid carrying itself into another that had been fired soon after.

Deciding the damned souls did not deserve to be so harshly erased just yet, Adam propelled himself forward. Covering hundreds of feet in a split second, he imposed himself between Legion and the oncoming attack.

Reaching within, he called upon Keter. Only available to Adam in his true Samaritan form, the Alabaster Core combined the energies of all other Cores together into a dwarf star of limitless energy, which he could then shape into any form he desired.

From his hand, Adam summoned a bolt of blinding lightning, which flashed outward and carved through the angel's attack like a knife. The ray of light dispersed harmlessly while Adam's attack continued forward, slamming into Uriel's crystal body and finally interrupting the creature's mindless barrage.

Turning his masked head to face the cloud of spirits, Adam silently willed it to return to its master. Legion obeyed without hesitation, dispersing in a shower of black ash. Stryfe would likely be irritated at having his spawn commanded by another, but now that Adam had awakened, its presence was no longer needed.

Uriel did not immediately move to attack, floating before Adam like a silent beacon. Though they had no face, Adam could feel the angel's gaze upon him, trying to comprehend what they were seeing.

Then, like a spark had been lit, Uriel's halo burst with a flare of angry white light, and another melodious scream pierced the air. It seemed that the angel did, in fact, remember their long-lost little brother.

For just a moment, Adam allowed himself a pang of pity. Poor Uriel, once blessed with a light that was loving rather than searing. The youngest of the archangels, Adam had always gotten along rather well with them whenever they joined him in his devil hunts across the ages. They would often assure him that one day all would be well, that the world would be made right.

Seeing them now, just as mad and lost as the rest, filled his heart with pain. But this was not the first time he'd been forced to put the Angel of Light down, and he would not hesitate.

The battle began in earnest as Uriel summoned three separate crests and fired a stream of light from each one. Adam took off, breaking through the sound barrier in less than a single breath. The beams moved to follow him, but he evaded without difficulty, making sure to stay high so none of the cityscape below was turned to salt.

He fired three more bolts of lightning from his hand, each crashing into and shattering one of the crests, before launching a fourth at Uriel directly. It impacted, and Uriel let out another song-like scream.

Though Adam's attacks took the form of lightning in this state, they were not genuinely destructive. What he cast was not electricity, but rather the energy of pure Creation. His goal was not to destroy his foe, but instead overwhelm its being with the dynamism of Life itself until it could no longer sustain its physical form.

Uriel did not seem keen on making this task easy. Dozens of smaller crests appeared along the length of their crystalline body, and from each one burst forth a single large diamond. Brimming with holy light, each was shaped like a long, thin pyramid, and looked to be deathly sharp. Propelled by Uriel's will, the crystal missiles rocketed towards Adam at supersonic speeds, each one capable of tearing through his supernatural body as if he were any mortal man.

Adam zoomed about in all directions, looping and turning and diving to avoid the sailing crystals. The projectiles were just as agile as he, circling around and cutting off every vector of escape. Before long, they proved too fast and too numerous for him to properly evade, and he found himself encaged on all sides as they closed in around him.

Drawing himself in tight, Adam called a swirling cloak of Keter to envelop his body in the form of powerful whipping winds. Just as the crystal missiles threatened to skewer him, Adam unfurled his body and flung his arms out to the side.

At the same time, he released the pent-up gales all at once, creating a miniature hurricane of White in every direction that smashed apart the incoming diamonds. They erupted together with the horrible sound of exploding glass, and the broken shards quickly dissipated into light.

Though he had succeeded, Adam could already feel his energy beginning to dwindle. Joshua's shared reserves were vast, but the Keter Core was one that took an immense amount of effort to utilize, to say nothing of the void draining him even further. He needed to end this as quickly as he could.

Raising his right hand to the sky, Adam generated as much energy as he was willing, shaping and expanding it into the form of a massive greatsword that towered into the heavens, twenty feet wide and a hundred feet tall. Swinging with all of his immeasurable might, Adam swung the blade in a downward chop towards Uriel's form.

The mad angel attempted to fire several streams of light to intercept the attack, but Adam's sword cut through them like mist. His blow struck true, carving a long, deep gash down the length of Uriel's body and severing the bands of golden script that encased it in the process. Another high-pitched wail rang out, but Adam had closed his heart to the angel's pain.

Uriel hung motionlessly in the air as the glowing white wound pulsed and seared their crystalline body. Gradually, a flood of bright turquoise energy began to erupt and flare out of the gash, and the angel's melodic screams seemed to reach new heights.

To preserve energy, Adam willed his massive sword to disperse but did not lower his guard. Despite the mighty strike he had landed, his true target had been the golden seals across Uriel's body. He would not be able to finish this so long as the angel was hiding in their restrained form, and now that the bindings had been severed, the true contest could finally begin.

In mere moments, Uriel was completely encased in the mass of blue-green light, which promptly burst away in an explosion of force that briefly left Adam deaf and blind. When his senses returned, Uriel's body had expanded and evolved. Much like Adam himself, the angel had unleashed their true form.

Their body was still composed of crystal, but this was where the similarities ended. Rather than the clear white from before, it now shone a deep and fathomless aquamarine. Their "head", if it could be called that, was now shaped like a massive, pointed steeple. The shining halo remained, circling the new spire.

Moving downwards, the single unified diamond began to splinter off into dozens of branching points, some large and others small, all jutting outwards in various directions. At the bottom, another large, sharp spire emerged from the mass of smaller ones like a gigantic lance.

From either side of the creature extended two titanic wings, at a total of four: the appropriate number for an archangel of their rank. Rather than feathers, the wings were also comprised of countless sharpened crystal segments, all shimmering beneath the blinding golden light from the tear in the sky. All in all, Uriel now resembled a colossal turquoise chandelier more than anything, both awesome and terrifying in their sheer resplendence.

Gathering more power into his hands, Adam readied himself for the next phase. Rather than immediately attack, however, Uriel surprised him by blinking out of sight completely in a split-second flicker of light.

Looking around in anticipation, he was just barely alerted to a surge of power, and whipped his masked head upwards in time to see the mad angel reappear barely fifty feet above him, four crystalline wings flared outwards.

Before Adam could react, Uriel gave a single mighty flap of said wings. A sound like that of every bell and wind chime in the world ringing at once overrode his senses, and he had just enough time to bring his forearms to bear in a cross guard before hurricane-force winds and a blast of sheer angelic power slammed into him.

The impact of the gale sent him rocketing towards the earth, and although his star-forged body was nigh-indestructible, the metaphysical power of Uriel's energy shot through him, searing his spirit and threatening to eradicate his entire being.

Barely managing to hold himself together, Adam focused his energy and forced himself to halt his meteoric descent. He came to a stop about a hundred feet above the crater, *far* closer than he intended to be to his companions below.

Now high above him, Uriel righted themselves and extended their wings to full length once more. They seemed to shimmer more intensely, but Adam soon realized that the glimmers were not a result of the golden light glinting off of Uriel's body. They were coming from *within* the angel itself, tiny pinpricks of blue light accumulating at the tip of each individual "feather."

Just as Adam realized what was happening, the collected glimmers all shot forth at incalculable speeds, each wingtip firing volley upon volley of azure light. The projectiles were so dense in their number that they resembled an all-encompassing rain which threatened to shower Adam and those below him in a ceaseless hail of purifying comets.

With mere seconds before impact, Adam raised both hands and created a titanic white shield that covered the entirety of the space above the crater. Uriel's rain fell upon the shield with merciless abandon. Despite their relatively small size, each one struck with greater force than any of Stryfe's demons had been able to muster, like hundreds upon thousands of meteor impacts delivered all at once.

Again and again they fell, a never-ending supply streaming from each of Uriel's glorious wings. Adam felt each impact upon his shield as if it were his own body. He forced more and more energy into the construct, strengthening its density to conceptual levels that defied the laws of physics. But the force behind Uriel's barrage was equally unfathomable, and despite his efforts, Adam could see the barrier begin to crack and buckle beneath such a relentless assault.

More out of desperation than anything resembling an actual plan, Adam took hold of his shield and focused all his strength into one mighty *push*. The barrier shot upwards with such force that it successfully pushed its way through Uriel's downpour of light.

The shield rocketed ever higher until it finally slammed into the angel, launching them even higher into the sky until they were nearly knocked back into the golden portal from which they had emerged.

With a gasp of exertion, Adam allowed his shield to shatter and dissipate, doing his best to recover strength for the next attack. But rather than warp back into range, Uriel chose to remain where they were, their form now an ominous silhouette beneath the golden portal.

Adam warily stared his foe down, then tensed when he saw the angel bring all four of their wings in tight. They came together to lightly touch the sharp end of the massive spire which formed the angel's lower body.

Each of the five converging appendages began to glow at their tips, their energies gradually coalescing and combining in the space between to form a sphere of sheer, blue-green power. The sphere was modest in size at first, but began to expand rapidly as Uriel's holy light flooded into it.

Adam found himself recalling a similar sight from his battle with Bahamut, but this coming disaster would be nothing like the globe of black water the demon had used. He could sense that Uriel was bringing the entirety of their might into one final attack. If it was successfully unleashed, not just the city, but the entire region would likely be reduced to a flat, featureless landscape of purified salt, wiped clean of anything even resembling life.

Adam looked back over his shoulder to the crater below, where the others watched him fight. He could still make out the plasma barrier Stella had erected, but such a defense would be utterly useless against Uriel's power.

Guess I have no choice.

Adam had hoped to avoid using this ability; his energy was running dangerously low by this point, and with the ever-present void still nipping at his heels, he wondered if he would even be capable of calling it forth. Seeing as it was his only option, however, Adam braced himself and called upon all he had left.

Raising his right arm, he angled his hand and pointed a single index finger in Uriel's direction. At the tip of the digit, a single mote of light materialized, pulsing rapidly with the power already building inside. Calling upon the strength of all ten spheres at his back, Adam proceeded to funnel every last ounce of White he could muster into its form.

He put the entirety of his will into the task, refusing to leave even a shred of power within himself. Before long, the concentration of energy at his fingertip had reached a level of intensity such that it rivaled an exploding star; if Adam's willpower wasn't containing it, its heat would have already incinerated the land below.

Another high-pitched wail told Adam that his time was up. He looked up to see Uriel's wings disconnect themselves from the now-massive sphere, at which point the collection of energy erupted into a colossal beam of blinding aquamarine light headed straight for the city.

Without a sound, Adam released his gathered White all at once, and the star at his finger erupted into a small, controlled supernova that matched the angel's beam in size and shape.

In addition to the gigantic pillar of Alabaster, several smaller streams emerged from Adam's finger to encircle his attack: Crimson, Azure, Laurel, Gold, Violet, Rose, Amber, Silver, and Umber. Nine glowing trails spiraled around the outside of the larger beam and collected at the top, forming something akin to an iridescent drill.

This shaft of light, laden with all the life Adam could muster, soared into the sky to meet Uriel's attack. The twin powers came together in an explosion of such force that it seemed like the world might shake itself to pieces. They reached an instant stalemate, crashing against each other while their casters each struggled to overwhelm the other.

Adam focused wholly and completely on nothing but pushing back the cleansing light, but knew he was outmatched. The angel had gained a significant head start in gathering their power, and Adam's energy levels were now all but depleted.

Try as he might, he began to feel the unmistakable pressure of his beam slowly being pushed back by Uriel's. It was only a matter of time before he was overwhelmed completely.

Suddenly, a surge of unknown energy shot through Adam's being, eliciting a gasp. Whipping his head around, he looked down to the ground where Joshua should have been. He hadn't moved, but next to him now was Stryfe, standing tall in his flamboyant ballroom attire with a hand on Joshua's back as he joined himself to their link and offered up his own power. The Devil seemed to notice Adam's stare, looking back with a prideful sneer.

Adam nearly laughed aloud. Evidently, he and Stryfe beating the hell from each other had been better therapy than expected. Though he would certainly never verbally express his gratitude, Adam accepted the additional energy and turned his attention back to the struggle at hand.

Straining from the effort, he began to expel Stryfe's proffered power into his attack. The iridescent beam now matched Uriel's in strength and even began to slowly push it back. He could do it. With this final gift, Adam would be strong enough to—

The pit opened again.

It swelled up inside him like a black hole, eating away at his insides with boundless hunger. Adam let out a cry of pain and convulsed, barely managing to keep his finger pointed towards Uriel while his other hand clutched at his chest.

Looking up, he saw his beam begin to warp and destabilize. He fought to regain control, but then he saw it: deep within the White core at his fingertip, small sparks of Black began to flicker.

No. No, no, NO! Not now! Why NOW!?

It was happening again. He'd let down his defenses, focused so intensely on the enemy in front of him that he'd expended all of his Color without regard to what would be waiting behind it.

Just like with Belphegor. Just like with Michael. He was going to fail. He was going to fail *again*.

Please, he prayed, though he knew there was no one there to hear him. *Please don't let this happen! I have to protect them this time. Oh God, I have to protect her!*

Everything disappeared.

He blinked, wondering if he'd somehow just died, but that wasn't the case. There was simply nothing around him but a blank infinity, silent and calm.

Looking down at himself, Adam saw that he was somehow Creed again, adorned in his usual leather coat. He noticed that his right hand was clenched into a fist; he was holding something. Confounded, he slowly opened his hand to see what it was.

The seed. He'd forgotten he still had it. But it was there, resting in his gloved palm. She had given it to him, a desperate attempt to save something that couldn't be saved. A pointless gesture that would never change a single thing.

Now, it was everything.

Creed closed his eyes, gripped the seed tightly in his grasp one more, and shut it all out: the void eating at his soul from without, and the Black gnawing at his heart from within. They weren't there. There was only him and the seed in his hand. It was small. It was weak. It was so fragile he feared it might break apart at any moment.

But it was enough.

Then, for an instant so quick it might have been an illusion, he felt as if someone was standing behind him. A whisper came to his ear. The gentle voice of someone he hadn't heard since the day everything ended:

I believe in you.

His eyes snapped open, and he was Adam again, floating in the sky above a dead city and wielding his own star in a battle of wills against a mad angel. He looked high into the atmosphere where the pitiful creature loomed, and no longer felt fear. He was strong now. Stronger than he had ever felt before in his long, long life. There was no doubt anymore. No hesitation.

With one last defiant shout, Adam gave a final push. His beam of Colors burst forward, pushing back Uriel's holy light as if it wasn't even there. The beam pierced upwards, straight for its target, and Adam roared the whole way. The supernova reached Uriel and, with one final song of despair, the angel was consumed in a maelstrom of vibrant light.

Pure radiance rent their crystalline body asunder, but did not do so with a ruthless burst violent explosion. Uriel's body simply came undone, unable to sustain its form in the face of sheer, overwhelming Life. Their body bloomed into a mass of pure, untainted White before finally dissolving into countless fragments of light without a sound.

The shimmering particles were slowly drawn upwards, pulled into the endless golden void by the myriad angels hidden within. Adam watched in silence as his poor friend's soul was drawn back to a place he could not reach, doomed to one day repeat this tragic cycle all over again.

When the last of the angel's light had vanished, the massive wound in the sky seemed to repair itself in reverse, rapidly closing and erasing all evidence that anything had ever occurred.

The world was quiet again.

Chapter XXII
"Little Lights"

Neveah hadn't thought it possible to miss the barren grey sky she'd been living under for the last eternity, but when the golden vortex sealed itself back together, and the harsh light finally vanished, her knees felt weak from the relief.

She didn't have time to fall, of course; as soon as Stella allowed her domed barrier to dissipate, Neveah rushed to meet the shining figure that was slowly descending upon the center of the crater.

It was quite a distance to jog, made harder by the bulky coat in her arms, but she scarcely noticed her fatigue. She drew near just as Creed—or Adam, she supposed—softly touched down to the earth.

She'd come within a handful of feet when he held up a hand to stop her, which she reluctantly obeyed. The others, who had been approaching at a much calmer pace than she, soon joined them. Together they watched as Adam raised his hand higher, like a conductor calling for a high note. For a moment, nothing happened, but soon Neveah heard a rustling sound at her feet.

She glanced down to see numerous small shapes emerging from the dirt; the clay markers, which had been pushed underground for protection before Creed had begun his fight with Stryfe.

Neveah had almost forgotten about them, and gaped as they were magically pulled back upwards. Rather than return them to their original positions, Adam drew the earthen stakes fully from the dirt, where they then rose high into the air above their hands.

Adam twisted his hand, and the floating markers began to move about in the air, arranging themselves in some sort of new pattern. Looking back down, Neveah realized that he was suspending them directly above the enormous black stain of the dead angel that marred the crater's floor; the pattern they had taken was the shape of Michael's remains.

She turned back to Adam just in time to watch him give a sharp *snap* of his fingers. As he did, the clay stakes flared with light all at once. In an instant, they had transmuted from solid objects to wisps of pure, white flames.

They flickered high in the air like hundreds upon thousands of dazzling white candles, and for just a moment, Neveah could almost convince herself that there were stars in the sky once more.

The ethereal sight did not last long. Adam dropped slowly and reverently to his knees, bringing his hand down to the ground as he did so. The moment his palm touched earth, the countless white flames shifted again, taking on the form of shimmering water droplets.

They fell to the earth like rain, landing upon the ashen stain beneath them. Each one left a mark of bright light where they touched, which then spread out to conjoin and meld with the others. In mere moments, the frightening black shape of the dead angel had turned a glimmering ivory.

Adam's strong voice rang out: "Be free."

At his command, the white shape burst into a shower of particles, not unlike those which Uriel had become when Adam defeated it. The motes of light—their number impossible to even estimate—drifted upwards, like a gentle snowfall in reverse. Many of them passed closed Neveah as they rose, and she felt a warmth the likes of which there hadn't been since the true sun shone in the sky.

The sheer majesty of the sight stole a single tear from her eye. She realized now that the "void" Adam had inadvertently created that day was more than just a dark force that drained his color. It was a tomb, a sinister vacuum which had trapped all of the lives were lost. He had planted those stakes as both penance and punishment, forcing himself to experience the pain that came with remembering the names of each person he'd failed to save.

At her side, Neveah noticed both Joshua and Stryfe give deep intakes of breath. They stood a little straighter, like a weight had been lifted from their shoulders. Though she already suspected, Neveah asked, "What did he do?"

Joshua seemed briefly too awed to answer, but managed a quiet response. "He purified the void."

"I should have done it a long time ago," came Adam's voice. He was staring at the little lights as they ascended, and even with his expression hidden behind the opal mask, Neveah could guess what he must be feeling. "I cared more about punishing myself than helping my children."

Suddenly anxious, Neveah resumed her approach, still basking in the warmth of the ascending lights. Adam turned to meet her, looking down on her with his blank face. Everything she had planned to say abandoned her, and she found herself unable to form the words. In the end, it was he who broke the silence.

"Howdy."

As soon as he said it, Neveah saw the Dove fly in from nowhere and land unnoticed on the top of his head. The sheer absurdity of the image finally broke through Neveah's trepidation.

"H-howdy," she replied with an exasperated chuckle.

"Questions?"

"About a million."

His head suddenly twitched as if he could hear something, which thankfully prompted the Dove to flutter off his head and out of sight. "They'll have to wait."

He turned over his shoulder, and Neveah followed his gaze to see that Maveth had once again materialized before them, two hands empty and two occupied with the massive scythe. The monster's pale-green skull was angled upwards, taking in the rising starlights.

"Mournful wights, so long confined. Seek rest within this soul of mine."

The creature raised Its two free hands, and the lights ceased their ascent. They changed direction, moving towards Maveth like a river of stars. One by one, each little flare made its way into one of the Preceptor's palms, where they promptly disappeared inside Its being. In mere moments, all the glimmers had vanished and the familiar chill of the empty world returned.

At first, Neveah felt repulsed. The sight of those beautiful souls being drawn into this terrible creature's body seemed an affront. They had only just been freed, and now were forced into yet another prison? The very thought made Neveah sick, but it was then that she recalled something Creed had said to her before:

"Even once your ashes are scattered, your soul will go nowhere. It will be stuck right where you were burned, left to float screaming and tormented in the aether for the rest of eternity."

Joshua had told her that the Preceptor's role among the Samaritans was to gather up lost souls. Neveah would never fully understand how it all worked, but Creed had made it fairly clear that a spirit left adrift was *not* at peace. As much as she feared and detested Maveth, it seemed that whatever fate awaited the souls within Its being was preferable to a torturous eternity left wandering a non-existent afterlife.

Neveah's musings were interrupted when the Preceptor turned Its gaze upon her. The twin voids that served as the creature's hollow eye-sockets bored into her own, and Neveah felt instinctively that the Pale Rider wished for her own soul just as much as the myriad It had consumed.

Though the thought frightened her, Neveah was startled to realize that Maveth's presence no longer seemed to strangle and immobilize her. The pressure was still there—she could feel it pressing in from all sides—but somehow it felt more bearable than before, if still unpleasant. Perhaps it was because she was standing next to Adam?

Or maybe it was just because Maveth seemed far less intimidating after running away to let Its goons do the fighting.

Adam himself took several slow, deliberate steps in the lead Samaritan's direction, standing between It and the rest of them in an undaunted stance. Its line of sight broken, Maveth met his masked face instead.

"Crusader bold from battle won. Restrain thyself. The work is done."

Adam didn't respond for a moment, but eventually his body was encased by another swirl of myriad colors. When they dissipated, Creed was standing before them, his hair again shorn, lower body again clothed in leather, and the three-pronged brand again emblazoned on his back.

Turning to her, he held out a hand, and Neveah happily returned the coat she'd been holding. He took a few seconds to put it on, and Neveah was surprised at how much more at ease she felt. Adam's shining form had been beautiful, but *this* man, it seemed, was whom she preferred to stand beside.

Maveth was looking between the five of them. "Confess doth We to be confound."

Neveah opened her mouth to speak, but Creed responded first as he finished zipping up the coat's high collar. "It's like the girl said, Boss. We just had to remind you that you need us."

Neveah raised an eyebrow at the words. *Look at him, acting like he thought this was a great idea all long.*

"An angel mad, called knowingly. Thou thought this would appeaseth We?"

"What we think is that I've made it clear I'm still more than capable of fighting the Adversaries. Of course..." he motioned to Joshua and Stryfe, "given the state I was in, I can't deny that I wouldn't have been able to succeed without our Crucifer and Apostate here, so I'd like to think we *all* managed to prove ourselves today."

"A frenzied plot to forestall death. 'Tis little more than wasted—"

"Oh, *do* stop with the fucking pontificating!" Stryfe interjected, the profanity clashing sharply with his haughty accent. "If none of this was truly enough to impress you, then by all means, shut your Shakespearean gob and feel free to resume our battle once more. But do not assume we shall make it easy for you!"

"He's right, Boss," Joshua chimed in, fixing the creature with a rather intense stare for someone without eyes. "We may be half-dead, but if you think we're gonna let you 'rewrite us', you can think again. If we have to, we'll come at you again and again, and I swear we won't stop until you *have* to kill us."

"Thy boast is made with little weight. Thou hast no choice in meeting fate."

"We all have a choice, Boss," Creed declared. "And so do you. You can choose to accept that I regret the things I've done, and the things I *haven't* done. And if you so choose, you can let *me* choose to atone for it."

For once, there seemed to be the slightest pause before Maveth responded. "Thy words are brave, but like a dream; ephemeral and oft unseen. Could strength not fade, as hath before? How knoweth We thou wilt endure?"

"You're a fan of oaths, aren't you? Allow me to make a new one." Creed raised his arms as if in praise and then, in quite possibly the most deadpan and patronizing tone Neveah had ever heard, declared:

"O' mighty Preceptor! I beseech your mercy so that I may atone for my weakness and cowardice. From this day forth, I swear to re-dedicate myself to the Covenant which binds we Samaritans body and soul. I shall resume my worldly travels, combatting the Adversary wherever they should appear and defending the Lambs until your mighty presence accepts them into your being. And if ever the day should come where my heart wavers in its conviction once again, I swear I shall willingly subject myself to whatever fate you, in your fathomless wisdom, see fit to bestow upon me!"

Everything was dead silent. Neveah's mouth hung open at the utter audacity of what she'd just heard, certain that all of their souls were about to be reaped. However, to her utter bafflement, Maveth remained still and motionlessly regarded Creed's unconvincing words for what felt like ages. Just as Neveah couldn't bear it any longer:

"T'would seem despair which veiled thine eyes has at long last been cast aside. 'Tis true that We did not expect such forthright vows of deep respect."

Neveah nearly fell onto her ass from the shock. That condescending crap had actually *worked*? Was this thing that susceptible to flattery, or did it just plain not understand sarcasm?

But indeed, Maveth was already turning its glowing green skull in Joshua's direction. "What say thee, of this contrition? Dost thou share thy kin's devotion?"

Devotion!? Neveah balked again. Could it be this eldritch monstrosity was some kind of stupid?

Joshua held up his hands. "Hey, my loyalty was never in question! I was only standing up for my big brothers! Long as we're all friends, I've got no problem with how things were going.

He gave a slight grin that Neveah could have sworn seemed almost dangerous, "Besides, let's be honest. I'm the only thing that's been keeping our merry little band from tearing itself to pieces. You were never really gonna deal with me."

Neveah was once again stunned by the audacity, but Maveth still did not lash out at the taunt. In fact, did It seem slightly... *cowed* at the words? Neveah was reminded once more that for a nice as he appeared, Joshua was still by far the most mysterious one here.

"Thou speaketh of obeisance plain. And yet one truth remains unchanged." Raising one of its skeletal hands, the Preceptor pointed a single menacing nail in Stryfe's direction.

The demon hung his head and sighed. "There we are."

"Forget thee not the impetus. The deed which rightly summoned Us. We yet demand a soul be rent. Accordance with the Covenant."

Neveah felt her heart sink, but Joshua surprised her with a quick response:

"Hold on there, Boss! I've been doing a lot of thinking, and the fact is, our dear Apostate's role isn't quite finished yet!"

The declaration seemed to surprise everyone present, including Stryfe himself, who jerked his head in his brother's direction, causing his voluminous mullet to sway in a positively ridiculous manner.

"Transparent lies deceive Us not. This demon's life shalt not be bought. Apostate's role hath been fulfilled. Lost devils claimed, as was Our will."

"But that's not *quite* true. Isn't there still something out there, Boss? Isn't there just *one* last stray to claim?" Joshua leaned forward, and though his next words were hushed, everyone present could hear them clearly: "The Nephilim?"

Maveth's skull jerked back, the first visible show of emotion It had yet expressed: It was stunned. So too were Creed and Stryfe, the latter shooting Joshua an especially heavy glare.

"Absurdity, of greatest kind. What foolishness hath gripped thy mind?"

"We all know it's something that should have been taken care of a long time ago."

"Seeking that accursed soul was never the Apostate's role."

"Why not *make* it his role, then? If we're talking atonement, I can't think of a better trial, *especially* for him."

"*Joshua...*" Stryfe growled. Neveah noted that the posh accent was nowhere to be found, which meant the demon must have been apoplectic at whatever it was Joshua was suggesting.

"The Nephilim cannot be held. It slips all bonds with powers eld."

"We've never sent a Samaritan after them full-time. Stryfe's got an entire army of demons under his control to search with now, and I'll stay with him to make sure it gets done. I swear it."

Stryfe was positively seething, but Joshua ignored the burning stare. "C'mon boss. You lose nothing from this. Stryfe gets to live, and in exchange you get the one thing you want more than every last Lamb put together...."

The ominous words hung in the air. Neveah had no clue what the hell a "Nephilim" was or why it seemed to be such a dramatic subject for all involved, but she certainly wasn't about to start asking questions in the midst of this standoff.

Eventually, Maveth turned to face Stryfe once more. "What sayeth thee, first incubus? Wouldst thou bring thy kin to Us?"

Stryfe looked ready to tear Joshua's head off, but managed to pull his glare away and face the Preceptor. "It could take *quite* some time..."

"Our soul was old when time was new. Patience was Our first learnt virtue."

The devil looked beyond less than thrilled, but grit his teeth and declared, "Well. Seems I've not much of a choice, have I? I suppose it's preferable to dying, at least." He didn't sound especially certain about that part.

The head Samaritan's gaze went back and forth between the three brothers for a short while, apparently mulling over everything it had heard. Neveah began to feel the pressure of its presence more intensely as the silence dragged on, her breathing becoming noticeably more difficult.

Eventually, Maveth's scythe vanished from its grasp, and it raised all four of its arms. Neveah tensed, but all the creature did was bring them together in twin sets of prayer.

"Thy chance at rest this day hath passed. When next we meet shalt be the last."

With that, Its monstrous body was consumed by a flare of bluish-green fire, and when it dispersed, all that remained was

Rictus, wrapped head to toe in tattered robes. He raised his masked face as if waking from a long slumber and regarded everyone present. Compared to his true form, this one now seemed far less intimidating.

"It seems," he began in his strange radio voice, "that the Preceptor has passed you by this day. I hope the weight of this mercy is not lost on you."

"Trust us," Joshua said, "it's not."

"Be warned: You have held on to your lives through foolishness and circumstance. They will never again prove your salvation. If this kind of defiance stirs within your hearts once more, know that we shall be there, and your story will end."

Creed looked Rictus right in the white pinpricks of his eye sockets. "That's fine. We've got some stories left to tell."

Rictus did not react to the declaration. After a pause, his dark gaze turned to Neveah, and she immediately felt the oppressive force close in around her.

"Congratulations, Lamb. You have proven yourself most clever. I know not how you came to be among us, nor how you have managed to survive for this long. But I implore you to take your leave while you still can; our world is one of chaos, and if you wallow in its depths for too long, it shall consume you. I promise it will not be as merciful an end as the Preceptor would offer."

Despite the gravity of the words, Neveah couldn't help but feel somewhat irritated at the tone. Overcoming the pressure around her, she managed to choke out a sarcastic, "Thanks for the concern."

Unlike Maveth, Rictus seemed to recognize irreverence when he heard it. He might have glowered slightly at her words, though it was difficult to tell with the mask. "If ever you decide that you have tired of this farce, know that all you need do is call to us. We are always there... in the dark."

And with that, the dark man disappeared. There was no warping of space of gust of wind to accompany it; he simply wasn't there anymore. The crushing aura that pervaded the air lifted, and Neveah found she could breathe properly again.

At that precise moment, Stryfe whipped around and swiped at Joshua's head with a claw of black fire. The scruffy man ducked out of the way as if he'd seen it coming a mile away, a rueful smile on his face.

Stryfe seethed. "You *will* pay for that, you son of a bitch."

"Watch what you say about my mother," Joshua replied. "Besides, I think we know *you'll* be the one paying for it." He gave a taunting shrug. "You'll thank me for it in the end."

Stryfe let out an animalistic growl and turned his back in a huff. It was at this point that Neveah experienced a feeling of something unwinding inside her. A wave of dizziness hit, and she realized her legs had no strength left in them. She fell onto her rear end in an undignified manner, and Creed looked down at her with an eyebrow raised.

"You alright?"

She was unable to keep her voice from quaking. "Y-yeah. Just hit me that I'm still alive, is all."

Creed nodded. "Fair enough."

He turned his attention to Stella at Neveah's side, who met his gaze evenly. "Now, about you—"

But the woman swiftly raised a hand to cut him short. "Before anything, you should know that my post-combat assessment is telling me your defeat would have been a complete mathematical certainty if I hadn't intervened."

Creed's eyes widened slightly, and he appeared to be pressing his tongue against the inside of his cheek. He rocked back and forth on his heels as if searching for a response.

In the end, he settled for asking, "What *exactly* are your energy levels at right now?"

Stella hesitated for a moment before looking down at the ground. "Three percent."

Several veins in Creed's neck seemed to take on a life of their own.

"Right," he whispered, face turning red. He turned to Joshua, looking *very* insistent.

"Get us the fuck out of here."

Chapter XXIII
"Can't Say Goodbye to Yesterday"

"So *this* is what you meant by 'rest?'"

Neveah furrowed her brow and narrowed her eyes as she tried to comprehend the bizarre contraption before her. It stood about ten feet tall, nearly reaching the ceiling, and was shaped in a fashion that reminded her of an egg, albeit a rather angular one.

Its exterior was a smooth, glossy black, but the front of the "egg" was currently split open like a door to reveal a stark white interior. There was a sort of protrusion that resembled a bench for one to sit down, with several thick wires hanging down from the top. The inner walls were adorned with various small screens, though they were currently blank and non-functional.

"Correct," came Stella's voice, and Neveah turned to see the woman laying a new, well-folded nun's habit on a nearby table, though she did not move to put it on.

Aside from this futuristic-looking device, Stella's quarters located at the back of the church more closely resembled a storage shed than it did a living space. The room was box-shaped and seemed roughly the same size as the church's basement. Its walls were lined with shelves and racks, which were in turn lined with boxes and crates, which were in turn filled to the brim with a wide assortment of—for lack of a better term—random crap.

Some things Neveah recognized, like the cloth and sewing machine that had been used to stitch her new dress. Most of it was metal objects and pieces of machinery she couldn't even begin to guess at. She imagined much of it was used for maintenance of the bizarre egg-chamber.

In the center of the room was a sizable iron table with long benches on either side. Neveah supposed this was where Stella did most of her work—whatever that entailed—but for now it had been cleared off. Creed was seated at one of the benches, looking anxious. Joshua sat directly across from him, fiddling with a fresh piece of straw.

Stryfe was present as well, though he was currently leaning against a corner some ways away smoking a cigarette. Upon repeated insistence from all of them, the demon had reverted to the initial form he'd taken upon his revival: stylish dress clothes, a black waistcoat, and slicked-back blonde hair.

Stella continued to explain as she finished smoothing out her change of clothes. "Doing so requires me to enter a period of significantly reduced activity and sensory awareness. The process is comparable to sleeping. It's also why I was unable to notice your... kidnapping."

Neveah quickly decided to move on, lest she endure another round of apologies.

"Alright, look. I'm not *totally* in the dark here. Everybody at least heard about the Eidolon Project at some point, but I thought they were all supposed to be building-sized war machines. I'm *definitely* sure none of them were as pretty as you!"

"I was created as the last unit produced by the Project. As I understand it, the vast majority of humanity's remaining resources were put towards my creation. As for my design, I assume my creators thought it would be more advantageous in approaching hostiles."

"Oh, most certainly," Stryfe snarked from the corner. "Those older toys made such obvious targets!"

Stella fixed the demon with an empty stare, and he held up a hand. "If it makes you feel any better, you *were* the only one of your kind that put up any real sort of fight..." he grinned, "for as long as you were able."

"What's that mean?" Neveah asked.

Stella looked away from the demon. "By the time I was deployed, the Final War was drawing to a close. I only saw combat against demonic forces once before the Anomaly occurred."

Neveah supposed "Anomaly" referred to the death of God. She found herself wondering how someone of Stella's nature perceived the significance of such a thing.

"So, you're basically the most advanced thing ever, right?"

It was Joshua who responded. "She sure is! Humanity's final weapon! Everyone told them to leave the fighting to the angels, but you see how that worked out!"

Stryfe scoffed. "Oh, indeed. You Lambs can get so *creative* when backed into a corner. A shame everything was already over by the time you built something worthwhile."

"You should see her when she's at full power," Joshua continued. "She can hold her own against any Samaritan."

"Irrelevant," Stella stated, and Neveah got the sense she was absolutely *done* with the two of them. "Also incorrect. My nano-machines are versatile, but the strength of the Samaritans surpasses them.

"I don't know," Joshua responded. "I remember you punching Stryfe's head off a few times when you first met."

Stryfe scowled. "I grew them back."

"Both of you shut up," Creed ordered. He was tapping an impatient gloved finger on the wooden table.

"Anyways," Neveah said, "how did the most powerful Eidolon ever end up in a church dressed as a nun?"

"After the Anomaly, my prime directive had been failed, and there was no longer anyone left who could provide a new one. I returned to my deployment terminal and remained there until Creed found me."

"He found *you*?" Neveah couldn't resist a smile. "And then he brought you here so you wouldn't be lonely anymore? That's so romantic!"

"I think it's unlikely that Creed was motivated by feelings of attraction. As a primordial being, he doesn't possess the typical human sex drive, nor does he possess—"

"Alright!" Creed snapped, slapping a hand on the table. "I get that this is all very interesting, but maybe we can save the full story for *after* you're not on the verge of shutting down?"

Neveah struggled to contain her laughter but knew he had a point. Stella seemed to as well.

"Understood," she stated, and proceeded to make her way over to the large machine.

"I'm surprised something like this still runs after so long." Neveah mused.

"With time having ceased to flow, the terminal is no longer capable of deteriorating. In addition, it contains its own self-sustaining internal power source. By connecting it to the wiring of the building, we've even been able to power the church's old lighting."

"I noticed." Neveah glanced again at the dim bulbs that barely managed to illuminate the room. Frankly, the idea of electric lights was about as alien to her as angels and devils these days.

"Enjoy it while you can," Creed stated. "Once Stella turns on the terminal, all the power will be drawn into it until she's done."

"Makes sense."

Neveah glanced back at the egg-like machine. "Still, it's pretty amazing. Never thought I'd *actually* see a working machine ever again."

Stella gave a nod. "It was built very efficiently."

With that, she stepped into the machine. The moment she did so, the various blank screens flickered on, displaying all sorts of numbers and readouts Neveah couldn't begin to make heads or tails of.

"I don't want you coming out of there until you're at *least* twenty percent," Creed demanded like a stern parent.

"Understood."

Stella sat herself down on the stool segment of the pod, placing her arms on two small armrests beside her.

"You want Stryfe and me to wait until you're up before we leave, Stelly?" Joshua asked.

"No," came the immediate response.

"Oh. Really?"

"Yes." After a moment, she added, "It's because I don't like either of you."

Joshua seemed to deflate a bit. "Didn't... really ask for a reason, but... alright." In the corner, Stryfe looked more amused than anything.

Within the pod, the hanging black cables suddenly sprung to life, extending themselves downwards behind Stella's body. They seemed to connect to something unseen at her back, prompting a short jolt in response. After it passed, she fixed Neveah with her violet eyes one last time.

"I'll see you upon my accepted level of recovery, Neveah. I'm sorry again for hiding my true nature all this time."

Neveah just gave her a smile. "Sweet dreams, Stella."

"...An illogical statement," the woman replied, but left it at that.

Lowering her head, the nun went motionless. The pod doors drew shut and sealed themselves with a hiss, though Neveah could still see a soft blue light shining from between the seams and heard a low humming sound as it began whatever process was needed to keep Stella alive.

Once the humming began, the pale-yellow lights lining the room flickered before going dark, plunging the room into blackness. As Creed had stated, it appeared that running her process would leech all other power from the church's basement until she was finished. Luckily, the room was soon bathed again in a calm, pleasant orange light courtesy of a palm-sized ball of flame that suddenly materialized in Creed's hand.

Neveah crossed her arms and raised her eyebrows at the sight. "Wow. I just watched a robot nun step into a giant egg to recharge her batteries, and somehow she's still not the thing I have the most questions about." She looked Creed dead in the eyes. "Your turn."

"You're~ in~ trouble~," Joshua sang.

"Who are you?" Neveah asked, then quickly added, "I mean, I *know* who you are. Everyone knows who you are. But does this make you my... way-great grandpa or something?"

Creed rolled his eyes. "No. It doesn't."

"That's not what I was told."

"All you've ever been told are very old stories that have passed through millions of years and languages. The truth is more complicated."

She gave a small shrug. "I literally have all of eternity."

Creed sighed but didn't put up further argument. "Alright. Firstly, don't misunderstand what I am. I may have been the first man, but that doesn't mean I was the first *human*." At Neveah's befuddled expression, he elaborated, "It's more accurate to say I was your 'prototype.'"

"You and your wife," Neveah recalled.

Creed made a slight pained expression at the word, but nodded. "We were made in more or less the same forms that you would come to have, but that's about it. Frankly, I have more in common with an angel than I do with humans."

"How so?"

"For one thing, my body was built from a star."

"Oh. Neat." Neveah decided she didn't need him to elaborate on that particular bit of absurdity. "So, you're really *not* my grandpa?"

"Of course not. You think all of humanity was actually born from two people? That's not how life works."

"Come now," Stryfe drawled from the corner. "Don't blame the Lambs because you never thought to make sure they wrote the stories down properly."

"Says the one who made sure they were written down wrong whenever he could," Joshua muttered. Stryfe just gave a self-satisfied grin in response.

"The *point* is," Creed continued, "that we were a test. To see what happened when something was given a soul and free will at the same time." He looked down at the table, and when he spoke next, his voice was laden with shame.

"We failed." He shot a venomous look to the corner. "Although not entirely on our own."

Stryfe studied his cigarette as if he was completely innocent. "All I did was offer a choice."

"Is that what you call it?"

"I'm not the one who forced free will upon you."

"*Please* do not get into this again!" Joshua begged. "It should not be possible to have the exact same argument since the *literal* dawn of time!"

"I get it," Neveah interjected, also wanting to avoid any more drama between the two. To Creed, she said, "So what really happened after that? Where did we come from?"

Creed glared for another moment at Stryfe, but continued, "After we failed, our punishment was being forced to bring you into the world even though we'd tainted it. Our mistakes ensured your lives would be difficult, but we had to make you live them regardless."

"Oh," said Neveah, then blinked as she realized what he was really saying. "So when you said that you worked with God..."

Creed nodded. "We were making *you*. It wasn't easy; it took us several tries to get things right, and even then, we always felt we could have done more. But in the end, we were patient, and you all came as you were, for better or worse."

"Wow," Neveah whispered. He'd explained it so simply, but the magnitude of what Creed described was not lost on her.

"Once there were enough of you, and we were sure you would actually make it, she and I... stepped back. Let you grow on your own. But we were always there. She stayed behind in His Kingdom, taking care of you when it was time to come home. And I," he once again looked to Stryfe, "took up hunting. Tried my best to keep the monsters out when I could find them."

"And you did a splendid job!" the Devil mocked. "You stopped us more often than not, to be sure!" Another slimy smile appeared on his face. "Of course, you never seemed able to stop your children from hunting *themselves*..."

"That's enough," Joshua interjected, a rare hint of severity in his voice.

Neveah managed to swallow her own anger at the demon's taunts. "Actually, I was just getting to you."

Stryfe looked at her like she was a particularly loud yapping dog, but she continued, "You're really supposed to be the Devil? *The* Devil?"

"Why so skeptical?"

"I never expected the Devil would dress up like Ziggy Stardust."

The three men all started at her words, looking at her in bewilderment.

"What? I still remember *some* things from before."

Stryfe couldn't seem to stop an impressed chuckle from escaping his lips. "Well, I suppose you must have had good taste, at least."

"Doesn't remember Jedi, though," Joshua muttered.

Stryfe took a drag on his cigarette and continued, "What can I say? I have good taste, too."

Neveah wasn't quite sure if stealing the faces of dead men counted as "good taste" by any metric.

"Whatever. What's that Rictus guy's deal? I get that he's possessed or something, but when he transformed, that... *thing* called itself—"

But the name seemed to catch in her throat for some reason. Furrowing her brow, she repeated, "It called itself—"

The result was the same. She felt a flash of alarm, opening and closing her mouth repeatedly, but try as she might, the name just didn't seem to come to her. A worried hand went to her throat.

Joshua winced. "Sorry, we should have mentioned that; it's part of the Covenant. Our names were sealed along with our power. Unless we're in our true forms, you can't speak them, and neither can we."

Neveah's brow furrowed in absolute confusion. "How does that even...?"

"Try not to think about it," Creed sighed. "We don't really get it either."

That only muddled things further, but Neveah decided to let it drop. She was rapidly losing her ability to wonder at the impossible things that surrounded these people.

Shaking her head to rid herself of the bizarre choking sensation, she continued, "Alright, then. Whatever Its name is, what *is* It? Some kind of demon?"

Stryfe scoffed at the notion, shooting an exasperated look at Creed. "*Do* explain it to the girl."

Creed glowered but did as he was asked. "In a word, It's 'Death.' And no, It's not a demon. Not an angel, either. It's more like a force of nature. It was born the moment God brought life into the world."

"Really? He didn't actually create it?"

"Not intentionally," Joshua said. "Luckily, all It ever cared about was maintaining the natural order. It did as It was told and took dead souls wherever they needed to go. As time went by and humans evolved, three others like It were born: Conquest, War, and Famine."

"The Four Horsemen," Neveah said quietly. Even she remembered their names being whispered during the final days.

"Not at that point. Eventually, when it was time for everything to end, God gave them the task of making sure the world was ready. *That's* when they became the Horsemen. The Pale Rider was the last one to show itself, and It was given absolute power over what souls were left. Your last judge and jury."

"Not that It got the chance to finish," Creed said.

"What happened?"

"What do you *think* happened?" Stryfe snarked from the corner.

Creed silenced him with a look and continued: "The End. Almost everything died, but seeing as you can't kill Death as long as *any* life is left, It managed to survive even when the other Horsemen didn't." His tone turned bitter, "It was able to take their powers for Its own, though. It used their strength to bind six other poor bastards who'd managed to survive."

Joshua raised a finger. "Instant Samaritans: just add eternal servitude!"

"It sees Itself as the closest thing to God that's left. But all It does now is wander around, gather up what lost souls it can find, and take them into Its being because It doesn't have any clue what else to do—"

"—while leaving you guys to handle what It can't," Neveah finished for him.

"She *is* paying attention!" Stryfe said as he finally finished his cigarette and tossed the butt to the floor, earning him yet another glare from Creed. He rolled his eyes, and the butt vanished into dust.

"You know," Neveah pointed out, "you still haven't told me exactly *what* happened at The End. Believe it or not, just saying 'God is dead' raises more questions than it answers."

A grim shadow seemed to overtake the room, and Neveah almost immediately regretted bringing it up. All three were quiet for a short while, but it was Stryfe of all people who spoke up first.

"The Beast." His voice was as grave as she'd ever heard it. "The Destroyer."

"The *what*?" Neveah whispered. Even with her poor memory, she was fairly certain she had never heard of such a thing.

Stryfe barely seemed to be addressing her as he spoke. "It wasn't supposed to have a mind. It shouldn't have had an ounce of its own will. All it was born to do was cleanse what remained of the world and wipe the slate clean.

His tone turned venomous. "And yet, the moment we set it loose, it ran to *Him* like a screaming child. Anything in its way was destroyed without so much as a thought, and in the end, it tore Him down from Heaven and wiped Him from Creation. I don't..." his crimson gaze grew unfocused. "I don't think it even realized what it was doing...."

The tension in the air was practically strangling her, but Neveah managed to ask, "Why? How did things go so wrong?"

But Stryfe's patience had apparently run dry, and he snapped, "Enough questions, Lamb! It's gone, and the world gone with it! You need not know anything more than that!"

"Settle down," Creed growled. He turned to Neveah with a look of caution. "He's right, though. Some things are better left unknown."

Neveah's mind still whirled with questions, but the sheer gravity in Creed's expression told her to drop the matter. For now.

Suddenly feeling light-headed, she let out a long breath and sat down at the table, running hands through her hair as she tried to process the mountain of information she'd been bombarded with.

Pinching the bridge of her nose, she began, "Let me see if I've got this all straight..."

She pointed at Creed, "You're the prototype human made of stars..." she pointed at Stryfe, "you're the actual fucking Devil..." she pointed off in a random direction, "your boss is *Death* Itself," she pointed at Joshua, "and you... what? You secretly God in disguise?"

The shaggy-haired man seemed bemused by that. "Ha! I wish! That'd make my job a *whole* lot easier! Sorry, but I'm exactly what I said I was."

"Don't be fooled," Stryfe chimed in yet again. "He fancies lies of omission. The truth is, we all wore a crown at some point in our lives."

"Ignore him. All I've ever been is a vagrant. And unlike them, I really am a full-blooded human. No different from you, aside from some better-than-average ESP."

Neveah felt skeptical. "A full-blooded human who just happens to be brothers with the first man and a demon?"

He shrugged. "If we're being honest, it's more of a metaphorical relation."

Neveah groaned and briefly laid her head in her hands. "Alright, you know what? I'm just gonna be glad we all made it out alive and leave it at that."

"Couldn't agree with you more!" Joshua clapped his hands together and rose from his seat with a cheery smile. "And on *that* note, I'd say it's time to be on our way!"

As they reached the top of the hill leading from the church, Creed noticed Neveah was breathing rather heavily and remembered that she had yet to rest since they'd returned. He would need to insist on that as soon as things quieted down. Annoyed that she'd even been forced to make the climb, he turned to Stryfe and Joshua.

"Why are we coming up here? You can leave from wherever you want."

"Just taking one last look," Joshua said.

His and Stryfe's backs were to Creed and Neveah, and Creed realized they were looking upon the distant shadow of the city.

"I think it's safe to say we won't ever be coming back here. Figured we'd pay respects from afar, is all."

"Nothing left to pay for," Creed grumbled, though in truth, he understood what his brother was saying.

"Maybe. But I figure we owe it anyways."

His brothers stared at the broken metropolis for a few seconds longer, and Creed couldn't help but wonder what was running through their minds.

At his side, Neveah had caught her breath, and asked, "Not to be annoying, but is anyone going to mention what exactly this thing is that the two of you are headed out to look for?"

Stryfe answered without turning. "Just a last bit of sport. One more monster to bring home."

"The way your boss reacted made it seem like there was a little more to it than that. You called it 'Nephilim', right? I've never heard that name. Does it... have something to do with the Beast you mentioned?"

Joshua sighed. "She's a perceptive one."

"It's nothing you need to worry about," Creed insisted, perhaps a little too forcefully. "Just a leftover piece of something we killed a long time ago. It's been running free for too long, and Rictus wants it. That's all."

The girl didn't hide her dissatisfaction. "Really? All that sharing and *this* is what you clam up about?"

"Remember what he said about things left unknown," Stryfe said.

"Ooh, *very* ominous." She still looked unconvinced but merely crossed her arms with a pout. "Whatever, I guess."

Joshua and Stryfe finally turned from the city to face them, and Creed regarded the duo in turn. For once, Joshua seemed like he wasn't quite sure what to say.

"Well... guess this is it for now."

"Not gonna try to drag me along?" Creed asked.

Joshua chuckled. "Nah. You've got your own role to play. In fact, you'd probably better get moving before too long. Don't want the Boss coming back, right?"

Another silence passed, and the three of them began to shift uncomfortably. Creed briefly wondered if perhaps this awkwardness was how it was supposed to be among real brothers.

"Hey..." he started, grimacing at how awkward it sounded. "Look, I..." Frustrated, he forced himself to swallow his pride and looked the other two in the eyes (and blindfold).

"Just... good luck, I guess."

They both seemed somewhat taken aback at his words, but Joshua quickly broke out into a grin.

"You too, big brother."

He began to raise his arm to Stryfe in preparation to depart, but froze as Neveah spoke up.

"One last thing!"

The three of them stared at her, and she raised a finger to point at Stryfe. "Before you go, I want an apology."

You could have heard a blade of grass fall in the stunned silence that followed. Stryfe blinked, and after a moment seemed to realize that he *had* heard correctly. "Excuse me?"

"You threw me to one of your demons as bait!"

"Well... yes." Stryfe looked as if he didn't understand the offense. "The Devil tends to do things like that."

"Yeah, well, you're still an asshole, and I want an apology."

Creed kept his expression neutral, but it was all he could do not to start rolling on the floor in hysterics. Joshua seemed equally stunned, and Stryfe looked less than amused.

"Is that so? And why, pray tell, should I give you one?"

"Maybe because she saw you crying on your back in the dirt?" Creed suggested, making sure the sheer amusement he was feeling wasn't evident in his voice.

Stryfe held up a blackened finger as if to object, but no words came. His eyes flitted back and forth between Creed and Neveah before he lowered the finger and stalked a few steps closer, looming over her and sneering like he was trying to frighten her. She didn't flinch.

After several seconds, Stryfe raised a hand again and, with a flourish of his fingers, willed a blood-red rose to appear in his grasp, which he promptly held out to Neveah. Creed was baffled by the gesture, but the girl reached out and accepted it without hesitation, careful to avoid the thorns.

"Take care, Little Lamb."

With that, Stryfe stepped back to Joshua's side, whose mouth was hanging open in wonder.

"Oh my goodness gracious..."

"Shut up."

"I am *so* proud of you right now!"

Stryfe closed his eyes, seeming exhausted. "Oh, I should have let Rictus kill me."

"Come here!" Joshua exclaimed, and proceeded to wrap his arms around the other man's shoulders in a ridiculous embrace. Stryfe's eyes snapped back open, a look of utter fury on his features.

"I will *fucking kill—!*"

And then they were gone, vanishing in a warping of space. Creed and Neveah were left alone at the top of the hill, drinking in what they'd just seen.

"You guys are weird," Neveah declared.

Creed wasn't about to argue. "Yeah."

"So... what's next?"

He tensed at the question, but supposed he'd known it was coming. "I suppose I'll be leaving soon. Like Joshua said, Rictus won't let me stay much longer. Have to be a real Samaritan again."

The girl nodded at his words, but she was looking at the ground. Feeling uncomfortable, Creed asked, "What, uh... what about you?"

Neveah was silent for a long time, lost in thought, but eventually seemed to come to some sort of decision. Looking up at Creed, her gaze hardened, and she reached out to grab hold of his hand. "Come help me with something."

Without warning, she turned around and began to drag him back down the hill towards the church. He was surprised but did not resist.

They reentered the building and approached the flowerbed at its center, still dimly illuminated by the weak grey light coming through the hole in the roof.

Neveah released her grip and stepped forward. Bending over, she took the red rose Stryfe had gifted her and slipped it into a random spot in the small garden, adding its bright crimson to the garish mass of uncoordinated color. She then stepped over the ring of flowers onto the soil within, right where Creed had removed the wooden cross long ago.

Dropping to her knees, she began to dig and scrape at the dirt with razor focus. Creed watched her in silence and was reminded of when he'd come across her digging a similar hole in the valley where he'd battled Adrammelech.

It seemed so long ago now, and their relationship so very different. Creed had regarded her as little more than an anomaly, a strange Lamb who didn't seem to realize how helpless it was. And she... well, he didn't know what she'd thought of him at the time. He'd tried to hurt her then, to chase her off so he could continue to wallow in his misery.

He was glad she'd been too strong for him.

When she was finally satisfied with her work, the girl rose to her feet and dusted off her dirt-stained hands. Seeing as she'd just gotten winded from climbing a hill, Creed didn't know where she'd found the energy, but she seemed practically wired. Standing, she turned and smiled at him.

"Alright. You do the rest."

"Excuse me?"

"Come on. I did the hard part. Now you just gotta drop the seed and fill in the hole."

So that was her game. Creed's first instinct was to argue, of course, but he had long since realized that was a useless past-time with her.

"You *do* still have it, don't you?" Neveah asked.

"Yeah..." Creed responded, reaching into one of the several pockets of his coat. He pulled the tiny seed out and held it in his palm, staring at it in apprehension.

The girl didn't know it, but the seed had saved him in his fight against Uriel. He couldn't tell her how, as that would require him telling her about the Black, and that was something he would not do.

Regardless, he found himself wary of parting with the seed. It shouldn't have mattered. Hell, he could probably just ask for another one afterward, but something inside him couldn't bear to let go of this specific grain.

After a few seconds, Neveah sighed. "Not ready, huh?"

Creed blinked at her perceptiveness; how did this girl keep managing to read him so well? She didn't seem offended, at least.

"It's okay." She reached into the pouch at her waist, "we'll use one of mine."

Creed instinctively wanted to deny the claim, but realized that he couldn't and quietly returned the seed to his pocket. Neveah knelt back down, placed the seed into the hole, and began to fill in the soil she had displaced.

"You sure that's even a flower?" Creed asked. She had barely even looked at the seed she'd chosen.

"It's *probably* a flower."

Creed rolled his eyes. Neveah finished her work, rising and dusting her hands once more. "Don't worry. You don't have to plant one right now. Just hold on to that seed until you're ready. It's gotta mean something when you do."

"'Mean something,'" Creed repeated, feeling a flash of melancholy. "Neveah, I appreciate that you've taken it upon yourself to... heal my spirit or whatever it is you're trying to do. But don't get too hopeful. I'll admit you pulled me back from the edge, but that doesn't mean I'm some brand-new person. I'll accept that there *is* more going on out there in the world than I thought, and I intend to see it. That doesn't mean I think things will ever be fixed, and it's not something a few dramatic speeches and some gardening are going to fix."

Neveah absorbed his words without flinching, though her smile did turn a little sad. Creed felt sorry, but didn't take back the words; much as he disliked them, they were the truth.

"Yeah," she said. "I guess you're right. I know you have to leave and go fight again, but that's not really what you want, is it?"

"I'll admit, it's more a matter of keeping Rictus from tearing me to pieces at this point. Don't get me wrong. I remember what you said: I've got a responsibility to protect what's left. And I will. But that doesn't mean I think this fight is suddenly worth anything."

His throat began to feel tight. "The truth is... I don't know what I want anymore. And I don't know what that means."

"It means you want to change," Neveah responded. "Or maybe it means you want to change *something*. Anything. If you ask me, that's a good sign."

"Is it? What good is fighting again if I don't believe in it?"

"Hey, remember what I said? It's okay to start small. You may still not believe in what you're doing, but *I* do. For now, maybe that can be enough."

She stood up a little straighter, placing a hand on both hips, then declared in a loud, confident voice: "If you can't find your own reason to keep going, there's nothing wrong with borrowing someone else's!"

Creed stared, wide-eyed, for several seconds, then promptly burst out laughing. It was a deep, uncontrollable laugh, one that forced him to double over and grab his stomach. Neveah practically leaped back in shock, and inside, Creed was just as surprised himself, but at that moment, he could do nothing but guffaw like an utter fool.

"What the hell...?" she said, looking at him like he was a madman. He couldn't quite argue.

"S-sorry..." he managed to choke out between his chortles. "It's just... that was *so* dramatic! And... that pose! You really thought that was a line, huh?"

Somehow, Neveah seemed to take offense at the words. Crossing her arms and turning her head away in a pout, she huffed.

"Jerk! I thought it sounded pretty cool..."

This only prompted another series of howls to overtake him.

"It was!" he exclaimed, forcing his laughter down to chuckles, "It was *very* cool!"

He finally managed to get himself under control, standing and taking deep breaths to calm himself. He wasn't sure if he'd ever felt anything like this in the entire span of his existence.

He let out a sigh, feeling something inside him unwind; a pressure he hadn't even noticed was there. He stared at the pale girl before him, pouting and grumbling to herself, and suddenly felt certain what to do next.

"Neveah. Come with me."

The girl started, uncrossing her arms and gaping at him. "What?"

"I've got to wander the world again, and so do you. Why not do it together?"

She just continued to gawk, so he asked, "What's the problem? I know you've been planting seeds all this time, but you're still just one girl on foot, right? How much ground have you really covered? The way I see it, having a Samaritan's powers on your side will help you reach places you never could on your own."

Neveah still seemed unable to respond, and Creed grew more serious. "You say I can borrow your reason to keep going. If that's true, then I have a responsibility to help you with it, don't I?"

He looked the girl right in the eyes, those bright green lights that had so easily broken down all the walls he'd built around himself.

"I may be a Samaritan, but that doesn't make me strong. So please: come with me. Stay by my side, and teach me how to be like you."

Neveah's mouth fell open slightly, and she suddenly ducked her head, blonde hair falling to hide her face. She stayed like that for a long while, her shoulders beginning to tremble.

Just as Creed was starting to fear he'd somehow offended her, she raised her head, and he saw her eyes were shining. She gave a single, vigorous nod and fixed him with the broadest, most radiant smile he'd seen since the day he met his wife.

"Okay!" she whispered through the tears.

Elsewhere, in some far-off, indistinguishable part of the world, a large cliff loomed over a dead, colorless countryside, itself littered with other cliffs and rocky crags. Atop this largest of outcroppings, a warping of space heralded the arrival of Joshua and Stryfe.

Joshua took several quick steps forward as they emerged, just in case his brother tried to tear his throat out, but the well-dressed demon stayed where he had appeared. Relieved that his prank hadn't cost him his life, Joshua made a show of raising a hand to his brow and peering out past the cliffside as if we were capable of taking in the sights.

"Welp, I've got absolutely no idea where we are, but at least it's more interesting than where we were. Those hills were *so* boring to look at!"

As usual, Stryfe didn't play along. "Why let him stay behind?"

Joshua grinned. "I said why, didn't I? He's got his role, and we've got ours."

"This hunt will take us lots of places. He'd be able to do his job just fine. And besides, if we actually *do* end up finding the Nephilim, it's only a matter of time before we're forced together again."

Joshua sighed. He swore he used to be able to get more past his brothers. "If that's the case, why rush things? Besides, he probably needs a break from us after all that mess, don't you think?"

"Or perhaps you're just trying to protect him."

"Stryfe, our brother has just found the first thing resembling any sort of peace he's had in a *long* while. What say we just leave it at that and let him enjoy it while he can?"

The two of them stared each other down for a moment before Stryfe finally scoffed. "Fine, then. But when he realizes everything you neglected to tell him about Testament, it will be *your* head, not mine."

"Fair enough." Joshua turned his back to the demon, then added, "We'll probably be both dead before that anyways. You know we'll have to go see Salomé, right?"

A flood of discomfort came from Stryfe's aura. "Is that truly necessary?"

"You know it is. If we're gonna find the seventh Beast, we've got to start with the one holding the other six. The Nephilim can be literally anywhere at any time, so unless you've got an idea where else to start, I don't see us having much choice."

He could feel the demon's mood worsen, but there were no further protests. Letting the matter drop for now, Joshua turned his focus to the empty world before him. He uselessly beheld a landscape he couldn't see, feeling just as dull and lifeless as anything else under the Black Sun's glow. For a moment, his thoughts turned back to Creed:

Make the most of what time you've got left, brother. Once this fight reaches you, it'll be a long while before any of us rest again.

Chapter XXIV
"We Will Rise Again"

"Hey," Neveah said from around her bright pink—albeit still flavorless—lollipop, "you should make me a gun."

She was currently lounging on the front steps of the church. Creed sat beside her, and for once he wasn't engaged with a sucker of his own. He didn't look at her when he responded to her request, but the exasperation in his voice was evident enough.

"I am not going to make you a gun."

"Why not?"

"I don't like guns. They made it too easy for you to kill each other."

"Alright. How about a sword?"

"I'm not making you a weapon, Neveah."

"C'mon. We're gonna be fighting angels, right? I should have *some* kind of magic thingamajig to protect myself, shouldn't I?"

She could almost hear how hard he was rolling his eyes. "You won't be fighting angels. You'll be watching from no less than a mile away while *I* fight angels."

"What if we're attacked by robbers or bandits?"

Now he *did* turn to look at her. "What the *hell* are you talking about?"

She gave a sheepish shrug. "It could happen..."

"Putting aside the fact that there are less than a million people left in the world and *none* of them care about stealing anymore, I'll remind you that I'm a primordial being who can literally make myself as strong as I need to be. You're five-foot-nothing and weigh all of ninety pounds."

She huffed. Who did he think he was, making sense like that? "Whatever."

"'Whatever,'" he mimicked. "Just because you have to look like a child forever doesn't mean you have to act like one."

"Oh yeah? Well, just because *you're* a billion years old doesn't mean you get to—"

"If this is going to be a common occurrence, I don't know how confident I am in this arrangement."

Neveah turned to see Stella emerge from the church doorway, hands behind her back. Her new habit was a bit more faded than the original, and this one had not yet been altered to slit its way up the thigh for easier movement.

"Sorry," she and Creed responded in unison, shooting each other annoyed looks in response.

After making their plans, Creed had immediately forced Neveah to lie down and rest. Though she had felt wired at the time, she found herself losing consciousness the moment she rested her head on a ragged bedroll Creed had brought up from the basement.

She had no idea how long she'd slept, but it must have been a *very* significant nap; by the time she awoke, Stella had already reached an acceptable power level and emerged from her pod.

The nun had listened quietly while Neveah and Creed explained their intentions to her. It hadn't been a long discussion, and once it was over Stella had stood, claimed she was going to find something they'd need for the journey, and disappeared into her room.

That had been some time ago, though Neveah couldn't be sure. If only Joshua had been there to count the seconds like a crazy person. She and Creed had spent their time waiting outside, mainly in silence.

Presently, Neveah rose from the church steps and turned to face the nun. "Did you find what you were looking for?"

"I did. But first, I'd like to give you something."

Stella took a few steps forward and pulled her hands from behind her back. She was presenting Neveah with a pair of faded brown items, long and made of cloth. They looked so foreign to her that it took several seconds to realize what they even were, and when she did, she let out an audible gasp.

"Are those... boots?"

"They are."

"Like... the kind you wear on your feet?"

"I believe those are the only kind."

More than any of miraculous things Creed and Stella had produced thus far, Neveah found herself in utter awe at the footwear presented before her. She'd been traveling barefoot for untold ages—the last pair of footwear she'd owned had disintegrated too long ago for her to remember.

By now, her feet had essentially become two large callouses that could withstand all but the harshest terrains. She'd long since given up hope of ever finding anything to cover them again, and had even convinced herself that she could get along fine without them. But as she beheld the glorious pair before her, that resolve crumbled in an instant.

"Where... where did you find them?"

"I didn't find them. I made them."

It was true. Upon closer inspection, Neveah could see that the boots had been stitched together out of several different types of cloth, mostly brown but with a few grey patches here and there, with tough-looking cured leather used on the soles. Much like her dress, they were fairly shoddy patchworks with prominent stitching. And much like her dress, she couldn't have cared less.

Sensing her hesitation, Stella stepped forward and placed the boots directly into Neveah's hands, where she held them as if they might burst into flames.

"Creed," she whispered loudly, turning and presenting them like treasures. "Shoes! They're *shoes,* Creed!"

"I see the shoes."

She gave Stella one last wide-eyed stare, then plopped down on the top of the church steps, and slipped them on. They were long, reaching up to just below her knee, and of course Stella had somehow stitched them to perfectly fit Neveah's legs.

Once she'd pulled them on, she gaped at them in silence for what could have been hours, marveling at the alien sensation of having something soft and warm on her feet.

"I'm still not fully accustomed to reading expressions without using my sensors," Stella said from behind, "but I'm correct in thinking that you approve, yes?"

"I do." Neveah was unable to keep her voice from breaking. "I really do. Thank you."

"You're welcome."

Standing, Neveah took several deliberately hefty steps down the stairs, then proceeded to lose herself and danced around in the dirt, stamping her feet as hard as she dared just to revel in her new ability to do so without rocks digging into her flesh. She felt positively giddy, and couldn't hold back several childish giggles. She would have continued for an embarrassingly long time if Creed hadn't approached and grabbed hold of her head to stop her in her tracks.

"Try not to wear them out right away"

Neveah struggled to regain her composure. "Right. Sorry, I just—"

"I get it." Turning to Stella, he asked, "Did you find them?"

The nun nodded, and reached into the pocket of her habit as she approached. She pulled something out and opened her hand to reveal two small spheres resting in her palm, each seemingly made of the same solid-black material as her charging pod. They were smooth and featureless, save for a small band of dim blue light wrapped around their centers.

"Cool!" Neveah mused, then furrowed her brow. "What are they?"

"Communication devices. Stored in my charging station for emergency use. If at least one is active, I will be able to link to it with my internal systems and achieve high-quality radio transmission regardless of where your travels take you."

"Whoa. They'll work anywhere? Don't they have a range or something?"

"They will function anywhere that the Network is present."

"Wait, there's a Network now?"

Stella raised her gaze to the grey sky above. "Correct. A system of satellites released into orbit to help facilitate functionality of the Eidolon Project. Despite how long it has been, most of the satellites remain functional. Their coverage includes the majority of the planet's landmass, and they will provide adequate power to these devices in most locations, just as they offer energy to my charging station."

Neveah didn't understand most of that, but took one of the black spheres from Stella's palm. Creed promptly took the other. "That's great!"

She smiled, but as she looked at the device in her hand, then to the wonderful boots she'd just been given, a wave of sadness and guilt washed over her. "Are... are you sure you can't come with us?"

Stella gave a slow shake of her head. "I'm sorry."

"But..." Neveah's voice sounded childish to her own ears, "you said this Network gives that pod its power, right? And no offense, but you're *very* strong! You sure you can't just... carry it?"

Her voice went small at how stupid that sounded, but she was desperate. She looked over her shoulder at Creed, who wore a melancholy expression.

"I'm afraid that wouldn't be viable," Stella said. "Unlike the transmission devices, my charging station requires significantly stronger signal strength from the Network to function. This area is one of very few I've ever found where such a signal is available."

Neveah felt her heart sink. She couldn't pretend to understand the ins and outs of Stella's functions and what she needed to survive, but if the nun was certain she had to stay, then she had to stay.

"It will be okay," Stella assured her, motioning to the communication devices. "With these, we'll be able to speak as often as you like. I'll be looking forward to the stories you have to share any time."

"Not quite *any* time," Creed chimed in, shooting them both a rather parental look. "Keeping in touch is fine, but don't neglect your rest. We *will* be back here one day, and until then, keeping your levels high is your top priority."

"That is the fourth time you've repeated those instructions since we began discussing your departure, Creed. My memory systems are perfectly functional."

Creed rolled his eyes at the pseudo-sarcastic response, and Neveah stuck her tongue out at him in jest.

Turning back to Stella, she said, "He's a jerk, but he's right. I don't know how all this stuff works, but I definitely don't want you that close to running out of power again. Be sure to take care of yourself."

"I will. I promise."

And with that, Neveah realized that they were out of things to say. The three of them stood in silence, nobody willing to break it first. In the end, Neveah decided to take the burden.

"I'll miss you," she whispered, feeling a bit silly at how much she meant it.

It still hadn't been very long since she'd met the woman, and shorter still since she'd learned enough about her to truly consider her a friend. And the sphere in her hand meant they'd likely be speaking again before too long, right? Even so, this parting was proving far more painful than Neveah had expected.

Perhaps that was how she knew it had real meaning.

"I am very glad that we met each other, Neveah." For once, Neveah could audibly hear the warmth in Stella's tone. "And I know that we'll see each other again."

She stated it so matter-of-factly that Neveah wondered if she'd just run some kind of probability check in her head, but the words filled her with confidence nonetheless.

Stella's violet gaze then drifted to Creed, who fidgeted just a bit. Neveah took a step back and allowed the moment to pass between them uninterrupted. She had no way of knowing just how long these two had been each other's sole companions, but knew that however hard this goodbye was for her, it was magnitudes more so for them.

Creed spoke first, his voice tight with emotion. "I'm... I'm sorry. For everything."

Stella responded with a tilt of her head, which Neveah had slowly learned was her equivalent of surprise. "There is nothing you need to apologize for."

"There is. I've been... for so long, I've been nothing but cruel to you. I was so busy wallowing that I didn't even—"

"Forgiveness without needing to ask is one of the final forms of love," the nun interrupted. "That's something you told me when I first began to ask about love. If that's the case, then you shouldn't need to ask for my understanding. It's already been given."

Creed swallowed noticeably at the words, but gave a nod in return.

"Right." He let out a sad chuckle. "How could I forget? Guess I need to make sure to call often, huh?"

"Correct."

"We'll be back." There was an iron-clad certainty in his voice.

"I know."

And with that, there was nothing left to say. Creed turned to go, and Neveah turned with him. Together they walked down the steps of the church, following the featureless dirt path up the hill. Their steps were slow and deliberate, desperate to last as long as they could. Once they reached the top, they turned over their shoulders one final time.

Stella was still there, hands clasped before her, looking on unflinchingly as she saw them off. Knowing they would never be able to leave otherwise, the two of them turned their backs once more. Together, they crested over the hill, refusing to look back until even the steeple was out of sight.

Observation: This Unit is now alone.

Clarification: Unit has been left in solitude before. Creed often left to journey into the city by himself.

Rebuttal: Circumstances differ; previously, Unit's expectation that he would return prevented self-classification as "alone."

Observation: Communication with both Creed and Neveah will continue to be possible. Unit will be able to allocate more time for energy renewal. Aspects of current circumstances appear to be exclusively beneficial.

Question: Why then is Unit dissatisfied with the outcome?

Recollection: Neveah's Statement— *I'll miss you.* Unit comprehends this notion.

Conclusion: Unit will miss its companions.
Question: How can Unit resolve this irregular conclusion?
Processing... Processing...
Recollection: The expression on Neveah's face when she received the boots This Unit constructed for her...
Conclusion: Unit must rejoin her companions.
System Alert: Energy levels at 19%.
Illogical: Diva Unit does not possess the means by which to do so. Current power reserves will not allow for extended time away from Station.
Solution: Unit must increase energy reserves.
Movement: Retreating into church. Closing doors. Building sealed. Retreating to personal quarters.
Observation: Diva Unit's energy levels have not been at 100% for approximately 108,000 system cycles.
Calculating: Achieving 100% energy capacity will take approximately 10,000 system cycles. This will allow for approximately 17,500 system cycles of activity under reduced consumption conditions before re-charging becomes a priority.
Affirmation: Unit will allocate as much time as possible to replenishing energy levels. Interruptions will occur only to communicate with companions.
Question: Should Unit reveal its intentions to companions?
Answer: No. An explanation will certainly invite well-intentioned protests. Unit will not abide by these protests. Thus, discussion would be irrelevant.
Affirmation: Unit will achieve 100% capacity. Unit will depart from this region. Unit will join with its companions once again.
Conclusion: This Unit will no longer be alone.

Creed and Neveah didn't stop walking until they came to an intersection of various dirt roads. This stubborn march had been necessary; had they stopped too close to the church, they might have been too tempted to turn back.

On all sides stretched rolling grey hills, all indistinguishable from the rest. From where they stood, even the looming shadow of the city couldn't be seen.

Looking down, Creed saw that Neveah was already breathing rather heavily. He'd have to remember to slow his pace from now on. The girl was permanently malnourished for all eternity, and it wasn't as if they would ever need to hurry anywhere in a timeless world.

"Y'know," Neveah said between short pants of breath, "not to sound spoiled right out of the gate, but couldn't any of those colors you got back make it so we don't have to walk the whole way? Or maybe you could do the spooky chant again and bring out that magic wind that lets you fly?"

"I could. If you wanted Rictus to show up and kill me for breaking the Covenant by taking that form when an angel wasn't around."

"Ah. I mentioned your boss was a dick, right?"

"Yeah."

The girl didn't look pleased, but straightened up and put her hands on her hips, looking out among the vast empty hills. "In that case, where's our first stop in this fun little forever-marathon?"

"I thought we might pass through the city on our way out."

She raised her eyebrows. "Really?"

"Figured I should pay my respects one last time." He hesitated, then continued, "Besides, I thought maybe you could... plant some seeds... if you wanted."

The girl gawked at his words. After a moment, though, something seemed to catch her attention. Her eyes flitted into the air, head turning as if to follow something he couldn't see.

In truth, Creed had seen her do things like this several times since they'd met. It perplexed him, but he supposed everyone was prone to their own bits of strangeness these days. The moment passed quickly, and her gaze refocused as she broke into a pleased grin.

"I think that's a great idea. I'll lead."

"You even know what direction it's in?" Creed challenged. Where they were now, the landscape around them looked identical in every direction.

"Sure!" she replied, her gaze returning to the direction it had before. Creed was going to ask exactly *how* she knew this off the top of her head, but the girl took off in a jog, apparently no longer concerned with exerting herself. Creed once again wondered at her odd behavior, but seeing as she *had* somehow chosen the exact right direction to run off in, he decided not to bring it up.

With a quiet chuckle, he moved to follow her, but froze as a black spark flashed through his mind, accompanied by a sudden hollowness inside him.

He went stiff, hand shooting up to clutch at the pocket of his coat and the seed within. By the time he could feel it, the moment had passed. The sensation was gone, but a new coldness served to remind him of what he was.

He'd allowed himself to grow complacent, even if just a moment. How foolish. He may have felt lighter now than he'd been in a long time, but that did not mean anything had changed. The world was still dead, and he was still a monster. His fight was not finished, and it never would be. Not so long as—

"Hey!"

Creed looked to see Neveah's head poke above the hill she had clambered over.

"What's wrong?" she called.

Creed pushed his dark thoughts down into the void from which they had emerged. "Nothing!" he called out, voice level.

He dropped his hand back down and began to walk after the girl with nary a hitch in his step. He reached her shortly at the top of the hill, looking down at her. "Just surprised you picked the right direction."

She gave him a rather smug grin. "Woman's intuition."

"I don't think that applies here."

"Whatever," she scoffed, turning her back to him. She made to resume her jog but hesitated and looked back over her shoulder. "Hey... What does the world look like to you right now?"

It was the same thing she'd asked him when they'd first met. Creed looked up into the sky, as he had so many times before. He beheld the fathomless ebony vacuum, a black hole sun promising light that would never shine and an end that would never come.

"Still dark," he declared.

Her expression turned solemn at his words. After a moment's hesitation, he added, "But... that doesn't mean there isn't anything out there."

Her face brightened ever so slightly. "Fair enough!"

She began stretching her arms in preparation. "Now try to keep up, good Samaritan. I can go forever on these boots!"

She took off jogging again, and with a grin he couldn't restrain, Creed moved again to follow her.

Yes, the world was still dark. And no, his struggle would never end. He carried it with him wherever he went. But in that moment, it didn't matter. Creed kept his eyes forward and decided that, right now, he could content himself with following in the shadow of the strange little Lamb who ran ahead of him as if she didn't notice the sun wasn't shining.

In truth, it wasn't much of a comfort. It was small. It was weak. It was so fragile that he feared it might fall apart at any moment.

But for now, it was enough.

A Dream of Things to Come
"Ordinary World"

    Somewhere in a place that can no longer be reached lies a field that no longer exists. The Girl stands at the center of this field, beholding pastures as green as her own eyes that extend forever in all directions.
    She does not know how or why she has come to this place. Only that she does not belong. She stares into a vibrant blue sky, where seven figures hang high in the air, so distant they seem to be little more than dark specks beneath the vastness of Heaven.
    This isn't what I wanted. I'm so sorry.

    Somewhere in the twilight between life and death, the Preceptor stands upon a shore of silver sand. Behind him yawns endless, shapeless dusk, and before him stretches a fathomless sea of gold, swirling with the lost souls of pitiful Lambs.
    The Preceptor lords over Its purposeless realm, blind to the hollow world beyond. Its solitude is broken by the shifting of space behind It; It turns to see the Crucifer emerging from the dusk. From behind ragged hair, white pupils glimmer in the twilight.
    I've seen him, Preceptor. The Logos has returned.

    Somewhere in the mortal world, a city of delirium shines in the darkness. Its buildings tower high, strings of lights webbing between them and paper lanterns floating in the air by some unseen force. Below these buildings, the Apostate marches slowly through dimly lit alleyways.

His pale hospital rags and grey hair stand out in the dimness of the alley, as does the white bandage wrapped around his head adorned with small black marks where each eye should be. All around him ring the whispers of puppets within the shadows, begging him to step inside their homes and join them in their festival. The Apostate ignores their pleas.

If she wants me, she can have me. But I will not go quietly.

Somewhere in a vast field of fallen snow ringed by a range of mountains, the Crusader steps forward to do battle. Scattered across the land are countless titanic corpses, adorned in white and gold with bloodied broken wings.

Before a particularly colossal corpse sits the Prodigal, regarding the Crusader with glee. His wide, mad smile begs for a better challenge than the angels surrounding them provided.

Ya knew the road was always gonna lead ya back here one day, old man.

In the twilight realm, the Preceptor and Crucifer find their gazes drawn to the approach of another. From far along the endless beach, the Sacristan approaches with slow, burdened steps. They drag a heavy golden chest in the sand behind them, its top adorned with the figures of two bowing angels.

They fix the other Samaritans with a look of grim determination. The Crucifer and Preceptor stiffen as they approach; even from here, they can hear the sound of screaming echoing from within the chest.

They've bet their lives on the future. Do you think you can match that resolve?

The Apostate comes to a spacious square at the rear of the city. Before him looms a twisted castle of shadow and madness. The darkness around him comes alive, shaping itself into dozens of humanoid figures made from the void. The Apostate's hand alights with unhallowed heat, a hideous amalgamation of red, black, and purple flame.

He waves his hand, and the hellfire consumes the living shadows in an instant. When they have gone, the castle begins to stir. Several eldritch Beasts emerge, their bodies shifting and warbling like living static. They hang from the castle's ramparts like a plaything, their eyes glowing a sickly venomous green as they look down at their prey in unseeing lunacy.

Have you finally come to take me away, my Prince?

The Crusader calls a massive greatsword made of the purest silver to his hands, its blade nearly as large as his own body. With a cry of ecstasy, the Prodigal's body flares with crimson energy like fire made from blood. He crashes his fist into the corpse of the angel behind him, and it bursts into a shower of golden ash.

All I want's a fight that makes my heart dance again!

The Crucifer's bloody body crashes and rolls across the sands to land at the Preceptor's feet. The Sacristan stands across from them with an outstretched arm, having just thrown the iron nail now embedded in the Crucifer's chest.

In a rush of power, the Preceptor's lower body transforms into that of an iron horse with eight legs. Gripping Its scythe in all four hands, It leaps over the Crucifer's body and charges at its foe.

Undaunted, the Sacristan reaches behind themself and throws open the lid of the golden ark. The twilight beach is consumed wholly and completely by a flood of light as the screams within the chest reach their crescendo.

I've seen a path to the end. The only one that will have any meaning.

A pair of draconic black wings spring from the Apostate's back, and he rockets into the air. He hangs before the Black Sun, hands alight with his hellfire, as the Beasts snarl and roar.

From the highest balcony of the castle, the Anchoress dances into the open. She prances and stumbles along, drunk on her passion, watching her beloved loom before her. Coming to the edge of the balcony, the Anchoress smiles, drooling in ecstasy, and cups her hands in the shape of a heart around the Apostate's floating figure.

It's okay. Our family will be whole again soon.

The Crusader casts off his human form, white hair spilling out behind him. At his back, the brilliant shape of a flower materializes at his back. It is comprised of nine petals, each made from one of the Crusader's colors, with a core of white at its center.

From the carnage of disintegrating angels, the Prodigal emerges. In his grasp is a saw-like sword that appears to be made from the spinal cord of some unknown creature. The Crusader attempts to call upon his light, but a flash of darkness taints his heart. He doubles over in pain, and the white core of the flower behind him flashes pitch black.

The Prodigal is unmoved by the sight, and with a gleeful shout, rushes forward with weapon raised. Though he is breaking to pieces, the Crusader forces himself to stand tall. He readies his massive blade and slams against his foe in a clash of will and hatred.

The other side. It's waking up. I won't be able to stop it.

The shore in the twilight realm lies empty, with no sign of the three Samaritans. All that remains is the Sacristan's golden chest, lying inert in the silver sand. It is stained with blood.

High above the rolling ocean, a lone figure descends from the non-existent sky. Clothed in a seamless white robe, he gently touches down upon the aural waters with sandaled feet and walks across the waves as if they were solid ground.

He reaches the blood-wet chest on the sandy beach and places a hand upon its ornate lid. He feels the writhing of its contents; souls he can no longer save. Hidden behind long brown hair and a fatherly beard, a Messiah smiles, promising the Lambs within that he will not waste their sacrifice.

Tell me. Would you help reject this broken world of ours?

The Girl trembles as she beholds the figures in the sky. The whole of her being tells her to shy away from them, that they will bring her nothing but pain. But she cannot, for even in a world where destiny no longer exists, she feels certain that some final fate yet rests in their hands. She must witness it, no matter the cost.

    Desperate not to be left behind, the Girl steps forward.

        Please. Don't go where I can't follow...

SAMARITANS

Book I: The Sound of Silence
END

The (Un)Official *Samaritans: Book I* Soundtrack

A list of the songs that named and inspired the chapters of this story:

Title Theme: "The Sound of Silence," as performed by Disturbed
0. "Drink the Water" by Justin Cross
1. "Black Hole Sun," as performed by Nouela
2. "Where Did You Sleep Last Night," as performed by Janel Drewis
3. "God's Gonna Cut You Down" by Johnny Cash
4. "O' Death" by Jen Titus
5. "You Want It Darker" by Leonard Cohen
6. "Imagine," as performed by A Perfect Circle
7. "The Devil and the Hunstman" by Sam Lee and Daniel Pemberton
8. "Broken Crown" by Mumford & Sons
9. "Wayfaring Stranger" by Jack White
10. "The Rust" by Sivert Høyem
11. "Talk In Circles" by Cults
12. "Everything in Its Right Place" by Radiohead
13. "Lazarus" by David Bowie
14. "Good People" by Poor Man's Poison
15. "Don't Give Up" by Peter Gabriel and Kate Bush
16. "The Man Who Sold the World," as performed by Midge Ure
17. "Black Sabbath" by Black Sabbath
18. "Words That We Couldn't Say" by Yoko Kanno and Steve Conte
19. "Pale White Horse" by The Oh Hellos
20. "Everybody Wants to Go to Heaven" by Glenn Yarborough
21. "Hallelujah," as performed by Andre Rieu
22. "Little Lights" by Punch Brothers
23. "Can't Say Goodbye to Yesterday" by Carla White
24. "We Will Rise Again" by Dan Romer and Meredith Godreau
25. "Ordinary World," as performed by The Hit House

ABOUT THE AUTHOR

C. John Carter is a born-n'-bred Texas accountant, but he'd much rather be a born-n'-bred Texas author. Since childhood, the religions and mythologies of the worlds have captivated him, and he has long dreamt of writing a world where all of these beliefs come to life and clash in a fantastical epic. He also likes violent action movies, fantasy RPGs, and anime, so he figured he might as well throw those into the mix as well. He's just getting started, but he's got enough ideas to last a lifetime, and as soon as he's done with all those violent action movies, fantasy RPGs, and anime, he'll get right on jotting them down.

He can be reached for all form of inquiry at
cjohncarterpublishing@gmail.com